Advance praise for Mark W. Tiedemann's
Compass Reach

"Compass Reach is space opera for those who've outgrown starship battles and phoney heroics. Complex, mysterious and engaging, it's reminiscent of the early work of Samuel R. Delany. Mark Tiedemann is a fine writer, and this novel proves that he's one of the best new SF authors on the scene today."
—Allen Steele

"Compass Reach is a rousing, inventive, far-future adventure by one of the most distinctive new voices in the field."
—Jack McDevitt

"A vivid and unexpected view of the underbelly of interstellar society. Mark Tiedemann writes with an engaging energy, gritty realism, and a genuine concern for his characters. Here's a new writer worth watching!"—Jeffrey Carver

COMPASS
REACH

VOLUME ONE OF THE
SECANTIS SEQUENCE

BY

MARK
W.
TIEDEMANN

Meisha Merlin Publishing, Inc
Atlanta, GA

COMPASS REACH

An MM Publishing Book
Published by Meisha Merlin Publishing, Inc.
PO Box 7
Decatur, GA 30031

Editing & interior layout by Stephen Pagel
Copyediting & proofreading by Teddi Stransky
Cover art by H.Ed Cox
Cover design by Neil Seltzer

ISBN: 1-892065-39-8

http://www.MeishaMerlin.com

First MM Publishing edition: June 2001

Printed in the United States of America
0 9 8 7 6 5 4 3 2 1

Dedicated to the memory of
Earline Knackstedt,
friend and mentor.

Many people helped me along the way to completing this novel and becoming a published writer, either through direct input or through steadfast encouragement and support. I would like to express my thanks to—

Tracy Adams, Eleanor Arnason, The Advance Photo Crew, Robin Bailey, Gregory Benford, Tom and Nadine Butcher-Ball, Ray and MaryAnne Braun, Ed Bryant, Rob Chilson, Bill Clemente, Vickie Daniels, Ellen Datlow, Chip Delany, John Dobbins, Gardner Dozois, Scott Edelman, Timons Esaias, Kelley Eskridge, Jim Fournier, Sherman Fowler, Peter Fuss, Carolyn I. Gilman, Nicola Griffith, Laurell Hamilton, Bernadette Harris, Lucy Holmes, Richard and Shirley Hudgens, Peg Kerr, Larry and Karen Kettinger, Gene Knackstedt, Damon Knight, Lloyd Kropp, John Lowrance, Jack McDevitt, Maureen McHugh, Deborah Millitello, Linda Nagata, Stephe Pagel, Tim and Serena Powers, Eugene Redmond, Terry Ryder, Marella Sands, Donna Schultz and gang, Sharon Shinn, Nancy Springer, Allen and Linda Steele, Drea Stein, Gordon Van Gelder, Erich Vieth, Terri Windling, Kate Wilhelm, Russell Wilhelm, Terry Winkelmann, and Gene Wolfe.

My apologies for those I may have missed—all my friends have been terrific through this.

An introduction to Mark W. Tiedemann
by
Nicola Griffith

Before Mark Tiedemann was a writer, he was a photographer. He excels at documenting people in the moment. He can be at a wedding (he was there for mine) or a workshop (we met at Clarion in 1988) and he will take a series of pictures that capture nuances—without interrupting the life in progress. You can look at the photographs a year later, five years, ten, and you are back there. There are no intrusive, irrelevant memories of having to pose, of him fiddling with light meters, no "look at me, I'm looking at you, I'm an important artist," nonsense. As a photographer, Mark is interested in people and how they fit in their world; he chooses the quiet route to art. He brings exactly the same concerns and skills to his fiction.

Fiction, of course, has one advantage: the subject does not have to exist. With science fiction this often leads to exoticism for its own sake, to wild wish-fulfillment fantasies of the superhero variety, and to the ascendancy of Idea over Story. There's nothing wrong with a novel stuffed with big skiffy ideas—I like telepathy via nanotech, paranoid artificial intelligences and aliens as much as the next reader—but some writers seem to think that's all there is: a big idea plus a few characters running around to give you a slam-bang plot. A plot, though, is just a series of events; the story is what makes us care and remember.

Story lies at the heart of any piece of good fiction. It is the account of an emotional change, a character's inner journey from one place to another. The better the writer, generally, the better the story, because the wellspring of story is a character, a human (or, as we're talking about science fiction, any artificial or organic intelligence) the reader can both believe in and sympathize with. To be a good writer, you have to do a certain amount of work. Many in the genre don't bother: this is SF, after all, and it's so much easier to trot out the old clichés of the freak IQ, the freak birth, or the freak talent. Mark Tiedemann's characters are not clichés; he never loses sight of the individual. His people, then, are, for the genre, quite unusual. They are ordinary heroes, as likely to fear failure, or commitment, or fear itself as they are to face invading cultures or rogue AIs, or nasty nano-viruses.

Having said that, there are nanotech, paranoid AIs, and strange aliens in *Compass Reach* (along with telepathy with a scientific rationale, interstellar hobos, and power-mad corporate titans). Tiedemann uses this first volume of his Secantis Sequence to lay out in detail a coherent and diverse universe, complete with necessary systems: economics, politics, history, sociology, religion, culture. We understand how people earn their money, and spend it; how they choose their government, and use it, and lose it; how they deal with the threat and actuality of change. His people, being ordinary enough to understand the way their world really works, are more likely to attempt change within a system than to try to overthrow it by revolution. They understand that one person is unlikely to mean much if s/he acts alone—no matter how big her muscles, how sharp his brain, how cool their clothes or great the rage.

The major concern of *Compass Reach*—and this is true of much of Tiedemann's short fiction; see, for example, "Passing" in *Bending the Landscape: Horror* (Overlook, 2001)—is how perfectly ordinary people deal with being insignificant in the general scheme of things. They are competent but not superhuman. They are often disenfranchised, disenchanted,

and estranged from family, and friends, and—most impor-
tantly—from themselves. In the course of the story they
find ways to return to themselves, ways to affirm themselves
without destroying planets or species or belief systems. His
characters are adults.

Compass Reach is the story of Fargo, an ordinary man who by
a series of believable incidents finds himself alone and largely
emotionally closed up while simultaneously being stuck in
the middle of significant events. His subsequent actions may
or may not have galaxy-wide implications but he knows that
whatever he does becomes part of his own history and will
ultimately affect who he is.... But Mark Tiedemann, remember, is a photographer; he never forgets the necessity of balance in his composition. So while we're focused down hard
on the people moving through their world, we also see, in a
series of both set pieces and fluid improvisations, strange
and beautifully imagined places. We walk, with Fargo,
through the maintenance levels of a well-used spaceport, are
shocked along with him by the grip of a machine mind, and
journey through the vast and ancient water cisterns beneath
Istanbul...and such is the author's skill at placing people in
their contexts that it's the earthscape that is the more won-
der-filled and alien.

Fargo makes mistakes, he learns and changes his mind and
occasionally he falters, but he keeps trying, keeps doing his
best. And we follow. For all that this is science fiction, for
all that "home" and "human" are not quite the same in this
imagined world as they are in our more recognizable one, the
place where the two come together is deeply familiar. This is
what the best books do: take us somewhere just strange
enough, with someone just familiar enough, that we have
fun, learn, and bring back food for thought.

Nicola Griffith
February 2001

COMPASS REACH

Chapter One

Fargo finished packing his bindle and took a last walk through the freerider sanctuary. When he had arrived six days ago there had been one old man still haunting the place, himself ready to leave, bellowing about monsters and impatient with Fargo's questions. Fargo liked his privacy, even enjoyed being alone days at a time—one of the benefits of freeriding—but not when he grounded. No one else had shown up since the old man left and the empty chambers had lost their appeal. The place was too quiet. Debris cluttered the floors, palimpsests of graffiti that went back to the early days of the colony crowded the walls, and anything useful had long since been picked over. Fargo's forays out into the colony proper for food and whatever else he might scrounge did not compensate for the company of other freeriders. The solace of solitude gave way to abandonment, an oppressive void. Time to leave.

A few of the old light panels still glowed along the corridors. The facility had once been part of a tubeway that the colonists had never completed. Most of the equipment had been stripped out and used elsewhere and the shunt tubes had been blocked. The installation had been forgotten, fenced off and posted against trespass. The colony was nearly ninety years old now and for a good part of the last sixty, freeriders had gathered here upon arrival, unbothered by the locals.

Fargo knew about sanctuaries on other worlds that had been abandoned for various reasons—new laws regulating freeriders, local reclamation of useful material, a move to a better facility—but he never expected to be the last to leave one.

He shouldered his bindle and switched on his headlamp, then started up the last flight of stairs to the access. He widened his beam to fill the narrow tunnel until he reached the door. He switched off his light, glanced back down into the darkness one final time, then pushed his way out into the night.

The colony of Eurasia occupied a hundred kilometer section of a feature they called the Great Plain Rift, a twenty-five hundred kilometer long gash in the face of the storm-swept northern hemisphere. It was the only surface feature constantly visible from orbit; the rest of the planet was continually obscured by massive dust storms. As Fargo descended the ramp from the sanctuary, he looked across to the opposite wall a kilometer-and-a-half away, at the clusters of habitats dug into the rock, and down into the domes and towers and streets huddled on the canyon floor. Fargo was impressed and bewildered at the human insistence to live on the surface of any world it claimed, regardless of the obstacles. Eurasia was a violent world and Fargo was glad to be leaving. Before this ride he had never been here. Six days had proved too long.

At the bottom of the ramp he unlocked the tall gate and let himself out onto the service road. He locked it again, though he could not imagine it effectively keeping anyone out, not even children, and started on his way to the spaceport. He glanced upward at the muddy brown night sky. During the day the light of 40 Eridani was just bright enough to turn it a sickly yellow-orange. Fargo preferred the night here. The rock walls rose nearly a kilometer to the wind-blown plains of Eurasia. Constantly flowing sands struck the energy shield that stretched over the colony and sparked in dim swirls that stirred the bleak night, making the sky look like a dark river.

Three days earlier he had been close to that fatal nature, high in the crags. The air was almost breathable near the top, where the energy moving through the shield tickled the fine hairs over his body even below his insulated clothes. He had perched above the spreading urb and played his synthet, looking down at the repellant beauty of the city. The colony was still growing, still mutating in a parody of organic evolution.

A door opened and closed somewhere ahead. Fargo slowed. Most of this side of the urb was manufactory, warehouse, related service facilities, and the abandoned shells of workers' barracks from the days when the tubeway was under construction. Three buildings on, he stopped opposite what appeared to be a small factory. A row of pressurized spheres lined one wall; pipes ran from each to various parts of the multilevel main structure. At a rear entrance someone had set out two large plastic boxes with the letters "FR" drawn on them in bright red.

Another freerider was busily rummaging through them.

Fargo stared for several seconds, surprised, pleased, and annoyed. He scurried across the service road and dropped to a crouch beside the other person, who glanced up quickly, eyes wide and suspicious. They were dressed similarly in patched-together black and grey clothes infused with cables and tubes that linked small black boxes and bubbles of electronic components. The effect seemed almost organic. Both carried backpacks.

"Hey," he said.

After a moment, the other frowned. "Hey."

"I was wondering if anybody here ever set anything out," Fargo said.

"It's rare," the other said. The voice was slightly nasal, female. "After this I'm heading for port."

"Me, too. May I?" He gestured to the boxes.

"Go ahead."

Fargo turned his light on the refuse between them. In a glance he saw little that might be salvaged.

"At least food hasn't been a problem," he said. "They're not bad about food, but adaptables..."

"I've been through it once now," the other said. "Some chips, a few boards with platinum and processed ceracon. Nothing intact and operative, but maybe salvageable."

"If there were an artisan here."

"Hmm."

Fargo found a patchboard covered with ruby red chips which he scraped off and dropped into a pouch at his hip. She pulled out some thick fabric and examined it under her light for several seconds, then discarded it. Fargo untangled a length of gold cable. It was burned in places, but there seemed to be sufficient quantity unscored to be usable.

They went through it layer by layer, like archaeologists, silently, until she whistled. Fargo shone his light onto her hands.

"Battery packs," he whispered, staring at the string of black disks she held. "Probably completely dead."

"No, not these. They're special units for lab equipment. Have to have a specific charge or they're useless. It's just possible..."

She pulled off her pack and opened a flap. She took out a small box with a silvery plate below a pair of gauges. She set one of the disks on the plate and watched the numbers shift on the box.

"There's one with a quarter charge," she said, then tested the next one. "Half charge. Looks like we got lucky."

"One of us, anyway," Fargo said.

She tested all the disks. Only one was completely dead, which she broke off the string and tossed away. "I'll dump the charge into our own batteries later," she said, tucking the remaining disks into her pack and putting away the tester.

"'Our' batteries?" he asked.

She paused and looked at him, an odd pout shaping her mouth, lending her, in the upwash of his lamp, the look of someone old, bitter.

"You don't want any spare juice? Fine."

"No, that's not-"

"Shh!"

He listened. He heard the faint sounds of an entertainment district in the distance, music rhythmically thundering from a nightclutch somewhere. Below that, though, was another sound, indistinct. Voices...?

She closed up her pack and shouldered it. "Never seen such edgy people," she said under her breath and started down the service road in the direction of the port. "I'll be glad to get off this rock."

Fargo rifled through the discards one more time, quickly, and found nothing else of much use. He snatched his own pack up and sprinted after her.

He caught up and fell into step.

"Where bound?" he asked.

"Tabit. You?"

"Don't know. Frontier, I hope." He shifted the pack on his shoulders. "This inner Pan shit is getting thick."

"Mmm."

"I wasn't sure if there were any other riders on Eurasia. I waited around the sanctuary but no one came by."

"Sanctuary's been abandoned for months I heard. I had a stake at a refinery till today. There were two other riders there, but they left last night. Owner was worried about inspections. He said they'd been doing them more frequently in the last year." She shrugged. "Maybe the Frontier is the way to go. It seems fewer and fewer of us gather this deep in."

"He pay you in scrip?"

She shook her head. "Bed and board. How've you managed?"

"I play synthet. Scrounged meals for public performances. A couple coes paid in scrip, but it's getting harder to come by."

"All credit quotient anymore. No Q, no access. I heard it's even getting that way in the Distals, out on the Frontier. Where'd you learn to play?"

"I always did play something. I learned when I was little. A few years back I spent time in a radical hermit's Monad.

That's where I picked up synthet. In fact, that's where I got this one."

"You're a monk?"

Fargo laughed. "Not me. But it was a place, you know? I did it before I started riding. They gave me sanctuary for a time while I made up my mind. Much as they would have welcomed me, it just wasn't where I wanted to stay. They let me keep the synthet."

"I always thought I'd like to learn to make music. Never had the patience."

"A Monad would be the place to do it. There's not much else." Fargo felt himself smile, remembering. "They had a cycle of twenty-one pieces, sort of a mantra, that supposedly produce a state of harmony. But I never felt anything more than just pleasure at playing them. Of course, I probably did it all wrong. They're supposed to be played in sequence for the proper effect, but I found all kinds of ways to rearrange them so they sounded better–or different. I even cut and spliced bits of them to each other. All wrong. Maybe they were glad to see me go."

The sound of voices came to them again, louder this time.

"Natives are restless tonight," she said.

Fargo glanced back the way they had come. The sense that people were getting nearer grew stronger, became almost a certainty. "This is the most uncharitable place I've been to," he said. "I don't think they'd even feed us but they can't stand throwing food away."

"Getting that way all over," she said.

"Since I've been here I haven't seen one of the local Invested look skyward. Not one, not once."

"Makes you wonder why they want to live here." She unzipped a pouch in her pack and pulled out the string of batteries. "You want some of this juice?"

"Sure, if you're offering." They walked in silence for several seconds. Then he said: "You want some chips? Found that boardfull–"

"Have plenty, thanks."

"Ah."

"Where did you come here from?"

"Last place I grounded was Homestead."

"Tau Ceti," she acknowledged, nodding. "Even deeper in. How was it there?"

"Crazy, like everywhere else these days."

"Mmm. I know it's crazy on Denebola. I was there six weeks ago. The Invested passed legislation to prohibit setis from leaving their assigned areas around embassies and the port."

"What? But Denebola's always been open to setis. That's where the first conferences were held–"

"I know. I told you it's crazy. Some coes were angry about it, but most were–I don't know, I guess 'frantic' is the word–frantic to get the laws passed and have any nonhumans removed from human sectors. I saw one riot, heard about six or seven more. But there's a heavier Armada presence now, too, so they didn't go very far." She shook her head. "I don't know why I thought it would be any saner deeper in."

"Maybe because there are fewer setis?"

"Maybe. I haven't seen one in months. They're getting as scarce as freeriders."

"There's still a sanctuary on Homestead, at least. Couple hundred riders."

"Still in the Old Stow warehouse district?"

"You been there? Yeah, it is."

Fargo let himself fall into the easy patter of freerider complaint, relishing the contact, the almost ritual grousing about the state of the universe. Still, it was uneasy talk, because so much of it was true, especially that things were getting worse.

Less than a kilometer from the port he gestured to a lighted brick-walled pit that contained three large bins.

"Good," she said. "This won't take long."

They moved behind the bins, against the wall, and dropped their packs.

In the light Fargo looked at her more closely. Her face was thin, almost gaunt, the lines stretched with a trace of a self-tightening intensity that simultaneously attracted and repelled. Her short hair was dark brown and her eyes were amber.

She pulled out a rectangular box from her pack and set it on the ground. She threw a couple of switches; readouts flickered blue.

"Where's your juicesump?"

Fargo opened a flap on the inside surface of his pack and showed her the dull metal plate. She nodded and attached cables to the surface then into the smaller unit between them. She laid a battery disk on the metal panel of the box. The numbers shifted quickly. She pressed a contact. A moment later a red light winked on. She discarded the drained battery and set another on the device.

Of the seventeen disks on the string she had salvaged, she gave him the power from nine and took eight for herself.

"I tested them," she said. "We get the same amount of power." She folded up her gear and replaced it. "How's your bodysheath? Been checked lately?"

Fargo's hand unconsciously went to the control at his belt that activated the sheath. "Checked it when I grounded here. Needs a new chip, but it works well enough." He frowned, remembering the uncomfortable static sensations from the last ride. The isolation field was weak in spots, inconsistent, and had failed to protect him completely from the g and the temperature. He had hoped to find an artisan here.

"Any of those chips you salvage work?" she asked.

"Don't think so." He pulled a couple of them out and ran his finger over them, checking their codes. He shook his head. "Wrong capacity. These are all data processors."

She leaned forward and studied them. "Maybe we could rig something. I have a small isolation field, I can split 'em for you, see how—"

He held up his hand. She stared at him blankly until she heard it, too: a crowd, nearing.

Fargo crawled between two bins. He blinked to force his eyes to adjust to the darkness beyond the pit, even while reaching for his nighteyes. The voices were louder but he still saw no one. He left his nighteyes in their pouch and crawled back to her.

"Later," he said, shouldering his pack. "Let's move."

"What is it?" she asked, following his lead.

"Don't know."

Fargo hurried from the pit and started down the road. There was a glow up ahead that seemed to form a curtain against the murk–the port, a few kilometers away.

One moment the road was clear, the next it was thick with people. He froze. His companion bumped into him. The mob roiled, low voices filled with resentment and nervous fear. They moved in unison like a band of stalking hunters. Fargo stood perfectly still, afraid to move.

Someone shouted, "There!" and Fargo's heart slammed in his chest, but the mob was moving quickly away, almost running.

She tapped his shoulder and pointed upward. An instant later, before he could say anything, she hurried to the canyon wall. Baffled, Fargo followed. She scrambled up the rocks and onto a narrow, half-finished trail carved into the cliff face. Below, the mob looked like a sluggish flood oozing along the service road. Lamps bobbed on the current. Fargo estimated maybe fifty or sixty coes in the group. Their voices rippled through the air, intense and threatening. Fargo and his companion quickly raced ahead of them.

"Does this run all the way to the port?" Fargo asked.

She nodded, her eyes on the road below.

Suddenly, she stopped, grabbed his arm, and gestured down.

A trio of robed figures hurried up the service road toward the port. They seemed to limp, their gait jerky and uneven. Perhaps, Fargo thought, one of them was injured and the other two were having trouble supporting their companion.

"The Invested," she said, "are playing cat-n-mouse with setis. That explains a lot."

Fargo stared. Setis, nonhumans–they walked oddly, that was the strangeness. What world? he wondered immediately, how far have they come to be here? Then: why are they being chased?

She motioned for him to follow and jogged ahead of the group below.

When they had gained about a hundred meters on the setis, she started down the canyon wall to the service road. She moved swiftly, with impressive ease over the crags. Fargo's heart beat faster as he guessed what she intended to do.

On the road, she scampered to the other side, into the shadows. Fargo watched the darkness near the buildings. Suddenly she reappeared. She started to say something, then looked down the road.

The three setis came around the bend.

They stopped.

Cowls hid their faces. Fargo stared, fascinated.

"We can help you," she said. "Trust us. We can get you to the port."

The three setis seemed to confer with each other, but Fargo heard nothing.

One of them came froward and extended a hand. Fargo started to warn her, but she reached out quickly and touched it. The seti stepped back by its companions. A moment passed and the three nodded.

"Fine," Fargo whispered, anxious. "Now what?"

She indicated the shadows into which she had disappeared. "There's an alley here that opens onto the port road. If we–" She took a few steps, stopped.

A crowd came out of the alley.

Another group came from the north down the service road.

The first group caught up.

The setis moved closer to Fargo. In the shadows immediately off the road he saw more people. Now, he guessed, they numbered closer to two hundred.

This close, in the glare of their lamps, Fargo saw the human faces clearly. He shuddered. These faces were familiar, though he had never seen any this extreme, so twisted with anger and fear, hate and rage.

The woman stepped backward. Fargo was suddenly aware that they were now a group of five and he wanted very much to not *be* there. They backed up automatically, off the road, across the uneven stone and dirt shoulder, against the canyon wall.

"Sorry," she whispered to Fargo.

He shrugged.

"There is no other way," someone said. Three someones, Fargo thought, three singers, alto, tenor, soprano, the timbres blent in rich harmony...he looked up at the nearest of the setis. It reached out a hand, quickly, and touched his face. Fargo flinched.

The mob took a step toward them. Another.

A powerful hand shoved him from behind and he staggered into the front rank of the mob. He reached out to catch himself. Hands grabbed at him, pulled him roughly. He tried to apologize as he was passed from one to another, shuffled through the crowd, but could not manage a complete sentence, very glad that he had taken the time to connect his catheter before leaving the sanctuary–

Fargo blinked, stunned for an instant by a flash of blinding darkness. A moment later he looked around to find himself being carried by one of the setis. He felt disoriented. He did not remember being picked up. His arms flailed out as he twisted to get his bearings. The seti placed him on his feet. His head swam; he reached out for balance, felt something soft, warm. Abruptly, his equilibrium clicked back into place.

The mob lay collapsed on the pavement, some of them twitching grotesquely.

"We must hurry," the seti said. The beauty of the voice undercut the urgency of the words.

The other setis were some distance ahead, one carrying the other freerider.

"How–how long before–"

"We have a short time," the seti said, setting a brisk pace on the road. "Are we on the right path to the port?"

"Yes," Fargo said. "We...were heading there ourselves."

Fargo ran alongside the seti and caught up with the others. The woman was on her feet again. She looked dazed.

"Thank you for your attempt to aid us," one of the setis said. "If we arrive intact tonight we will gratefully repay your kindness."

"No trouble," she said. She glanced at Fargo as if for corroboration. When he nodded she smiled. "By the way, my name's Lis."

"Fargo."

They walked quickly on in silence. Fargo began to relax when they crested a rise and he could see the port platform high off the ground on its many pylons, near the lip of the canyon.

"What happened?" he asked. Lis shrugged.

"We were conducting business with a local diplomat," one of the setis said. Fargo listened to the voice and almost missed the words. "Our work was concluded. We expressed interest in seeing the community. Our host was reluctant, but he escorted us. There was a misunderstanding involving our presence at a...nightclutch. Other patrons objected. When our host defended our right to be there, trouble began. We left with our host at that point. Several people followed us. A struggle occurred and we were separated from our host. We thought it best to return to the port. I hope our host will be safe. We have been trying to get back to the port since."

Fargo glanced back again, relieved at the empty roadway.

"What did you do to the mob?" Lis asked. "They acted–I don't know–nerve stunned."

None of the setis answered. Fargo tried to think of something else to say to get them to speak; his curiosity itched, and the music in their speech...he wondered, briefly, what it might be like to play synthet while they simply talked.

They came to the last stretch before the gates of the port. Beyond the gate Fargo could see the maze of columns that rose up to the port platform, each one housing a lift. Sharp blue lights spiked the darkness between the columns, casting conflicting shadows on the filthy, litterstrewn polycrete. Only ID scans guarded the seldom-used gate. A public shunt carried most people into the port–that or a private taxi lifting directly to the platform.

"How were you planning to get inside?" he asked Lis.

Before she could answer, one of the setis stepped up to the gate and inserted a chit. The gate rolled aside. The seti waved them through.

Their bootheels echoed high overhead, chittering like distant insects. The air felt thick, humid. Steam haloed the lights. On each wide pylon was a large red number, the code to the port platform high overhead. The setis wound a snaking path among them.

"Toadlickers!"

Fargo stopped, crouched.

"Frog lovers!"

He strained to see something through the confusing shadows, fog, and distance. Bootsteps clattered somewhere, but he saw no one.

"Come on, co," Lis tugged his sleeve.

They followed the setis through the maze of columns. The nonhumans moved very fast, despite their seemingly awkward gait. Finally they stopped at one of the lifts and again used an ID chit to open it. Fargo and Lis crowded in with them.

Fargo drew a deep breath. They smelled faintly of sawdust.

"You shouldn't have gone into the city without a police escort," Fargo said as they ascended to the platform.

"We had an escort at the beginning of the evening. But they disappeared later on. We were left to fend for ourselves.

We were prevented from reaching the shunt and no taxi would stop for us."

"Did you try to contact your embassy?" Lis asked. "Maybe the Armada could have—"

"We preferred not to involve the Armada. And it did not seem reasonable to endanger anyone else from the embassy."

"It's getting bad," Lis commented.

"Yes," the seti said.

The lift opened and they stepped out onto the port platform

The lift opened onto a promenade that overlooked the landing field. Smooth polycrete bridged the gap between the canyon walls for ten kilometers. Blast pits dimpled the tarmac in neat ranks. Most of them were unoccupied. The few shuttles waiting to lift off bulged out of their pads like unopened flowers. The bright lights set their aging, discolored hulls with dull jewels. Fargo turned and looked down the long row of buildings huddled against the edge of the platform: embassies, warehouses, the Armada garrison, hostelries, hangars, and corporate offices. The port was a small town in itself. Fargo could make out a few human shapes far down the line of structures. Over it all the force shield coruscated with the dark oil-and-water patterns of the windblown sands. To Fargo the port seemed more alive, more vital than all the rest of the Eurasian settlement. He was not at all unhappy about leaving this bleak place.

In the distance a shuttle lifted off. Fargo pressed against the transparency, rapt.

Light grew beneath it, leaking out from the spaces between the hull and the cradle, brightening from dull orange up through red-tinged yellow to white. The fires flickered rapidly in an even pulse and the vibration rose through the scales to an audible rumble.

The shield above it puckered and irised open. Sand swirled down in a column for a few moments, enveloping the shuttle.

Then it rose, the fires of its engines strobing through the curtain of dust, shoving up through the thick atmosphere. The hole in the shield snapped closed. Fargo watched the bright trail of the shuttle quickly fade to a pinpoint, then disappear.

"The embassy is this way," the seti said, pointing.

"We'll leave you here," Lis said, moving closer to Fargo. "You can get protection from this point on."

The setis all reached up and pushed their cowls back. Large, dark eyes caught pinpoint highlights; a ridge emerged from just below the brow to push outward above the small mouth, which was a dark, moist line; soft, saffron-colored fur covered the face and head from the jawline up, leaving clear a pair of three-slitted vents that hugged the jaw from where ears *ought* to have been down to the chin. The throat was a complex webwork of tissue that fluttered slightly when they spoke.

"You will not come inside with us?"

Fargo shook his head, then laughed self-consciously. "Thank you, but we have ships to catch. Got to be on schedule."

The "leader" extended its hands. Fargo saw that they were covered in fur except for a round area in the middle of the palm and a small spot on each fingertip. The fingers seemed too long, with extra joints, and the wrist bent at an odd angle.

"I am Voj-Nehan of the Ranonan Trade Legation. I am a resource you are welcome to use if you need anything."

Fargo smiled and hesitantly took the hand extended to him. Lis accepted the other hand.

For an instant his vision doubled. He blinked hard, then closed his eyes. *The light changed—he recognized the color of that sun, he thought, and the group of nonhumans moving away from him were Rahalen, tall and distantly elegant, the most humanlike of the several seti groups—he opened his eyes to look at Lis, though it seemed briefly that he saw only himself. He felt for a moment as if he were falling down an endless tunnel, air rushing through him, around him. Electricity suffused his mind and the world seemed very bright.* Lis gaped, caught her breath. Fargo closed his eyes again, but he could still *see* the setis, clearly, though it felt like he held the wrong hand. He began to pitch forward, opened his eyes, and caught himself against the door of the lift.

He looked up and saw the setis disappearing down a walkway, heading for one of the buildings.

"The evening's catching up with me," he said, laughing. He rubbed his hand absently; the skin tingled warmly.

Lis stared at her hand, mouth open. "I think I'm going to be more careful with whom I shake hands from now on."

Fargo laughed again. She looked up and smiled tentatively.

"Maybe you're right," she said, straightening. She rubbed her hand against her hip. "Everything *is* catching up. I think we ought to see about our ride, eh?"

Fargo nodded. He stared at Lis, unwilling to look away. She looked toward the field, at the shuttles, and he felt an odd rush of excitement at the way the shadows accented her cheekbones and the curve from her lower lip to her chin.

She looked in the direction of the setis with a sudden expression of longing. It startled Fargo by its familiarity. He felt it, too, and glanced back. But Voj-Nehan and its companions were gone.

"The Seven Reaches hold nothing but strange," she murmured. It was an old saying, but Freeriders still used it, when they talked among themselves about the chance to Ride out of human-settled space, leave the Pan Humana, and see what the seti realms, the Seven Reaches, had to offer. No one Fargo knew of had ever gone.

"Come on," Lis said suddenly. "Time to get off this stone."

Fargo followed her along the walkway to a stair that led down to the loading level. At the bottom she switched on her bodysheath. Fargo hesitated, then turned his on. The field coursed over him, giving him an unpleasant chill.

Drones ran cargo trains out from warehouses to shuttles. Fargo saw no passenger ferries, but he had expected none. Eurasia was not a world tourists frequented and starship crews could find better shoreleave on the transit station. Port personnel were replaced from time to time and occasionally there would be garrison rotation, but other than the infrequent government mission few people came here.

The forest of service modules, storage bins, and gantries was threaded by invisible tracks the robots followed. All loading and maintenance occurred here, below a ceiling of polycrete fifteen meters thick.

Lis tapped his arm and approached a polycom set into the wall near one of the drone tunnels. She pulled an earplug from her belt and inserted it into her left ear, jacked another line into a port on the polycom, entered a few sequences of code through its touchpad, then bent her head to listen. Fargo blinked and looked at the roster of shuttles that scrolled onto the screen. There were heavy lifters belonging to the huge starships waiting in orbit, as well as slightly smaller robot shuttles. The bigger ships were manned, bonded carriers and built to haul perishables and sensitive manufactures to orbit. The robots, which belonged to Eurasia, lifted big supplementals filled with raw material or bulk nonvolatiles to orbit, shepherded the huge nacelles to a waiting ship, then detached and drifted back down to the surface. Fargo hated hitching rides out of gravity wells on such drones. He was glad to see the larger shuttles. He selected one at random–pad 29.

"Found mine," she said, unhooking. She turned to him. "You a lonerider?"

He nodded. "Are you?"

"Usually."

They stood like that for several seconds. Fargo felt an urge to say something else. But he was confused and he had always remained silent when confused. Suddenly, Lis drew a deep breath and looked away.

"Well, let's get to them, then."

He hitched up his pack unnecessarily and fell into step beside her. They hurried out into the maze of service machinery. The bodysheaths kept most of automated security from "seeing" them, but it was never certain when a human might be monitoring the field. Fargo searched for his number, vaguely uneasy, vaguely aware it was connected to Lis and the setis, and unwilling to voice his disquiet.

"I'm going this way," she said.

Fargo jerked to a halt and looked in the direction Lis pointed. A number of loaders tended the cargo shunt that angled up into the side of the shuttle. The tube entered the shuttle and spilled the contents drawn from the shunts into stowage. Somewhere overhead, obscured by the mass of the boat and the tending machinery, was the sealed bottom of the blast pit.

"Wouldn't want to come along, would you?" she asked.

Fargo swallowed. He had been afraid of the question–afraid she would ask, afraid she would not.

Bluish light colored half her face, pooling in her left eye. Machinery began hammering off in the distance. He opened his mouth to say "Yes," then closed it. He wanted to go with her but did not know why. The image of the Rahalens walking away under another sun intruded. Suspicion replaced the immediate desire, and he shook his head, not so much at her offer as at his own bewildered feelings.

Lis nodded and looked away. "I see. You don't know what the freight is."

"No, I–"

She smiled thinly. "You don't want to be obligated. I understand. I feel the same way."

"You do?" He felt certain she did not.

"Well," she said, "safe travel, co. Maybe we'll meet somewhere else, eh?"

"Sure..."

She slapped his shoulder, causing a bright spark between their sheaths. Then she pulled her hood over her head. She looked at him for another moment, frowning, then leaned abruptly forward and kissed his cheek. Blue-white light flashed briefly in the corner of his eye.

And she was gone. Fargo touched his face. He considered following her, but he hesitated just long enough for the feeling to pass. He travelled alone, always had since leaving the Monad. It was better that way. He relied on no one, no one depended on him, and he enjoyed the illusion of freedom. It gave him a kind of equilibrium, as though he were a universe unto himself, centered and complete.

Through the soles of his boots he felt a heavy vibration building. Even down here the force of the lift-offs penetrated.

He moved on. He checked the numbers on the service drones, watched for cargo nacelles marked for the pad he wanted. If he was lucky his next ride would take him further out to the Frontier, into the Distals, away from the growing craziness of the inner Pan. Maybe, he thought, I should've asked Lis to verify it for me. He glanced back in her direction. No. It would have obligated him. Not a lot, but a start, and he felt himself fortunate to have pulled away at all.

The next three pads he checked were not his. The fourth was.

Only one train of cargo remained connected to the shunt tube. Fargo chided himself for cutting things so close and went to the last car of the train. The manifest posted on the rear hatch declared the contents to be several tons of long chain polymer enroute to Finders. That was a fairly new colony, younger even than Eurasia, out among the Distals, the farthest reaches of human settlement. It was possible he might find real work there and plenty of loose scrip.

He walked the length of the train to the car that was currently uploading into the shunt. Along the length of the big tube were trapdoors in case of a jam, which almost never happened. The nearest one was several meters along its length, about three meters off the ground. The tube was sheathed in strutwork for the small robot tenders to climb along. Fargo jumped up once, missed. Jumped again and caught hold of a thick bar. He let himself hang until he stopped swinging, then worked to get a better grip–

–and was painfully torn from the metal and thrown to the ground. He hit the polycrete and rolled backward, his breath exploding from his lungs. His fingers stung. Maybe, he thought, the damned thing's electrified.

As he began to stand, something slammed into his ribs.

He rolled again and came to his feet in a low crouch. All around him stood hunched, angry shapes, faces partially visible in the chaotic light of the port. Someone reached for him; reflexively he slapped the hands away.

"Frog lover," someone said.

"Suckhead!"

"Toadlicker!"

"Suckshit!"

Fargo shifted his gaze from face to face, realizing that these were either part of the mob he had thought they had escaped or a new mob with the same mind. He noted a couple of port maintenance coveralls.

They stood between him and the train.

"I'm a nid, coes," he said. "No ID, no existence. Don't want a reputation for seeing the unseeable, do you?"

Two of them stepped toward him from opposite sides. Fargo spun, drove his leg straight out in a solid kick into the midsection of the largest of the two. Fargo staggered, though, and lost his balance. Long enough for the other one to punch him in the head.

The tension broke and they attacked him. He uselessly fought back until he fell limply to the pavement. Bright sparks clouded his vision and the world beneath him heaved and turned.

Chapter Two

When he opened his eyes the mob was gone. He pushed himself up to his hands and knees. He did not know how long he had been unconscious. Every part of his body ached and his breath came painfully, with a sharp stab at the apex of every inhalation. He wondered how many ribs were broken.

The sounds of the port were louder, meaner. Carefully, he rolled over into a sitting position.

Before him, strewn across the polycrete, were all his belongings. His pack had been ripped open and everything pulled out.

"Children will be nosy," he muttered, shaking his head. He craned his neck back and saw that the train was gone and the shuttle itself had been taken up. The way his ears rang it had probably left already.

He managed to get to his feet. The pack itself lay beside him. It was undamaged, only emptied. Fargo began moving from item to item. Each intact piece went into the pack. He winced when he found his synthet, completely smashed. He dropped to his knees and hefted the largest pieces. Inexplicably, he felt ashamed. The synthet was a gift, a responsibility, a part of a past to which he could not return, could never repay. In his mind he devised a number of tortures for the mob, to be carried out the day he was voted Chairman of the Pan Humana, or even God, whatever that might be.

With a kind of ritual care he bundled the pieces together and placed them inside his pack. He closed his eyes for a second, then gathered up the rest.

He heard voices then. His hand went automatically to his bodysheath–

"Shit!" he hissed, cupping in his right hand the dangling remnants of the control box. He stared at it and weighed the options. Without it he would have to go through lift-off unbuffered from any g not absorbed by the shuttle's own isolation field. But more immediately he could not long evade port security.

He looked back toward the port buildings. There was the seti offer. If ever he needed anything...? He scowled and dismissed the idea. He had no idea what the freight might be. Lis had gotten that right–if he did not know the cost, he did not accept help.

He pulled the box off his belt and shoved it into his pack. He looked up at the sealed-off bottom of the pad, then out through the tangle of machinery around him. About a hundred meters away another shuttle was still being loaded. He weighed the risks, wondering how bad it could be without his sheath. He might be lucky, hop aboard with a load of perishables on a boat with a well-monitored isolation field. Normally even a loosely controlled field that let through some of the g would be tolerable. But he was hurt and he did not know how badly. The sound of voices reached him again and he decided. Whatever else, he had no wish to remain on Eurasia. "Can't be any worse than a broken heart," he muttered.

He walked stiffly to the other shuttle. The voices receded. The shunt was drawing from the second to last car of a fifteen-segment train. He did not bother to read the manifest–it made no difference now. He stared at the strut he needed to catch for a long while, trying to force the pain out of his mind. Suddenly, he crouched and jumped. His torso ignited in agony. When he opened his eyes he was holding firmly onto the strut.

He pulled himself up into the webwork of metal. Every motion made him wince. Carefully, he began to climb.

He finally reached the access port on the tube. He rested for a few minutes and studied the surface before him as if he had never seen one before.

Fargo pulled a small tool, his multijack, from a sheath inside his left boot. He fumbled with the ring on its base and a bit extruded from the other end. The head fit perfectly into a small hole beneath the panel. He twisted; the panel irised open.

He slipped the multijack back into his boot, then hoisted himself into the dark tunnel. Packages tumbled up the shaft, bumped and jostled him, setting his aches afire. He let the suspensor field carry him into the boat.

Just within, robot handlers snagged the packages and handed them off to other manipulators for stowage. Fargo winced away from one as it tried to grab him. The pain cleared his head for a few seconds and he found the handrails that led away from the sorting area. The suspensor field released him with a viscous sucking sensation and he felt his weight return.

Breathing raggedly, ears ringing, he climbed the twenty meters to where the tunnel let him into a small spherical chamber. Numbers and glowing switches starred the blackness. He groped for his lamp and scanned the control panels. He pushed the contact that resealed the access iris, then checked the environmental integrity. This was only a loading bay service node, so it was possible that it might not maintain atmosphere well, but–no, it was tight.

Fargo relaxed then. He only had to worry about lift-off killing him. Still, he took out his breather mask. As far as he could tell it was still sound. Then he propped his pack up to make a cushion. He took a couple of *episoph* pills to ease the pain.

He stretched out against the pack and tried to list mentally all the individual bruises and broken bones he had, but they kept overlapping each other into one overwhelming ache. Exhaustion became his focus.

The rumble was heavier, more solid here within the ship. He blinked, swallowed, and thought very clearly that, really, he should have gone with Lis. At the thought, he felt a strong, almost desperate desire to see her again.

The rumble became a constant explosion and a large, steel hand pressed him against the pack. An eternity later he lost consciousness.

"Who is he?"

"You don't know?"

Fargo concentrated on the low voices. He felt packed in cotton. He could not open his eyes. Even the words he heard seemed to come from far away.

"If by that do you mean does he work for Estana, I wouldn't know."

"He's probably just what the shipmaster said. A freerider."

He could not feel his limbs. He remembered, vaguely, pain, but even that was just a hazy memory. Fargo worked on opening his eyes; he felt a delicate tearing along his lashes. He drew a deep breath. His ribs shifted; there should have been a lot of pain. He remembered the maintenance node, the lift-off–he did not remember being found. He worked at his eyes again and was rewarded by his left lid peeling apart stickily.

"He's waking up."

Water sprayed across his eyes, cool and startling. Someone wiped at them gently and Fargo managed to open both.

A face hovered above him, framed in blackness. Light hair, delicate features, large grey eyes. Fargo blinked to clear his sight.

"Wha–" he croaked and immediately a tube slipped between his lips and a trickle of water filled his mouth. He swallowed, took more, began to suck. Working the muscles of his throat felt wonderful. He turned from the tube, coughed. "Where am I?"

"Easy, co. Monitor's got you sedated, don't fight it."

"Oh."

"You're lucky you didn't die in there, co. We were ten hours out from Eridani before we found you."

Eridani? Oh, yes, he remembered: 40 Eridani, Eurasia's primary.

Fargo looked past the man. The lights were low, but he made out the shapes of other beds, hulking biomonitors beside each one–standard med facility–and another man standing by the hatch, staring at Fargo.

"You're a freerider?" the man beside him asked. It was politely asked, none of the scatological curiosity Fargo usually heard from Invested who chose to speak to a nid. He did not even seem put off by Fargo's body hair.

"Maybe."

The man smiled. "We found no ID of any sort on you. Just your clothes and your pack and your physical condition." He waited. When Fargo did not respond he continued. "You're badly bruised and you were bleeding internally. You've been under the healer for three days now. You're pain is still being blocked and will be until our medtech decides you can bear it on your own."

Fargo studied him. His smile was quiet and young and he seemed very patient. He watched Fargo intently, as if waiting for Fargo to recognize him. Uneasily, Fargo realized he felt willing to trust this co.

"I'm–yes, I'm a freerider."

The man turned to the other. "Satisfied, Daniel?"

The one at the hatch shrugged. "I don't see why you just didn't let me have a look inside, we could have left him asleep."

"Because it isn't polite–"

"Oh, no, we must be anything but impolite!"

"–or necessary." They stared at each other for a long, silent time. Fargo watched until he thought he heard voices. He turned his head to see if anyone else was present, too quickly, and he felt dizzy.

The hatch slid shut with a dull thud. Fargo looked back and saw that the one named Daniel had left.

"My name is Stephen."

Fargo stared at him.

"Are you going to tell me yours, or do I just call you nid?"

"Fargo."

"Fargo." Stephen nodded and stood. He reached toward the biomonitor. "I'm going to let you sleep some more, Fargo. We'll talk later."

Before Fargo could say anything, the thickness around his senses increased and he faded off to sleep.

Gradually, over the next few days, the biomonitor withdrew the sensory block. Fargo woke a couple of times in discomfort. His torso ached and his left wrist felt sprained.

The morning of the fourth day, Stephen came with a set of grey utilities and placed them on the next bed. He deftly canceled the remaining biomonitor functions. Fargo groaned as sensation returned to him fully. He wrapped his arms around his ribs and rolled slowly onto his side. Stephen helped him to sit up. Fargo laughed weakly at the effort it took.

"You'll recover quickly now," Stephen said. "The bones have all knit, the clots are gone, and all you have to do is work through the stiffness."

Fargo nodded, then gestured at the utilities. "Where are my clothes?"

"Elsewhere. You'll get them back when you leave us. For now, though..."

Fargo sat still, letting himself get used to the aches and pains, and watching Stephen. The man waited, apparently glad to see Fargo up, willing to help.

Finally, Fargo slid to the deck and held onto the pallet behind him till his legs steadied. He sighed and crossed to the next pallet and picked up the shipboard coveralls. Each step was an effort, as much from apprehension as from pain. Stephen moved to help him, but Fargo held up his hand. Grunting with every twinge, he managed to step into the utilities and pull them up.

"Well," he said with forced good humor, "if I can do that I can do anything."

"Like manage a real meal?"

Fargo gave Stephen a long look. "What's the freight, co?"

Stephen looked at him innocently.

"I've been caught," Fargo said. "I owe passage. What's the freight?"

"Simple enough. You do as I say till the next port. You work for me."

"And just who *are* you?"

"Stephen Christopher."

"So? Do you own this ship?"

"No, but my employer is leasing it at the moment. Which means, effectively, that the shipmaster works for me." He smiled. "Still, it took some persuasion to keep him from shoving you out a lock anyway. Now, about that meal...?"

"I guess if I work for you, then I do as you say."

Stephen nodded. "And I say you eat, co."

"Not co. I'm not Invested."

Stephen motioned him toward the hatch.

Fargo stepped out onto a broad walkway that ran the length of the central access shaft. He went to the rail and looked up. Five other walkways marked off equidistant points around the circle. Light panels spaced every couple of meters threw cross-hatching shadows. From where he stood, Fargo counted five transfer rings that rotated from segment to segment, one pseudograv orientation to the next. He estimated the shaft to be about one hundred fifty meters long.

"What ship is this?" he asked.

"The *Caliban*."

"Independent?"

"Of course."

Fargo nodded, relieved. Stephen started walking aft and Fargo followed. Other people came out onto different walkways, tilted at angles to his perspective. Fargo looked away, his equilibrium still off from the pain and the wobbly feeling in his legs. He touched the railing to steady himself, embarrassed.

The mess hall was a short distance from the med center, right next to a transfer ring. A half dozen crew, wearing pale green or blue utilities, clustered around one of the larger tables. Fargo saw them look up, felt them focus on him. He stayed close to Stephen. Stephen gestured toward the dispenser.

"Select whatever you want," he said.

Fargo glanced at the crew again. Only a few still watched him and now they turned quickly away. He punched in his requests and moved to the end of the line. A panel opened and his tray slid out. The aroma filled his sinuses; he reached automatically for a piece of meat, then stopped. He carefully lifted the tray and walked to a table, conscious of the surreptitious looks from the crew. His belly made small noises, but Fargo went through the proper motions–napkin, knife and fork, waited for his "host" to join him. Stephen sat down across from him with a glass of water.

The food on Eurasia had been good, but he never knew when he might be forced back into scrounging excess supplement from a processing facility or digging in refuse bins for discards. Even on Eurasia he had been fed mostly sandwiches, protein and carb loaf, rarely hot, always something quickly prepared that did not require any co to spend much time on him. He closed his eyes and savored the meat–he did not recognize it–the potatoes, the mixed vegetables, the fresh bread. And coffee!

When he opened his eyes he found Stephen Christopher staring at him intently, with open curiosity. Fargo blinked, then scowled. Stephen reddened slightly and looked away. The group of crew suddenly burst into laughter. One of them stood and left the mess. None of them were looking at Fargo, though.

"Does it bother you to be invisible?" Stephen asked.

"Sometimes. Does it bother you to be visible?"

Stephen looked at him uncertainly. "How did you become a freerider?"

Fargo filled his mouth with food and took his time chewing. He rinsed his food down with coffee.

"Why do you want to know?"

"I'm curious, that's all. If the question offends you—"

Fargo chuckled. "It's difficult to know what questions are offensive when they never get asked. Funny. We don't care for being invisible, but we like the privacy. In some ways we have more privacy than you Invested. There's nothing to be known about us, even if someone were interested. We don't exist, we have no reality. No future...no past." He shrugged. "Fargo the freerider didn't exist before he was a freerider. He didn't do anything to become one. Someone else did and he doesn't exist anymore."

"So what did this someone do to create Fargo?"

"You'd have to ask him, co." He sopped the rest of the gravy with the bread and popped it into his mouth. He daubed his lips with exaggerated delicacy, wiped his fingers, and dropped the napkin on the plate. "Thanks for the meal. What's next?"

Stephen started to answer, then closed his mouth around a frown, and glanced toward the entrance. The one called Daniel stood there staring at him. In the light of the mess Fargo could see him clearly now. Daniel's black hair made his pale skin seem pallorous. His jaw was wide and his eyes piercing green.

It seemed to Fargo that Stephen and Daniel seized each other's attention, physically held it for several seconds. Fargo watched, unable to look away, until Daniel gave a half smile and ducked back out.

"Come on," Stephen said abruptly, looking apologetic. "I'll show you where you sleep."

Fargo hesitated. Phantom noises danced through his mind, like a recent memory of a conversation he had overheard. He struggled for a moment to focus on individual words, but they slipped between the attempt and faded.

"Fargo?"

Stephen was halfway to the exit. Fargo laughed self-consciously and stood. He placed his tray in the recycle chute and followed Stephen.

Stephen led him forward, toward the bridge. They entered a booth on the first transfer ring. Seats folded out from the wall of the small chamber. Stephen touched a contact beside the hatch and the ring took them two segments around. Fargo's stomach lurched slightly at the shift in orientation as they passed from one pseudograv field to another; the system needed adjusting.

Two doors aft of the ring, Stephen brought him into a spacious, comfortably furnished cabin. A second compartment let off the main room. A fully equipped polycom stood against one wall.

"This looks more like the shipmaster's quarters," Fargo said. He wrinkled his nose at a faint burnt odor.

"Almost," Daniel said. He stood in the connecting doorway. "The exec's. Privilege of position. Stephen's owner–"

"Employer."

"–expects the best for his pets." Daniel stared at Stephen. Tensions raised the hairs on Fargo's neck and he suppressed a shudder.

"Daniel has a slightly dramatic descriptive sense," Stephen said. He seemed to flinch at something. "Fargo is going to act as our valet till we reach our destination. But he'll take direction from me." He stared at Daniel.

Daniel grinned at Fargo, then stepped back through the connecting hatch.

"Valet," Fargo said. "Been awhile since I had a title. What do you want me to do?"

At first Stephen did not answer, only continued to gaze at the connecting door, his face rigid. Fargo looked over the cabin uneasily. A couch ran the length of one wall; fold-out chairs; a set of shelves bore various objects, the sort of bric-a-brac spacers tended to collect over time; little else, almost nothing personal.

"You can bring us our meals here," Stephen said suddenly. "We won't be leaving these cabins if it can be helped till we reach our port. Take care of laundry, other errands for us."

"Do you really think you can keep me locked up all the way to Markab?" Daniel called from the other room.

"Help me make sure my friend doesn't wander off. And–"

He suddenly winced, eyes squeezing shut, teeth bared. Fargo stepped back, toward the exit. The smell seemed stronger. Fargo's pulse quickened. He wanted to run. A second later, Stephen, face white, opened his eyes wide. He glared at the connecting door for several moments, then crossed to it. He leaned through.

"You'll stay where I tell you to stay!"

"Mind that temper, Stephen. Hanna wouldn't approve."

Stephen hissed sharply. "Don't even think you can tell me about–"

Fargo came against the wall. He glanced to his left, at the door. It might be possible, he thought, to hide in the transfer ring crawlspaces, work my way to the cargo bays through the maintenance ducts–

Not without my clothes–

Half my gear is smashed–

Fargo looked back as Stephen's arms dropped to his sides. His hunched shoulders relaxed and he glanced sheepishly at Fargo. The tension faded palpably.

He said to Daniel in a much quieter voice, "Please. Don't fight with me over this."

If Daniel replied Fargo did not hear. Fargo let out a long, shaky breath. His legs quivered and he let himself slide to the deck. A mild headache pressed around his sinuses. In a fair universe, he thought, this should have covered the freight. He closed his eyes. Fair is a fable, he thought. There's only you and whatever happens next.

Fargo dozed on the sofa and came awake with a start. Stephen sat at the polycom, motionlessly intent on the screen. Fargo rubbed his eyes and stretched.

"Good," Stephen said. "You can get us dinner."

Fargo looked around. "How long did I sleep?" When Stephen did not answer, Fargo stood. "Sorry. What do you want?"

Stephen shook his head absently, then blanked the screen. "We've been eating what the crew eats. Just bring a variety. Get yourself something, too."

"Do you want me to eat here with you?"

"That might be best for now."

Fargo went back to the same mess. He paused outside to look down the length of the ship. He had crawled through dozens of vessels like this with his father...

Two crew approached him and he self-consciously turned from the rail and entered the mess.

Three others sat at a table far from the dispensers. Fargo went directly to the counter and began tapping in orders for various dishes.

"Do you work for those two in the exec's cabin?"

Fargo looked around. "Excuse me?"

The three exchanged amused looks. The one on the left said, "I asked if you're working for our passengers."

Fargo nodded. "It's freight."

"You're a freerider."

Dispenser doors slid open. Fargo pulled plates out and set them on the tray.

The man leaned against the counter beside him, folded his arms. "The reason I ask," he said conversationally, "is that we all have a wager running that they aren't really human."

Fargo paused. "Why would you say that, co?"

"Little things. You *have* noticed some peculiarities about them. Eh?"

"Well...to tell you the truth I haven't. I only got out of your infirmary a few hours ago."

The man nodded and looked down at the tray. "That's not all for you, is it?"

The last panel opened and Fargo gratefully transferred the plate. He sighed and gripped the edges of the tray. "No, this is for my–your–passengers. If they eat all this, I'll let you know. That'll prove they're human."

The man frowned. "How so?"

"This is ship's mess. Do you know any setis that could survive it?" Fargo held his breath. The joke was an old one, but using it here, now, was a risk.

He smiled, patted Fargo's shoulder, and went back to the table. Fargo emptied his lungs and lifted the tray. The three crew chuckled. Fargo kept his eyes on the exit as he crossed the deck.

"Hey."

Fargo stopped.

"What's your name?"

"Fargo."

"See you around, Fargo. And let me know if they finish."

Fargo gave them a quick look and a smile and hurried out. Daniel met him at the cabin door, grinning.

"Food! Wonderful! I'm starved!"

He took the tray from Fargo and went back to the other chamber. The connecting door slid shut. Fargo looked back down the corridor and considered exploring. He patted his belly and went back to the mess.

The same three crew looked up when he came in.

"Forget something, Fargo?" the one who had spoken to him before asked.

"*My* dinner."

They laughed. Fargo punched up a meal and prepared to go back to the cabin.

"Fargo, come here. Sit."

Uncertainly, Fargo set his tray on the table among theirs and sat down. "Thanks, co. You're sure you don't mind...?"

"You used to work ships, didn't you?"

Fargo nodded. "Been some time, but...this is a converted Kraken class in-system, isn't it?"

Eyebrows went up, glances exchanged.

"Fifty-six years old," another said. "Converted fifteen years ago."

"They're one of the easiest," Fargo said. "Hard puller. If I had my choice it's what I'd run. What system?"

"Homestead, originally. Shipmaster Sterg's from Neighbors, though, so our tag says."

"Been to both places."

"I'll bet you've been to some places."

"Well..."

When he returned to the exec's cabin he found the connecting door still closed. Relieved, he sprawled out on the sofa and thought about Dieter, Midec, and Royce, his new crew acquaintances. Like most independent spacers, they did not care for freeriders as a class–or, Fargo thought, a non-class–but they were fascinated by them individually. Given the opportunity and the proper encouragement, spacers and freeriders bridged the gap easily.

Royce had offered to take him around the *Caliban*...

He stretched and triggered small pains the length of his body, so he made himself simply lie still while consciousness faded.

...the bar, half-bar, no, there was an omnirec attached, it opened out on a launch field, pits to the horizon, ships coming, going, faces crammed against the mirror behind the bench, talk talk talk, want a drink, there, tall red fluted glass, smokey contents, thanks, Lis, you're welcome, been here too long, no, not long enough, where did you go, long story, a ship rolled up to the window, his father riding the nose, a wrench in one hand, a synthet in the other, isn't that your dad, yeah, let's get out of here, sure, out the other door, onto a ledge overlooking a valley, clouds pale blue, bubbling over too-green, hey, I know this place, it's Aquas, sure, that's aqual in your glass, what glass, Lis reaches out, take his hand, don't run off anymore, okay, okay, I won't, didn't mean to last time, but, hey, don't explain, it just makes it tougher, where to now, there's our ship, over by the ledge, hovering, big clamshell carrier, three setis standing in bay, waving, Lis dragging,

no, wait, where, this is it, this is what you want, I know you do, but I don't know I want this, well, figure it out, I'm not taking you back to nothing again, my glass is empty...

Fargo opened his eyes. The room was dark. He shifted and his utilities sucked damply at his back. He rubbed his face and sat up. He listened intently for a time, but no sound came from the other room.

He pulled off the sweat-soaked clothes and tossed them into the darkness. The hygiene cubicle was in their room. He wanted to shower, wash the stink off, but he did not want to wake them. He lay back down, rolled onto his side, and tried to sleep.

"Lis," he whispered and peered intently into the lightless press around him. He winced at a sharp internal pang, surprised and scared. "How do I sleep with this?" He grunted, not knowing what it was that prompted the question, and worried at it until, mantra-like, it shoved him into a light sleep.

Chapter Three

In the morning he woke with a painful bladder. The room lights were low–he saw his utilities crumpled against the door– but the connecting door was still shut.

Fargo rolled to his feet and knocked. "Coming in," he called. "Need the cube."

He pressed the contact and hurried in as the door slid aside. He tried to aim for it without looking around, but he glimpsed Daniel and Stephen in the bed, sheets tangled around them. He reached the cubicle, stepped inside, and sealed it.

He sighed in relief as he urinated.

Fargo showered. The spray of water felt wonderful and there was plenty of it. He wondered how much the crew got, if any. Defoliant sprays and sonic scrubs, maybe, while the shipmaster and exec got this.

He stepped out in full light. Daniel sat crosslegged on the bed.

"Nice bruises," he said. "Looks painful. I could clear some of that up if you want."

"Fargo!" Stephen called from the main room.

Daniel waved at the door. "The master calls."

Uneasily, Fargo left the bedroom. Stephen sat at the polycom, his hair tousled, his eyes narrow and bloodshot.

Fargo shook out his utilities and smelled them. Not too bad, he thought, but I should've hung them up. The fibers needed room to let loose the particles of dead skin, hair, and dried sweat. He stepped into them and zipped it up.

"Pardon, co," he asked, "but did you say we were going to Markab?"

Stephen nodded. "Why?"

"Just curious. Need to plan my next ride. Helps to know where I'm going."

"Get us breakfast please. Then I have an errand for you to run." He typed desultorily on the keypad.

Fargo went back into the bedroom. Daniel had not moved. He watched Fargo with a grin. Fargo took the tray of empty plates and left quickly.

He did not see his three crew in the mess or on the walkways. He filled another tray and returned. Stephen handed him a disk.

"For Shipmaster Sterg."

"You're sure? I mean..."

"It's all right. He knows you're working for me."

"And after that?"

Stephen shrugged. He seemed preoccupied. It was easy to see how the crew might think these two were setis; their behavior was certainly unusual.

The shipmaster's cabin was along the same passageway, about thirty meters forward. A small plaque was set center in the door.

M. Sterg
Shipmaster
Caliban

Fargo touched the bell and waited. The door slid open.

Sterg sat behind a desk. His left hand rested on a square interface panel. Sterg's eyes shifted sightlessly. The polyceramo implants in his fingertips connected him directly to the ship's cybernetic systems. Fargo had seen few of these systems, knew they were becoming more common, especially among spacers. They made him uncomfortable. Part of him wondered what it must be like to become one with a computer, to expand one's awareness and mental capacity, or through another such interface link with a human being. It was a little like telepathy. The thought brought Lis sharply to mind.

"Yes?" Sterg said.

Fargo started. The man was half-in, half-out of the interface, eyes tracking as if watching something in the air between them.

"I have a message from Co Christopher," he said.

"Leave it."

Fargo dropped the disk on the desk before the man, nodded politely, and backed out of the cabin.

"Looking for something?"

Fargo turned. A tall man with short salt-and-pepper hair stared down at him. He stood very close; Fargo stepped back reflexively and bumped against the now-closed door.

"Uh...no, co, I already found it. Him. I–"

The man frowned suddenly. "You're the nid we found, aren't you? What are you doing in the shipmaster's cabin?"

"I had to–"

He raised his right hand toward Fargo's face. The motion was unhurried, almost casual. Fargo stiffened. The fingertips stopped centimeters from his mouth and hovered there.

"Don't," Fargo said quietly.

The hand withdrew slowly. "That's my cabin Co Christopher and his friend are using."

Fargo swallowed. "It's a nice cabin."

The Exec raised his eyebrows.

"I mean–"

"Don't explain."

Fargo grew angry. "I'm working my freight in Co Christopher's service. If that's not all right with you, take it up with your shipmaster or Christopher's employer."

"Janacek."

"What?"

"Kol Janacek. Do you know the name? He's Co Christopher's employer. And ours, for this trip." He stepped back. "Tell Co Christopher that any further communications with the shipmaster go through me. A lease doesn't change the way this ship is run."

"I'll mention it, co."

Fargo glanced back once as he hurried down the corridor. The Exec was gone.

Fargo found Royce three levels around, in one of the cargo supplementals running updates on sealed atmosphere containers. Fargo kept him company till he finished, then let Royce take him on a tour.

Fargo understood the basic design. The forward section contained navigation, engineering, the polycom data core, environmental support, everything permanent. The central shaft connected it to the aft assembly where the translight envelope generator was housed. One hundred twenty degrees apart, three TEG vanes extended outward from the shaft. Between them the supplementals attached to the shaft. For a conversion, the design was elegant.

The *Caliban* carried a permanent crew of twenty and took on temp crew, short haul workers, depending on the kind of run and number of cargo supplementals—anywhere from ten to thirty extra. Passenger supplementals were generally self-contained and often passengers never left them for any other part of a ship.

Fargo let Royce talk. The spacer seemed glad to have a knowledgeable audience. Fargo remembered all the times he had crawled through ships with his father, often reciting the location, function, and design requirements while his father listened, corrected, criticized. Despite the fact that he had hated those days, often he missed them. He wondered if his father would appreciate the irony of how those lessons had paid off for his son. Fargo was familiar with most starship designs, a good portion of in-system ship designs, and had an intimate knowledge of the way the basic components fit together and operated. It was not so difficult once you understood that almost all ships and stations were designed and built according to prefab protocols that were over a century and a half old, designs that left "gaps" for anticipated retrofits that, often as not, were left empty when older equipment became obsolescent and was removed, or provided shafts for maintenance motiles. It had been cheaper to build from ready-made components. Now, no one thought to question it. Freeriders took advantage of the ignored spaces and Fargo knew other paths, cracks, and crevices left by rote designs. What he did not know had not yet killed him and he learned more all the time. But this ship, the *Caliban*...for all Fargo knew his father might have been her refitter.

The *Caliban's* shuttles clung to the rim of the forward section. The four lifeboats lay in a row against the shaft. They were equipped with single-use TEGs, so the survivors would have a chance to get to a nearby star system and a better chance at rescue.

Fargo ate with Royce in the mess. Because of Royce they accepted him. For a time, at least, he had ceased to be a nid. They spoke to him, laughed with him, treated him like anyone else. Once he left the *Caliban*, that would end. They were Invested, he was disenfranchised. For a time, here on a ship that itself had only minimal existence in the "real" universe while it traveled at plus light speeds, Fargo enjoyed a change of status. He felt cheated that he could not simply enjoy it without constantly fishing for information. Maybe they understood, too. They seemed innocently open now, giving him what he needed, perhaps easing their consciences for the time when they would again treat him as invisible.

Fargo stepped through the door of the suite and immediately wanted to leave. It seemed too warm and the burnt odor was stronger. Stephen sat in a chair, his legs drawn up, arms wrapped around his knees, and Daniel leaned against the wall beside the connecting doorway between the two rooms, arms crossed.

For several seconds neither man looked at Fargo. Fargo considered leaving. Then he noticed that both Stephen and Daniel had been crying. Their eyes were red and their cheeks shone with drying moisture.

Daniel sighed suddenly. It was a faint whisper of air, raspy and desolate and, Fargo thought, very old.

"You just won't understand," Daniel said sadly, and retreated to his half of the suite.

Stephen leaned his head back, swallowed loudly, and closed his eyes.

"Did you deliver my note, Fargo?"

"Yes."

Stephen glanced at him. "And...?"

Fargo shrugged. "Shipmaster was busy. Interfaced. So I put it in front of him and left. It didn't seem polite to stay and stare at him."

Stephen nodded.

"Ran into the Exec, though, in the corridor. He's not a very happy co, is he? Told me from now on all communications for the shipmaster should go through him."

Stephen gave him a sharp look, frowning.

"You work for Kol Janacek?" Fargo asked.

"Yes."

"Mm. I worked for him once, long time ago."

"Oh? How long?"

"Oh, a lifetime, I'd have to say. How about you?"

"Just a few years. You don't care for Co Janacek?"

"I don't have an opinion. I never met him, actually, just did some freelance work for him. He probably didn't even know I existed then, and I was Invested at the time." He looked up at Stephen. "I don't think I would care to know him. Or meet him."

Stephen stared at him intently. Finally, he nodded. "I think I can see to that. I only need your services till we reach Markab."

"Do we have any stops between now and then?"

"None scheduled. Eurasia was our only one."

"Stroke of luck, eh?"

"No. Convenient, yes. I don't believe in luck, though."

You'd never make a freerider then, Fargo thought. Stephen said no more. After awhile Stephen returned to the polycom.

"Avoid the Exec from now on, Fargo. If I give you something for the shipmaster it goes directly to Sterg."

"Of course." Fargo went to the sofa. "How long?"

"Mmm?"

"To Markab. How long?"

"A few days." Stephen glanced at him. "Tired of our company already?"

Fargo laughed and Stephen went back to his study.

Janacek. Stephen did not believe in luck, but Fargo could find no other explanation for this situation. Janacek meant certain things to him, things that really had nothing to do personally with Kol Janacek, just associations. Business. It was one name he wished never to hear again, but even deep in the Pan, down where the Vested hid, people talked about Janacek, and Cambion and Hall and half a dozen others out in the Distals, the emerging Vested on the frontier. Fargo had heard them called heroes, liberators, dictators, and race traitors. They were none of those. What they were caused talk, probably even among the Vested on Earth and Homestead. They were powerful and growing more so. A lot of Q. Trade with setis, expanding economies on new worlds, open market possibilities, and all of it scaring the Inner Pan.

And I'm going back there, he thought, back home, where I never wanted to go ever again.

He had been working for Stephen Christopher five days and so far had done nothing more demanding than fetch their meals. Fargo used the empty time to explore the ship and scavenge odds and ends that might be useful. He stowed his booty in one of the life boats.

He had gotten to know several of the crew. In the past few days he had seen almost all of the ship. He was beginning to feel to comfortable on board. He looked forward to leaving. Comfort was deceptive, comfort was a trap.

Stephen and Daniel remained enigmatic. No one knew much about them, except that they had been taken on at

Epsilon Eridani Transit Station, deep Inner Pan, close to the heart–close to Sol. Fargo could not figure them. They did not leave these rooms, though Fargo believed that Daniel was chafing under the constraint. Stephen talked to him often, curious conversations that had a quality of naivete Fargo found amusing. He wanted to know about some of the people Fargo had known, where he had been. He wanted to know why he lived the way he did and probed at Fargo's answers. Fargo enjoyed the talks–no, he relished them, as troubling as that was to admit. An Invested was paying close attention to who he was. It disturbed Fargo to think he was that easily seduced out of his pride. But Stephen seemed genuinely interested, rather than someone with a cruel sense of humor toying with a nid.

Though Stephen sometimes surprised him with the extent of his knowledge, the gaps in his understanding baffled Fargo. Stephen understood that some people lied sometimes to hide things or to protect themselves, but he did not know why some people lied simply to lie. He understood why people sought close involvement with others, but not why those same people refused intimacy, pushed it away, and became angry with those who sought it. He understood the pursuit of material comfort, but not the pursuit of power. He knew that people carried sensitivities that were better left untouched, but not that those sensitivities might have no visible relationship to anything real. Fargo conceded to himself that he did not have a very good grasp on these things himself–but he knew how to recognize them and how to act according to that information. He knew how to avoid the traps people unconsciously laid all around them, waiting for someone to trip one and start a snagging, suffocating series of entanglements. Stephen did not seem to possess *that* knowledge, the visceral awareness that is part of the process of growing up human.

Perhaps he was not human. Fargo thought about the seti on Eurasia. No, he thought, there are others, people so involved in a singleminded obsession that nothing else impinges on their awareness. People who grow up in institutions, apart from most of ordinary humanity. Academics, scientists, radical religionists. His own time in the Monad, seeking release from these very things, had brought him face to face with people who had successfully broken the connection that allowed understanding. He had yearned for that freedom himself, but not even there could he dissolve those unconscious recognitions.

Still, theirs was a rejection of understanding they already possessed on some level. Fargo had the feeling Stephen had never possessed it.

He came awake in the middle of nightcycle; his dreams evaporated instantly. He searched the dim room. The only light came from a handful of power lights on the polycom, and the adjoining room.

Annoyed, Fargo rubbed his eyes and chased the shadows of his dreams. Lately they were more vivid than he ever remembered, though they still made no sense once he woke up. Lis was in most of them.

A sound came from the next room. A sigh or the shifting of cloth. Fargo told himself to roll over and go back to sleep. But he was curious. He had heard no sound till then, no words, nothing to give any indication that they were awake.

He stood and padded silently to the door.

The two men sat on the deck, back pressed to back, heads touching at the crown. They were at an angle that hid Stephen's face; Fargo could only see Daniel. His eyes flickered open and closed erratically. His mouth worked occasionally; a trickle of drool trailed down his chin. All the other muscles in his face were relaxed, still, producing a look of *absence*, as if Daniel was not there. His fingers twitched, curling, stiffening, one wrist flexing now and then.

Fargo stared.

Suddenly Daniel's eyes opened wide, cleared, and he looked at Fargo. Fargo stumbled backward and Daniel smiled sardonically. A moment went by and Daniel's face lost its intelligence again. He was gone.

Fargo retreated to the sofa. His heart hammered and his breathing sounded too loud as he struggled to control it.

The light from the other room faded to black. Fargo stared into the sudden dark, trying to will his eyes to see, wishing for his belongings and his nighteyes.

A sliver of greyish light swept out of the air near the door, something reflecting dimly from the polycom lights. Fargo heard the faint swish of fabric.

"Calm down."

Fargo jerked back. The voice–Daniel's–was from right in front of him. He seemed to sense the outlines of a face then, very close.

"No one's going to hurt you." A hand came to rest on Fargo's knee. "Stephen's sleeping. He fights so hard these days to avoid this, but...well, they say you never forget the first language you knew, and never pass up a chance to use it again. Calm down, Fargo, it's all right."

Fargo felt his breathing slow, his heart return to normal. Despite his fear, his body was calming.

"You have no idea why Stephen's retained you, do you? He thinks I'll behave myself in front of strangers. After all, he believes he's rescuing me and he expects me to behave appropriately. I haven't been, so when they found you–*I* found you, actually–he interceded with Sterg, who's really not very imaginative or particularly pleasant, and took you in to help keep me in line."

Fargo licked his lips. "Rescuing you from what?"

"The world, the flesh, corruption...Tesa Estana."

"She's Primary Vested."

"She is that. Some say she's related to the Chairman of the Pan. I wouldn't know, I've never met Erin Tai Chin."

"You've met Estana?"

"No."

"Why would Stephen have to rescue you from her?"

"Well, that's a good question, isn't it? Hanna says I've attracted her attention. And Stephen has always been an obedient child when it came to Hanna. They *did* offer me a job, and the terms were very good." He sighed. "Stephen never adjusted to leaving the nest. He never came to terms with his differences, how to use them to advantage. Or maybe he did. He works for Kol Janacek, after all. I can't honestly see any difference between working for him and working for Tesa Estana. Hanna says there's a difference. The universe is changing and Hanna wants to have a say in how."

"Who's Hanna?"

"Mother, master, mentor, maker." He laughed softly. "I was glad to get away from her, to be honest. I've been having a good time since she let us go." He was quiet for a long time. "But I guess she never did let go." He tightened his grip on Fargo's knee. The skin under his touch itched.

"Listen, freerider. Stephen imagines he's taking me out of harm's way. Maybe he is, maybe he isn't. But he was wrong to involve you. A word of warning–whatever may happen it won't be a good idea to get in the way. Play servant for Stephen, see that he doesn't come to any harm. Get him back where he belongs, get him home. He's not very clever about staying out of danger. He doesn't understand the way things work very well. See that he's safe, then go. Don't look back. That won't be hard for you. You like to run. You have no trouble leaving things incomplete, unfinished. Just follow your nature and you'll be all right."

Fargo thought of several replies, voiced none of them. His fear was back, nearly full force, coupled now with a growing resentment. Daniel had touched raw nerves, named a pain Fargo had learned to ignore, one benefit of the Monad. He felt Daniel staring at him, felt an intense scrutiny.

Then, very softly: "You've seen them..." Daniel grunted and took his hand away. "If I could only convince Stephen to have a look at you then he'd know."

"Kn-know what?"

"That Estana isn't the enemy. And maybe Hanna's wrong."

"I don't understand."

But Daniel had withdrawn. Fargo sensed the man pull back, return silently to the other room.

Fargo sat there, watching where he imagined the doorway to be, and tried to control his thoughts, tried to achieve the calm Daniel had somehow produced by a phrase and a light hand on his knee. But he could not stop thinking about what Daniel had said: "You've seen them." Fargo wanted to find some other meaning for those words, but he could not. He was certain Daniel meant the setis on Eurasia.

Fargo came awake from a hand on his shoulder, shaking him. He opened his eyes and saw Stephen glaring at him.

"Where's Daniel?"

Fargo had fallen asleep sitting up. His neck was stiff. He sat forward and rubbed the tight muscles.

"Where's Daniel?" Stephen repeated.

"I just woke up, co…"

"I—" Stephen broke off and turned away. He paced the cabin a few times, then stopped before the polycom. "The ship has dropped out of translight. We're not moving."

Fargo looked up, frowning. "Where are we?"

Stephen shrugged. "I don't know. I'm not very good at reading these things."

Fargo went to the polycom and studied the screens. The ship had no velocity. They had slowed to sublight a few hours ago and now had come to a relatively complete stop. Fargo touched contacts, requested more data. The screen shifted, information scrolled down.

"We aren't near anything," he said. "We're in the middle of empty space. Nearest colony is…Fornax…but we're a good fifteen light years away. Why don't you ask the Shipmaster?"

"I tried. He's not answering his comm."

A deep bass vibration ran through the deck. Fargo frowned and stabbed at the polycom.

"What was that?" Stephen demanded.

"I hope not what it sounded like."

Fargo sat down and began making a series of data requests. Stephen's access code had opened the system for him. He discovered that he could get into anything in the datacore. He worked quickly, scanning the replies and moving to the next subject, hoping he was wrong and, if he were not wrong, that his luck held until he had all the information he needed. Stephen kept silent, as if sensing that this was not a time to interrupt.

"We're being boarded," Fargo said. "The *Caliban* masses right around a hundred and ten thousand metric tons. There's a mass alongside us massing about half a million. It's matched vector and velocity, come to a halt with us. The reason we've stopped is the translight envelope generators have been shut off and the reaction drives are on standby. The sound you heard was a grapple hauling us against a lock. Main locks have opened. The ship's systems have been overridden and the comm has been shut down."

"Where's Daniel?"

"Can't trace anybody." He changed protocols and began isolating the lifeboat he had accessed from the ship's systems.

"What are you doing?" Stephen demanded.

"Getting us a way out." The polycom suddenly went blank. Fargo slapped it's console angrily. "Damn! Where are my things?"

"What?"

"My clothes, my pack, my belongings. Where?"

"Shipmaster Sterg took them—"

"Get your stuff together, get ready to move."

Fargo stepped into the passageway and headed toward the shipmaster's cabin. As he touched Sterg's nameplate and the door slid open, a hideous metallic ripping echoed through the ship, dancing edgily across his nerves.

Fargo found his belongings shoved in a cabinet beneath a rack of weapons. He contemplated the rifles and sidearms for a few seconds, then decided against them; he did not know how to use them in any case and felt certain Stephen did not.

He stripped off the grey utilities and pulled on his own clothes. He checked his pack quickly. Everything was still there, including his broken synthet. He hoped he had hoarded enough parts to make repairs.

Fargo tried to access the shipmaster's polycom, but it too was dead.

The metallic ripping sounded again.

Shouldering his pack, he hurried out of the cabin and headed back to Stephen.

When he reached the cabin Stephen was gone. He checked the other room, the hygiene cubicle. Stephen's clothes were still in the closet.

"Damnit, co," he hissed, then shrugged. He had tried, though he could not say why. Stephen was no longer his concern. It was time to think of himself. The ship that had grappled the *Caliban* was, he had no doubt, a megacorps vessel. Few independents massed that much. No independent could hope to get away with piracy, at least not like this. Given all that, Fargo was sure the *Caliban* would not be allowed to return to any port.

He stepped into the passageway again.

The Exec stood there.

Along with him were three people Fargo had not seen on board the *Caliban*, two men and a woman. The woman was tall and slender, sharp-faced and dark. She regarded Fargo unblinkingly. One man wore body armor and a communications headset. The other man was taller than the woman, wide through the torso, with a slender neck and long, graceful hands. He had a neatly-trimmed white beard and light reddish hair. All three wore a metallic headpiece that hugged their skulls closely.

"Who is this?" the tall man asked.

"A nid," the Exec said and shoved Fargo back into the cabin. "Where's your employer, nid?"

The woman swept into the suite and explored it as Fargo had done.

"He isn't here," she said.

The Exec reached for Fargo. "So where is he?"

Fargo shook his head. "Couldn't say, co. He was gone when I arrived."

The woman looked at him narrowly again, then shrugged. "We have Daniel. One of them is enough. We're finished here, Andrew. Dake, recall your people." She left the cabin.

The one with the communication headset–Dake–nodded curtly and switched on his gear. He subvocalized, then switched off. He grinned at Fargo.

"You a freerider?" he asked.

"Not now," Andrew said to him impatiently.

The two men gave the room another cursory look, then began to leave. The Exec started to follow.

"Not you," Andrew said, turning. He put a hand against the Exec's chest.

"I thought–"

Andrew shook his head with mock sadness. "We appreciate your help, especially in shutting down this barge. But we're not taking you with us."

"We had an arrangement!"

"Our arrangement was that in return for betraying your shipmaster and helping us get our property, you would get a ship of your own." Andrew gestured at the cabin, the passageway. "So it is."

The Exec stared at Andrew for several seconds. Andrew smiled and walked away, out into the passageway. Suddenly the Exec screamed and rushed after him. There was a loud bang, then silence.

Fargo eased up to the door and peered around. The Exec's body lay crumpled across the passageway, blood pooling beneath him. He shuddered: explosive weapons on board a starship were dangerous to everyone. Clearly, they did not care. Fargo knew then that the ship was forfeit.

Fargo hurried the other way.

He crawled through a service conduit running between the transfer rings. It was hot and close and he was breathing hard when he opened the hatch on the fourth ring. He was outside the booth, in pitch blackness. He switched on his lamp and climbed around to the emergency access that connected to the belly of the lifeboat. The launch hatch was open. Fargo scrambled up into the small airlock.

He sealed the outer hatch, waited for the ready light, and pushed his way through the inner hatch.

The interior was warm and pressurized. Fargo removed his mask and went forward to the cockpit. He could see the console already illuminated by function lights.

From around the edge of the pilot's couch Stephen looked back at him.

"Did you find Daniel?" Stephen asked.

Fargo shook his head. Stephen frowned and turned back to the console.

Fargo dropped his pack behind the copilot's couch and looked over the monitors. Stephen was intently studying one that displayed operating instructions.

"You don't know how to fly this?" Fargo asked.

"Do you?"

"No." Fargo grinned and sat down. "Can you bring that up over here? Between the two of us we just might be able to figure this out before we're found."

Chapter Four

Fargo isolated the skiff from the remaining automated maintenance systems. Vibrations thundered through the hull. Fargo
tried to ignore it and concentrate on the protocols displayed
on his screen; he understood most of the lifeboat system, but
a great deal had been added on.

Suddenly it was still. Fargo looked over at Stephen, waiting for the sounds to resume. When they did not, he shrugged
and continued reading.

The deck bucked beneath them. Fargo clutched at the
arms of his couch. The shock ended immediately, leaving
Fargo's pulse racing. He stared at the still-blank main screen
above them, expecting a final, fatal impact. He felt himself
begin to float up from the couch and grabbed at the restraints.

"There," Stephen said.

The main screen winked on. The star field seemed to fall;
the lifeboat was drifting, slowly spinning. Then the two ships
came into view from the top of the screen.

The megacorps merchanter filled the view. For all its immense size it did not seem bloated. The lines swept back from
a blunt nose to a mushroom-like aft cap. Six TEG vanes traced
delicate secants along the aquatic body. Against it, the *Caliban*
looked small and vulgar, the empty spaces along its shaft giving an irregular, incomplete appearance. It was old, worn.
Debris drifted away from it in a slowly expanding cloud.

The pair disappeared from view at the bottom of the screen.

"We need to stabilize," Fargo said.

"I don't think we should power up anything," Stephen said.
He tapped at a keypad. "Let me see...ah."

The view locked onto the two starships and held.

All the lifeboats had been ejected. As they watched, a faint beam leapt from the mega and touched each one. A puff of instantly crystallized atmosphere billowed as the beam breached each hull.

"Shit," Fargo hissed.

The beam began punching holes in the *Caliban*, evacuating its air, destroying its TEG, the vanes, slicing a line down the shaft, through any supplementals in its path. Fargo watched the soundless destruction, fascinated at the prospect of death. He had always imagined that he would die slowly, on the ground somewhere, alone.

The beam stopped.

After a few hours, the big ship withdrew its grapples and pushed the *Caliban* away. The space between the two ships widened slowly. A series of faint gaseous jets spewed from various points on the mega hull. It powered up and shot off, dwindling quickly to a pinpoint, then vanished as it reached transition velocity and fell headlong into translight.

"Damn," Fargo whispered.

"What?"

"See if you can magnify the view."

Stephen worked briefly and the scene jerked forward vertiginously. Scattered across nearly a kilometer of space were several small shapes. Transfixed, a pressure growing behind his eyes, Fargo watched as Stephen isolated one and magnified it.

The body was spreadeagle, fingers clawed as if trying to hold onto something–life, Fargo thought bitterly, the pressure becoming numbness. It was difficult to tell if it had been male or female in its hodgepodge freerider suit. The face mask hung several centimeters from its face.

Stephen shifted to another. Then another. And another.

"What happened...?" Stephen asked quietly.

"Mega transports have been venting freeriders. I've heard, but this is the first time I've seen..." He closed his eyes. "Shut it off."

"Why would they do it here, though?" Stephen asked.

Fargo shook his head. "Who knows?"

After a time, Stephen said, "It's not just freeriders. Crew, too."

Fargo thought of Royce. Anger warmed his chest and stomach, tightened his throat.

Stephen sniffed and Fargo looked over at him. His eyes glistened.

"I heard them say they have Daniel," Fargo said. "For what it's worth, he's alive."

Stephen nodded and closed his eyes.

"Who were they?" Fargo asked.

"Estana. Her people."

"Why?"

Stephen did not answer.

"Never mind, co," Fargo said. "None of my concern anyway."

An experienced operator might have accomplished as much as Fargo in minutes, but Fargo nevertheless felt a spark of pride at managing these systems. The retrofit of new components confused him and the tutorials did not cover everything. At least it possessed pseudogravity. He might have made more guesses, but as this small skiff represented their only connection to survival he was afraid of doing anything that might crash its systems. He proceeded cautiously.

Stephen seemed asleep. Annoyed, Fargo ignored him and busied himself trying to learn how to pilot the boat. Finally, after he had reread the same paragraph four times without understanding it, he gave up and got out of the couch.

He was stiff and his head ached from concentrating.

There was food in the small autochef and a full watertank. He quenched his thirst, ate a little, and stretched out on the narrow bunk just aft of the cockpit.

Between the fear, the anger, and the study he was bone weary. Still, his mind continued stubbornly to tease at things. The corpses–some of them might have been friends. Fargo thought of inspecting each corpse to see, but he could not find the will. One more thing unfinished, incomplete. No one else was aboard the *Caliban* anymore and he had to be careful how he played the odds for survival. Sleep seemed not only allowable but absolutely necessary. Choices made from fatigue could be fatal. Eventually, sleep took him.

...you've seen them, Ranonan, furry faced and large eyed, Lis took hold of his hands, grinned, eyes bright, yes, we've seen them, haven't we, and more, walking across the fields on Neighbor's naked, sky mild green, Daniel runs across their path, waving, leading a gang of setis, Lis says never mind, there's a place I know, and Stephen says we can get there if you tell him how, just give him the code, the book, the word, the path...

When he opened his eyes the lifeboat was under way. Fargo felt the difference through his spine, a distinct vibration. He lay awake for a time, puzzled over when he had gotten up to program the TEG and set the boat on course for Fornax. He was certain he had done it, but he could not remember when. There was no break in his sleep to account for it, but he clearly remembered—

He jumped up and rushed to the cockpit. He had dreamt it, not done it.

Stephen was awake. He looked up at Fargo and smiled.

"We'll be at Fornax in two days," Stephen said.

"But..." The text on his screen remained unchanged, exactly where he had left off.

"Something wrong?" Stephen asked.

"No...just..." He shook his head and pushed away from the couch. His bladder ached dully. He headed for the small cube at the rear of the aft cabin. Fragments of dreams mixed jarringly with reality. He felt disappointed. He had never operated a TEG before, he had looked forward to programming the run to Fornax himself.

"Fargo?"

He paused at the cube door. "Hmm?"

"I want to thank you."

"For what?"

"Helping...wanting to help."

"Just freight, co. Besides, I didn't do much. You were already gone when I got back to your room."

"No, you've done a lot. I couldn't do this with–anyway, I want to say thanks."

Fargo shrugged and entered the cube. As he emptied himself he could hear Stephen continue to talk.

"I didn't know what else to do. They'd caught Daniel, they were armed, I didn't know who they were, what they might do. I hid in one of the transfer ring booths. Then I crawled into a maintenance node when the power went off in the rings. I couldn't tell when they'd left, if it was safe to come out, I didn't know. Without you..."

Fargo listened intently, but Stephen said no more.

He switched on the small sink; the pumps whirred audibly in the cramped space. Fargo cupped his hands under the flow, dipped his face in it, took a little into his mouth. It tasted flat, lukewarm.

He went forward. Stephen gave him a cowed, guilty look.

"You used to freeride," Fargo said. "Didn't you?"

Hesitantly, Stephen nodded.

"And you went back?"

Stephen looked up. "'Back?'"

"Reinvested. Back to an identity, a place. Back Inside."

Stephen reddened. "I didn't have a choice."

Fargo grunted. "That's what you say when you become Disinvested. How did that work? Once a freerider, always a freerider, isn't that what the Invested say? Once a nid, never a person again. So how did you merit an invitation back Inside?"

"It's not all that hard. You could do it if you wanted. Any of you could."

"'Any of you could.' Did you hear that? A distinction. Came out automatically, you didn't even have to think about it."

Stephen's lips pressed tightly. His hands danced briefly over the keypads; information shifted from one screen to another, new data appeared in its place.

"You're a quick study," Fargo said. "So what did you used to be? A pilot? I understand they have the hardest time adjusting. Always a passenger, never crew. Most of them find a place and stay on the ground somewhere. Most radical hermits used to be crew. Is that it? I could see that, if you were. Taking any chance to reinvest."

"No," Stephen said. "I was never a pilot."

"Oh. Well, then, I want to know. Is it so much better In There that it's worth your integrity?"

Stephen scowled, but did not meet Fargo's gaze. "You don't know anything about my integrity."

"True enough. But I know about mine. I wouldn't reinvest for anything. They can all kiss my ass."

"Easy to say when you have no choice."

"Oh, but I thought we did. That's what you said. 'Any of us could.'"

"But not you."

"Why not?"

Stephen glanced at him. "It's true, isn't it? You can't."

Fargo jabbed Stephen's shoulder. "When we get to a station I go my own way. You won't have any trouble. Just show them your ID, the great Pan Humana will be glad to take you back into its smothering arms. Meantime stay away from me."

Fargo fell onto the small bunk and turned his face to the bulkhead.

"How long have you waited to say that, Fargo? Ever since you became a freerider? I guess in four years you could get it nearly perfect—"

Fargo snapped out of the bunk. Stephen, standing in the gangway, stepped back.

"How did you know that?"

"You told me—"

"I never *once* talked to you about that! How do you know that about me?"

Stephen started to turn away. Fargo snatched at his shirt and Stephen slapped at his hand. His eyes grew large, fearful, and he held his hands out, palms facing Fargo.

"You have no right to know that," Fargo said. He paced the width of the cabin, clenching and opening his fists. "Maybe it's everything since Eurasia. Maybe it's catching up."

Stephen seemed fragile, defenseless. It would be simple, Fargo thought, to reach out and break his face. He silently tallied everything that had happened to him in the last ten days, since Eurasia, and concluded that the scales were out of balance by a significant amount. He was due.

"What is it about you and your friend that was worth all those lives?"

"I'm not your enemy, Fargo," Stephen said.

Fargo laughed explosively. "That's a pretty useless thing to say."

Again, the expression of mild bewilderment crossed Stephen's face. He simply did not react the way Fargo expected him to and that disjunction with expectations was too consistent to be a fluke. It meant something.

Fargo sat down on the bunk. "What are you?" he asked. "Why did Tesa Estana want your friend?"

The bewilderment vanished, replaced–once more–by wariness, caution, a closing down. He began to retreat into the cockpit. Fargo jumped up and grabbed his arm.

"Working for you nearly killed me. I think that deserves an explanation. Last time freight was this expensive..." Fargo remembered then what the Exec had said. "Janacek."

Stephen frowned and pulled his arm free.

"You work for Janacek. That's how you know about me." He watched for a reaction but Stephen kept his expression fixed. "But why? I mean, Kol Janacek didn't even know me. I thought he didn't. But–is that why Estana wanted you? Because of something to do with Janacek?"

"Perhaps," Stephen said quietly. "I don't know why Estana wanted Daniel. Daniel didn't work for Janacek."

"But you do and Daniel's your friend." Fargo shook his head impatiently. "Come on, co. You nearly got me killed, you owe me some answers."

"Maybe. But I can't."

Fargo waited for more, then sighed. "Fine. I really didn't expect anything else. Once Invested always exclusive." He turned away. "I'm tired. Wake me when you want to sleep."

"I didn't kill all those freeriders, Fargo."

Fargo stood listening to the sound of his own pulse and worked at not seeing bodies float past his eyes. He did not answer. Stephen was right, he was not to blame for that, but...

In a smaller voice, Stephen added: "I didn't kill those people."

Fargo was not really tired, but he did not want to deal with Stephen anymore. In the confines of the boat sleep was the only privacy. He lay on his side, facing the bulkhead, and tried to find a still place inside. Sleep came as a surprise.

...translight opened space, a hole in the middle, a chute down which he fell, weightless, frictionless, intertialess, nonplace, the field generated around him isolated him from the space he had been born into, separating everything from everything, Lis grinned with the pleasure of the fall, reached for him, furry-handed, held on, "Over there, maybe we can go over there, be someone" but what Fargo wondered, and took her hand, and saw stars slide by, slip from their grasp, and the language ahead spoke in numbers, vectors, axes, polar interpolations, direction was not quite the same, but Lis knew where to go, Lis knew how to go, Lis knew...

Fargo blinked. He could not remember a time since childhood when he had dreamed so much, so vividly. He rolled with the images walking through his mind–Lis was there again, as were Stephen and Daniel; the *Caliban* and its shipmaster, hands sunk into the deck, face empty but for constantly changing symbols in his eyes; and the seti–and wrestled with the gnawing sensation of being watched. Even as he tried to dismiss it, the feeling deepened. He dreamed the events on Eurasia, then dreamed it again. He wanted to move on, shift to something else, but still once more he was hurrying with the setis through the mob, helping them away, ending on the tarmac of the port, beaten, while overhead the corpses of freeriders floated and stared down at him...

But he was awake now. These were not dreams but memories and he could not shut them off.

He twisted on the bunk, and looked at Stephen. He sat on his haunches less than a meter away, fixedly watching Fargo. For a moment neither moved. Then Stephen reddened, embarrassed, looking like nothing more than a small child caught at something forbidden.

You've seen them...

Fargo gaped at him. "You read my mind."

Stephen's eyes widened fearfully and he started to turn away. Fargo lunged from the bunk and tackled him. Stephen threw his arms up, tried to push Fargo away, but only gave Fargo leverage. Fargo spun him around easily, wrapped an arm around Stephen's neck, and pulled him up against the storage lockers opposite the bunk. Stephen struggled. Fargo tightened his hold.   Fargo's breath came raggedly. "What are you, co?"

"Please, don't be afraid."

"I'm *not*–!" He stopped. Yes, he was afraid. Terrified, in fact. "How do you know that? Are you still reading my thoughts? Quit it!" He jerked his arm tighter, making Stephen wince.

"No, I'm not! Please–I promise, I'm not looking..."

Fargo frowned. "Looking. Daniel said something about that, if you'd just let him have a look...both of you?"

Stephen went limp in Fargo's hold.

"No need to answer, co," Fargo said, mock conversationally. He worked at slowing his heart rate, regaining control. "It's obvious now." He suddenly felt foolish holding Stephen this way and started to release him. Then he wondered if that thought had been injected by Stephen to get him to let go, and tightened up once more.

"What now?" Stephen asked.

"I don't know." Fargo's mind worked frantically. They had well over a day of travel left before reaching a system, then however long it took to attract rescue. The skiff was too small to effectively isolate himself from Stephen. He frowned, seeing no evident solution. Frustrated, he pushed Stephen away. "Stay out of my mind."

Stephen slowly stood. He shook as if cold, his eyes red and anguished. He stumbled back and fell into the bunk.

"It's called telelogging," Stephen said, his voice a hollow monotone.

"I don't want to know about this! I don't want anything to do with this!"

"I try not to use it anymore, but it's difficult. It's like trying not use an arm or a leg. I only use it when there's no other choice."

Fargo caged his skull with his hands, as if trying to find the entrance and block it. He almost laughed at the idea and carefully placed his hands on the deck, palms flat; the faint vibration of the engines was restful, calming.

"Why wouldn't you use it?" he asked suddenly.

Stephen looked at him, a flicker of hope in his eyes.

"You'll laugh," Stephen said.

"Oh? You know this for a fact?"

Stephen shrugged. "It's not right, not fair."

"Impolite?"

"Yes..."

Fargo grunted. "So how much did you do to me? How much of me do you know about now?"

"It doesn't work that way. Quite."

"How much?"

Stephen looked uncertain. "Daniel found you in the shuttle. I telelogged you in medical just to see if there was any brain damage. Then, yesterday, when you went to sleep, I recovered everything you'd learned about running the lifeboat."

"And this last time?"

Stephen drew a deep, shaky breath. "You–there were images of–things you've seen–I needed to know–"

"*Then why didn't you just ask me!*"

"How do I know you'd tell me the truth?"

"You say you used to freeride. Did a freerider ever lie to you?"

"No."

"And you know that, because you checked."

Stephen nodded.

"Then why–?"

"Because I don't–" Stephen hissed between his teeth. His face reddened and twisted with frustration. "I don't understand people."

"I don't see–"

"No, you don't. Nobody does. Can you tell when someone is lying to you?"

Fargo stared at him, baffled. "Well...not every time, but often enough. You *have* to be able to, just to stay alive."

"How do you tell?"

"I just–"

"You just do it. There's no trouble. You grew up learning how so that it just happens now. Not me. I don't understand, I can't recognize, I never know. If I have to have information from someone the only way I can be sure of it is to telelog them. What you're talking about is a language I never learned." Stephen folded his arms and drew up his legs and huddled in the bunk, face set, staring at nothing.

Fargo watched him for a long time. Between his anger and fear he could not quite grasp what Stephen was telling him. Slowly he got to his feet and went to the autochef. He did not turn his back on Stephen while he punched up a meal. He took the tray and moved sideways toward the cockpit.

"You stay away from me," Fargo said. "I need to think."
Stephen's eyes flicked his way. He nodded.

Fargo set the tray on the console and dropped into the
copilot's couch. The food was nearly cold when he remembered to eat it.

Stephen's eyes were closed when Fargo came back. He stared
at the young man, his thoughts muddled and distasteful, but
clearer than they had been. He recognized that the distance
between the cockpit and this compartment was purely symbolic. It probably could not keep Stephen out of his mind–
Fargo wondered what the range was for a telelog–but symbolism, like ritual, often carried sufficient authority to achieve
real effects. He was fairly sure Stephen had not telelogged
him but he had no way of knowing for certain. In the end, it
was a matter of faith.

"Are you asleep?"

"No," Stephen said.

"I have questions."

Stephen sat up, swung his legs over the edge of the bunk.
He rubbed his face, then went to the autochef and drew water. "All right."

"Why'd you give up freeriding?"

"I didn't have a choice. I was found."

"Janacek?"

"I ended up with him. He offered sanctuary." He regarded
Fargo narrowly, as if weighing how much to give, how much
to hold back. "I stayed out on the frontier as much as I could.
I used to do tricks for loose scrip. Magic tricks–cards, telling
fortunes, palm readings–"

"You must've been very good."

"On Markab Transit I was doing my act when a seti joined
the audience. I–they–I ran. I can't–"

"They scare you?"

"Terrify me. I must have gotten a little from it, though,
because I passed out. I woke up in a private room. Janacek

had seen the act, saw what had happened. He figured out what was going on–he knows information systems, has a knack for figuring odds–"

"I know his reputation."

"Anyway, he offered me a place."

"He's not an altruist," Fargo observed. "What do you give in return?"

"I attend business meetings with him, telelog the others. It gives him an edge. Occasionally I travel. I'm a very important negotiator for him."

"And in between these jobs you try to refrain from telelogging so you can learn something about people. Janacek himself is a case study in the worst sort of human being."

"No, he's not."

"Trust you on this?"

Stephen met his eyes. "He's not the worst."

Fargo shrugged. "What are you going to do when we reach Fornax?"

"I suppose I'll contact Janacek and go back to Markab. I've lost Daniel, I don't know what else to do..." Pain briefly flashed in his face.

"It's not going to be that simple. There's a dead freighter we left behind. Questions will be asked. All the answers point to something you might not want to admit to anyone."

"I don't see that we've got a lot of choice."

Fargo sighed. "When we reach Fornax, I have decisions to make. I'm not happy with the idea of ending up in a detention cell while the port authorities try to decide if I had anything to do with the *Caliban's* death."

"You're a nid. Why would they even notice?"

"Oh, in something like this I'm sure they'd make an exception. We're invisible only as long as we don't make large enough messes to attract attention. This is a large mess."

"So what are you going to do?"

"If possible, not be around to be questioned."

Stephen looked up. "Or?"

Fargo smiled thinly. "You're not reading my mind?"

Stephen scowled. "I told you–"

"Sure. I have one more question. Are you thinking of going after your friend?"

"I–maybe. Why?"

"Well, we can possibly help each other then. If you go back to Janacek is he likely to *allow* you to go after Daniel?"

"Probably not. This trip wasn't exactly allowed."

"Didn't think so." He absently scratched his chin. Beard was beginning to grow out again. "I'll see you get to the freerider sanctuary on Fornax. From there, I don't know."

"Why?"

"Why what?"

"Why would you help me?"

"Who says I'm helping *you*?"

"But–"

Fargo raised his hand. "I said I have decisions to make. One step at a time, co."

It was a good question, though, Fargo thought. Why help him? *You never finish anything*, Daniel had said. *Just follow your nature and everything will be fine...*

He wanted his synthet. He wanted calm, peace of mind, escape. He was mildly disgusted at the desire. It was, though, his nature. Maybe it was a nature he no longer wished to follow.

The hatch opened and two men in drab brown utilities climbed into the steam-filled cabin. They stood in the center of the small room waving their hands and turning slowly, frowning. One stepped into the cockpit.

"Nothing," he said. "Check aft. See where that vapor leak is coming from." He squinted. "Piss, it's hot in here."

The other grunted and headed for the hatch that led into the small engine room.

Fargo pressed close to Stephen, his arms around the telelog's shoulders. Sweat ran down his face, filled his clothes.

There was barely room for the both of them in the cube. Stephen was tense, every muscle tight. Fargo urged him forward, out of the cube. They walked quietly. Fargo felt Stephen's concentration through the periods when Stephen seemed to fade out of existence right in front of him.

At the hatch Fargo had to let go of Stephen. Through the mist he saw the shapes of the dockworkers, fore and aft.

"Found it," one of them called. "The evaporator in the recycler–"

"Just turn it off! I don't need a description!"

"Pardon the piss out of me."

"Now! I'm melting!"

"Hold on, hold on."

Fargo crouched, hands on either side of the hatch, and lowered himself through.

As he neared the bottom of the shaft, he curled around and reversed direction. He eased his head below the rim and quickly checked the dock.

The cradle rode a long rail from the bay doors of the airlock. Beyond its edge, on the floor of the bay, stood a truck stacked with diagnostic equipment, but Fargo saw no one else. What he could see of the bay gave the impression of unfinished work. Good, he thought, and let his legs fall. He somersaulted out of the hatch. He hung from the bottom rung for an moment, then fell to the cradle.

A few seconds later Stephen dropped Fargo's pack into his waiting arms and emerged himself.

Stephen's face was pale and glistened with sweat. Fargo shouldered his pack, then scurried forward to the lip of the cradle. Above, cables hung amid the shadows of strutwork and beams, bare conduit showing through the spaces where plating had yet to be put up. Despite the harsh white arcs, the place was gloomy. The air was cool and drew the perspiration from his face quickly.

They climbed over the side. The skiff was a small bullet shape resting on six spindly legs in the middle of the overly-large cradle. Fargo let himself drop to the floor of the rail bed. Stephen landed and nearly fell. Fargo grabbed him. Stephen pulled away with a curt nod.

At the far end of the rail bed the shaft entered a large housing. Beside this was a maintenance access. Fargo pushed the handle down and grinned when the door opened. He shoved Stephen through first, glanced back at the little life-boat, and followed.

Bluish light panels glowed dimly along the ceiling. The shaft bulked ominously to their right, merging several meters on with the huge tractor mechanism that filled the back half of the chamber. Fargo shone his lamp over the accretion of machinery.

"Fairly new," he whispered. He looked meaningfully at Stephen, but the other man did not respond. Fargo grunted and killed his lamp.

They squeezed through a narrow gangway that ended at another door. Fargo tried it and again it was unsealed. He pushed it open.

They stepped into a machine shop. Fargo squatted low and surveyed the space. When he felt sure no one else was here, he stood and moved through the loose maze of machines.

There was a polycom near the exit. Stephen tapped it, entering his ID, and requested a station guide while Fargo checked the corridor outside. The entire section seemed to be still under construction. Fargo listened intently, but heard no one.

He jumped at Stephen's touch. Stephen stepped past him, into the corridor, and motioned for him to follow.

Minutes later they emerged into a broad public circuit. Offices, shops, hostelries, omnirecs, restaurants, nightclutches –so much to do, yet the place felt deserted. The few people present seemed to be station workers or bored crew.

"I was right," Fargo said. "They picked us up for salvage and brought us to a perimeter station. Looks like they're still building it."

Stephen nodded silently.

They found a credit booth and Stephen tapped in his personal code. Several seconds later a dull grey card extruded. ID in hand, Stephen took a room for them at a nearby automated hostel.

Fargo watched him slump in a chair, eyes closed.

"Are you going to be all right, co?"

Stephen shrugged. "I'm not used to doing that. Blocking Daniel is one thing, but keeping invisible to normal senses..." He swallowed hard. "I need food, sleep."

"Give me your chit, I'll do some shopping."

Stephen listlessly handed Fargo his new card. Fargo watched him for a time, then gently pulled him from the chair. Stephen tried to brush Fargo's hands away, but there was no force, no energy, and Fargo managed to guide him to the bed. He eased Stephen down and pulled a blanket over him. Stephen's breathing deepened at once.

Fargo opened his pack and pulled out the dark blue utilities he had scavenged from the skiff. As he peeled his own suit off, he thought of what had just happened and shuddered. He might, he decided, get to a point where it did not frighten him, but he doubted he would ever get used to it. The chance had been slim, Stephen had explained, one sabotaged by any loud sound or physical contact. Fargo still was not sure he understood about the steam, but Stephen had said it was necessary for the trick to work.

Trick. Fargo almost laughed at that. Stephen had rendered them invisible to the two dockworkers by force of will. Some trick.

Stephen snored quietly. Fargo zipped up the utilities, pocketed the card, and left, feeling mildly guilty at his relief at getting away from Stephen.

Fargo could not believe how scarce loose scrip had become. Beta Fornax was sixty light years from Sol, one of the Distals. Further out lay Dawnrise, Etacti, Gamma Aquarii, Markab, other younger colonies, but Fornax was not that much older, still technically the frontier. The line was fluid, measured more by population density and market traditions than distance, but Fargo had been here less than a year ago. The drive to become fully Pan was strong, pushing out those traditions, tucking the fringes of life into a well-ordered path. Conformism through mass bribery. The benefits of the Pan made it difficult to remain apart and Fargo did not blame people for wanting the security of the credit quotient system. That did not mean he approved.

It took the better part of a shift to find a scrip dealer and the price was higher than he expected. Somehow, though, the idea of being overdebited at Janacek's expense alleviated the sting of being used.

As hard as it was to find someone from whom to buy scrip, he found no such reluctance among vendors to accept it–they all must have had ready ties to the grey market.

When he returned to the room Stephen was awake. He lay on the bed staring at the ceiling. He looked better, Fargo thought, not so washed out and weak.

"Someone was here," Stephen said.

"Who?"

"Police."

Fargo's pulse quickened slightly. He set his packages on the dresser. "What did he want?"

"Questioned my sudden appearance on the station. Wanted to know if I knew anything about a derelict skiff registered to the *Caliban* that had been picked up by salvage operators."

"Damn. That was quick."

Stephen sat up. "There must be an alarm tagged to my ID. I expected that. I just didn't think it would be this fast."

"Hmm. Things've changed out here since my last visit."

"What did you get?"

Fargo laid out his purchases. "Two new bodysheaths, clothes, a new power transferal unit, food, and a little information. I found out what in-system ships go where and when and which ones are independents."

Stephen nodded. "I've decided to go after Daniel."

"Really? You don't even know where he was taken."

"There's only one place that makes any sense. Earth."

Fargo chuckled. "Only the hardest place to reach in the Pan Humana. That makes perfect sense." He glanced at Stephen and saw no change in his expression. He still looked tired, but his eyes were set, determined. Fargo nodded. "I admire your ambition."

"I'd like your help, Fargo."

"I'm giving you help. One freerider to another, even if you did reinvest. I'll help you off this station and see that you get a ride to another."

"I appreciate that, but I need more."

"Why should I? Daniel is your friend."

"I can get you reinvested."

Fargo spread out his new bodysheath and started calibrating it. He pulled a meter from his pack and worked with the controls.

"I can help you get back at Janacek," Stephen added.

"I'm not stupid, co. There was a time I'd have loved to hurt Kol Janacek–"

"I sensed that. I didn't get a clear idea why."

"–but I'm too realistic to believe I can, even if I particularly wanted to. It's none of your business why."

Stephen shrugged. "Fair enough. But I'd like you to think about it."

Fargo tossed him the other bodysheath. "Come on, get to work. We need to be off this station before they place Stephen Christopher as a passenger on the *Caliban*."

They did not check out of the hostel; the room would remain registered to Stephen Christopher until someone discovered that Stephen Christopher had not used it for however long it would take for someone to notice.

Dressed in brown worktogs, they strode purposefully down the commercial circuit until Fargo found a vacant storefront.

He used his multijack to get them in, then sealed the door behind them. They switched on their bodysheaths and crawled up through the ceiling access into the service ducts. They made their way through the maze to the docks, then into the hold of an in-system freighter. Fargo kept looking over at Stephen, waiting for him to slow or falter, but he seemed to have fully recovered.

The cargo bay of the freighter stank richly of semi-processed organic compounds. Fargo climbed among the support struts upon which hung the octahedral nacelles like giant egg sacs in a huge web. Thick shock padding nestled against the bulkheads between the outer edge of nacelles. He clipped a safety line to a strut and settled his pack securely between frame and cargo.

"This is great," he said, grinning. "How could you give up this kind of life for one of ease and plenty?"

"It was a hard choice," Stephen said dryly.

"This is going to be a fairly long ride. Maybe you can tell me about it on the way in."

Stephen looked around. "What do you think they're hauling?"

Fargo shrugged. "By-product from carbonaceous asteroids? Rendered comet? Human feces?" He glanced at Stephen. "You're not going to tell me about it, are you?"

"About what?"

"You and Daniel."

"I shouldn't."

"Are you two the only ones?"

"No."

"How many? A dozen? Two dozen? A hundred?" When Stephen remained silent, Fargo asked, "Are the others in danger from this?"

"They could be."

Stephen secured his safety web and stretched out, staring out at the labyrinth of nacelles.

"Well," Fargo said after a while, "I guess it's just as well you don't tell me anything else. I mean, once I get you on a ship headed for Earth, I'm shut of you. You're on your own. It'd be risky to have me wandering around telling everybody what I know. Of course, if I *were* to help you I'd insist on knowing everything. But since I'm not I can understand your reluctance. After all, you know for a fact that my mind's made up, that there'd be no convincing me to go along. I don't mind. I guess I can talk about my own fascinating and varied life all the way down to the inner system." Fargo snapped his fingers. "Hey, I could tell you how I came to be in that shuttle all beaten up!"

"I know how you got there. That's one of the reasons I'd like you to come with me." He looked directly at Fargo. "You've seen them."

The ride took four days. For most of it they could not talk because of a heavy vibration that rattled through the hold. Fargo had earplugs, which reduced the noise to an annoying hum and rendered conversation impossible. They ate sparingly and found brackish water available from a recirculation line.

Fargo slept fitfully. The din of the ship and his own growing reluctance to enter his dreams kept him too close to wakefulness. The only good part, he decided, was that Stephen could not badger him. Fargo wanted to extricate himself from the younger man, leave him on his own. Fornax was not far from Markab, there were regular runs between them. If Stephen insisted on going after his friend, there were plenty of avenues for that as well. Fargo told himself his freight was paid, he owed Stephen no more.

The problem was he could not keep the image of those dead freeriders floating in space out of his mind. As soon as sleep became imminent, he saw them, swollen faces, arms and legs extended, clouds of frozen blood around their heads.

What is it, Fargo wondered, makes you worth all that?

His anger ebbed and flowed like a tide. It required a lot of energy to keep it full and volatile. The helplessness he felt robbed him of focus, turned his mood dark. There had always been a name or a face against which he could direct his bitter-ness–his father, Kol Janacek, a woman he had once loved who had left him, the jurist who had ruled against the claims of the Monad and expelled them all–but in each instance a part of him knew that he had been partially responsible. His father had had expectations of him and he had stubbornly refused to accommodate them. There were other members of the fam-ily, brothers and sisters, who did not mind repaying the kindnesses of home. Better they receive the benefits of the leg chains his father offered while Fargo went out on his own, cut off. He had offered his services to Kol Janacek, and will-ingly participated in the marginally legal trafficking of private information–Fargo had a flair for it, he could get in and out of guarded systems. But Janacek–not personally, but his people, his corporation–had used that information to hurt a friend of Fargo's. The guilt had taken Fargo by surprise. There was the possibility of legal retribution, but...well, Fargo had surren-dered his status, joined the hermits, tried to immolate himself, and along with that his pain. The woman–well, after all, he was disinvested, no longer a Person in any legal sense. She had never actually said she loved him as much or in the same way as he loved her. He had made assumptions again, allowed himself the illusion that there was more. Sometimes he won-dered if he would have supported her had she been the one stripped of her citizenship. Her leaving simply made joining the Monad easier.

The jurist was just doing her job. The Monad had been on private land. They had had a lease at one time, but through inattention and the vagaries of financial arrangements they had lost it. There had been no reason to believe anyone would ever throw them out, but when the original owners transferred title to someone else, everything changed. The universe was no longer what it had been and stability–ever an illusion–van-ished without a sound.

He might have reinvested then. Nothing stopped him.

No, that was a lie. He had backed out on an arrangement with Janacek. That had cost him. The jurist–his name was among those in the Monad and none of them had been allowed back in. There were reasons he could not. Maybe if he tried hard enough...but no, freeriding was easier.

He could blame all of them, but it was hollow blame, impure outrage because he had handed them the knives and even shown them where to cut.

But this was different. All those people, flushed from the bowels of the ship, given no chance, from the look of it no warning, life snuffed out and no possibility of redress.

Freeriding was a risky life, one of only a few options open to the disinvested. Death could come instantly through any of a thousand carelessnesses. But after a century and a half of Pan economic management certain traditions existed that, till now, it seemed, had the authority of law. Freeriders who were caught by a shipmaster were made to "pay their freight" by working the voyage. It was a kind of indenturing, an opportunistic slavery.

They were not murdered.

The megacorporations seemed to be changing that tradition. He had a name now, too: Tesa Estana.

They say she owns the sun...

Fargo turned it over and over, worked at it while the freighter fell noisily on its path to the inner system, and began to focus his rage.

Chapter Five

All ports on all worlds, Fargo decided, are breathtaking. Some, though, take the breath pleasurably while others wrench it out.

The freighter had linked to a station in orbit. Offloading was automated and Fargo and Stephen simply rode a nacelle out. From the processing facility it had been no trouble to find a ground bound shuttle carrying finished organic product.

Now they reached the crest of the ridge north of the port and Fargo paused to look down at the colony.

Port Fornax was a fifty kilometer long plane dotted by blast pits four abreast, flanked on the north by a wall of ancient striated stone and on the south by the customs facilities, warehouses, offices and maintenance facilities of a hundred mercantile shippers. A kilometer further south, connected to the port by dozens of rail lines, Fornax Prime, capital city of the system, spread over the bottom of a shallow valley.

"I still don't see why we didn't just stay up there," Stephen said, jerking his thumb toward the sky.

"We can't make the right connections. Fornax doesn't have a full orbital complex, everything's automated, minimally crewed. Not much room for freeriders. It'll be easier to get the right ride from down here." He looked at Stephen. "Besides, I have friends here. It wouldn't do to pass them by."

Stephen shook his head doubtfully. "I've never been here before."

"Then you're in for a treat. Rull runs a fine sanctuary."

A collection of abandoned buildings huddled near the edge a short distance west. The cracked walls and discoloration showed their age and neglect. Fargo strode toward them, his anxiety lifting with each step.

Within, the floors were littered with debris mingled in thick dust, stirred slowly by the breeze through open windows. Shadow-shapes on the walls showed where equipment had once been. Fargo led the way into the center of the complex. It grew darker, cleaner, until finally they stood in a bare room with almost no light.

"Traveled far, traveled well," Fargo said. "Now we're filled with things to tell."

A deep, rumbling laugh came out of the blackness. "You must be the only one still uses that, Fargo. What is it, you got a thing for bad rhyme?"

"I'm a fool for useless traditions."

A line of bright light appeared in a wall, widened, became a door. A large man with a long, dirty-looking beard stepped out of the blackness into the sharp light.

"Rull!"

"Fargo! You son-of-a-bitch!"

Suddenly Fargo felt his shoulders squeezed painfully in the big man's embrace. He slapped his hands against Rull's flabby waist, laughing.

"Shit, it's good to see you!" Rull let him go.

Fargo swung at him playfully and Rull almost thoughtlessly intercepted the blow, pushed it away, laughing.

"Who's your co?"

"Rull, this is Stephen. Stephen, Rull Rex, king of Fornax."

Rull groaned. "Stop with the poetry, Fargo, or I'll hurt you. Welcome, Stephen. Friend of Fargo's and so forth."

"Now that the introductions are done," Fargo said, poking Rull's gut, "can we go down?"

"What's your hurry?"

"I have to *piss*, you fat rat."

"One more like that and you can piss yourself." Rull laughed again and waved a heavy arm. "Come on."

Rull closed the door after them. A cheerily-lit hallway stretched away from them. At intervals a wide doorway opened onto other corridors. The last one ended at a ramp.

At the bottom they stepped into a cavernous space filled with a town.

Stephen hesitated.

"Never been here before?" Rull asked. When Stephen shook his head, the big man laughed and patted his shoulder. "Well, then, let me tell you about it. This used to be the main warehouse for the colony back when it was starting up. Three square kilometers. Matter of fact, they thought they might have to build the whole colony underground. Beta Fornax is a variable. It was at low ebb when the site was picked, burning with god's own fury when they arrived. Long period variable, though, they figured it out before they finished all this. People like living above ground, they like a sun shining on them, don't ask me why."

Fargo shook his head and watched Rull guide Stephen ahead, pointing at things and talking. Partitions and huts formed a grid of streets. Smoke drifted up from kitchens spread throughout the sanctuary. The babble of hundreds of voices filled the air continuously.

"–just left a lot of equipment behind. A lot of it was broken, but we've managed to repair it. We have a continuous feed from the port, we have our own communications–not a TEGlink, mind you, but good enough for in-system." Rull looked back at Fargo. "That's how we knew you were coming."

Fargo cocked on eyebrow at him. "I know."

Rull nodded and continued. "We have artisans that can fix damn near anything."

"How many people are here?" Stephen asked.

"Oh, a thousand, fifteen hundred maybe. Our numbers are down, we used to have a constant population of two thousand or more."

"What happened?" Fargo asked.

"Migration. Lot of coes are heading further out."

"Fargo!"

A young girl hurried forward, a wide smile on her pale face.

She wrapped her arms around Fargo's neck and kissed him quickly, then stepped back, blushing. Fargo laughed.

"Alli!"

"I got excited when Rull said you were coming back," she said and stepped closer again. "Are you going to play for us?"

"Ah, Alli, I'm sorry. My synthet's broken."

"Oh."

"But I brought some good stories." He leaned over and said in mock-conspiratorial tones, "I touched a seti on Eurasia."

Her eyes widened. "You did! What was it like? What kind?"

"Alli," Rull interrupted, "don't pester Fargo now. Why don't you let your da know he's here and needs a place."

"Oh, no, I can manage my own berth somewhere," Fargo protested. "I don't want to put you out."

Alli was nodding vigorously and moving off. "That's all right, Fargo. We've got room. It's only for a short while anyway." And she was gone down a narrow path between two kiosks.

Rull shook his head. "Next year her da says he's going to take her on her first ride. I worry for her."

Fargo nodded, suddenly uncomfortable. He waited for Rull to say more, but the big man shrugged, swatted him on the back again, and said, "Well, come on. Let's get you settled in. We want to hear everything, Fargo."

Fargo went up to the ridge at twilight each evening to watch the shuttles arrive and depart. The fires of their engines, meteor-trailed and sun-bright, threw the port and the wall of rock into a blaze of hellish color. Shadows danced insanely around them, flickering in time to the false thunder. Once in a while, a lull happened, deeply silent. Fargo's ears hummed and, after many seconds, he could hear the faint, faint crackling of the blast pits cooling.

After seven days Fargo itched to leave, but Rull asked him to wait. He had told them all what he had seen on Eurasia, what had happened since, leaving out the central fact of

Stephen's and Daniel's talent. He did not like lying to them, even by omission, but Stephen said nothing, either, so it was a lie they shared. He wanted, more and more each day, to be off Fornax Prime. Before he changed his mind.

When he had told them what had happened to the *Caliban* and the venting of the freeriders it had started an ongoing conference. Fargo had confirmed what had till now been only rumor. Freeriders tended to avoid megacorps ships anyway, but now it took on new significance. He was certain this was why Rull imposed on him to wait.

He could think of worse places. He had no lack of company and there were musicians among the permanent residents. There was food, plenty of energy, work in Fornax Prime if he wanted it. At times he considered staying on, making a place for himself.

But.

It was hard enough keeping accounts squared riding. Staying meant never squaring them, always owing freight to someone. Too much like living Invested.

Night closed in and he went back down. He threaded his way through the rich smells and friendly noises of the sanctuary to the hovel he and Stephen were sharing with Alli and her da, Ben. Rull was waiting with Stephen.

Stephen looked up. "Fargo..."

"We've found you a ride," Rull said. "A longshot maybe, but there's an independent headed for Sol. The *Isomer*. They're taking on no passengers, just leaving a few off. Can't get data on their charter, so we don't know what they're hauling, what their other stops may be, but they've got a Forum permit clearing them into Sol."

"And they're independent?" Fargo asked dubiously.

Rull nodded. "You've got an eight hour window. Pit ninety-two. We can get you aboard, you don't even have to worry about that."

Fargo dropped into a crosslegged posture beside Stephen. "That's great for Stephen. What about me?"

Stephen lowered his eyes.

Rull said, "This one's for both of you."

Fargo looked at him. "I don't understand. I wanted a ride further out. I'm not leaving the Distals, especially not for Sol."

"Fargo..." Rull hesitated. He looked embarrassed. That and angry. "Look. The news you brought us–we're asking. We want you to go."

"'We'?"

"We, yes, the freeriders."

Fargo felt himself tense. "You're asking or calling in freight?"

"Now, Fargo–"

"Fargo," Stephen said, "please."

Fargo glared at him until he looked away again, then glared at Rull.

"Why?" he asked.

"This friend of his," Rull said, nodding at Stephen. "He's important. I don't know how, but it cost us lives. Besides that, things are changing. We see fewer and fewer coming out, more and more moving into the Distals, nobody coming back. It's got to do with setis and Vested and god knows what all. We need to know what's going on. We need someone to bring us information."

"Stephen's going anyway, have him spy for you."

Rull frowned. "You're refusing?"

Fargo opened his mouth, then caught a glimpse of Alli in the back of the hovel. She had been present, though silent, through the whole discussion. No reason for her not to be, it was her place, and freeriders did not keep secrets. Usually. He sighed heavily.

"This squares us," he said.

Rull's eyes widened. "Fargo–"

"I don't want to owe *anybody!* You knew that, and you're calling in freight!"

Rull looked hurt. "I thought you might do it because we asked, Fargo. This isn't freight. You don't want to, fine. Nobody'll think the worse of you."

Fargo's breath came hard. Finally, he nodded. "All right, I'll do it. Never been to Earth. This might be my only chance."

Rull relaxed. "Thanks, co. I'll let the others know."

Fargo nodded. "Great." He tapped Stephen's arm. "Get your personals, co."

Stephen nodded and moved away.

Rull regarded Fargo evenly. "Co, I–"

"We'll talk when I come back."

Rull nodded.

"I have to get ready," Fargo said finally.

"Travel safe, travel long."

Five other freeriders took them down to the warehouses. Fargo and Stephen followed as they threaded the path through old doors, down refuse-choked alleyways, and into connecting shafts that finally deposited them inside a building half-filled with cargo supplementals.

Fargo waited in the shadows while two of them went out to find a suitable shell. Stephen carefully avoided Fargo's eyes. Even in the dark Fargo could tell he was embarrassed and uneasy. Fargo said nothing. Let him suffer, he thought. He's been too damn much trouble as it is.

One of the scouts appeared and waved them forward.

The supplemental rested on an agrav skid. As Fargo stepped onto it the whole thing dipped a centimeter or two, then stabilized with the new weight. The other rider was waiting, crouched, beside the inspection hatch. He straightened when he saw Fargo and ducked inside.

Within, in the light from their combined lamps, Fargo saw racks of drawers filled the space top to bottom, leaving enough room between for a co to walk.

"What are we going up with?" Fargo asked.

"Scent," the rider replied and grinned. "There's a fungus here, distills down into some pharmaceuticals. What's leftover makes perfume. Colony gets more for that than for the medicine."

Fargo grunted, shaking his head. "Who wants this stuff?"

The rider shrugged. "There's a class nine stasis field on this one, keep the stock free of g. Give you an easy ride upwell."

"Thanks, co."

"Travel well, travel long." The rider patted Fargo's arm, then squeezed by to say good-bye to Stephen.

The inspection hatch sealed. Only their two lamps lit the cramped space. Fargo dropped his pack. "This should be easy enough."

"Thanks, Fargo," Stephen said.

"For what?"

"Coming. You could still have said no."

"Uh huh. And let down Rull and every freerider there."

"They wouldn't have held it against you. They were asking."

No, Fargo thought, they might not have held it against me. But I would have.

"Must be some independent," he said, "to rate access to Sol. Last I heard only megacorps ships went in and out. That and Armada."

Stephen did not answer.

"Be interesting if we get to Earth," Fargo continued. "I've never been there. I hear the whole planet is climate controlled, just like pleasure parks on Pan Pollux. Always the right weather for whatever a co might want."

"It's not like that. It's...well, there's some climate modification, but not like on the terraformed colonies."

"Really? And I imagine you know this from experience?"

For a time Fargo thought Stephen had gone silent on him again. But then Stephen said, "Yes. I was born on Earth."

Fargo felt the slightest shift when the supplemental began to move. The internal field did not quite sync with the external agravs and the difference allowed the smallest effects through. He slipped on his breather and switched on his bodysheath.

He stretched out on the deck, back against his gear, and turned off his lamp. A few moments later Stephen did the same.

"Fargo?"

"Hmm?"

"Just how angry are you?"

"About what?"

"Going to Earth."

Fargo did not answer, partly to annoy Stephen. But, he realized, he was not so much angry as frightened. Frightened and excited, repelled and curious. He had no answer, just as he had had no answer to Lis's invitation, her observation. His reactions were jumbled and complex and he did not trust naming them.

Another jar told him the supplemental was being loaded onto the shuttle. He checked his chronometer and closed his eyes. His heart raced, but he thought he might manage a nap before lift-off–

A deep groan rumbled through the walls of the supplemental and Fargo jerked awake. He looked at the time again. Rull had given him an eight hour window, but this was a good three hours ahead of schedule.

The air seemed to thicken, but this was illusion. Fargo felt no increase of pressure. The stasis field maintained a constant g. He relaxed a little, but he could not sleep now.

The trip upwell took just over an hour. The shuttle juddered loudly into dock. Fargo felt himself float gently off the deck; the stasis field was not directional. Faint vibrations shivered through the air as the supplemental was maneuvered into its berth on the body of the ship. Fargo counted seconds, adding up the distances, the time required for pressurization, for all the necessary sensor apparatus to link in. Counted the time till he could be fairly certain it was safe to leave. Ship's g gradually pulled him back down to the deck. When it seemed to remain constant for several minutes, Fargo switched on his lamp and found Stephen.

Stephen hugged his legs close, eyes wide. His face looked old in the sharp light, drawn in anxiety, as if he had been wrestling with demons on the trip up. Fargo wondered if Stephen ever lost control of his ability and wrestled with someone else's demon by mistake.

"Hey," he said. Stephen looked at him. "Time to move."

"We're not staying here?"

"No. Don't know what the inspection schedule is. I want to be somewhere else, where maybe I can tap ship's data."

Stephen nodded. Fargo, relieved, stood and pulled on his pack. There was no reason not to stay right here for the whole run. But he did not trust this ride and he did not want to try to explain that to Stephen. Instead, he just wanted to be elsewhere.

He opened the hatch and lowered himself through. The inspection corridor deck was less than three meters down and he landed quietly in the still-low g. The lights in the corridor were off, except for red panels at each access. Stephen followed and landed with a loud metallic crack.

Overhead the corridor sealed against the row of supplemental inspection hatches. Fargo gestured for Stephen to follow and trotted toward the nearest access. He knelt by the panel in the deck and studied the control, quickly identifying the manual override. He tapped it and sighed, relieved, when it irised open.

He bent over and lowered his head through the hatch. The next level looked like an in-hull storage compartment. Bins stretched away. Luggage. The *Isomer* carried passengers, then. Fargo smiled to himself and dropped through the hatch, somersaulting deftly. He swung for a few seconds from the edge, then let himself drop.

"Your pack, co," he called up to Stephen. "This ought to be a fine ride anyway. Passenger services. Good food, plenty of internal hold space to hide in–" Stephen's pack fell and he caught it. "We could've done a lot worse." Stephen lowered himself, hung briefly, and dropped. "Maybe Rull wasn't completely open with us, but he at least came through–"

Light flooded the passageway and hands closed on his arms.
He tightened up, tried to set his stance, but he was jerked
backward, off his feet. He bounced against a bin and slid to
the deck. He twisted around to see what was happening.

Three men held Stephen. Fargo jumped up.

The shortest of the three turned. He held a pistol at his
side. His wide face was etched with deep laughlines and fur-
rows rippled his forehead beneath short grey-brown hair. He
casually brought the pistol up and pointed it at Fargo.

Fargo sighed and shrugged.

They stepped out of the shunt into a crowded arcade. Fargo
glanced curiously at his captor; the man had tucked the pistol
inside his tunic. He nodded Fargo forward among the passengers. Fargo smiled and nodded with exaggerated politeness at
the stares of the Invested. To their left a railing ran the length
of the deck. Fargo drifted close and looked down into a busy
promenade. He glimpsed trees and fountains, shop fronts,
benches. A light touch on his arm guided him away.

"This is the long way to detention, isn't it, co?"

"It would be if that's where you were going."

They turned down a short side passage. Stateroom doors
lined both sides. They stopped at the fourth and last door on
the right.

"This is yours. My name is Barig. I'm ship's First. You need
to talk to anybody, you let me know. Welcome aboard *Isomer*."

The door opened. Stephen stepped inside. Fargo turned
to Barig.

"This is really very nice, co. What's the freight?"

"I don't know. Myself, I'd have you scouring the solid
waste system till we found someplace to dump you off. Shipmaster Cana says no."

"And who does Shipmaster Cana work for?"

Barig's face darkened. "For herself, co. And I work for
her. Don't make it difficult for me to do what she wants." He
nodded sharply toward the stateroom.

Fargo went inside. The door closed.

"I'm sure it's locked," Stephen said.

"Not for long." Fargo dropped his pack and reached for his multijack.

"Why not just wait and see what happens?"

Fargo glared at Stephen. The telelog had slouched into a chair, his fingers laced over his stomach, and was staring straight ahead at a wall.

"We don't know *what* they have in mind!" Fargo snapped. He narrowed his eyes. "Or do *you?*"

"I got the sense that we were expected and that we're not going to be harmed."

"It took nearly ten minutes to get from the storage bay to this room. You couldn't get more than that?"

Stephen scowled. "I told you, telelogging isn't that simple. I can't just lift things out whenever I want. If they're on the surface, sure, that's not hard. For instance, would you like to know Barig's opinion of us?"

"I think I can guess that, thank you."

Stephen shrugged. "But as for complex details or specific information, it takes longer and it's harder work. Usually, I need to get someone to think about what I want to find. Key words, phrases, a couple of pertinent questions, and generally it surfaces. You have to think about it even if you don't intend to tell me."

"That's why you're so useful at business meetings?"

"Everything's on the surface. But otherwise...human minds are terribly chaotic places. It's really simpler to have someone just tell you something."

Fargo nodded and crossed the room to the couch. "You can sense people at a distance? I mean, if someone were coming here now..."

"No, not unless–" He frowned uneasily. "Look, it's not telepathy."

"You read minds, right?"

"Yes and no. It's–look, I have to touch someone. It's partly–"

"So you can't sense people coming."

"If I've had physical contact with them within the last day or two, yes. Otherwise..."

"What about when Daniel was taken?"

"If you're wondering why I left Daniel alone, I didn't. He left me. I felt the exec coming for us and I tried to convince him to run, but..."

"Well, I suppose four against two aren't good odds."

"Four?"

"Yes, four. The exec and the three from Estana's ship. In fact, one of them was addressed as Tesa. I think it was Estana herself and two of her aids."

Stephen looked troubled. "I've been told Estana never leaves Earth."

"She must have this time."

"She's a recluse..."

"We'll find out when we get there, co. Don't worry about it for now. We have a more immediate problem."

"Oh?"

"Why are we in a stateroom instead of detention? This is pleasant, but the shipmaster could still put us off, then we have to find another ride."

"You asked me once if a freerider had ever lied to me."

Fargo looked at him.

"Rull did. To both of us."

Fargo shrugged. "I've figured that out."

"He lied the first day. He told us they didn't have a TEGlink. They do. I just thought he wanted to keep it a secret, I had no idea if it was general knowledge."

"A TEGlink? Then..."

"There's a lot of information coming in through Fornax." Stephen shrugged. "I didn't think it was important."

"Anything else unimportant enough not to mention to me?"

"He lied about this ride."

"Obviously."

Stephen looked at him as if he had been struck. "You *knew* he lied?"

Fargo nodded.

"Then what was all that about freeriders never lying?"

"Freeriders are human. We lie when it's convenient, just like everybody else. I was surprised when you said none of them had ever lied to you. I was trying to make a point."

Stephen stood. "This isn't easy for me, Fargo. It took me a long time to figure out that not all lies are intended to hurt. I keep people's privacy. I don't know how to sort it out."

Fargo watched him pace the room for a time. He sat down in a different chair and chewed at a thumbnail. He suddenly straightened and leaned forward, his face urgent. "There's something familiar here. I can't tell what it is, but..." He looked at Fargo. "Why are you coming along? What changed your mind? You agreed to Rull's request too fast. Don't tell me it's because he asked or you're afraid of letting others down. You're not. You're a lot more afraid of having people owe you something."

"Lots of reasons. I'd just as well leave them unsaid. But for now you've got a travelling companion."

"Thank you."

Fargo suddenly felt acutely uncomfortable. Stephen's face was earnest, almost innocent. He seemed genuinely appreciative and Fargo did not want to be appreciated. Stephen was right about that. He avoided any obligations as a rule. Obligation necessitated dependence and made betrayal possible.

With startling suddenness his attention centered on Lis. He winced, shocked at the strength of the memory, the feeling. He had not thought of her in the last few days. He had not dreamed, either, he realized.

"Fargo? Are you all right?"

He blinked at Stephen. "Just what were you 'rescuing' Daniel from?" When Stephen hesitated, Fargo said, "On the *Caliban* I heard Tesa–or whoever that was–say something about recovering her property."

"I–"

A sharp tone sounded. Both of them looked at the comm panel by the door to the bedroom. It sounded again and Stephen went over and tapped the accept.

"Yes?"

"Co Christopher?"

"This is Co Christopher..."

"This is Shipmaster Cana. Welcome aboard. I hope your accommodations are adequate. I understand you're travelling with a companion. If you'd like I can arrange a separate stateroom for him."

"Well, I–frankly, Shipmaster Cana, I'm a bit confused..."

"Of course. My apologies. Would the two of you please attend me this evening at Table? I'm sure things can be clarified then."

"Uh–"

"We'd be delighted, Shipmaster," Fargo called out.

"Excellent. I'll expect you both at eighteen hundred."

Stephen looked dazed. "Thank..." The light on the comm went out, the connection broken. "...you..."

Fargo stood, chuckling, and came up beside Stephen. "Never pass up Table. You don't know when next you'll eat that well." He studied the comm for a moment, then stabbed a contact.

"Who do you wish to communicate with?" the computer asked.

"Ship's First Barig."

A moment later: "This is Barig."

"This is Co Fargo and Co Christopher, your new passengers. It seems we've been invited to Table with the Shipmaster."

"...Yes?"

"We'll need some suitable clothes, I think. It wouldn't be right to show up looking like a couple of nids, would it?"

Chapter Six

Fargo could not recall the last time he had worn silk. The fabric seemed to float a few millimeters away from his skin, allowing air to slip through and tickle the fine hairs on his arms and legs. He stared at his reflection while Stephen finished dressing. He found that by concentrating on details–the fold in the sapphire fabric as it fell from the small pearl catch at his throat, the shadowplay from shoulder to wrist when he moved his arms, the shift of his dark eyebrows and the crease in his cheek as he tried out different expressions that might go better with his fine new clothes–the person he examined in the mirror became unfamiliar, a stranger he wished to have introduced to him. There was some comfort in seeing such reticence in someone else, a measure of confidence gained from knowing that whoever this co might be he seemed even less sure of himself...

"Ready?"

The illusions ended and Fargo nodded to Stephen. Stephen's tunic was ivory, belted at the waist. It fit him, Fargo thought, matched his paleness, his light hair, his milky skin. And still he looked out-of-place, like some seti dropped in the midst of humanity, the more alien for being so humanlike.

A pair of escorts waited in the corridor. No weapons showed, but Fargo assumed both were armed.

Fewer people strolled the arcade now. Nightcycle approached. Fargo heard the thrum of music from an omnirec on the mall below. He walked along the rail, looking down appreciatively. The *Isomer* was obviously a much larger, newer ship than the *Caliban* had been. Not a conversion of an old in-system hauler, but a starship from the first.

The escorts took them to a shunt and rode forward with them. The shunt let them out before the wide double doors to the Shipmaster's suite.

Fargo hesitated at the threshold. He glanced back at the escorts and one of them waved him on. Stephen was pale, frowning uncertainly. Fargo forced a smile and stepped forward.

The room was twice as long as wide and seemed jammed with people. Fargo saw bright colors, a smear of faces, soft light rimming glasses held waist high; thirty guests, perhaps a few more. All the self-assurance he had brought fled. He could feel the smile frozen in place and hoped he did not look too transparently terrified. The new clothes did not quite substitute for genuine confidence and he found himself wishing that he *were* that stranger in the mirror. At least that co belonged at functions like this.

"Well?" Stephen whispered.

"Well...I want something to drink. Now."

Stephen pointed and Fargo saw the bar at the far end of the hall. Near this end, a few steps from the doors, the floor rose, three shallow steps, to become an island upon which stood the table. Fargo nodded and wound his way nervously through the small groups, thankful that no one had spoken to him between the entrance and the bar. He leaned against it for a time, half-listening to the babble of conversation behind him, hearing little of it. He had never liked these events. His father had insisted he attend for years, so he could become familiar with them, accustomed. It was business and he would need to understand. He had managed familiar–he never grew accustomed to them.

He punched up a drink at random and drank it straight down. He ordered another, cradled the glass, and turned toward the gathering.

He saw Stephen talking with two men. He did not seem pleased. Fargo watched, wondering if he should interrupt, "rescue" Stephen, but their conversation ended abruptly and Stephen came toward him. Fargo leaned back against the bar.

"Some of the mystery is cleared up," Stephen said. "Kol has been looking for me." He ordered a drink, then gestured toward the two men. "Bosh Macken and Sren Kovitcz. They both work for Kol."

"What are they doing on board?"

"The Panlateral Trade Commission talks. I didn't think they were scheduled this soon." He shrugged. "I had intended to be back on Markab beforehand, but..."

"I don't follow."

"Sorry. Chairman Tai Chin called the talks a few months ago. This is her last big effort to formalize relations with the seti, the Distals, and the Primary Vested. She wants an open border policy, less trade restriction, more interaction."

"And Janacek is part of this?"

"He's one of the speakers for the Distal mercantilists. Oh, not just him, but he's one of the keys. Tai Chin has asked for the conference to settle the issues. I thought we had another month, but evidently I was wrong."

"Really. So this ship just happened to be in-system at Fornax when we just happened to need a ride?"

Stephen shook his head. "This is one of eight different missions. All of them apparently had instructions to pick me up if found."

"Is Janacek on board?"

"No, he's on another ship. He'll be told, though."

"Well, that explains what you're doing here. My presence is still a mystery."

"What do you mean? You're with me."

Fargo laughed softly. "I don't think that would be enough to get me invited to Shipmaster's Table, do you?"

Stephen did not answer. He kept looking at Macken and Kovitcz and sipping at his drink.

"So is there anybody here I might find an acceptable conversation with?"

Stephen blinked at him, then began to scowl.

Fargo raised a hand defensively. "Sorry. I should know better than to ask for favors. I'll find out on my own."

He drifted from island to island, eavesdropping on the conversations. The guests were a very mixed group. People from several worlds were present. The rich soup of clashing langish dialects–none so harsh or untempered by Pan Standard as to be unintelligible–possessed a musical quality for Fargo. The sounds of the words, the way a co from Neighbors pronounced them compared to the way someone from Faron spoke, blent in harmonies. When he stopped trying to hear one person speaking and listened to the crowd as a whole, the effect was almost soothing.

Topics varied from group to group. Fashion, business, music, dramas, politics, travel. Fargo followed little of it. He was grateful for the number of people; he had an excuse to avoid joining a conversation he was sure he could not carry. He continued around and through, wandering among the well-dressed Invested, soaking up bits of information, and losing himself in the sounds.

The walls held graphics from several worlds. A few he was sure were seti. The lines, the proportions, the play of color–none of it made human sense. The rhythms were off. Fargo found it difficult even to look at them for very long, as if the images continually slid from his conscious apprehension.

He came around to the bar again. Stephen was gone. Fargo set his empty glass on the return plate and punched up another. He quickly scanned the nearby guests but did not see Stephen. Drink in hand, he set out on another circuit of the room.

"Looking for anyone in particular, or just a friendly face?"

Startled, Fargo lurched around–liquid sloshed from his glass across his hand–and stared at the unfamiliar woman beside him. He began to beg her pardon, then looked closer.

"Lis...?"

She smiled, lower lip tucked under teeth, eyes glimmering with moist highlights. She wore a maroon jacket and loose

white pants and her hair was shot with corundum. She looked
nothing like the woman on Eurasia, yet the moment he said
her name she looked like no one else.

Fargo laughed. "What—?" He noticed his wet hand then
and laughed again.

Lis took him by the elbow and led him back to the bar.
She tapped the panel and a moment later handed him a damp
towel.

"I've been watching you since you walked in. Took me a
bit to realize it was you," she said. "You clean up almost as
well as I do."

"What are you doing here?" he asked, wiping his hand
clean.

"You mean you didn't expect to see me here?"

"Should I have?"

She shrugged. "Shuffle a deck of cards enough times,
eventually you'll get the same hand twice. Complaining?"

"No. Just…well, how are you?"

"I'm interesting. At least, that's what my employers tell
me."

Fargo blinked. "Employers…?"

"Don't look so crestfallen, there's plenty to go around."
She raised up on her toes and looked across the room. "Ah. I
think Shipmaster Cana is about to seat Table."

Fargo followed her gaze. A tall, slim woman with light
brown hair, dressed in deep emerald, stood at the edge of the
platform. Beside her, half a head shorter, was Barig.

Lis touched his shoulder. "Fargo, I'd like to talk to you
later, after all this."

He ordered himself another drink, avoiding her gaze.
"Uh…"

"Welcome," Shipmaster Cana said. Her voice was sharp,
almost nasal, and cut through the moil of conversation easily.
"I'm Shipmaster Sea Cana of the *Isomer*. I'm glad you could all
attend this evening. Before we seat, I would like to introduce
a special guest for this evening."

"That's my cue," Lis whispered. Before Fargo could respond, she was gone.

"*Isomer*," Cana continued, "is privileged to be transporting a number of representatives to Earth for the upcoming Panlateral Trade Commission conference. We have coes from major frontier mercantile houses, three members of the Forum from the Distals, academicians, local representatives, several journalists. *Isomer* hasn't been so graced by such a showing of the best and brightest in some time." Quiet laughter chittered across the room. She smiled.

"I have invited a select group representing each of these interests for tonight's Table. You've all had a chance to become acquainted with each other. I'd like now to introduce to you a representative you have not had an opportunity to meet."

Barig moved aside and Cana turned. "*Isomer* is also privileged to be transporting the Ranonan Legation representing the Seven Reaches and seti interests. May I introduce and would you all please welcome Ambassador Yol-Maex."

A tall figure emerged from a door on the opposite side of the table and came around to stand alongside Cana. Fur-covered hands pushed back the light blue cowl to reveal the face Fargo had seen for the first time on Eurasia.

You've seen them...

Then Lis stepped up onto the platform alongside the seti. Fargo stared, stunned.

"And this is the human liaison to the Ranonan legation," Cana said. "Co Lis Falco."

For nearly a full minute no one reacted. When it began it escalated quickly. A whisper was followed by a cough, then several people spoke at once, and one man shouted something Fargo could not make out over the several shouting voices that, halfway through, joined his. A ripple seemed to move through the assembled guests.

"I will not!" someone snapped loudly.

"–nonsense–"

"Let's not be shy, we'll have a show of hands–who's a bigot?"

"That's it! This has to stop!"

Suddenly a group of about ten coes moved to the exit. Laughter bubbled from one end of the room, answered by low grumbling from another. Fargo saw indecision, fear, puzzlement, and impatience in the faces around him. He had never cared to be in the middle of crowds, especially crowds where the general mood was in flux between ambivalence and ugliness. He glanced at the door, wishing to leave, but he did not want to be counted among those who had already left. He remembered the mob on Eurasia. I'm different, he thought, I'm not like that. He tightened his grip on his glass and stood still. He counted the faces– those who looked indecisive outnumbered those who seemed pleased with the seti presence. The mood had not coalesced into anything definite and it seemed all too likely to shift to the worst.

He drew a deep breath and walked forward. "Welcome, Ambassador! I'm glad you're here. That means we can eat and I for one am starving."

He glimpsed a few astonished expressions. He hoped no one would try to stop him reaching the platform. He felt a rush throughout his body, as if some part of him tried to move faster. He fixed his gaze on the table, then saw Lis watching him.

Someone laughed loudly. Someone else sneezed.

Just as he reached the three shallow steps, people began moving forward. For a moment he was terrified. But they were coming up to take their places at the table.

He stood by a chair–there were no place cards that he could see–and he felt the guests assemble around him. He looked up and saw Lis across from him. She nodded, her face eloquently grateful. He looked toward the head of the table.

Shipmaster Cana cocked an eyebrow at him. "Welcome to Table, Co..."

"Just Fargo. Thank you for the invitation." He turned to Yol-Maex, who stood at the opposite end. "A pleasure to make your acquaintance. I think I've met a relative of yours."

The Ranonan bowed slightly. "And I, yours," it said.

Fargo caught Stephen's eye as the telelog skirted the edge of the platform. He was pale and regarded the seti nervously.

When everyone had found their place, Fargo did a quick count. Eleven places were empty; over a quarter of the human guests had left.

Shipmaster Cana sat down and nodded. Everyone took their seats.

He leaned toward Lis. "I suppose I have you to thank for being invited?"

She nodded. "And a good decision it turned out to be, too."

"Mm. Well, let's hope the food lives up to its reputation."

A complex cascade of feelings ran through him, as if presenting him with his choice from a buffet. All he needed to do was choose the right one, but they went by so quickly. He recognized one feeling clearly: foolishness. His emotions were playing with his balance and he felt like an adolescent.

Two servers rolled along opposite sides of the table. Extensors carefully set plates of salad and soup before each human. As the devices moved back to their portals, a third emerged and rolled directly to the Ranonan and began setting dishes before it. The largest plate contained something that resembled a normal salad except for the coloration–salmon, ocher, and white.

Carafes of wine arrived.

"Surprised?" Lis whispered.

"Not in the least," Fargo said with exaggerated casualness. He poured wine in her glass, then filled his. They raised the glasses toward each other, touched them lightly together. "I'm astonished," he said.

The wine was dry. Conversation erupted in small, quiet groups, here and there down the length of the table, finally coming together, weaving the guests into one fabric. A ritual. There were rules. First the salad and wine, unimportant pleasantries, meaningless phrases passed back and forth, up and down, like passwords to verify that everyone present belonged here, had a right to participate in the more important things to come.

Then the main course, the substantial food, and bolder topics.

"May I ask, Shipmaster," a heavyset woman in gold and sapphire silks to Cana's left said loudly, "why you've waited till now to let us know a nonhuman was travelling aboard your ship?"

"You may ask," Cana said. "But it would be more appropriate to ask Co Yol-Maex."

The woman raised her eyebrows and glanced toward the seti, who looked up and met her eyes directly.

"I will consider the question put," the Ranonan said, the words carefully enunciated. "I am the nexus of a trade group approaching your government for modifications in the laws restricting interaction between the Pan Humana and the *Sev N'Raicha*–what you call the Seven Reaches. As to why we waited till now, that was my request. I wished to be more familiar with you through observation before I attempted a social interaction."

"Wise tactic," someone said. "We can be touchy."

"You make it sound," another man said, "as if the restrictions were unreasonable. They're not just blind bigotry, there are legitimate–"

"Of course," the woman across from him interjected, "there are always justifications for intolerance. You don't even have to look hard, they're lying around. Most of them haven't even been used yet."

"That's not what I meant," the first man objected. "The stability of currency is not a question of prejudice, it's a very real issue."

"It wasn't until we found the setis."

"Why would you want to modify the restrictions?" the first woman asked.

"Same reason *we* want to modify them," another woman said. "Damn nuisance, all this xenophobic–"

"Excuse me," the first woman said, "but perhaps the seti has a different reason."

"Excuse me," Yol-Maex said, "what is your name?"

"Hella Caxender of Nine Rivers."

"Thank you. Co Caxender, we are restricted in many ways in dealing with humans. The frontier–what you call the Distals–seem to be the only places where some degree of diverse interaction occurs. Your people have been welcomed into the heart of the Seven Reaches, into the core of many congregations. It is our intent to try to obtain similar privileges."

Privileges. Fargo looked at the Ranonan narrowly and wondered if it really understood what it was asking for. There was more at stake here than just privileges.

Until Fargo joined the Monad the inherent ritualism of life had been invisible to him. Like air and breathing, it just was, and in the same way he was aware of the medium and process of oxygen and oxygenation without really noticing it, he had moved through the rituals of his life without really questioning them or understanding them as anything more than part of living. He listened to the conversation now with a secret pleasure. He recognized it as a ritual. That and no more. He doubted Hella Caxender–or any of them–had any interest in learning anything new. Like most coes, their minds were made up, their opinions preset long before this encounter. He wondered if the Ranonan understood this.

In the Monad, structure was nakedly visible. The cells spiralled round a central chimney, rising toward the blue-black sky of Etacti, visible through the iris in the center of the arching roof. The doors faced inward, a small window faced outward. There was nothing around the Monad. Desert, the color of a vein through pale flesh, bounded in the distance by a ragged ridge of mountain.

In the Monad there was a time for breakfast, a time for reading, a time for meditation, and time for exercise; a time for ablutions, a time for dinner, a time for sleep. Most of the time was silent. They were radical hermits, turning their disenchanted backs on the Pan and all other aspects of their time and their culture. The structure of the Monad gave them four directions to look–out at the desert, which could kill them, in at the common far below, which could comfort them, and within at their souls, which might do either. Few ever looked up at the sky. It was there, but it was part of a universe they rejected. To be offered the view and refuse it meant acceptance of that rejection.

What comfort there was in the common was made spartan by the rules of Common Table. Conversation could not be conducted directly, only through third or fourth parties. They were hermits, they did not seek direct contact. To address directly the one you wanted to talk to would have negated any freedom the hermitage allowed. Discussions took on the ethereal quality of prayers in an empty cathedral. The third party form was the basest: recitations made to anyone and everyone, like thoughts uttered aloud in private, became the preferred manner. By indirection, implication, and a subtle code never codified but quickly learned, the limitations of the fundamental ritual were transcended. The format lived, a ritual turned custom turned artifact. The constraint of the ritual produced an art and often Fargo had wished for a way to record the results.

And still, even with so complex a system, the things spoken of were as meaningless as any conversation anywhere between anyone. The particular shade of dark the sky was that day and who had broken discipline to notice it; the coughing fit echoing round the Monad, who could it have been; why did co so and so rate a cell that high, that close to the top, and some other, certainly not the speaker, but someone the speaker knew, rated one at the base...

No different than the society they had left. Except here, with the rules made explicit, the rituals so obvious, Fargo learned for the first time the structure of human interaction. Now he could no longer ignore it. And the implied honesty of the Monad structure suggested that they understood something basic about the lies most people told themselves and others.

Even so, it was possible to reach a point where the rituals became so integral as to sink from conscious regard. No different. People looking for a way to be together that did not require intimacy, that denied vulgar connection, that did not degrade into emotional anarchy.

Then, once every five days, the Harmonics. Synthets wove melodies in the air above the common, sound issued from each cell. The twenty-one mantras were constructed to blend with each other. Some were farther along than others, but there was no disharmony.

It was here Fargo knew he was no hermit, radical or otherwise. He loved the commingled sound, the beauty of all the joined voices. Instead of finding his way inward and apart from the others through the mantras, he only found connection. Instead of finding the Unique Aspect that was supposed to be at his center, the defining element of who he was, he found a complex medley of responses that shifted and sifted with the music. He could not lose himself in the Monad, as he wished. He could not give up the thing that was him, because, he discovered, he was too many things.

Still, it would not have been difficult to stay. No one would have had the temerity to ask him to leave. They were hermits, they were not supposed to notice that he was different than they. For all he knew, none of them had achieved what they claimed, or implied, they had achieved. The rituals were easy enough, and in time second nature. Fargo was sure most of them no longer thought of what they did as ritual. Some had been in the Monad so long Fargo imagined that they had been born within the bulging flue.

He left and saw the structure of ritual in every circumstance. With the Invested it was so well entrenched, so much a part of their thoughts and feelings that it seemed they could have no thoughts or feelings without their rituals. Maybe, he thought, their rituals *are* their thoughts and feelings. They're just not mine...

The Monad would have fallen apart without ritual. It defined them, as perhaps it did everyone. Maybe, he thought, that was the Unique Aspect that everyone defended without knowing they defended it.

A server took his empty plate and he looked around to see if anyone had noticed his absence. Lis smiled at him conspiratorially and he covered his sudden ill-ease with his wine glass.

"–zero inflation has always been a goal of the Forum," a man was saying. Fargo recognized one of the two men Stephen had been speaking with, Bosh Macken. "The greatest curse of pre-Expansion Earth was the shaky economy. Since the early colonial days we've been terrified of local collapses. Remember Faron. Nobody wants to see something like that again."

"What exactly does an open border policy have to do with old horror stories about debtor systems?" Lis asked. "We abolished that policy after Faron, no colony since has gone into receivership."

"Not to Sol," Macken said. "But there's no way of knowing how the seti would treat a system that found itself unable to service its debt. We're talking about the possibility of drawing the entire Pan Humana into a destabilizing arrangement of supporting unviable trade arrangements."

"You mean we might all have to cover our bad investments?" Lis shot back.

"No. But why should, say, Nine Rivers be responsible for a trade agreement between Markab and a seti concern? If Markab loses liquidity and can't service its note, why should Sol bail us out?"

"Why shouldn't it?"

Macken shrugged. "The fact remains we just don't know."

"It intrigues me," Yol-Maex said. "It would seem reasonable that if what you do not know is what frightens you, then you must learn as much as you can about it. Make the unknown known instead of hiding from it."

"What if what you learn," Fargo asked, "changes forever what you are?"

The Ranonan blinked. "Why should that matter?"

"For some people, to change is to die." Fargo glanced at Lis, his heart hammering.

"It seems," Yol-Maex said, "that this fear has to do with identity. One feels comfortable with what one is. To lose it is, indeed, a disquieting thought. But what is the likelihood of that? Identity is a complex thing. To perhaps lose one or two components in the course of gaining new knowledge will hardly destroy the totality."

"Unless," Stephen said, "you base your concept of identity on only one component."

Hesitantly, Stephen raised his eyes to the seti. Fargo watched, fascinated, as they regarded each other silently.

Abruptly, Hella Caxender asked, "What do you do, Co Fargo?"

Fargo started, then smiled. "Oh–my field is the Brownian redistribution of waste."

Lis burst into laughter. The tension broke and Stephen smiled thinly at Fargo.

"May I say, Shipmaster," Fargo said, "that you set a fine table. This is excellent. I think we should toast our host."

Glasses were raised toward Cana.

"I, also, would like to toast," Yol-Maex said. "I toast humans. Among you I have met none who are so limited as to possess only a single component of identity. You are a most admirable and promising race."

The conversation lost its edge. Smaller topics broke the table into groups again and Fargo sensed the general relief.

Stephen was still pale, but he no longer seemed quite so uncomfortable.

After dessert Shipmaster Cana presented a new piece of music–quasi-symphonic, resembling a tone poem but with less structure and a free-flowing improvisation line that wove in and out at unpredictable moments. Fargo smiled mechanically and longed for a synthet. Yol-Maex thanked Cana and retired. Lis went with the ambassador, but returned.

People stayed for more drinks then began leaving by ones and twos until finally only Fargo, Stephen, and Lis remained.

Stephen leaned against the wall near the bar. He looked worn out.

"Are you all right?" Fargo asked, handing him a brandy.

Stephen nodded. "I didn't know..."

Lis came up to him. "Shipmaster Cana wants us to stay for a time." She studied Stephen. "Are you up to this?"

Stephen opened his eyes. "Will any seti be present?"

"No."

"You work for them?"

Lis nodded. She smiled at Fargo. "We were both offered jobs."

"I see," Fargo said, "that you took advantage of the offer."

"Not entirely by choice. After we parted, I went looking for my ride. What I found was a gang of port bulls looking for freeriders. They were between me and my shuttle. I tried to find a way around them and kept finding more gangs, so I went back to the embassy and asked Voj-Nehan if the offer still held."

Fargo scowled. "I wasn't so lucky. They saw me first."

"You're alive, I'd say you're lucky."

"I don't believe in luck."

Lis nodded, a look of uncertainty on her face.

"Why are the setis on board?" Stephen asked.

"Just as Yol-Maex said. They are an official trade legation to Earth. None of the megas would let them book passage, even though they have official invitations and diplomatic vouchers from Chairman Tai Chin. I'm working as sort of a liaison."

"Liaison to what?"

"Humans. They don't understand us very well."

Fargo grunted. "Where have I heard that before?" When Stephen gave him a dark look, he asked, "What was going on between you two? I felt like the rope in a tug-of-war."

Stephen shook his head and sipped his brandy.

Cana came up and poked Fargo with a finger.

"I don't much care for freeriders," she said.

Fargo moaned, mock serious. "Oh, and I thought we were making such progress!"

"Shipmaster, I'm shocked," Lis said, "I thought we were getting along very well."

Cana started. "You–?"

"All of us," Stephen said. "At one time or another."

She raised her eyebrows, then grunted. "Maybe you find it amusing, but I sometimes depressurize my cargo holds. I carry biologicals occasionally–pets and such for passengers, research organics–and it's simple to clean everything out by exposing it to hard vacuum. I've found freerider corpses from time to time. It's not pleasant."

"Do you just vent or do you try to find us first?" Fargo asked tightly.

"Oh, we search. I try to find you before we make transition."

Fargo nodded. "Then you and I have no problem with each other."

"Barig said we were expected," Stephen said. "Were we?"

"Yes. Please, come with me."

"How did you know about us?"

"Kol Janacek has been looking for you." She glanced over her shoulder. "You were on board the *Caliban*?"

Stephen nodded.

"I'd like to hear what happened." They reached the opposite end of the dining room and Cana led them through a door into a private suite. "But we were making a general search for you–unofficially, of course–at Co Janacek's request. We weren't certain you were on Fornax, but considering where the *Caliban* was found it made sense. Your ID turned up at a perimeter station, but you'd disappeared again."

"We might have taken a ride with any of a dozen ships, though," Fargo said. "Janacek's resources are impressive, but I don't think this is all his doing. Is it?"

"We were informed that you'd likely want to go to Earth."

Stephen frowned. "Informed by whom?"

"I'll come to that."

Fargo glanced around at the room. The light was pleasant, indirect. Art panels were set into two of the walls–a few representational works of various planetscapes, an impressionist style of the Great Nebula in Orion, and a couple of pure abstracts, one done completely in silvers and greys and alabasters. The chairs were all arranged in the opposite corner facing the paintings. Cana waved them into seats.

"I'm an independent," Cana said. "I do what I want as far as the law allows. In a lot of ways we independents are like freeriders."

"Not to hear some of you talk," Lis said.

Cana nodded. "We're caught in a bind about you. You legally don't exist, but there are subtler laws to deal with people who give aid to you. The Pan Humana doesn't like loose ends. You're a loose end. So are we. So are the Distals. Do you know anything about the conference we're going to?"

"The Chairman called it," Lis said. "She's bringing together the prime movers of the Distals and the Inner Pan to try to hammer out an agreement about the borders. She specifically invited a seti legation."

"And the Primary Vested are fighting her. Even if she wins this one, Erin Tai Chin is likely not going to remain Chairman. If she loses, she won't have any real power anymore. Publicly, the question is whether the borders will be open or sealed. The issue, however, is what the Pan Humana will be like forever after."

"Why are we talking?" Fargo asked.

"Because you're with Stephen Christopher."

Stephen looked up. "You said you were informed I'd want to go to Earth. By whom?"

"Someone you know."

He shook his head. "I don't understand..."

Cana pursed her lips. "Indulge me a little further. The forces shaping the future are not obvious ones. The Seven Reaches sit out there with all they imply and affect us by little more than their presence. The Pan Humana is manipulated by the megas. Those are the obvious forces, the ones everybody knows about. But they are hardly the only ones. The Pan Humana itself shapes. It's a slow, largely unself-aware process, but inevitably one of the strongest. Even the freeriders have an effect. The competition developing between the core and the Distals contributes. In all this, direction becomes a foolish thing to expect. We have to look for gross changes, lumbering shifts that have no precision. The key to understanding the various forces is in understanding motives. Why the various facets act the way they do. When you know the motive you can determine the goal. Depending on who we're talking about, you can determine the likelihood of achieving that goal."

"Basic political theory," Fargo said. "What does this have to do with who asked for Stephen?"

"As I said, some forces are subtle. Some are not at all obvious to anyone, even though the effects of their presence are felt."

"Ghosts in the machine?" Lis said.

"Something like that," Cana said.

Fargo began to say more, but a movement caught his eye. He looked around until he focussed on one of the paintings. The silvery abstract was shifting. The textures oozed and flowed, pulled inward toward a locus. Fargo watched, fascinated and frightened, as a pair of eyes formed and peered out at them.

"Hello, Stephen. The years have been long."
Stephen stood woodenly. "Hanna?"

Chapter Seven

Stephen stretched his arm out and let his fingertips brush the surface of the image. Patterns shifted around the points where he touched. He jerked slightly, then turned to look at Fargo and Lis.

"She wants to communicate with you," he said. "Directly."

Fargo hesitated. Stephen was excited, eyes wide, boyish. Fargo could easily, it appeared, topple him back into his moodiness by refusing. He looked past Stephen to the image. The eyes seemed fixed on him. They were not human eyes, though they were good imitations. It was not just their colorlessness, but their ambivalence. Fargo was reluctant to give over any control to them.

Lis squeezed his hand and he almost snatched it away. The sensation shocked him.

"What does that mean?" she asked.

Stephen opened his mouth, then shrugged. "It's hard to describe. Communion? I–"

"Why?" Fargo asked.

Stephen's enthusiasm diminished slightly. "There's a lot of information we all need...and she needs to know if she can trust you..."

"I'm willing," Lis said. She tightened her fingers on Fargo's hand slightly.

Fargo nodded.

Stephen grinned and held out his hands to them. Fargo let Lis pull him forward. He lifted his left hand and let Stephen grasp it tightly. His palm tingled and he resisted the urge to yank it away. Stephen gripped Lis's right hand.

Then he released them and turned to the image. He pressed both hands against it. His head bowed.

Fargo started to say something, but it was lost within the sudden presence in his mind. At first there were no words, only the sensation of a vast Other. The room felt too small, then *he* felt too small, floating. The room was as big as it needed to be, he saw, as big as the universe. The eyes locked onto him, fixed him in place, and she burrowed into him. He held his hands out uselessly to fend her off.

The molasses quality of his thoughts undermined his attempts to resist. The futility of trying to block what was happening gave way to a warm cushion of intense interest. His mind enveloped, flower-like, the strong kernel of Being in its center. He turned away, but took it with him. The others were dim, unreal shapes clouding his field of vision. Nothing was solid, nothing relevant except what was inside.

His senses tingled with activation. Bright flashes coursed through him. He fell, but the floor was a vague impression only partially noticed amid the coruscating layers of neural activity.

I am not me.

Yes, you are. That, and others.

?

Stephen, Lis.

And they?

Contain you, too.

All this...

All.

And you?

I am here.

How?

There was no reply...

Fargo twisted inside out and "looked" around. Warm masses glowed and pulsed in a huddle around him. They were yellow, orange, white, with fine veins of cerulean, pleasant and inviting. Intrigued, he reached to touch one. A wispy fibre extended from him to the nearest. The surface scintillated where the fibre touched, then swelled toward him. For an instant he was afraid, wanting to pull out, but it reached him and–*I I I, YOU YOU YOU, WE WE WE*–core, center, reason–Soft considerations, warm expectations, innocent bitterness.

Introduction to Alternate Viewpoint, class begins–

?

The orchid split in half, opened, and swallowed–

Happy memories interlaced with unkindnesses done for no apparent reason, no purpose, no motivation.

None of this makes sense.

What do you know?

Nothing.

What do I feel like?

Seti...

!

Please, I'm lost.

...

There was never much hope alone. Always there existed the conviction of being incomplete when isolated. But isolation became a salve, an ointment, to heal the hurt. Only to get strong enough to lose it all again.

Things never change, really, but I keep hoping.

Who?

In each of us there is the potential of everyone else.

Sounds like parlor sophistry to me, a little verbal ballet set to sympathy.

All I want!

Yes?

Is what I've always wanted.

?

One possible way to understanding, he found, was in the repetition of events undergone through no conscious effort, without control, without recognition, without more than vague apprehension. Patterns emerged and displayed for him a willful insistence on partial surgery on emotions that demanded feeding but only achieved a brutal sort of transfusion insufficient for more than mere existence. Intrigued, Fargo looked closer, deeper. In response, he was taken in further. The belief of incompleteness became stronger until he reached the center, the core. Then it dispersed. The tide broke against a rocky abutment of independence. At the heart of it, strength.

Let me show you something.

?

Here, right here, in here...

The core opened again. Within Fargo saw a bedlam of images. Vertigo took him as he groped for something to hang onto, and he pitched downward, falling. He passed tier after tier. When he looked back he saw a vast columnar flue stretching to a diminishing circle of light–

He turned again and saw a brownish mist rising toward him. A cacophony of chittering surrounded him, distorted laughter or a billion contentless conversations.

Who the hell am I in?

The mist swallowed him.

Hanna wore a metal body below a hairless flesh and bone head. Her eyes glittered but she did not smile. She raised her left hand and gestured to the stars that surrounded them. Fargo saw the paths of starships spreading out from one star to dozens of others. The bright paths rayed out like the arms of an explosion, lacing together the heavens.

"Look closer," Hanna said and Fargo, wary, bent toward one of the suns.

A ship came to a world and sent people and equipment down to mold it. As Fargo watched, the planet changed from a dirty grey and waxen hue to blue and green and white. Cities appeared and then ships came back up its well into space and stations were built. More starships arrived and the world changed further, a place for humans, beautiful and warm and welcoming.

"Closer."

Fargo saw roadways reach from town to town and city to city; businesses thrived; farm fields flourished, patterning the landscape. Graveyards filled. Within the largest city, he saw a faint shape form that seemed to hover over it and grow out of it. Ghostly at first, it solidified into another image like Hanna–but it was not Hanna.

Fargo looked at Hanna for explanation. Instead, she gestured across the stars to other worlds. Fargo followed her gaze and saw more embodiments of planetary matrices.

"How many of you?" he asked.

Hanna touched her chest and worked her fingers into a seam Fargo had not noticed before. She pulled it aside and opened herself. He backed away, but Hanna reached for him. She seized his wrist and pulled him closer. He stared into the corridor, terrified, unable to break her grip. The corridor stretched away to a vanishing point. Hanna shoved him inside and he fell to the floor. When he rolled over he saw the ceiling close over him, the slit become a pucker, the pucker smooth out.

He pushed himself up to his feet. He was shaking. The hallway was a dirty white, plain, lined with black, unlabeled doors. He heard voices. He followed the sounds, walking on legs that felt infirm, watery. Abruptly, the hallway ended at a door marked "A.V. Class 102." He hesitated. Turning, he saw that the corridor had become a small room and there were no other doors. He opened the door and stepped through.

Stephen paced before an empty blackboard, an open book in his hand. He spoke in a monotone to the packed lecture hall. Fargo did not understand him. The words were senseless, a different language. Fargo recognized no one in any of the seats nearby.

"You're late."

Stephen was looking at him, expectantly. Fargo smiled timidly and held up his hands in apology. Stephen indicated a chair in the back row.

Fargo scooted between knees and the next row of chairs and sat in the one empty seat, in the middle of the section.

"What," Stephen continued, now in perfectly understandable langish, "was the purpose of constructing the World Matrix Databases? Fargo?"

"Uh...I–"

"Anyone else?" Stephen glanced from face to face.

"Collation of information throughout the world, global communication organization, standardization of governmental services," someone said.

"Exactly. And what did we end up with?"

"A sentient, self-aware, self-contained system–"

"Wrong! Wrong, wrong, and wrong!" Stephen slapped the podium. "None of you pay attention! Fargo! What's wrong with the description just given?"

"I don't know," Fargo said.

"Exactly! I'm glad to see at least one of you pays attention! Hanna is not self-contained! She needs communion! She needs contact! She needs other minds! Heuristically Automorphic Nonlinear Neuronal Analog! That's what that means, that she is patterned on a human mind, and a human mind kept unstimulated by new things stagnates and eventually collapses and dies! Fargo! When did First Contact occur?"

"Oh...forty years ago?"

"Thirty-eight to be precise. And what did the Forum and the Chairman do when it happened?"

Fargo fidgeted in his seat. He hated being lectured to. He hated being in class. He hated classes.

"Exactly!" Stephen jabbed the air emphatically with his book. He was obviously enjoying himself. "They panicked. Wouldn't you? I mean, aliens, for godsake! Different creatures with nothing–presumably–in common with us. Really different, species that looked nothing like us, that thought nothing like us, that possessed language trees whose roots we couldn't begin to comprehend. Panic. Panic was the only acceptable response, because all our institutions had been designed primarily to deal with emergencies that create panic. Threats. How did the panic manifest? Anyone? Fargo?"

"How should I know?"

"Exactly. No one knew what to do. Send representatives, send the military–yes, send the Armada, see if they shoot back–send someone who can deal with aliens. Nonhumans. Other minds that are really different. After all, didn't we have people who had been studying exactly that problem? Well, yes–we did. But the entire community was seized with the same panic. This was real, this wasn't theoretical, and while there were certainly individuals more than willing–in fact, *eager*–to go have a look at these new neighbors, there was no functioning mechanism within their institutions that could sanction and send them. Panic. No one had a sensible suggestion how to go about doing this. Except Hanna. And what did she do? Fargo?"

"She sent you, telelog!" Fargo waved angrily at Stephen, a dismissal. "Asshole," he said under his breath.

"I'll speak to you about your lack of proper respect after class. But you're right. She sent me. And about fifteen others she had gathered together as infants and raised as telelogs. Now, does anyone here understand the difference between a telelog and a telepath? Anyone?" He shrugged. "I'm not surprised, there's no reason you should. Research into telepathy had been abandoned early in the twenty-first century after it had finally been demonstrated that research would never produce a verifiable example. It became common knowledge that telepathy was a myth, a fairytale, with no basis in reality. But Hanna had access to all the research that had been done and she reconsidered the idea from a technological angle."

Stephen straightened, rocked on his toes. "A telelog is an artificially created telepath." He tapped his forehead and the blackboard behind him suddenly contained a brilliantly colored cross-section of a brain. Stephen indicated a dark mass that threaded its way from the prefrontal lobe back to the occipital and down into the medulla by way of the pituitary and thalamus. "A factory," he said and gave the image a rap with his knuckles. "Biotech. An implant designed to manufacture nanopoles and distribute them. Simple skin contact passes them on and they then find their way throughout the nervous system of the secondary host. To the brain and along the axon structure of the cerebral cortex, into the visual cortex, the auditory response system...in short, an infection that permeates the brain and sets up what amounts to a transmitter." He struck the blackboard again. "The receiver is there, controlling everything. The invaded brain is deciphered and its sensory processing patterns are translated. Transmission can then take place in a meaningful way and the receiver further decrypts the signal into usable images. A manufactured telepath."

He ran his hand over the blackboard and the image disappeared. Stephen dusted his hands. "The idea was a good one, if a little crude. Language was bound to be the chief barrier in communicating with actual nonhuman species–but not if you could read the thoughts of the person or being you're talking to. You can derive exactly–supposedly–what his, her, or its meaning is. So what's wrong with that notion? Hmm? Anybody want to guess? Fargo?"

"No, I don't want to guess. Why don't you tell me?"

"I'll do better than that."

Fargo clutched the arms of his small chair as the room dissolved. Stephen was suddenly right before him. Around them the murk of moiled colors congealed into purple-blackness. Stars appeared. Fargo glanced down and sucked a lungfull of air as he saw a planet rising up fast. His fingers ached from gripping the chair. He closed his eyes, but behind the lids he could see shadowshapes of mountains and rivers rushing by.

Motion ceased. He opened his eyes and looked up at a thin porcelain tower rising out of a plaza stretched between two walls of red stone. Stephen touched his arm and he jerked away. Stephen smiled at him; behind Stephen were a dozen people Fargo did not recognize–no, Daniel grinned at him from beneath a blue silk cowl. Stephen pointed to the tower.

"There," he said and walked off toward it. The others followed, leaving Fargo behind.

Fargo ran after them.

A peaked archway opened into the tower. There Fargo saw dozens of people, waiting. He looked closer, frowning. They were not people. Not humans, he corrected himself. Seti. All the different kinds: Rahalen, Cursian, Distanti, Menkan, Coro, others for which he had no names. No Ranonan.

The air shimmered, shifted, as through heat waves. Three seti stepped forward–two Rahalen and a Coro, the Rahalen elegantly humanoid in their layered gowns and austere, smooth faces, the Coro an indistinct mass of reddish flesh wrapped round and round by multicolored belts.

Stephen stepped forward.

"We are the representatives from Sol, capital of the Pan Humana," he said. He offered his hands. The Rahalen touched him. The Coro rolled closer and a pseudopod stretched out between a blue and a green belt and brushed Stephen's palm. He closed his eyes.

The three setis stepped back. Fargo's brain filled suddenly with terror, cloying fear that froze him in place. He saw the other telelogs buckle, some clapped their hands over their ears, one clawed at his eyes and screamed soundlessly. Stephen seemed caught on a hook, dangled, his body jerking with muscle spasms. Daniel was on his knees. A girl fell to the ground and Fargo knew somehow that she was dead. Daniel crawled toward her, tears streaming down his face, his mouth open so wide Fargo expected the skin to tear. He lifted the dead girl to his chest and heaved silently. A few managed to run, but they collided with each other and the walls.

"What–what–what–what–what–" he shouted over and over. The floor rolled and he spread his arms for balance.

Daniel snapped his mouth shut suddenly, laid the corpse down, and stood. He tackled Stephen. He draped his friend over his shoulder and tried to run, but the floor had become a bog. With each step his feet pulled out with a loud, wet sucking sound. Fargo's fear was thick, syrupy, suffocating.

The seti rocked back and forth. Several had come forward to help the first three, touched them, and now reeled under the impact of terror, adding to the staggering weight of sensation. A few held each other, some had advanced menacingly on the humans, stopped, and staggered back.

The roof of the tower peeled open like a giant flower. Hanna appeared against the distant stars. Tears streamed down her face.

"They don't want us," she said. "They're afraid. Run. Hide. Run."

Everything dissolved around Fargo. He fell. He was in a black room, curled in on himself, repeating "What–what–what–what–"

Eventually he focused on a shape lying across the room. Painfully, his muscles cramping from being held so rigid so long, he crawled over to it. A woman. He rolled her over.

Lis's face turned up to him. Empty eye sockets and blood from cut lips. To Fargo's horror, she moved. She tried to smile.

"We fucked up, didn't we?"

"Any questions?" Stephen asked.

Fargo looked up and saw him standing a few meters away, book in one hand, pointer in the other.

He opened his eyes. Bright flashing pulses rimmed his vision. He concentrated on dimming the glare. The aftersmell of burnt plastic filled his nostrils. After a time he recognized the bed nearby. It was a medunit pallet. Someone was on it, but that was too hard to work out. He swallowed and resumed working on the glare. As the brightness faded and his headache began to diminish, he raised his head to look down at himself.

He lay on his side, hands folded between his drawn-up legs. His throat was dry and there was a small but growing itch on the left side of his lower back. He did not trust himself to move just yet, so he tried to ignore the itch.

The light was low. The throbbing glare was almost gone now, replaced by a coarseness to his vision that matched perfectly the scoured feeling in his mind. His raised his eyes slightly and saw the end of a drinking tube. It was close; just a slight shift forward, crane of the neck. He stared at it for a long time. The itch worsened. His throat hurt.

He moved.

The water was cool.

He looked at his neighbor. She seemed familiar, but her face was turned away from him and besides it was too soon, he felt, to try for names just yet. Images danced through his mind as he looked at her. At some point he noticed that she was naked. Then he realized that he was naked.

She's seen me...

They've seen me...

She shifted on the pallet, began to turn her head toward him. He forced his eyes shut. Inside, the view opened out and he looked down an endless shaft. At the bottom things moved, tried to crawl up the walls. Wisps of memory drifted up like fumes. Eyes looked back at him. Silver eyes.

Terrified, he opened his eyes again.

She faced him, eyes open, and he was startled and relieved to see that they were not empty, there was no blood.

Her chest moved gently with her breath. She blinked; her mouth flexed into a weak smile.

She's seen me, he thought again, and closed his eyes, pressed his chin down against his chest. His arms trembled.

The shaft was gone now, but in its place was the memory of his father's shipyards. Vast, skeletal places, scaffolds dwindling in the distance, harboring—indeed, nursing—the growing forms of new ships, refitted ships, cannibalized ships.

Fargo had never been interested in how they were built, only in where they went. His father never left the system. All he wanted to do was build them, never ride them. The man had been uncomfortable even in the brief shuttle rides up and down from station to planet to station again.

He rolled over, pulled one hand away from the other and reached back to scratch the now intolerable itch. He groaned and opened his eyes.

The med facility was comfortingly immobile. The shapes were machines, neat and precise and unchanging, and they demanded nothing. They merely watched, monitored him, took care of him. They knew his insides.

He coughed. The spasm grew quickly, uncontrolled, until his chest felt squeezed repeatedly. He rolled over again, bit the drinking tube and sucked. The water collided with the cough, sprayed over the pillow, but he did not vomit.

"Fargo...?"

He stopped moving, lay perfectly still. Maybe, he thought, she would not notice that he was awake. Maybe she would leave him alone.

He felt defenseless.

Her voice was raspy. "Fargo?"

He looked up. She had swung her legs over the side of the pallet and sat there rubbing her eyes. Her body was sinewy, tightly-muscled. A scar ran from just below her right breast all the way across her stomach and ended at her left hip. Frowning, he searched for other features, found a pucker between her left armpit and clavicle. He wondered what her back was like.

She raised her head and looked at him.

"You awake?" she asked.

He managed to nod. He did not want to speak with her. He did not want to know how much she had seen. He shuddered.

"My brain," she said, "feels flensed." She chuckled. "I feel terrible."

"Flensed..." His voice was a croak, a harsh shadow.

The door opened and Cana stepped in. She looked worried as she studied them both.

"How is it?" she asked.

Lis shrugged. "I'm...not sure. I–" She frowned and closed her mouth.

Fargo realized that they were waiting for him to speak. He did not want to. What did they know? Had both of them seen him? Seen everything? Cana did not appear worse for the experience.

Lis glanced at her. "You weren't..."

"No," Cana said. "I didn't do it. I couldn't risk being incapacitated." She smiled thinly. "But I've been through it before."

Fargo coughed again, took another drink, and pushed himself up. He ached.

"That was...awful," he said.

Cana went to a cabinet and pulled out robes for them. "When you're up to it I need to talk to you about all this."

"I'd like to go back to my cabin and sleep for ten days," Lis said, easing herself to the deck and pulling on the robe.

Fargo nodded. "Sounds like a plan."

"Would you like escorts?" Cana asked.

Lis shook her head. "I think we can limp along with each other. Thank you."

Fargo's heart hammered briefly. He wanted an escort. Being alone with Lis now–he was too close to being obligated. He did not want her kindnesses. Any more and he would owe freight.

But Cana left just then. Fargo managed to stand and put on his robe.

"Come on," Lis said, holding out a hand. "I'll walk you back to your cabin."

His time sense was off. The shunt ride lasted far too long, the walk to his stateroom–he discovered then that he had been moved to his own, away from Stephen–an heroic trek. Lis spoke little and when she did she said nothing that required Fargo to give more than a cursory response. For that he was grateful.

The time alone, though, was all too short. Lis returned, brought him food, sat with him while he ate. When she was gone he lay on his bed and stared at the ceiling until his eyes hurt. When he slept he chased ghosts in his dreams. He did not bother to dress, except for the sickbay robe. On one of her visits, Lis pushed him into the hygiene cubicle and cleaned him. The sting of the spray, the tickle of the sonics, the warmth of drying off, it all felt good, but his distrusted it. She depilated his face, chest, belly, transforming him–physically at least– into Invested. He pushed her away then and sprawled back on the bed. Later he remembered her yelling at him about something. He did not care to listen, he did not bother to remember. You've seen me, he thought, or maybe he said it, you've been inside, you should know why I'm like this.

She badgered him into dressing and she took him for walks. He wandered the corridors with her. On the third or fourth such excursion he began pointing out details of the ship's construction, explaining how it had been designed and manufactured. Like a mantra, the monologue soothed him. She took him from section to section and he told her about each one. Maybe, he thought, there were twenty-one of these to describe and close the circle. It felt good to talk about it. There was familiarity here, security, and it kept her smiling. Gradually, he saw the strain in her face, the pain. He understood vaguely that she had gone through the same thing, was suffering from the same trauma, and that her attention was as much for herself as for him. He felt guilty then in a distant, unfocussed way for resenting her company at first, then for relying so much on her visits without giving anything in return. But it slipped away, muffled in the healing anaesthesia of denial as his mind rejected any responsibility, refused to let him worry over anything other than himself.

During the eighth walk, he stood on a rail above the atmosphere recycling plant. A few crew were busy doing a routine systems check far below, and Fargo explained it to Lis.

He stopped abruptly. He blinked at the sudden clarity around him. Frowning, he looked at her, saw her regarding him anxiously. For a moment it baffled him. What was she afraid of? She was obviously afraid...

He gripped the railing and stared out. He remembered. He closed his eyes and felt ashamed. He wavered, almost fell, but Lis was there, shoving up under his arm, catching him around the waist.

He gulped air and sobbed once.

"I'm sorry," he said. "I'm–it's–I'm so sorry."

He recognized himself as more than a name again. He was back.

"I don't mean to sound sentimental," Lis said, "but I haven't stopped thinking about you since Eurasia."

The words–just the sound of them apart from content–abruptly released the tension and Fargo almost laughed with relief. She had continued to come take him for walks. In the last couple of days he had started taking care of himself again. Lis still came by everyday. He looked forward to Lis's visits, but he was nervous about them. He owed her a lot of freight. He was obligated. He had hoped she would just forgive the debt and let him go.

"You're direct, aren't you?" he observed.

She raised her eyebrows. "Are you going to try to tell me it didn't affect you?"

"No."

"But you don't want to talk about it."

Fargo heard accusation in her voice, defensiveness and a little anger.

"What's to talk about?" he asked.

She frowned.

"I mean," he went on, "we were heroes together. What we did was unique, wasn't it? It's only natural that you'd remember the co you went through something like that with."

"That's very good. Very convincing. But you know that's not what I'm talking about. That's not how I've been thinking about you."

"Isn't it?"

After a long time, she nodded. "Maybe you're right. Maybe it was only the nature of what we went through."

Part of him relaxed. He was safe, there was no need to run. But something frail crumbled inside, embittering his relief, and suddenly he wanted to apologize to her, talk about what he really felt, ask her if it was, after all, the same for her. In the end he was too afraid. Momentum carried him past the opportunity to be otherwise.

They had turned down the corridor to Fargo's room. Now they stopped before his door and faced each other. All at once, as if it had been waiting for the chance, the tension and awkwardness reemerged.

"Well," Fargo said. "My head is bursting. I need sleep."

Lis's mouth flexed briefly in disappointment.

He touched the contact and the door opened.

"I thought you were happy to be with me, Fargo."

"I am."

"Then I guess I keep reading you wrong, but you seem to be trying not to talk to me."

"That's not true." No, he thought, he did not mind talking to her, as long as the subject was safe and did not center on his obligations. Ritual patter.

"I can understand you not wanting to talk about what happened with Hanna. I'm not sure *I* want to talk about that. But when I talk about Eurasia, you turn it into something else, like what happened wasn't the same for both of us."

"I'm not convinced anything *did* happen on Eurasia."

"Why? That makes no sense. What is it, Fargo? You admit to the horror, but not to the wonder. Am I too tall? Is my sense of humor too strange? Why don't you want to be with me?"

"I–"

"Yes?"

Fargo closed his eyes. "I don't want to talk about this."

"Ah."

"You don't know anything about me."

"Nor, it seems, am I likely to."

"It's none of your business!"

"I see."

"No, you don't! It doesn't have anything to do with liking you or not."

"That's reassuring."

"I–there's–look–"

"Yes?"

Fargo turned away. "I like you, Lis, but–"

"I have the patience of a diplomat, Fargo, but there are limits."

"There's too much to explain. I can't."

"You mean you won't. Fargo, what are you so afraid of?"

He glared at her. Helplessly, he clenched his fists and sucked in his lips. He willed her to go away. He resented that she was so thick that he might have to say the words.

"I'm not afraid of you," he said.

"Then you don't like me?"

"I do like you! Damnit–!"

"But it's a sterile kind of thing. You don't want to get your psyche soiled."

Fargo looked away.

"Fargo, I'm sorry, I didn't mean that."

"Leave me alone."

He thought she would touch him. He braced himself for the sensation, the light hand, the attempt at salving the wound. Instead, he heard her footsteps recede, then silence.

He entered the stateroom and closed the door. His head pounded now. All he wanted to do was see this one thing through, get Stephen to Earth and help him retrieve his friend. That would be enough to balance the scales. Then he could leave, and go on as he had been. Why did everyone assume that just because a person is willing to do *one* thing, there is automatically a willingness to do another? And another. An on and on, into irrevocable involvement.

She had asked the magic question–why are you afraid? He understood very well why, but he did not want to tell anyone, did not want to share that. If he did, he believed, he would bind himself and lose–

He frowned. Lose what? The seti ambassador, Yol-Maex, what had it said? That no human was so simplistic as to possess only one facet of identity? Was that true? Fargo had talked as if he believed it, but did he?

He stumbled back against the door and slid down. He knew what he was losing. Clarity. He remembered the word, but what it defined was hazy, indistinct. Perhaps he had lost it already, the way he had given up freedom from obligation by helping Stephen. Certainly his experience with Hanna had left him unclear. Clarity, freedom–what was left? Security? He saw the murdered freeriders floating in space, floating *free* in space, and the image was very clear.

There was no security and he did, after all, feel like a fool.

Cana asked him to her cabin. When he arrived, Lis and Stephen were already there.

"We'll be making dock in another two days. I want to go over this with you. I want to know what's involved. Hanna has told me–us–very little."

Fargo walked up to Stephen. The telelog lowered his eyes, then tried to turn away. Fargo grabbed his shirt.

"Was that necessary?" he asked.

Stephen frowned. "What?"

"What Hanna did. Whatever it was."

Lis's hand rested on Fargo's shoulder. He looked around at her.

"It's not his fault," she said. "He didn't know it would hurt. Did you, Stephen?"

"No." He looked frightened. "No, I–I grew up doing that. It's how we all were with Hanna. It never occurred to me it would–"

Fargo let him go. "Right. Okay." He turned away. "So what exactly *is* all this about?"

"It's all about the World Matrix AIs," Stephen said.

Fargo blinked at him, for a moment uncomprehending. "You're talking about the mainframe databases that integrate entire colonies, right? They're computers."

"They're artificial intelligences," Cana said.

Stephen grunted. "There's nothing artificial about intelligence."

"I meant–"

"I know what you meant. Hanna is not artificial. A human template was used in the original program. She's almost two centuries old now and long ago developed into an autonomous being. But I didn't know there were others like her."

"Every colony that has a matrix database," Cana said. "They program each other through the TEGlink. At least, I think that's how it works."

"Wait," Fargo said, holding his hands up. "You're saying that Hanna is a sentient computer."

"Oh, more than a computer," Stephen said. "A data processor is a computer. Hanna originates data. I think that's more than a slight difference."

"I've never heard of this before."

Lis got to her feet and went to the bar. She entered a complicated series of instructions, her fingertips lightly clicking against the contacts. Four tall glasses of a pale blue liquid emerged and she handed them out.

"In a former life," she said, "I was a connoisseur of fine depressants." She grinned at Fargo and raised her glass in an exaggerated salute. "Cheers, fellow travellers."

Fargo took a long pull. It was cold, spicy. He nodded in approval and looked at Lis. He wanted to be alone with her, he realized, and the thought made him uneasy.

"How does Daniel fit into this?" he asked.

Stephen frowned and looked away. "He–" He seemed for a moment to be in pain. "Look, Hanna showed you what happened to us. What you went through from Hanna is only a shadow of what we went through with the seti. There are probably quite a few of us who would be glad to see the Forum succeed and seal the borders."

"Daniel was going to work for Estana," Fargo said.

Stephen nodded. "He'd been operating a small counseling service on Neighbors. I heard about him–he was having a remarkable success rate–"

"I can't imagine why," Fargo said sardonically. "If you heard about him out on Markab, then it's likely Tesa Estana had heard of him, too. Neighbors is a lot closer to Sol. I suppose she was pretty upset when she found out someone had snatched him out of reach."

Stephen glared at him, then turned to Cana. "I want to know why Hanna's in contact with you. You and the other independent spacers."

"You don't know?"

"I wouldn't ask if I did."

Fargo stood before the display and traced some of the patterns absently. "How is it possible for her to do...whatever it was she did...through the TEGlink? I mean..." He frowned at Stephen. "Is that what you meant by being used as a medium?"

Stephen nodded, still looking at Cana.

"You disperse the nanopoles," Fargo mused, "and she transmits...well, that's certainly efficient. You can't transmit, can you?"

"Not to a colony host."

"Colony host. *There's* an interesting term." He stepped closer to Stephen. "Tell me, once the colony is in place do you always have access to that mind?"

"Fargo–" Lis began.

He held up a hand. "Let me be clear about this, so everybody understands. I resent this. I'm a very private person. You did this without my permission. We've talked about this before, but I want all the answers now."

Stephen looked afraid. "Fargo, I swear–look, the nanopoles are not permanent. The colony can't sustain itself without constant reseeding. After a few days, it deteriorates and voids through the bloodstream."

"If I ever find out otherwise–"

"I think," Cana said, "that's enough, Co Fargo."

Fargo stepped back from Stephen. "For now."

"To answer your question, Co Christopher," Cana continued, "Hanna's been in contact with some of us as early as when the Project was closed down and some of you needed hiding."

Stephen started. "Then you knew about us, too."

"Mostly. Not in great detail, but I knew about the Project. Hanna's kept a lot of us in business. She's been our source of information on things that might otherwise have seen us shut down and farmed out."

"Why?" Stephen asked.

Cana smiled. "Information flow goes both ways. We're important sources for Hanna. The megas don't know about Hanna. She doesn't trust them. I don't think Hanna's entirely pleased with the direction the Pan Humana has taken."

"Sounds to me," Fargo said, "like Hanna is sponsoring the coming revolution."

Chapter Eight

Aquas was the first stop, Cana had told them, then Neighbors, Procyon, and finally Sol. The transit station floated in the center of the viewscreen that dominated one wall of the omnirec. Fargo estimated that nearly sixty people were gathered here to watch the docking. There were other omnirecs and lounges where many more watched. He stayed near the far end of the bar, away from the entrance, remembering the times he had visited Aquas. He had never been here as a regular passenger, Invested.

Aquas was a small bluish dot just to the left of the station. It was normally a mild world. Its eccentric orbit carried it through a period of intense storms every twenty years or so, driven by the moderately variable G4 primary. The inhabitants produced a fine liqueur, aqual, that was as mellow as their music.

Everyone was very quiet. Aquas Transit Station filled the screen until the magnification was automatically reduced. Then the scene shifted to the berth to which the *Isomer* was being directed. The ship followed the invisible cord of the station beacon into the vast maw. Station guidance then assumed control and brought them all the way inside.

Dozens of robots swarmed over the *Isomer* linking up the ship-to-station life support, commlinks, access tubes, conveyors, and diagnostic service equipment. Cana made a general announcement to the ship that they were in dock and the station would be open to them shortly, please wait. People began filing out, no one seeming in a particular hurry. For most this was only a stop along the way, a chance to walk off the ship and claim they had "been" to Aquas.

Fargo ordered another drink from the bar and carried it closer to the screen. He sat down and sipped, trying to remember which one this was–three? four? He told himself he was only mildly affected and looked back up at the screen.

The viewscreen now showed people moving unhurriedly down the transparent tubes connecting the ship to the station. Robots flitted about, working on various parts of the hull, monitoring equipment connected to the station, moving easily among the struts and braces, in the ill-lit berth. There was no sound, but Fargo imagined the thrumming of huge machines, metal against metal, the hiss and whine of equipment. Even on stations, ports possessed the same look, the same feel. In all his freeriding he had never boarded a ship, or even entered a port, in daylight. The dark was the proper stage for jumping a ride. As a result, Fargo saw all ports as enclosed places strewn with obstacles, a maze for him to penetrate, a puzzle to solve.

Cana had requested that he not leave the ship. He had been quasi-officially attached to some aspect of the conference mission and issued ID by the Ranonans. He left the chit in his room. It was embarrassing in a way. He had not planned to leave the ship in any case. The *Isomer* was scheduled to be in port for only ten hours.

He wondered idly if the Ranonans would be permitted off the ship. Even if they were, he thought, they couldn't. Even a freerider had more freedom than a seti. He toyed with the idea of slipping off the ship unnoticed, going somewhere and stealing a souvenir.

Inexplicably, his mood changed. He looked around the omnirec, expecting to see someone. The booths were empty, most of the patrons now gone. Those few remaining all kept to a table near the front. He was alone. Suddenly he found that condition intolerable.

Fargo set his unfinished drink on the bar and headed for the exit. Lis was in a stateroom near the seti, aft in a section that was isolated from the rest of the ship. He had looked its location up many times since their last encounter, he knew several ways to reach it from almost any part of the ship. He pictured one of those ways now.

He stepped out into the mall and heard his name called. He looked around and heard it again. He looked up. Stephen stood above him, on the arcade. Fargo waved to him and Stephen waved for him to come up. Fargo sighed and went to a lift. Stephen met him.

"There's a problem," Stephen said. "The ship's been placed under quarantine and Shipmaster Cana has been arrested by station authorities."

The bridge was roughly oval, the main operations consoles facing the center where a holographic projection tank served as the main screen. At the moment it was empty. Data flickered constantly on the multitude of flatscreens on the consoles.

Fargo straightened as Lis followed the Ranonan ambassador onto the bridge. Barig looked up from the communications station.

"Thank you for coming, Co Yol-Maex," Barig said. He sat down in the command couch and looked at the Ranonan narrowly. "I'll make a bet with anyone that this has to do with you."

The seti tilted its head to one side. "Indeed?"

"Frankly," Barig went on, "I advised Cana against taking the commission. But the Q was good and she wanted the prestige."

Fargo raised his eyebrows. Lis scowled behind Barig's back. None of them had spoken much with the Ship's First. He had been remote, unapproachable through most of the voyage. Even at Table that first evening he had said virtually nothing, choosing instead to watch and listen. He seemed completely absorbed in his station as Cana's second-in-command, to the point of having no other apparent interests. Fargo had seen dozens of Barigs, perhaps hundreds, all brief, dutiful, and efficient, all meticulous and unforgiving of sloppiness and laziness. The Shipmaster may have been "in command," but Barig ran the ship and that was his primary concern.

"I'm assigning you a personal guard till this is over," he said. "For now I'm treating this as a threat. I'm requesting all passengers to remain in their cabins."

"Incoming comm."

Barig straightened in the couch. "This is Ship's First Barig, commanding in Shipmaster Cana's stead."

"Stationmaster's Aide Aron Feif, Co Barig. Apologies for the inconvenience. I trust your passengers aren't too alarmed."

"They'd like an explanation."

"I'm sure. I–"

"Where is Shipmaster Cana?"

"We have detained her for questioning. Are you aware that you have violated Forum Transport Law?"

"In what way?"

"You are transporting nonhuman lifeforms, are you not?"

"Some of the passengers have their pets with them–"

"I'm referring to aliens, Ship's First, please don't be coy with me. You have on board a seti delegate and its entourage, bound for Sol."

"We have clearances through the Chairman's offices for that, and Representative Yol-Maex has formal invitations from the Chairman's liaison. None of this has been done without proper clearance."

There was a pause. Then: "There have been changes. Please transmit the applicable documentation for our assessment."

Stephen touched Barig's shoulder. Barig glanced up at him, then said, "Excuse me for a moment, Co Feif." He touched a switch. "All right, we're private."

"Get them on board," Stephen said. "Something's not right. Get someone here from his office, preferably Feif himself."

Barig frowned, then released the switch. "Co Feif, I will be glad to show you *Isomer's* clearances, but the Ranonan Delegate insists on personal contact. If you could come on board it would also make my problems with the passengers a little easier. A quarantine is a hard thing to explain."

There was a longer pause before Feif came back on. "Very well. For the sake of your human passengers. I'll come on board myself, with a security guard. Is that all right?"

"Certainly. We'll be expecting you." Barig stabbed at the panel. "Damn. What the hell is this all about?" He glared at Yol-Maex. "Those invitations of yours are legal, aren't they?"

"Absolutely."

Lis stepped forward. "Mind if I do a little exploring?" She held her right hand up and wiggled her porcelain-tipped fingers. Fargo stared; he had not noticed them before. Now he saw that she kept them covered in skinlike sheaths. "It's been awhile, but I used to snake my way around security screens pretty well."

"That's up to Jonson," Barig gestured toward the olive-skinned woman at the communications console.

Lis looked at her. "Do you mind?"

Jonson shrugged. "Have at it. I've been trying to break through for a half an hour."

Lis sat down beside her and cracked her knuckles theatrically. "Lemme show you a few tricks, co." Her hands descended to the board. In a few seconds she was in a deep trance.

They met in the passenger receiving lounge. Barig brought six crew, as well as Fargo and Stephen. Lis had remained on the bridge, working with Jonson. Yol-Maex had also stayed on the bridge, observing on a screen, while two of his aides accompanied the humans. Feif came on board with four of his own people.

Stephen had pressed his hand to Barig's for several seconds just before Feif's arrival. Now Barig greeted the aide with a firm handshake.

Fargo stared at the stocky man and felt cold. The face was familiar, the association unpleasant. Fargo still had occasional lapses in memory and it annoyed him to have to struggle to remember something that ought to be obvious.

Barig, hands on hips, glowered at Feif. "This better be righteous, co. Where's your authority for this?"

"Where are your clearances?" Feif demanded, giving Barig a startled look. He absently rubbed his hand against his thigh.

Barig gestured and an aide stepped forward with a handreader. Barig inserted a disk and the aide turned the screen toward Feif.

"And the seti's?" Feif inquired dryly, pointedly not looking at either of the Ranonans.

Barig removed the first disk and inserted another. Feif watched the scan.

He nodded. "These have been rescinded. Ambassador Maex is disinvited and is to be returned to the embassy on Markab and from there escorted out of the Pan Humana." He removed a disk from his breast pocket and inserted it in the reader.

Barig read it, his scowl deepening. He nodded curtly and handed the reader to one of the seti. Feif puckered his lips and rocked slightly on the balls of his feet.

"All right," Barig said. "As soon as Shipmaster Cana returns, we'll transport the Ambassador back to the Frontier."

"No, Ship's First, we will do that. The Ambassador and his party are to be turned over to us and we will see that it is returned. Shipmaster Cana is to remain in custody to face formal charges."

"Charges pertaining to what?"

"As I stated, laws have been violated."

"Which weren't laws until just now."

"Ignorance–"

"Don't quote at me. I know our rights."

"Do you wish to be brought up on charges as well?"

Barig pursed his lips. His hands uncurled slowly. "We'll comm you with the arrangements."

Feif raised his eyebrows.

"You are courteously," Barig said slowly, "invited to leave my ship."

Feif grinned lopsidedly and held out his hand. "My disk and yours, please."

"We aren't going anywhere. We'll hang onto these for the time being."

Feif frowned. "I must warn you that–"

Barig raised a hand. Four crew stepped forward, hands going to sidearms.

"Until I violate more than just courtesy, co, I am master here. Or are you rescinding spacing law as well?"

"You have four hours," Feif snapped. He retreated with his staff.

The lock was sealed.

"He was lying," Stephen said. "He's not even a government official."

Barig blinked at Stephen. "What do you mean?"

"He doesn't work for the government. This is an illegal action. I suggest we find out who's actually in authority here."

The memory clicked into place then. "Dake," Fargo said. He looked at Barig and Stephen. "Estana's in charge here. That co was one of the ones from the *Caliban*."

Lis seemed dazed. She leaned back in the couch, gazing at a point on the console before her, a quiet smile on her face. Jonson rested against the edge of the console, one hand on the interface plate, her half-lidded eyes flicking back and forth.

When Lis saw Fargo, her smile widened. "Hey."

"Hey. Are you...?"

"I'm fine, co." She drew a deep breath and looked up at Jonson. "What do you think?"

Jonson's eyes stopped shifting. She blinked rapidly, then took her hand away from the interface. "I'm impressed," she said. "I've been trying to navigate that configuration since it appeared."

Lis nodded. "It's hard."

"So what's going on?" Barig asked.

Jonson gestured at Lis. "She got through the security. I've never seen anyone do what she did in there."

"It's been awhile," Lis said, stretching. "But I haven't lost it."

"And?" Barig said edgily.

"This is an illegal operation," Lis said, rubbing her eyes. "Well, maybe not illegal. The clearances seem in order, but we're talking about a mega, so...anyway, we're locked in a berth leased and managed by Tower Enterprises. All the regular commlines are monitored and from what I was able to find out from credit records, no regular station personnel presently work in this section of the station. It's all Tower people. About fifty of them. It's likely that the stationmaster doesn't even know what's going on. They're operating under sanction from the Forum. How much about this the Forum knows, well, guess if you want. I'd be willing to wager a few representatives know."

"Tower," Barig said bitterly. He glanced at Stephen and Fargo. "You said he was lying. You said he works for Estana. Tower is Estana's company." Barig frowned at Fargo. "You recognized him?"

"I was as close to him as I am to you," Fargo said.

"Why didn't he recognize you?"

Fargo shrugged. "I dress better now. All he saw then was a nid." He paused, considering. "Of course, it doesn't matter. One way or the other they expect to get what they want."

"That fits," Stephen said. He kept his eyes on Lis and stood on the opposite side of the bridge from Yol-Maex. "This is all a hoax."

"Fine," Barig nodded. "Just fine." He crossed his arms and tapped his index fingers on his biceps, eyes slitted. "Hoax or not, it doesn't change much. We're still tied to the station with no way of getting away unless the station wants us to. Besides, they have Cana."

"We can't just turn the Ambassador over," Jonson said.

Barig glared at her.

"Sorry," she said.

He turned to Fargo. "You're a freerider."

Fargo raised an eyebrow. "Last time I checked."

Barig grunted. "You know all the ways in and out of a ship in dock that sensors can't cover."

"So the legend goes."

"Well..."

Fargo frowned at him. "What have you got in mind?"

The service tube stretched on, diminishing to a point. The three light strips exaggerated the convergence, colored the walls bluish. Fargo walked along slowly, watching for the way out.

"Another sensor coming up," Lis said in his left ear. "About...nine meters, overhead."

Fargo stopped and slid the infrared lens in place over his right eye and surveyed the ceiling. A brightly pulsing yellow dot jumped out in relief against the dimmer background.

"Is that my access below it?" Fargo subvocalized into the microphone at his throat. His breather mask muffled nearly all of the sound.

"As a matter of fact," Lis said.

"Can you kill the sensor from there?"

"Let me see."

Fargo glanced over his shoulder at the other three, Stephen and the two crew Barig had assigned to them. They looked back at him questioningly. Stephen looked edgy. The tube was claustrophobic and they had been in cramped spaces for almost an hour now, working their way through the nether crannies of the *Isomer's* gas exchange system into the complementary sections of the docks, slowly moving past sensors that had to be temporarily or permanently disabled. The coes from the ship still looked eager. Jesi cradled her rifle easily, rocking slightly on her toes as she crouched; Seth sat down behind her, arms wrapped around his legs. Fargo had been undecided about how many to bring–he had not wanted a crowd, but he did not want to be underprepared–so Barig had made the decision. Fargo needed Stephen–Jesi and Seth were insurance.

"Got it," Lis said. "Move quickly, I don't want to leave this one off too long."

Fargo gestured for the others to follow and hurried forward. In the floor beneath the now dead sensor a round section was recessed, a keypad on the wall above it. He punched a code into the panel. The hatch irised open. Fargo braced himself and lowered his head through it, into a lightless space. He switched on his lamp and saw a much larger corridor. Down the center of floor below ran a trough about half-a-meter wide.

"What is this?" he asked.

"An old shunt line leftover from construction," Lis explained. "A lot of the system is still in place."

"Couldn't we have just used this instead of crawling through the exchange system?"

"I said a lot of it is still in place, not all of it."

"Hm."

"Don't complain, I could've sent you through waste circulation."

Fargo let himself fall through. He landed softly and waved for the others to follow.

"Anyone watching over our shoulders?" he asked.

"Don't you trust me? You want to move to the right, turn left at the next junction, then proceed about thirty meters."

Stephen landed, then Jesi and Seth. Silently, they ran down the corridor. In the overlap of their lamps, Fargo saw gaping holes where plates had been removed, cables hanging, tangled piles of old parts. They passed a section of the trough that still held a length of the rail along which shunt cars once raced.

They reached the junction and sprinted the last stretch. The side corridor ended a few meters further on. This had once been a construction node.

"Now what?" Fargo asked.

"At your feet," Lis said, "there's a sealed panel to a circulation duct. It's isolated from the rest of the system because it connects to detention."

Fargo saw smooth surface at his feet. "All right, you're sure it's there?"

"Trust me, it's there."

"Great. We'll have to cut through. That should be a real inconspicuous event."

"I can reduce the heat sensitivity of the nearby sensors for a time. Stop picking nits and get on with it."

"At once, venerable guide. By the way, what are we supposed to do when we get to Cana's cell? Once we break in there alarms'll go off everywhere."

"That is a problem, isn't it? Actually you'll be going to a monitor station. I can't get access to any of the cells. I have no way to know which one Cana's in. You'll just have to do a search."

Fargo motioned to Jesi to go to work on the panel. Bright sparks leapt from the touch of her rifle on the metal. "Keep talking."

"The security sensors in all these corridors are linked directly to the stationmaster's database. Alarms will be routed back to the section by way of the central core. Inefficient, but I doubt seriously anyone expects this kind of intrusion. For all we know, no one's monitoring. It's possible we can keep anything from getting through. I'm having Jonson figure a way to block return signals. She thinks we can, so we'll bet on her for now."

"Done," Seth said.

Jesi and Seth used large pairs of grips to pull up the cut metal. They bent it back. Seth used his foot to push it to the floor.

Fargo dropped into the air shaft. The passage was less than two meters wide, little more than a meter high. He crawled forward as the others descended into it. He had to use infrared in the darkness; the walls glowed red and green from temperature variation. The air was humid, warm. "How far?"

"Fifty meters. Then you'll be at the monitoring station. From that point you're on your own. I don't have access to personnel assignments or anything."

"Then how did you know there were only fifty Tower people working here?"

"Food consumption."

"You're kidding."

"Hey..."

"All right, I believe you. What about the security sensors in place?"

"Can't break them. Sorry."

"I'm disappointed. I didn't think miracles ran out."

"I'll pretend I didn't hear that."

Ahead, Fargo saw light spilling in from a grate on the left. He came abreast and peered down a chamber about six meters on a side. A podium-like console stood in the center. Benches and lockers lined two walls. One man sat with his back to the console, working a small three dimensional puzzle in his thick hands.

The grate covered a rectangular vent a meter long and twenty, twenty-five centimeters high. Fargo pushed himself back from it.

"Problem," he whispered to the others.

Jesi climbed over him and studied the vent. She scowled darkly and shook her head. Fargo sighed.

"Got a small problem," he subvocalized. "Vent's too small."

"What do you want me to do about it?" Lis asked.

"Is there another way in?"

"Not unless you want to walk right in through the main entrance."

"Can you get us there from here?"

"Not without taking you through traffic. You'll risk discovery."

"I can cut this wider," Jesi said close to his ear.

"What about alarms?" Fargo shot back.

"Can't help you with those," Lis said.

"Not you. Jesi wants to cut the vent open."

"There *is* a time factor," Stephen pointed out.

Fargo glared at him.

"Shh!" Jesi hissed. Fargo looked toward her. She was back at the vent. She held her finger to her lips. As Fargo watched, she slipped a handgun from its holster, aimed through the grate, and fired.

Fargo heard the body hit the floor and shuddered.

Jesi quickly brought her rifle around and started cutting at the top of the vent. The glare made Fargo flinch. Sparks showered Jesi and she slapped at them where they struck her bare skin. The second cut released the grate and it fell forward and clattered below. Then she twisted around, braced herself, and kicked at the wide strip of metal. It folded outward grudgingly. Six solid kicks and the hole was wide enough for Jesi to climb through.

"We're in," Fargo said.

He landed and glimpsed the corpse. It sprawled toward the entrance, one arm flung out. The puzzle lay under one of the benches. Fargo looked away from the ruined head. There was little blood; the energy pulse cauterized as it killed.

Seth went to the console while Jesi leaned against the wall by the entrance. There were two doors off the chamber; the other opened on a corridor of cells.

Seth looked up. "No external monitoring," he said. "They evidently didn't expect anyone to break in here."

"Why should they?" Fargo laughed. "This is impossible, isn't it?" He did not expect much in the detention section itself, which was mostly used for vagrants or peace disturbers who were only in for a day or two at a time.

Stephen was frowning intently. He strode down the corridor of cells, looking at each door briefly, stopping at the eighth one on the left. "Here."

Seth touched a contact on the console. The cell door slid aside. Fargo hurried down the corridor and peered in. Shipmaster Cana looked at them from where she sat on her cot. She frowned deeply, then grinned, shaking her head.

"I suppose you have a way out planned?"

"The same way we came in," Fargo said.

Cana marched down the corridor and nodded to Seth and Jesi. She eyed the dead guard.

"Necessary," Jesi said.

"Okay, lead the way."

Fargo handed her a breather from his pack. Cana pulled it on as Fargo and Stephen climbed back into the air duct. Cana followed, then Seth.

Jesi tossed the grate up to Seth and pulled herself into the duct. Between the two of them they managed to pull the tongue of bent panel back down. Jesi pushed the grate up against it.

"That's not going to convince anyone," Seth said.

Jesi shrugged. "Maybe they won't look."

"You don't think this was too easy, do you?" Seth asked.

"Those people aren't Forum reps," Cana said.

"We know that," Jesi said. "This entire segment of the station is being run by Tower Enterprises for the time being."

Fargo was breathing harder. Adrenalin pushed at his nerves. He wanted to be out of the tunnels as quickly as possible. An irrational fear was mounting, as if something were following them, unseen, unheard, and unpredictable. He ran a mental checklist again–had he and Lis gotten all the sensors?

He stumbled. His shoulder slammed against the metal wall and he slid almost a meter, his wind leaving in a rush. He squinted his eyes and sat up. Stephen reached for him.

"I'm fine," Fargo said. "Just clumsy."

The crack of metal on metal jerked his eyes forward. A panel had fallen in place, sealing the duct. Fargo stared at it, uncomprehending for a moment. Another three meters...

"Now what?" Cana asked.

"I must've missed a sensor," he mumbled. He surveyed the walls through infrared to see if he had overlooked something, then craned his neck to look back the way they had come. "Is there a junction back there?"

"Not one that I saw," Jesi said.

Fargo worked his way past Stephen, Cana, Seth, and Jesi and crawled quickly back down the duct. Nearly a hundred meters from the new barrier he found another. The seam was too close; he could not work his fingers under the panel and probably could not have raised it in any case.

There were no sensors along the walls that he could see.

"Lis," Fargo called. "Are you still monitoring this?"

"Yes. I don't know what's going on," she replied. "You'll have to get out through the security section. Whatever's closed those panels I can't override."

"Great."

"Why don't I just cut through?" Jesi suggested.

Fargo thought it over and shook his head. "Don't know how many more are on the other side. Let's go back and see if we can override it internally."

He beckoned the others back to the grate and pushed it open again. Fargo went to the console. No alarms flashed, nothing to indicate that Cana had been removed from her cell. He looked at the others as they emerged from the air duct. Everyone watched him expectantly, perhaps a little warily. He shrugged. Seth came up to the console and touched some contacts.

"I don't believe it," he said, shaking his head. "Cleaning was scheduled for the shafts connected to this one."

"Cleaning," Fargo said flatly.

Seth nodded. "A corrosive is used to scour the surfaces. They seal off the sections directly attached to vents. It happens a segment at a time throughout the whole system. Just dumb luck we picked now to do this."

"How long does it take?"

"About twenty minutes for the initial flush," Seth said, studying the console. "Another hour to purge the system of the corrosives."

"Just out of curiosity," Jesi said, "what about the sections around vents?"

"I suppose they send someone or a robot to do that manually."

Fargo frowned. "I–"

Alarms sounded, drowning him out. His eyes darted back and forth while Seth studied the console. Fargo gestured for Jesi to watch the door, then turned back to the console. He looked down the corridor to the cells, and saw a thin pink smoke wafting out of the open cell door where Cana had been. He pointed.

Seth stabbed a button and the cells were sealed off from them. He pushed another and the claxon ceased.

For several seconds they stared mutely at one another.

"I think we better get out of here," Cana said finally, quietly. Her eyes were intense, almost frightened.

"Lis," Fargo said, "check all the links between the ship and the station and make sure everything is secured. We're going to have to use the main corridors to get back."

"What happened?"

"Gas. Have Jonson direct us out."

"Got it," Jonson came on over the comm. "Proceed out the door, straight down the corridor to the next junction, then left. Thirty meters will bring you to a mess hall."

"Way ahead of you now, co," Fargo said, hurrying to the door.

He led them at a run down the hallway. They saw no one in the corridors until they reached the mess. Two coes stepped out of the doorway, talking and smiling, and Fargo collided with the one on the right. They sprawled on the deck, back through the door into the mess. The man grabbed at Fargo's breather. Fargo slapped at the grasping hands and tried to roll off of him. Suddenly he was shoved to one side. Jesi straddled

the man and deftly slammed the butt of her rifle down onto
his jaw. Fargo scooted away. The other man slumped against
the wall by the door.

Seth pointed across the vacant tables. A spindly shape
moved among them, extensions loading empty trays into a cart
that followed it, cleaning tabletops. Jesi shot it. A black hole
appeared midway up its shaft; smoke wafted out and the arms
writhed briefly and locked in place.

"What–" Fargo started.

"Ears," Jesi said.

Fargo shook his head and got to his feet.

Banks of dispensers lined two walls. At the corner where
they met was a recessed panel. Fargo took out his multijack
and hunched beneath the counter. His hand shook slightly as
he inserted a bit into the locking receptacle. The tool whirred
almost inaudibly and the panel popped loose. He pushed it
inward, switched on his lamp, and crawled through.

Hot air and mingled aromas filled the cramped access. He
pulled himself along to the far end, about three meters from
the panel. There he entered a passageway that ran behind the
dispensers. Feeder conduit descended along their rear walls
and attached to large collared ports. Fargo heard the gentle
bump and shuffle of packages tumbling through them, like
the scuffling of large animals in the dark.

"Where the hell–?" Cana stood beside him. The others
climbed out of the access way behind her. Jesi emerged last.

Fargo touched Stephen. "Anyone around?"

"I told you it doesn't work like that!"

"Right. Sorry, I forgot." He looked up. The ends of either
passage were lost in shadow. Overhead the rows of conduit
entered the ceiling. "Up there is the main supply artery. That's
where we have to go." He looked at the others. "Any of you
ever been carried by a suspensor field?"

"I have," Jesi said.

Fargo nodded, unsurprised. He was beginning to think
Jesi had once been Armada, maybe a marine. "Good, then

you know what to expect. Shipmaster, Seth, when we enter the artery you'll experience extreme disorientation. It's a non directional agrav field. Within it you'll think you're in null-g. But the airflow drives everything along, so you'll also think you're falling, but falling *up*. Don't panic. If you have to, close your eyes. We'll take care of you. All right?"

Cana and Seth nodded.

None of the conduits looked large enough to get inside, but at the end of the passageway Fargo found a ladder. He climbed to the top and opened the maintenance hatch. In his lamp light he watched small, off-white packets tumble by in the pipeline above. He glanced down and saw the others waiting, watching him. He swallowed dryly, nodded, and climbed in.

The field seemed to tug at him. He drifted along in the air current. Behind him he heard a sharp intake of breath, a brief flurry of limbs flailing against the sides of the shaft.

"Here–" Stephen said.

The commotion stopped. Fargo let himself drift along a few meters before he looked back. Everyone seemed to be in the shaft. Stephen had his arms around Shipmaster Cana, who looked at the walls wide-eyed.

One side of the shaft was a series of holes. At each one a mechanism like a spider waved its long manipulators like anemone. The packets floated by. A sensor tracked them and, if one were needed to replace stores in any of the dispensers, a spider would reach out and snag it and feed it down the appropriate hole. They ignored the humans.

Fargo came to a junction. He knew from experience to take the lefthand shaft. There was a moment of dizziness when he moved from one field into the next.

There was no current in this artery. Fargo worked his arms and swam along. Several meters on he came to a barrier with a keypad centered on its surface. He tapped a short code and waited. Nothing happened, so he entered another. The barrier rolled aside, into the wall.

"Careful," he said, "the field ends here. Watch me to see which way is up."

He swam to the edge and took hold. Cautiously he pushed a leg out of the agrav field and felt it pulled "down." He oriented himself upright to that field and stepped out. The suspensor field sucked at him as he move away from it. He dropped sharply, belly seizing, and landed on a platform half-a-meter below the lip.

He turned and raised his arms. "Your turn."

He caught Cana. Stephen and Jesi both guided Seth out, then fell to the floor themselves.

Fargo went to the rail opposite the shaft and looked out. In the light of his lamp all he saw was a confusion of struts, platforms, cables, and clusters of spheres. To his right a ramp led down to another passageway.

Cana leaned against a wall.

"Let them get their legs back," Jesi said. Seth squatted, hung his head down.

"Not too long," Fargo said.

"Does anyone want to fill me?" Cana asked.

"We're not sure," Stephen said, "but it seems that Tower has gone to a great expense to turn back the seti delegates. We were informed that their invitation to Earth had been revoked. You are going to be brought up on charges for the illegal transportation of nonhuman life forms."

"That's obscene," Cana said.

Seth staggered to the rail and leaned across it. Fargo thought he would vomit. The man looked pale, his mouth hung open, and his hands trembled slightly. But Seth closed his eyes, drew deep breaths, and held it.

"Co?" Fargo asked.

Seth raised one hand and nodded. "A minute."

Fargo grunted, the turned to Cana. "You can't just blame Tower. They couldn't do this without some government co-operation."

Cana frowned skeptically.

"Think about it," Fargo went on. "This is a transit station. Leasing this much space to a corporation without some station personnel supervising? I've never seen that before. If station personnel were here this wouldn't be happening. Probably, anyway. Unless it had been cleared by Sol."

"If the government doesn't want the seti legation, why not simply disinvite them?" Cana asked.

"I haven't got that figured yet, but it seems likely that it's not the whole government. A faction, maybe a big one. In any case it's better to let a mega take the blame if something goes wrong—like it is. Jonson, where are we?"

"I've got you located between modules," Jonson said, "Do you see a corridor anywhere?"

"Yes. Just below the shaft. I'll go down to it."

He descended the ramp and stopped at the entrance.

"Perfect," Jonson said. "That will take you to a recycling module. From there, turn left, proceed twenty meters. There's a lift and you want to drop two levels. That will put you back to the supply nexus for our dock. Find the atmosphere interchange. It's stabilized at the moment."

"What about station alarms?"

"Nothing," Lis said. "We read that there was an accidental gas leak in detention, but no general alarm. I blocked that one from the core. So far you're doing fine."

"Is it possible they haven't gotten in there yet to find that Cana's gone? Does that mean we're going to make it, boss?"

"Possibly, possibly," Lis replied.

Fargo waved for the others to follow and plunged into the passageway.

It ended at a narrow walkway. In stark infrared relief, Fargo saw the recycling module, an immense blockhouse structure suspended amid catwalks and conveyors and meter-thick tubes. He followed the walkway onto a platform. At one end he saw the lift, a mechanism, like so much else within a station's skin, left over from the days of construction. It was cheaper to leave all these things in place, never to be used again, than

take them out, or even turn them off. In such enormous
projects, it was simpler to forget them. He waited for the
others to catch up, then crowded them all into the cage.

Two levels down they stepped into a jungle of girders, pipes,
strutwork, cages, tangles of modules; maintenance robots moved
like the fauna of some alien forest, shadows amid shadows.
Jonson whispered in his ear and he moved through it.

Fargo revelled in the mazelike configurations; he felt at
home here, in his element, moving in and out of places humans were not intended to go. He was only dimly aware of
the four people following him, trusting him to get them out of
this confusion. He paused at a railing and stared down. Steam,
illuminated redly by monitor lights, obscured details. It looked
like a mechanized version of the underworld. Massive air ducts
forced tons of atmosphere from place to place; gas exchang-
ers, water lines, waste recycling, power nodes. It was as familiar to Fargo as city streets or the circuits of a station or the
passages of a ship were to the Invested. Not home, no, he did
not think of it that way, he had no home. But he felt confi-
dent here.

He found an enormous snaking tube that ran alongside a
catwalk. Jonson said yes, that one, and he followed the tube
until it curved away and down through a platform, joined by
two others. Somewhere below was *Isomer*.

He ran his eyes over the surface of the tube until he found
the flush-mounted access panel. Jesi helped him take it off.
Within, it was pitch black. Wind blew loudly. Seth shined a
light into it; rungs were set into the opposite side.

"It's not...?" he asked.

"No," Jesi said. "Just a big pipe."

Seth nodded, visibly relieved.

"Anyone following?" Fargo asked Stephen.

Stephen was looking around. "Not that I've noticed.
But–"

Fargo watched Stephen survey the shadows. The telelog's
eyes locked suddenly and Fargo followed his stare.

Clinging to struts and braces, hidden partially by shadow, were a half dozen freeriders, watching them. Fargo started to raise his hand in greeting, then thought better of it. He was with Invested, dressed like them, working with them.

"Come on," he said sharply, turning back to the tube. "Jonson, are you monitoring the inputs to the ship? You're sure this is the right one?"

"That's what I said."

"What about alarms?"

Lis said, "Comm is starting to flow. They're probably talking about you, but there aren't any alarms."

Stephen led the way into the conduit. Cana followed, then Seth. Fargo and Jesi carefully replaced the coverplate from inside. The air roared around them.

Fargo took hold of the rungs and backed down the curve. He held tightly, climbed carefully. The wind snatched at his clothes, tugged at him.

The pipeline ended in a larger one, even windier. Fargo could barely hear Jonson's instructions. Find the one with no flow, he thought she said, and she gave a direction. He walked along, almost pulled off his feet at each pipe that opened in the wall to his left. Air rushed through them, forced to its destination by pumps at the other end, creating heavy crosscurrents.

He stopped before one which did not pull. Jonson yelled in his ear, yes, that one, and he pointed. Once more they squeezed into a narrow space and climbed downward. There were no handholds in this one. They braced themselves, legs pressing backs against the inside, and let themselves slide slowly down.

It grew quieter as they descended. Then their feet hit bottom. "Jonson?" Fargo called.

"You're aboard," she said. "Is everyone in?"

"Yes."

With a sharp grating sound, the connection to the air duct sealed above them. Fargo sat down.

"Where are we?" Cana asked.

"On board," Fargo said.

Cana led the way from there. They scrambled along until a hatch opened before them and Barig poked his head up. They climbed down into the *Isomer*.

Chapter Nine

On the bridge, Lis whooped loudly and the others clapped and whistled.

"Accolades later," Cana said, making a slight bow with mock drama. "Let's see if we can get out of here."

Barig nodded, a smile playing on his thin lips. "We've already isolated ourselves from station services. Although we are still connected, we're relying totally on shipboard systems."

"Fine," Cana said, sitting down in her couch. She rested her fingertips on the interface panels. She frowned briefly at Lis, who still sat beside Jonson at the comm station, but said nothing. "Jonson, send a message to the stationmaster requesting permission to leave dock." She blew out a nervous breath. "I hope all our passengers who debarked will understand why we can't wait for them."

Fargo looked over at Yol-Maex. The seti stood out of the way, hands folded before it, watching quietly, unobtrusively. Its large eyes seemed never to blink. Suddenly, Yol-Maex looked at Fargo and nodded once. Fargo nodded in return, uncertain how to read the gesture.

"We are instructed," Jonson reported, "to relink with station and admit station security. We're in violation of port authority regulations."

"Hm," Cana grunted, grinning crookedly. "Request regulations in question."

After a moment, Jonson shrugged. "They just repeat the same instruction."

"Fine. Inform station that we're leaving dock. If they don't want to be responsible for the damage they'd better disengage and open the bay doors." She glanced around at her crew. "Prepare for immediate embarkation. Mallory, are we in position to direct a narrow beam at the bay doors?"

"Affirmative. Thrusters are aligned for that, but I must caution–"

"I know, it could burn us up, too. I'll chance it." She glowered. "This is my ship, not theirs."

"New message," Jonson said. "Desist or face revocation of merchanter license."

Cana nodded slowly. "Mallory, have you adjusted the forward thrusters to counterbalance the blast? What I want is a series of pulsed emissions against the bay doors."

"Calculated and programmed, Shipmaster."

Fargo appreciated knowing what was happening. Through the interface, everyone on the bridge was linked to the ship and each other; they knew what was going on without the need of words. But Fargo, Stephen, and Yol-Maex could not link–this exchange was for their benefit.

"I've informed all passengers to remain in their quarters or secured in emergency couches," Jonson said. "People are complaining, but they're complying."

"Good. Repeat my previous message to the stationmaster."

"It's being intercepted," Lis said suddenly. "It's not getting to the stationmaster."

"We're being ordered to stand down and open up," Jonson said.

"Fine. Let's leave, shall we?"

For almost a minute there was silence. Fargo swallowed. Lis linked and was deep in a trance. Yol-Maex seemed perfectly at ease. Stephen gripped the edge of his couch.

"Shipmaster," Barig said, "the bay doors are opening."

"What?"

"The bay–"

"I heard. Get us out of here now!"

A brief quake shook the ship as the engines cut in.

"We're moving out," Mallory announced.

Alarms clamored. On the screen Fargo saw the bay receding slowly. The giant umbilicals that had serviced the starship were torn loose, dangling impotently in the sudden hard vacuum. Then they were free of the bay, the surface of the station falling away. On another screen Fargo saw stars.

"They're upset now," Jonson said dryly.

"Take us out to transition point," Cana said. "Get us the hell out of here."

"Smaller craft are moving to intercept," Jonson said.

"Mallory—"

"Give us a few seconds we'll be up to speed, we can outrun them."

"Why did they open the doors?" Cana wondered.

"I did that," Lis said, grinning. "A trick I always wanted to try. I fooled the system into thinking we were a different berth with a clearance."

Cana laughed too loudly and it rippled around the bridge. Nerves, Fargo told himself, and laughed with everyone else.

Tiny slivers drifted into view on the screens. The station was already taking on a visible curve. In another second the edges appeared.

"They're firing!" Lis snapped. "I don't believe it! They're damn well firing on us!"

"Mallory?"

"Speed increasing. Another six seconds."

The deck vibrated for a second.

The transit station was diminishing rapidly now. The attack ships were lost against the background of stars, but the bolts of energy they had fired were gaining, displayed on the screen as bright blue spears of light. *Isomer* was coming up to speed.

"Transition point in three seconds," Mallory announced.

"Your discretion, Mallory."

Fargo counted the time down. The bolts closed quickly. Then abruptly everything on the screen shrank "away" to infinity and there was nothing.

Isomer lay still in space alongside another ship. Passengers moved from one to the other. Fargo watched the other ship detach its umbilicals, drift away, then accelerate off. In seconds it was a star among countless others. Then it vanished.

Shipmaster Cana had gathered her crew and the few passengers remaining in the large common room below the bridge. The screen dominating one wall winked off after the *Netherland* disappeared into translight. Fargo found all six of the Ranonan Delegation–Stephen kept on the opposite side of the room from them–and the legation from Kol Janacek among the forty crew. All the private personnel who had worked in the leased shops on the mall had left the ship.

"You should have gone with the other passengers aboard the *Netherland*, Co Macken," Cana said to the human delegates. "The other representatives did."

"You're still going to Earth–"

"So is the *Netherland*."

"–our mission hasn't changed. My employer wouldn't approve giving up this easily."

"I'll see to it you aren't caught up in any consequences we may have brought on ourselves then." She looked at the others. "We're skipping Neighbors and Procyon and going straight to Sol, and the Ranonan Delegation has kindly offered to compensate us for the loss of Q, although I doubt that will help us now."

She frowned and shook her head. "It seems we're now criminals. We're no doubt going to be charged with destruction of public property and illegal transportation, namely the setis." She glanced at Fargo. "It *is* illegal to knowingly transport nids, too, though I've never heard of anyone being charged. They might just throw that in with everything else. I'll be damned if I'll let that bother me now."

"Perhaps," Yol-Maex said, "his status as a member of our legation will exempt him and you from difficulties over that."

"Perhaps," Cana said, smiling tiredly. "But that won't keep us in business once we reach Earth. Even if Tower was operating on its own and illegally, the truth is they carry more weight than I do. No matter what else happens, I'm out of a ship and a career. I may end up freeriding."

Lis laughed and opened her arms. "We welcome you, Shipmaster! Proud to have you among us!"

Smatterings of nervous laughter spread through the gathering.

"That may not be necessary, either," Yol-Maex said. "I would speak to you privately at another time, Shipmaster Cana."

"My door is open, Ambassador."

"So what's planned?" Fargo asked.

"I have a contract with the Ranonan to get their party safely to Earth. Right now that's a contract I intend to fulfill. Once we get there we'll have to see what happens. We're being pushed around by the megas, probably with Forum approval. I'm not sure where the Chairman stands, but I know the sympathies of the Colonial Forum. They don't want open trade with the seti. The one chance we have is that the Chairman is more agreeable. After all, the Ranonan were invited by the Pan Humana's executive arm, maybe she'll speak up for what we've done." She sighed. "I'm not betting on it, though."

No one spoke. Fargo looked at the faces of the crew. They faced disinvestment. He saw a few brave smiles, cocky postures, but mostly he saw worry, fear.

"Back to your posts," Cana said quietly.

The crew filed out.

Cana went up to Yol-Maex. "If you have a proposal that might get me out of this mess, I'd be grateful to hear it."

Fargo pressed the button on the door and waited. He rocked back and forth on his toes. He frowned at the door and started to press the chime again, when it opened.

Lis's eyes were red. "Hey."

"Hey. May I come in?"

"You're sure you want to?"

Fargo winced and she stepped aside.

"Want something wet?" Lis asked, heading for the bar.

"No, thanks."

"You want to talk?"

"Yes."

"Sit down, then," she jabbed a finger at the sofa. "I have some questions before you start." She lifted a glass to her mouth, drank half of it, and looked at him. "It's water, don't worry." She laughed hollowly. "I was pretty messed up after Hanna got through with us. I thought maybe I was just short-tempered, a little over-sensitive. I thought I might apologize for climbing all over your wounds when we both still needed time to heal. I thought about it." She shook her head.

"Lis, I–"

"I said I have questions. Maybe a couple of statements. First, it really riles me that you deny what happened on Eurasia. I certainly experienced something and I'd like to know what it was. You can deny it if you want, but–just be quiet till I finish, Fargo–but that doesn't change my mind. It did happen. I don't like being called a liar, even by implication. So I want to know what you think happened or why you didn't feel it. *If* you didn't feel it."

Lis sat down across from him. "Second, I want to know why you became a freerider. Most of us had no choice. I wonder about you, though. Thirdly, I want to know how you really feel about me. Because I feel in-between right now and mad as hell about it. I don't know what I'm going to feel when you get done talking."

"Are you through?"

"I'm not sure. I'll butt in if I think of anything else."

"What do you want answered first?"

"Take your pick."

Fargo drew a deep breath. "What happened on Eurasia–yes, it was real, yes, it happened. Our minds were joined briefly. Stephen calls it telelogging."

Lis nodded thoughtfully. "The Ranonan?"

"There's no other explanation. We shared consciousness–or something–for a few seconds."

"I think it formed a bond." She frowned. "I haven't stopped thinking about you since then. I thought I was getting soft-celled and sentimental."

"I've thought about you a lot, too. You're in my dreams." He rolled his eyes. "Now does that sound dumb or what? But it's true. It bothered me."

"Why?"

"That's a little harder to explain."

"It has something to do with you freeriding?"

"Let me ask you how you got started?"

Lis shrugged. "I'm not really sure. I used to work on a freighter, an independent, *Callipygian*, out of Homestead. We got bought out by a mega. Happens all the time, no big deal. We were even offered jobs. I took one, even though a lot of my crewmates didn't. Wouldn't." She waggled her fingers. "Got my implants from them. Had a nice cozy position, could've worked those ships for the rest of my life. But–well, I found a way to divert some business toward some independents. Nothing huge, just enough work to keep a few of them in business. I learned how to work my way through the systems. That's why I'm so good at it."

"Not quite good enough, though?"

"Not quite." She smiled ruefully. "I got caught, I was dismissed. I'm pretty sure that the word went out that any independent that hired me would lose its license. Nothing I can prove, but I could not get a post. I drifted from one port service job to another until the wanderlust got me so hard I had to leave. I didn't have the Q to buy passage, and anyway that wasn't what I wanted to do. I guess the next most obvious choice was freeriding. I bought all the necessary paraphernalia, dumped all my ID in a disposal, and jumped on a freighter to the Distals. That was nine years ago."

Fargo nodded. Most freeriders told similar stories. For one reason or another, their position opportunities dwindled until finally they had little choice. Especially the old spacers.

"You kept riding?"

"You mean unlike all those relics that refuse to look at the stars anymore? I think they cheat themselves. Not me." She jabbed a finger at him. "Your turn."

"In my case–after I left my home I drifted from one thing to another. I was a musician for a time. I managed a warehouse once. My last profession was...questionable. I put together data portfolios on people or businesses. Sometimes the information was of a personal nature, sometimes it wasn't exactly a matter of public record–"

"In other words you broke into private information systems?"

He nodded. "I'd put together a package for a client–details of investments, vacation preferences, business associates, lovers, family matters. A wide range of data. I'd just compile it until I was told to stop. I was very good at it toward the end. It's remarkable how much information is still unrecognized, unused, practically hidden. I have–had–no idea what any of it was used for. At least, not directly, not until–not until a friend of mine was ruined by it. He was petitioning to become Vested. His bid looked good until I discovered that there were certain liens still in place against a small portion of his holdings. He had a taste for racing, had bought a number of specially-built ships. He'd lost a few of them, one badly–totally destroyed, crew killed, and he attempted to blame the shipbuilder for faulty work. Well, the gambling debts from the loss resulted automatically in claims against him, but they were pending the outcome of his suit against the builder. My investigations were instrumental in proving that it was not the shipbuilder's fault–I'm the son of a shipbuilder, I grew up in shipyards, I...understood...the questions that had to be asked. The suit was dismissed, the liens fell into place immediately and his petition was denied on the basis of insufficient title to personal holdings." He smiled grimly. "In other words, he was too poor. Amusing, eh? Poverty isn't supposed to exist anymore. It became even more amusing when he suicided over it."

"You weren't responsible for that."

"No, maybe not, but I was involved. Intimately. Without my involvement...well, it might still have gone that way, but he might have lived a few more days, weeks, a year. He might have lived long enough for the liens to make no difference to his petition. He might have gotten over the depression. He might–well, he might. All I recognize is that *with* my involvement he certainly died."

"That's when you started freeriding?"

"No. I got pissed first and went after the co who commissioned my data compilation. I started searching *his* holdings, looking for any shit that might hurt him."

"And you got caught."

"Did I. Nothing so polite as being fired and unable to find work. I was beaten up, threatened with my life, and then had all my options closed. I kicked around here and there and ended up in a radical hermit monad."

"You're kidding."

"I'm not. It sounds incredible now, I know, but–I was looking for dissolution. I wanted to erase myself. If I became Not Me, then I–whoever I'd end up as–wouldn't be responsible. I spent almost a year seeking the transformation and destruction of who I am. It didn't work. Maybe because they weren't really hermits and the road to dissolution after all has to be sought alone. I don't know. Anyway, the Monad was shut down. It was on private land and the owner threw them off. We petitioned for court intercession, but the matter was uncomplicated in a legal sense. The Monad didn't own the property, there was no formal agreement. I left. I still had a little Q, so I used it up on the gear I needed and then I started freeriding."

"Do you ever think about reinvesting?"

"Occasionally. I don't pursue it. That's a trap, too. As to your third question–Lis, I don't know how I feel about you. I like you–a lot. But other than that I don't know."

She nodded slowly, then smiled. "Are you adverse to trying for more? Or are you so paranoid that you think this is another trap?"

Fargo looked away. "It's safer not to. Obligations–"

She leaned forward. "This is about *freight*?"

"You don't think so?"

She gave a short, cutting laugh. "That's for strangers! We've been inside each other!"

"But–"

"Don't you ever want to be close to someone?"

He shrugged, then nodded. "I just don't understand why you want to."

"Because I'm a goddamned romantic, that's why. I happen to like the idea of being in love."

"But if it was just what the seti did–"

"I don't care what the cause was!"

He drew breath deeply. "If I do this–if I admit this to you–I won't ever want it to end. If I admit how I feel and what I want, you've got to understand that it's as good as a commitment."

"Full disclosure? Warning to the customer before the purchase?" She laughed. "The terms are agreeable."

Fargo let out a long breath. "I feel foolish. I have to work up my courage to make love to you."

Lis laughed loudly and set her glass down. She stood and began unzipping her blouse. "Don't worry about it, co," she said. "I'll take care of everything–this time!"

Fargo explored her. Light caresses building into firmer pressures, on her stomach, ribs, and thighs, fanned an eager fire. He was immersed in a *déjà vu* daydream, amazed at the natural way he found her response points, the way he knew where they were, what they required. In return, Lis responded exactly the way he wanted. She knew what he liked, the way he liked it. For a few minutes it felt like an exercise, an intellectual exploration that transcended guessing. They stopped and looked at each other questioningly.

Fargo opened his mouth to say something, but Lis touched his lips with her fingertips and kissed him at the juncture of his throat and collarbone. The words evaporated, burned away by her mouth. She sucked at the spot lightly, ran her tongue in tiny circles over it, brushed it with her lips–and Fargo ran his thumb gently over her eyebrow, knowing beforehand the reaction. Lis groaned throatily and her pelvis moved against his thigh synchronously with the slow stroke of his thumb.

He kneaded the place between her shoulderblades with his other hand. Her body, stretched along his, was a satiny warmth, her odor sharp, heady.

Lis moved slowly, exploring things at leisure, though Fargo could sense–Fargo *knew*–she wanted everything now and was keeping herself in check. He was fascinated–Lis was making love to him the way he had always wanted to be made love to.

She moved her mouth down his belly. He sat up and ran his hands over her back. She pressed closer and worked her hands around his buttocks. A fine sweat coated both of them.

Lis liked to push herself to limits. Limits of endurance, limits of patience, limits of stimulus. She seemed to sense that his limits were very low. It had been many years since his last physical intimacy. He had fallen into a pattern of avoidance, travelling alone where possible, keeping himself aloof otherwise, even when he craved company and stayed for days in a sanctuary. Privacy was sacrosanct among freeriders; they had little else. Lis was the first to insist on more from him. Now she could do what she wanted with him.

She slid her mouth over his penis and with a convulsion Fargo climaxed. Startled, he gaped at her.

"I'm sorry! I–!"

Lis grinned up at him, then ran her fingers down his chest, onto his stomach, and continued what she had been doing.

Fargo, embarrassed, fell back on the bed. In moments his embarrassment merged with arousal, transformed by want into a delicate desire to please her.

He traced the patterns of her ears with his fingers. Lis gathered the radii of his awareness and drew them to a locus of intense sensation. Fargo arched his back.

Lis climbed up his body, kissing and licking his torso, pausing for seconds on a nipple until Fargo moved his left hand between her legs and stroked her. She eased herself up and pushed her tongue into his mouth. Gently, she guided him inside her.

Fargo wrapped his arms around her, pushing against her. Lis's breath was a tight susurrus in his ear, an even meter that matched his own. She pressed against him with the same intensity, as if their purpose was not intercourse, but fusion. The surfaces of their bodies interfered, keeping them separate and distinct.

But the distinction blurred for Fargo. He closed his eyes and rolled with Lis, and remembered her. Her breath suddenly grew louder, then burst in a series of deep, quick gasps.

Lis nestled against him, dozing. Fargo wanted to sleep, but too many things cascaded through his mind. He was angry at the wasted years, but he forgave himself–there was no way to know. Any other course, any other choice, and he would never have been here.

Fargo remembered loneliness, longing, searching–not his own, but Lis's. He remembered finding something resembling the thing sought, always learning with aching certainty that it was not right, was not what was wanted. But always the quest continued.

For himself? He had sought nothing but distance. He had gone toward no goal. The memory of purposeless years set against Lis's naïve optimism opened him up like a shell. She filled him, entered the empty spaces, and the bitter melancholy turned sweet with the certainty that he was not alone anymore.

He did not believe in fate or destiny or any superstitious causality in life. Like walking, life was a sequence of controlled falling, accidents partially guided by intent, desire, response. For once, it seemed, he had fallen the right way.

Chapter Ten

Fargo slitted his eyes open. The light, still dim, shattered through his lashes, haloing any object he saw. His limbs felt heavy, like slow thoughts, and he turned his head to the right. Lis stretched out on her side, back to him, and the heaviness became lazy warmth.

He blinked. Someone stood across the room, against the wall. Fargo noticed bright highlights in dark eyes. He raised himself up on his elbows, blinked again, then rubbed his eyes. Sleepers flaked away.

No one was there.

He fell back and stared at the ceiling. Finally, he decided he was very tired. Tired enough to see things, tired enough for his imagination to play with him. Except, he thought, I've never felt better...

"Hey."

Lis had rolled over. She touched his chest lightly.

"Hey," he returned.

"What're you thinking?"

He shook his head and shifted onto his side, facing her. "Just..."

She raised her eyebrows. "Just?"

"Exactly." He let his hand drift over her breasts, down her stomach. He hesitated at the edge of the thick hair below her navel and looked at her. She nodded minutely and he slipped his hand between her legs. It excited him to see her close her eyes and stretch ever-so-slightly in response.

As she pulled him over her, he hesitated and looked toward the wall again. For an instant he thought someone watched from the shadows...and then he saw that the light panel above the bed made a shadow of the back of a chair against that wall…and he looked down at Lis and forgot about it.

"You know, you don't have to ask permission every time you want to do something."

He selected a piece of cheese from the platter and bit into it. Homestead cheese; he recognized the tang. He nodded, but did not look up.

"Can't help it," he said.

"Freight?"

"No. Just…"

"Just?"

He swallowed a mouthful of wine and looked at her and thought: she's not beautiful. Sinewy, almost gaunt, except that she was in no way underweight. Lis was tightly-muscled, shoulders a bit broad. And Fargo thought: she's exactly what I want.

And looked away, embarrassed.

"What *is* it?" she asked. "Hey…"

"We're nids."

"So?"

He shook his head as if to twist away from the what was in it. "It's not ours. Nothing's ours."

Lis watched him quietly for a time, then nodded. "So you can't have anything. Nothing can belong to you."

"Something like that."

"Get over it."

"Just like that?"

"I'm not having any trouble."

He sighed. "I'll work on it."

"Do." She smiled. "In the meantime, let me make it clear. You have my permission. If there's something I don't want you to do, I will tell you."

They ate in silence until the comm chimed. Lis padded across the room to the console and touched accept.

"Yes?"

"Co Falco?" Yol-Maex–or one of the Ranonans, Fargo
could not tell them apart by voice–said. "Pardon any inter-
ruption, but we would speak with you."

"All right. I'll be there in ten minutes."

"Satisfactory."

Lis sighed and shrugged. "Duty, love. I need to shower."

"What's it like working for them?"

She pursed her lips thoughtfully as she headed for the cube.
"Hard to say. Their time sense isn't ours, so they do things
that don't always agree with my sleep schedule. But then, I'm
used to keeping odd hours myself." She grinned. "I have to
tend to this. We can talk about it later."

"Sure. You want me to go?"

"No, they didn't ask for you. Sorry." She stepped inside
the cube and the door closed. She came out a couple of
minutes later, went to the closet, and pulled out a bright red
outfit.

Fargo watched her dress, amazed. The motions were ordinary enough, but he had not seen a woman do this in over four
years. Not as an Invested, in normal clothes.

She finished, checked herself briefly in the mirror, smiled
at him, and left. He tried to dismiss his annoyance at not
going. They had extended him some kind of status as part of
their mission, but so far that had meant little.

Fargo ate a little more, then, suddenly restless, he dressed
and walked out of the stateroom.

He pressed Stephen's chime and waited, but the door remained shut. He knocked loudly. Stephen did not respond.
Fargo wandered onto the arcade.

He leaned on the rail and looked down at the empty mall.
The shops were dark. Overhead shutters blocked the view.
At sublight they were opened, but at translight the unmedi-
ated view was unwatchable. The geometries made no sense.
All the views available on screens were approximations, managed by the ship's systems and turned into something a co
could look at and understand.

Fargo looked around at the sound of footsteps. Bosh Macken came toward him, gazing down at the deserted deck below.

He stopped near Fargo and gripped the rail in both hands.

"Strange," Macken said.

"What?"

He nodded down. "Never saw one empty before."

"Oh. I have. But you're right, it's strange."

"Where was that?"

"Hmm?"

"Where did you see one?"

Fargo shrugged. "My father was a shipbuilder. He used to drag me along on his inspections."

"Ah. Where was that?"

Fargo straightened. "I have to go find a friend."

"Co Christopher?" Macken grinned. "He's in Shipmaster Cana's rooms."

"How do you know?"

"I asked her."

"What's he doing there?"

Macken shrugged elaborately. "I'd like to know myself. If you find out, would you tell me?"

"I don't know you."

"I'm just asking–"

"You work for Kol Janacek, don't you?"

Macken nodded.

"Then...I don't want to know you."

As Fargo walked by, Macken turned and gripped his arm tightly. Fargo tried to pull free, but Macken's hold was powerful.

"You don't fool me," Macken said. "You're a nid. Personally, I don't care. But I have instructions to watch Stephen, take care of him. If you get in the way, I won't have any problems killing you." He drew Fargo closer. "Do you understand?"

Fargo's heart hammered, but he did not look away from Macken. Eventually, Macken released him, but Fargo continued to glare at him. Macken made a shooing gesture and returned to looking down at the empty mall.

"Don't ever turn your back on me again," Fargo whispered. Macken's shoulders tightened and Fargo walked away, trying to keep an even stride, trying not to hurry. He managed. He even managed, to his surprise, not to look back.

Cana did not open her door, either. Fargo looked both ways down the corridor, then slipped his multijack from inside his blouse. He dialed a bit and worked it into the manual lock release on the door switch. Three twists and Cana's doors slid open. An alarm probably went off somewhere, he knew, but he did not care. His encounter with Macken had left him feeling reckless.

The shipmaster's quarters looked spartan. A bed, a single chair, a cube, another door, one cabinet with a few objects–small statuary, a row of books, artifacts Fargo recognized as seti, but could not categorize–and a closet. Fargo ran his fingers through his hair, suddenly self-conscious. He backed toward the door, intending to leave. Then he stopped and stared at the other door.

You've already broken in, he thought, and crossed the room.

The door opened on the reception hall where the dinner had been several days earlier. He stood on the table platform. Stephen sat on the floor in front of the Hanna display.

The shapes moved, oil-on-water thick. Stephen did not look around. Fargo descended the shallow steps, hesitated, then sat down. Stephen stared into the display, his gaze fixed. He appeared locked in a trance.

Fargo heard footsteps behind him. He looked back and saw Shipmaster Cana frowning down at him. He stood, hoping she did not see his nervousness.

"How long has he been like that?" he asked.

Cana looked at Stephen. "A couple days now. He's done it before, but this has been the longest commune."

"Commune?"

She nodded. "You understand what he is? What he does?"

"A little."

"Hanna created him. His ability, anyway. She devised the implants, taught him how to use it. Him and the others. She can communicate with him through it."

"How is she here?"

"TEGlink."

"But–"

"Hanna has a dedicated line. I don't know how. Power's not a problem, but keeping it secret–it's an impressive accomplishment. She doesn't use it often. This is the most time I've ever seen the display active."

"Hanna's–" He shook his head. "Where's Co Falco?"

"Uh, with the Ranonans."

"Mmm. I need to talk to them, too. Excuse me." She went back to her room.

Fargo, relieved, walked quietly toward Stephen. He glanced at the display but found he could not look at it very long. The geometries made no sense and his mind kept insisting on a recognition the slowly oozing shapes denied.

Stephen stared, unblinking, into it.

Fargo wrinkled his nose at Stephen's odor. Two days? He stepped back.

Stephen blinked slowly, his head falling forward. He looked up at Fargo and smiled wearily. "Fargo. I didn't hear you come in. What–?"

He winced, squeezed his eyes shut, and started to fall over. Fargo caught him and eased him down to the floor. Stephen's legs remained folded. His breath whistled through his teeth and he grabbed his thighs and worked his fingers.

"Too long–" he managed, then gasped. Carefully he straightened his legs. Sweat appeared on his forehead. Fargo held his shoulders and felt him trembling.

"Can I get you something, co? Water? Pain pills?"

"No, no...just...*ahh!*"

Stephen got his legs straight and rolled onto his back. He lay there, pale and still, breathing hard. Fargo remained kneeling beside him, ready to act, but with no idea how.

Finally Stephen opened his eyes. "Water would be good. I'm sorry..."

Fargo hurried to the bar and tapped for a glass of water. He helped Stephen raise up to drink, then kept his hand behind Stephen's neck.

Stephen laughed briefly. "Been a long time since I did that. Locked in one position for too long. Sorry. Didn't mean to scare you."

"Scare me? Hey, nothing scares me."

Stephen laughed again.

"Can you stand?"

"I doubt it."

"Let me help you to a couch."

Fargo set the glass down. Stephen put his arms around Fargo's neck and Fargo lifted him first to a sitting position, then, with a heave, managed to get him to his feet. Stephen clung to him, most of his weight on Fargo's shoulders. Fargo staggered slightly, kicking the glass over, then got his arms around Stephen's chest and walked him across the room to a couch.

Fargo picked up the water glass and refilled it. Stephen drained half of it.

"This has been...so good, Fargo..."

Fargo glanced at the display. The image was frozen into one configuration now, though he still found it difficult to "see" it. "If you say so."

"You wouldn't know," Stephen said. He patted Fargo's arm weakly. "You've never been joined to someone this way. Sharing thoughts, sensations...dreams..."

Fargo cocked an eyebrow. "No, of course not, co. I've never felt any of that."

Stephen continued to gaze at the display without reacting.

"So, co," Fargo said, "what've you and Hanna been...communing about?"

"Immense…it's so big." He looked at Fargo. "I never knew."

Cana returned then, followed by Lis and two of the Ranonans. Stephen frowned at the setis. He drew his legs up as if preparing to stand, but he only tried once.

"Now that you're all here," Cana said. "Co Christopher? Are you all right?"

Stephen nodded.

Lis came over to Fargo. She touched the back of his hand lightly and turned to stand beside him.

"I debated whether to say anything to you," Cana said. "I'm still not sure what all this is about. Things are moving and I'm not privy to all the details."

"You have decided, after all," Yol-Maex said, "to tell us?"

Cana nodded. "We're being followed."

"It's only a faint perturbation," Cana said.

They stood before an image that floated several centimeters from the wall, blocking their view of three of her paintings—including the Hanna display. Fargo saw a field of green, roiling in complex patterns—the universe at translight speeds, a realm consisting almost totally of effects without matter, only marginally translated into a manageable form—and in the center of it a faint yellow-green mote that came and went sporadically, but persistently.

"That's a ship?" Fargo asked.

"There's very little else it can be," Cana said. "Stars can occasionally register like that, but they're relatively stationary. Nothing else moves fast enough to register as that massive and stay with us that long."

"They can see us like that?"

"We have to assume so."

"What can they do?"

"In translight? Nothing."

Fargo turned to Cana. "But they'll be with us all the way to Sol?"

"It's possible."

"Which means that when we drop down from translight we'll have whatever ships will be waiting for us at Sol in front of us and this one—or more, we can't tell—behind us."

"Likely."

Fargo grunted.

"There is nothing you can do as well?" Yol-Maex asked.

"Nothing," Cana admitted. "I debated whether to tell you. But it really doesn't matter. You still want to go to Sol."

"Correct."

She shrugged. "Then we go."

"Then we will not be concerned."

Cana frowned at the Ranonan. Fargo looked at Lis, but her expression told him nothing.

"It's still probable that it's a coincidence," Cana said.

"We will accept your judgement," Yol-Maex said. "Pardon us, but we have on-going matters."

"Of course."

"Do you still need me, ambassador?" Lis asked.

"If you would."

Lis squeezed Fargo's hand and followed the setis.

"Well, hell," he said.

"I'm not sure," Cana said, "I will ever get used to them."

Cana sent him along with Stephen to make sure he got back to his cabin safely.

"I'd like to be alone, Fargo," Stephen said at his door. He shuffled inside and the door sealed. Disappointed, Fargo wandered the arcade again, then went to Lis's room.

Lis's cabin door opened for him. Lis was at the polycom, her fingers against the link panel. Fargo watched her for a time, disturbed and fascinated at once. Her half-closed eyes, her mouth relaxed, smiling—she reminded him of Stephen, communing with Hanna, and Daniel pressed back to back with Stephen, deep inside.

Suddenly she blinked and pulled away. She sighed deeply and stretched.

"Fargo. I didn't hear you come in." She yawned. "Hey."

"Hey. I hope I didn't interrupt anything important."

"Simulations. Been awhile since I used the link. It takes practice."

"You didn't seem to have any trouble with it back at Aquas."

"I used to be pretty good."

"Mmm."

"What's wrong?"

He went to the bar. "Nothing."

"Don't lie to me."

He glared at her, startled. "Don't analyze me."

She winced. Guilty, he busied himself pouring a drink.

"Ignore me. I don't know what's wrong."

"I don't want to ignore you."

"Why not? Everyone else does."

"That's shit."

"Maybe." He crossed the cabin and sat down facing the polycom. He stared at it and sipped his brandy. "Of the bunch of us, I'm the only real nid. You and Stephen...both of you are connected to something. Him to Hanna, whatever she is, and his friend Daniel and however many others like him there are. You to the Ranonans. Connected. I'm the only one that has no other reason to be here. I'm not connected to anything." He shrugged. "Just thinking out loud. Maybe I should go."

She sat down beside him and touched his hand. "You're bothered by the links, aren't you?" she said. "It's been a long time since I had a chance to use them. Ninety-nine percent of the interfaces in the Pan require a valid ID before they let you in. Usually I forget all about them." She frowned and kissed his temple. "But the rest...you're wrong. You and I...we're linked."

He pulled his hand away and swallowed more brandy. A half dozen clever responses came to mind, but he could use none of them. Not here, not with Lis. He cared for her too much to be snide. My best weapon useless, he thought. He was frightened. The setis were telelogs, Stephen was and had Hanna and Daniel and who knew how many others. Cana was Shipmaster with a loyal crew, most of whom could link through the ship's systems and merge in a kind of telelogging—and Lis could share that, too. He was the only one who was utterly isolated. Stephen had said as much. *You have no way of knowing.*

"We're linked..."

He looked at her, expecting anger, resentment, impatience at the very least. Instead she wore an expression he had seen often given to others, but it had been so long since anyone had intended it for him that he did not recognize it at first. For a moment it frightened him. It would have been easier to deal with anger and hate, he was used to that, knew how to defend against it.

But he had no defense against compassion. There was only rejection, and with that, rejection of the love behind it.

He reached for her hand and she took it.

"I've never finished anything," he said. "I didn't become a shipbuilder. I didn't become a musician, either, and instead of doing something worthwhile I ended up doing something stupid. I've been avoiding completing things since. The life of a freerider is perfect for me. No freight, no obligations, nothing to complete and no way to complete it if there were."

"Is that why you've stuck with Stephen? Something to complete?"

"Maybe."

"So let me help." She punched his shoulder lightly. "Shit, I'm perfect for you, too. You'll never be finished with me."

He started laughing, unable to stop. At some point it changed and he pressed his face into her lap and cried. Lis held him and rocked him. He was frightened, but he was happy, too, and he clung to her from both. He hoped she understood. He believed that she did.

The screen in the common room was filled with data. Sol system was surrounded by a cordon of habitats, battlestations, shipyards, robot monitors, and roving patrol ships, all in a loose ring outside the aphelion of the Pluto-Neptune circumference. The *Isomer* approached one of the stations.

Yol-Maex sat next to Fargo. "Now's the moment of truth," Fargo said.

"These facilities," the Ranonan gestured at the screen. "Their purpose is war?"

"Defense. Amounts to the same thing, I suppose. That station could obliterate this ship."

"Is Earth prepared for a war?"

"Earth has always been prepared for war."

Cana's voice came over the address. "This is Shipmaster Cana, commanding the Ranonan Diplomatic Vessel *Isomer*. Request permission to pass system perimeter and proceed to Earth. We are on official business. Our clearance can be transmitted at your convenience."

Fargo started and looked at Yol-Maex. The Ranonan cocked his head to one side.

"It seemed the best solution," it said. "Employing one of the human customs. Ownership is the greater portion of the law."

"So you bought the *Isomer*. Elegant, Ambassador. Elegant."

The voice of the station coordinator said, "We understood the *Isomer* to be an independent vessel. There are several complaints outstanding regarding unauthorized transit out of Aquas and violations against station facilities and personnel. Please transmit your pertinent data."

"It remains to be seen," Yol-Maex said, "if all humans observe such customs."

"Prepare to dock, *Isomer*," the coordinator said after a few minutes.

Fargo sighed, relieved. "Well, they could've started shooting."

The station grew larger on the screen. Smaller craft swarmed around *Isomer* and escorted her to a dock section that was essentially a long boom, with airlocks, stretching out from the main station. Two other ships were already there, one a hulking merchanter, the other a battlecruiser. Fargo frowned at the dark hull of the latter: it was smaller than the merchanter but projected an impression of enormous power. Fargo wondered whether the knowledge of its purpose lent it such a threatening look, playing on his imagination and fear, or if the skill of its designers had imbued it with the mien of innate threat, knowing that a deadly appearance can be a warship's most important aspect.

"Everybody meet me in the main lock," Cana requested.

Fargo walked alongside Yol-Maex.

"Uh, Ambassador...may I ask you something?"

"Yes."

"Just–well, it would help me to help you if I understood a little more of what's going on."

"What do you misunderstand?"

"Well, to put it simply, why are you bothering with this? I mean, what do setis hope to get out of straightening out relations with humans? I don't understand why you're here."

Yol-Maex was silent for several steps, then nodded. "I will tell you."

Fargo waited. They were almost at the lock area when he said, "When are you going to tell me?"

"When it is right to do so."

Fargo bit back a harsh response.

At the hatch, Yol-Maex put a hand on his shoulder. "You should not be concerned with your value. You would not be here if you were not necessary."

The seti stepped into the lock. Fargo followed automatically.

Stephen and Lis were already with Cana. Presently the rest of the Ranonan party entered the lock.

Stephen smiled at Fargo. "We're here," he whispered. "Sol."

"Hm. Imagine that."

Lis looked at him curiously and he bobbed his eyebrows. She smiled, shaking her head. Fargo pinched her waist. She brushed at his fingers and he caught her hand and pulled her closer.

"Maybe I have a misplaced sense of the romantic," he said to her, "but if you don't mind I'd like to tell you something."

"What?"

"I love you."

"Misplaced sense of timing, more likely," she said, her face slightly flushed.

The airlock opened. A party of five entered. The leader was a crisply dressed man with white hair and brilliant blue eyes. The others were uniformed in dark grey and sidearms– Armada.

"Shipmaster Sea Cana?" he said, pronouncing it "see" instead of "shay."

"I'm Sea Cana."

"I'm Commander Reese Albans of Sol Division, Armada. I've been given the authority and responsibility of dealing with this situation. Accordingly, I want you, your First, and Ambassador Yol-Maex and the other Ranonans to remain on board. Everyone else will be escorted to the station proper while I remain to question you."

"Very well. Everyone is here."

Albans nodded and ran his eyes over the assembly, lingering only slightly on the Ranonans.

Lis stepped up to him. "Excuse me, but two of us are attached to the Ranonan Legation, human liaisons. We should perhaps remain with them–"

"All humans off the ship," Albans said shortly.

"I will speak with you later, Fargo," Yol-Maex said.

Fargo walked with Lis and Stephen as the Armada contingent led them down the long corridor. At the end was a large antechamber where three more Armada personnel manned desks and requested ID. Fargo handed over the chit he had

been issued from the Ranonans; Lis handed the same to another officer.

"What's this?" the officer asked.

"ID."

The man shook his head slightly. "Pan ID, if you please."

"We're attached to the Ranonan Legation," Lis said. "I'm
liaison, he's my assistant–"

"Valid Pan ID please," the officer snapped, holding out
his hand.

"Sorry, co," Fargo said. "Don't have any."

The man looked up blankly.

"If you check," Fargo went on, "you'll find I'm attached
to the Ranonan Legation as an assistant to the liaison–"

"Nids," another man said. Lis leaned on his console, mouth
puckered distastefully. The soldier looked at Fargo's interrogator.

"We got a couple of nids here."

"No ID," Fargo's soldier said flatly. "You're disinvested?"

"Well–"

"Detention. We'll figure out what to do with them later."

"Hey, I said–"

"Provost Marshal, escort these two to detention. Next."

"I'm with the Ranonan Legation–" Fargo protested as he
was pulled from line. "Hey, would you let me–"

The Provost Marshal was a broadshouldered woman with
an impassive, unmemorable face. She shoved Fargo along.
Lis walked smoothly, slowing sometimes, only to be shoved
next to Fargo.

"Look, we're attached to Ranonan Trade Legation. We're
legitimate. You–"

The woman grabbed Fargo's wrist suddenly and twisted.
Fargo sucked air in pain.

"Nonhumans and nids," the woman said quietly. "I have
no use for either. Now move!" She pushed him forward.

Fargo rubbed his wrist and glowered at the soldier. Lis
touched his shoulder gently and nodded him on. He assumed
a stony silence.

They rode a shunt across the station and emerged in a starkly lit section. The troops here seemed less proud than the rest. Fargo could not quite identify the difference–their posture was correct, though barely, and their uniforms were clean, though perhaps older–but he saw no patience in any of them. He stiffened, knowing there would be no sympathy here, either.

"Nids," the Provost Marshal said to the warrant officer.

"Great, just what we need."

"I think you'd better check–" Lis began.

The warrant officer glared at her. After a few seconds he looked back at the P.M. "Ship them to Charon?"

"I don't care," she said. "Just get them off station. There's a shuttle in five hours."

"Nobody's interested in what we have to say?" Fargo ventured.

The P.M. spun, driving her fist into his ribs. Fargo clenched his teeth and clung to the desk edge, refusing to cry out. He slowly straightened.

"I guess not," he managed.

The warrant officer gestured and two guards came forward. They were taken down a short gangway lined with narrow, heavy doors. Lis was put in a cell and Fargo in the one across from her.

The cell was a small, truncated pyramid with a foldout cot and a toilet. Curiously, there was a polycom panel by the door. It was old and disused, covered with grime.

"What's that for?" he asked his guard.

"Last statements, communications with attorneys, public announcements."

It surprised him that the soldier answered. The man leered. "It's not used anymore, but it's the legal right of every prisoner to have such access."

"Oh. Thanks, co."

The door closed leadenly. Fargo studied his cell and shook his head.

"Welcome to fucking Sol."

Chapter Eleven

Fargo had just dozed off when they came again. Lis was already in the corridor. Six marines escorted them out of the detention area. They boarded another shunt. A few minutes later they stepped out onto a vast platform. No one else was present except a pair of women in brown shipsuits at the far side, waiting.

"Well, well," Lis said.

"No talking," one of their escorts snapped.

They crossed the platform. The corporal advanced to the waiting coes and handed them a disc and spoke briefly. The women looked at Fargo and Lis. One of them, the taller of the two with light, short hair and dark brown eyes, frowned.

"All right," the corporal said. "You go with them."

"Where are we going?" Lis asked.

"Charon. You'll learn more when you get there."

"What about our right to counsel."

The corporal laughed, surprised. "You're nids." He shook his head and walked away. The troops followed.

"Come on," the tall woman said. "They evacuate the atmosphere in a few minutes, make sure you go with us."

The women walked in the opposite direction. Fargo looked at Lis and was puzzled to see her smiling. She shrugged and followed.

They cycled through a small airlock and passed down an umbilical barely large enough for one person at a time. When Fargo got to the ship he saw that the little craft was bristling with internal guard monitors and automatic stunners. The women had no need of guards or weapons on their tiny transport.

Lis came out of the lock and looked at the taller woman, grinning.

"Been awhile," Lis said.

"Damn," the other said. "I never thought I'd see you again."

Fargo folded his arms. "You know each other?"

"Uh huh," the blonde said, grinning. "We served on *Callipygian* together."

"Saris!" Lis cried, holding her arms wide.

"No! Wait!" Saris held up a warning hand.

Fargo saw one of the stunners on the bulkhead above center on Lis.

Saris turned to the other. "Jen, turn those damn things off. These are coes."

"They're nids," Jen said grumpily.

"And so would we be if we hadn't sold our souls! Turn them off!"

Jen shrugged and left through the hatch. Presently the activation lights on the stunners went out.

Lis and Saris embraced enthusiastically.

They floated in the cramped common of the tug; it was an old ship and did not possess pseudogravity.

Fargo listened to Lis tell the two pilots about the last few weeks, impressed with her ability to leave out important details and fill the gap convincingly. He added a little here and there to lend her validity, but it was obvious Saris and Jen accepted it all.

Saris whistled appreciatively when Lis and Fargo finished. "Well, now, I don't know what things are like in the Distals these days, but Tesa Estana owns everything around Sol, if not outright then with favors and threat. Even Charon, where we're going, that's for her."

"What is it?" Fargo asked.

"Small rock that tags along with Pluto. They're digging it out. Used to be a research facility, long time ago, but it hasn't been used in more than a century. Estana's turning it into some kind of habitat, but there's more equipment than living space."

"You're going to take us?" Lis asked.

Jen scowled. Saris looked embarrassed.

"Wish I could help you, co," she said, "but this is our job. This is the best I could get short of being disinvested. At least it's work."

"Well," Lis said, "I know how that is."

Saris smiled and shrugged. "I wouldn't worry about it. Another couple weeks and things ought to be done there. Construction's almost finished."

"Then what happens to all the people there?" Fargo asked.

"I imagine you'll be transferred elsewhere."

"Maybe. Maybe not. Nids are disposable, you know."

Saris gnawed her lower lip, then glanced at the display in the corner of the room that gave telemetry from the control cabin. "We reach Charon in ten hours. This isn't a very punchy boat. I suggest you both get some sleep. I'll see you get a good meal before we dock."

Lis stretched, her body pivoting slowly. "I'm tired anyway. Hope we get to see each other some more, Saris. Be good to reminisce."

"Yeah," Saris laughed. "I'll see to it."

Fargo followed Lis down the short gangway, pushing gently along the walls, to the cabin opposite the small galley. Saris locked the hatch behind them.

"Might be the last time we get to sleep together," Fargo said, gazing dispiritedly at the narrow bunks with the zero-g webbing.

"Don't be such a pessimist."

He did not know what woke him. Fargo opened his eyes to the ceiling above the bunk. The lights were dimmed for nightcycle (or did this small tug have a nightcycle?) and the hum of the engines was the only sound.

He looked around. Lis floated by the door, working with a small tool in an opening alongside. She glanced at him and held her finger to her lips. Fargo pushed the rest of the web-bing away and let himself rise to the level of the "top" bunk. He stopped himself and hung there, watching her work.

The door slid open suddenly. Lis grabbed the side of the opening and pulled herself through. Fargo pushed after her.

She went to the galley and started exploring, looking for a weapon, but there was little loose in the cramped area. Lis shook her head impatiently.

"I–"

"What are you doing?"

Fargo spun too fast and his shoulder crashed into the bulk-head. Jen glared at them from the gangway.

Lis shot forward, and Jen pulled herself to one side. Lis caught herself against the bulkhead, twisted sinuously, and shot down the gangway toward the control cabin. Jen opened her mouth to shout and prepared to chase Lis. For a second she was framed in the hatchway. Fargo got his feet behind him, curled against the bulkhead, and shoved, hard. He slammed against her and they both bounced off the far wall and ricocheted, tumbling together, back down the gangway aft. Fargo's shoulder was in agony. He spread his arms and legs out to stop himself and caught the palms of his hands on jagged edges and protrusions in the wall. Finally he managed to stabilize himself and halt the tumble.

Jen floated limply at the far end of the gangway. Blood formed globules that drifted away from her mouth. Her eye-lids were half-closed.

Fargo rubbed his right shoulder. His arm was numb, per-haps dislocated. He pushed toward Jen.

He reached for her to check her pulse. Her hand shot out and grabbed his wrist. She twisted and pulled and he went over her, into the aft bulkhead. He tucked his head down barely in time and took the worst of the blow across his back.

Jen had bounded away in reaction, but was turned to face him. She looked right and left, then dived into the cabin op-posite the one Fargo and Lis had occupied. Fargo did not know what was in there but he felt certain he could not let Jen back out. He kicked off the bulkhead.

He caught the edge of her doorway. Within the small cabin Jen spun around, something metallic in her left hand. Fargo shoved himself back across the gangway, let his legs absorb the shock against the opposite wall, then sprang toward her, good arm extended, palm outward. He caught her in the collarbone as her hand flashed up. Pain lanced up his arm. His momentum knocked her straight back against a small cabinet mounted on the wall. He followed her in, arm still out, and connected with her jaw. Her head snapped back.

Fargo held onto her shoulders and steadied himself. Her fingers had opened and he saw a long, sharp knife float away. Across his forearm was a deep, crimson slash.

Jen was unconscious now. Ignoring the pain, Fargo went through the small compartments in the cabin and found the extra webbing for the bunk. He tied her hands as best he could, then tucked her into the heavy net. He tightened it around her, then anchored it to the light fixture in the ceiling.

His shoulder ached deeply. He kneaded it, searching with his fingertips until he felt the displacement. He winced and looked around for a solid handhold. He took hold of the webbing around Jen with his injured arm and reached for the edge of the hatch with his other hand. He gulped air, closed his eyes for a moment, then pulled. Jen's body straightened, the webbing held, and his shoulder lurched back into place with a sickening crunch. Fargo let go, his vision dancing with scintilla. He tried to remain still so his stomach would not heave. When everything settled down and the pain began to subside, he drifted back to the cabinets. Blood drifted in small spheres throughout the room. It floated from the cut eerily, spreading very little across his skin, through his sleeve.

He found some gauze in a half empty medkit and wrapped his arm, then cautiously made his way forward to the control room.

Lis was at the console, fingers dancing over the controls, eyes darting from her hands to the small screens as numbers flickered by. She glanced at him and grinned mischievously.

"Told you not to be a pessimist," she said.

Saris floated unconscious against the bulkhead behind them.

"We can't get to Earth in this boat," Lis said. "Even if I programmed a cometary course to conserve fuel–"

"Fuel?"

She nodded. "Fuel. This is an old craft. Even if I did that, we'd run out of food, water, and air before we made it."

"So what do we do? Can't go back to the station."

"Not that one, at least. According to this–" she tapped the chart on the screen "–there are dozens of places within range."

"Uh–what happens when the Armada starts looking for us? We'll be overdue at Charon in a few hours."

"Details, details."

"Are you really as reckless as you seem?"

"Possibly, possibly." She frowned thoughtfully at the chart. "We need a different ship, one with more range." She indicated a bright red circle. "That is supposed to be a mothball dock. The question is, what's stored there and who's watching it?"

"How far away?"

"Four hours." She reached across the console and pressed a series of contacts. "From now."

"Even if we get a different ship, Lis, we have a system-full of Armada and automatic surveillance to get through and I'm sure Earth's orbital defenses will take notice of an unauthorized landing. We could get shot through again and again between here and there and still not be able to land."

Lis shook her head at him, clucking her tongue. "Have you always been so pessimistic and I've simply not noticed before?"

"Practical, not pessimistic."

"Let's worry about what we can do before we wonder about what we can't."

"I'd prefer to rejoin the *Isomer*."

"Mmm. I have my doubts any of them will get through."

Fargo watched her uncomfortably. "Why don't we just run then?" He moved behind her and began slowing massaging her neck and shoulders.

Lis frowned. "What do you mean?"

"I mean–damn, Lis, we don't owe any of those people anything! They're Invested. We've got no business messing around in their affairs."

Lis looked worried. She stared at the console.

"Fargo, I–when Yol-Maex made us his liaisons I felt good. I liked that."

"Yol-Maex is probably in detention, probably about to be shipped right back to the Seven Reaches. Armada doesn't follow the same rules everyone else does."

"That's not the point. I liked–well, feeling important again. Freeriding is all right, Fargo, but it's–it's nothing. We're nothing."

"Compared to what?"

"You know what I mean! You pointed it out yourself, so don't try to tell me you haven't been thinking the same things. But beside that we don't do anything, Fargo! What? Going from place to place, playing hide and seek with the port facilities and the ship's sensors, hoping we don't catch a ride with a ship that flushes its holds, like Cana said." Lis blushed. "I'm thinking I don't want to do it anymore."

"Hm. And how do we stop? Maybe if this trade thing had worked you could reinvest, but what about me? I'm just a tagalong. And actually, I doubt you could become Invested again. The feeling against setis is strong. What you're doing is probably going to be a barrier."

"What about our position with Yol-Maex? With the Ranonan? Even if these talks fail, we still have status with them. What could the Vested do to you then?"

"That didn't do us much good this time, did it? Besides, it doesn't look like any seti are going to have much say within the Pan Humana. The Forum, the megas, even the average Invested seem determined to keep them out."

"Then we could go live with the setis! Why are you arguing with me, Fargo? What have we got to lose?"

"Our lives!"

"As freeriders? Not much of a life." Her eyes glistened. "Don't you even want to try?"

Just follow your nature, Daniel had said: run. He had been looking for an opportunity ever since. He thought back over the past days, going over it all looking for the places he might have used to get away. There had to have been at least one. Why was he still here? Running, freeriding, had been a natural rhythm, or so he thought, action easily taken, like breathing. Since Eurasia the rhythm had faltered, broken down. One step after another, stride by skip by jump, he had brought himself to this.

Finish it, he thought. Complete what has begun. See it through.

He swallowed hard and made a throwaway gesture. "Sure, let's try it. I guess I am getting used to being seen when people look at me."

Lis's mouth quivered around a smile. She reached for his hand. "All right, then."

They found the honeycomb structure by a faint beacon. It looked dead to Fargo, lightless and abandoned. Debris floated near a damaged section that appeared to have been struck by a heavy body; they were within a cometary belt that encircled the system, filled with chunks of metal-bearing rock and clumps of organic ice. None of the standard guidance systems on the station seemed to be functioning, so Lis brought them into one of the empty cocoons manually.

"No pressure," she said, frowning at the console. She looked over at Saris. "You've got shells on this thing, don't you?"

Saris nodded. She would not look at Lis; instead she kept her eyes down, her expression surly.

Lis sighed. "Saris, I'm sorry. But what would you do in my place?"

"Same thing," Saris said. "But I'm not in your place. I'm still Invested. Barely."

"If they take it away over something like this, it's not worth having."

"Fuck you! They already took yours away!"

Saris's lips trembled. She sniffed loudly. Fargo glanced at Lis, who continued to study the console. But her jaw twitched tightly. A single tear moved away from her face.

"Keep her company," Lis said, patting Fargo's thigh. "I'm going out and see if I can get us some atmosphere."

"Thanks."

He watched her swim down the corridor. Jen screamed at her as she passed the open hatch.

"Jen always was a bitch," Saris said. She gave Fargo a furtive look. "Lis tell you she used to be Armada?" When Fargo did not react, Saris grunted. "Thought not. Most of your kind wouldn't be too forgiving over that." She frowned. "You and her, there's something?"

"What do you think?"

A speaker on the console snapped and Lis said, "I'm going out now, love. I'll let you know how I do."

"I wouldn't be surprised if she's got a way out," Saris said. "And I wouldn't be surprised if she left you behind."

"What's going on at Charon?" Fargo asked, irritated at Saris.

"Told you, some kind of construction for Estana." She shook her head. "Wouldn't be surprised if she intended to live out here all by herself. She's a recluse, you know. Hates people."

"Really. I didn't know."

"You must be from the Distals."

"Markab, originally. Etacti after that."

"Thought so. You've got an accent. I'm from Neighbors myself."

"How did you end up here?"

"When *Callipygian* was taken over, I left. I didn't want to work for a mega. Trouble was, not many independents were taking on new coes. I couldn't get out of Centauri Transit. Local haulers was the only thing. So one day there was a general hire for Tower Enterprises, a regular run to Sol and back. I managed to make four of them before I got pulled and assigned to outer system tug work."

"Have you ever been to Earth?"

She laughed. "Not once!"

The console speaker cracked again. "Fargo, I've got it working. About another ten minutes you can leave the boat."

Fargo touched a contact. "Too bad. Saris and I were just beginning to get along."

"Should I come rescue you?"

"No. Ten minutes. Where are you?"

"Station cencom. It's all intact and I think I can get most of the systems active."

"Why do that? Are there any other ships in dock we can use?"

"Have to be able to access the system to find out."

"Oh. Sure."

"Ten minutes."

"I'd go in five," Saris said. "She'll leave you."

"I really don't think so."

"You think you know her?"

"It's pretty obvious you don't."

Saris scowled. "She's Armada. You can't fucking trust them. Whatever it is she's into, you'd better get away from it."

"How do you know she's Armada?"

"We crewed together for nearly three years. You notice things about a co. For instance, the way she fights. Good at it, isn't she? Where do you think she learned?"

"I took out your companion." He grinned at her. "How do you know I'm not Armada?"

Saris's eyes widened briefly, then she looked away. "You don't have the look." But she said nothing else and did not look at Fargo again.

At eight minutes, he unbuckled himself and swam toward the airlock.

"–goddamn shit! I'll *kill* you I get out of here! You toadlicker! Sucksilt–"

He pulled himself quickly by Jen's room.

In the lock he checked the equalization. Lis had timed it about right. He cycled through, into the station lock.

The passages were all tubes. A strip of pale blue light glowed along the way led him to cencom. He pulled himself down the handgrips until he came to bulkhead with a ladder. He swam up the short tube into a wide dome.

Fey energies danced over the ceiling. Lis hovered at a broad board, her hands pressed to an interface. A short line held her in place. As Fargo came up beside her, he saw her eyes rolled up, mouth slack.

Suddenly the ceiling went dark. Fargo flinched and looked up. The chaos of light had given way to a panorama of local space.

"That's more like it," Lis said. She smiled at him. "Hey."

"Hey."

"I wager Saris wasn't too happy to see you go."

"Oh, no. Saris was thrilled. Jen, however, cried."

Lis unhooked herself and turned. She studied the various consoles that rimmed the chamber, then pointed. "That one." She kicked off the edge of the board and shot across the room. She caught herself deftly and studied the console.

"What about ships?" Fargo asked. "And how about some gravity?"

"No gravity. The generator was removed." She shook her head. "It still amazes that they'd just leave something like this untended. I mean, it's not that old–it's got a link interface! Other than pseudogravity, everything here still works."

"It's less trouble to leave it than to take apart."

"Yeah, but–" She clipped a line to her belt and faced him. "Hasn't it ever bothered you? The waste?"

"No. In fact, I'm pretty grateful. Freeriders couldn't survive if the Invested didn't throw so much perfectly good stuff away."

"That's what I mean. We're supposed to be disinvested. We're not supposed to have what everybody else has."

"We don't."

"Have you ever gone hungry?"

"No, not really."

"Have you ever not had enough energy to run your gear? For that matter, look at your gear. Each one of us walks around with everything we need, right on our backs. And it's all free, we just have to scrounge for it."

"That's not what we're denied."

"No, it isn't."

Fargo shook his head. "What's your point?"

She blinked at him for a moment, then turned back to console. "I don't know. Just thinking out loud." She looked the controls over. "Good, it still works. Give me a minute, I've got to send a message."

"A *message*–!"

She pressed her fingers to the interface and the console gauges shifted brightly. When she finished, she unhooked and pushed herself back toward him.

"There. Now we just wait."

"For what? Message to who?"

"I don't know."

"You don't–Lis!"

"What are you worried about? Everything will be fine."

Fargo thought about what Saris had said and studied Lis to see if he could tell. Armada? It might explain some things, certainly, but...

But they were linked. He had shared her mind. He would know.

Maybe. If he had shared all of it. Or even the most important parts.

What had Stephen said? More often than not it was simpler to just ask.

He licked his lips. "Saris told me you were Armada."

"Did she? And you want to know if it's true?"

"I'm not sure. But..."

"I did *not* just message the Armada. After everything else I'd expect you to believe I'm on your side." She looked up at the star-filled dome. "You have to take me on faith. If you're not sure about me, I can't prove my innocence."

"So just tell me."

"Well...I was and I wasn't. I failed the course. Two thirds the way through, I burned."

"That's where you got your implants?"

She nodded. "I didn't think you'd trust me if I told you the truth."

Fargo laughed. "Well, it does help to be given a chance to forgive something. At least I know you're not perfect."

She swatted at him and he snatched her wrist. They started to rotate slowly. He tightened his grip, hard, until she winced.

"Never again," he said evenly.

She nodded. "I won't."

He let go.

The communications board signaled.

"Hey, hey," Lis said, and kicked toward it. She touched her fingertips to the panel for a moment, then punched the air. "Our ride is on the way."

Lis prepped an old in-system courier. She gave Saris and Jen tranquilizers and untied them.

"Let them figure out how to explain it," she said.

They took the courier out of the dock. Lis tapped in a set of coordinates she had gotten from the reply to her message and the old boat headed out.

"Where did this all come from?" Fargo asked.

"Yol-Maex. Just in case, he said. I have no idea what to expect, but I don't see that we have very many options right now."

Fargo considered a few, but kept them to himself. The cockpit was quiet and he enjoyed it at the moment. Lis closed her eyes. In seconds she started breathing heavily.

He was tired himself, but he could not bring himself to sleep. He stared at the display of stars. They seemed so far away now, but he picked out several he had been to. It's a small universe, he thought. And patient. It never ends.

He leaned forward suddenly.

A patch of the sky vanished. Black on black, stars that were there a moment before gone...

"Shit..."

The patch widened, occluding more stars. The courier closed with the black seti ship.

Chapter Twelve

Fargo woke Lis as the seti ship blotted out more than half the sky. She tapped the comm panel and sent another signal. A blue light winked on and she smiled.

"Our ride," she said.

A minute later the black ship enveloped them. Fargo started at a heavy vibration that ran through the courier. Then it was silent.

"Now what?" he asked quietly.

"I don't know."

Fargo made an adjustment on the console and studied the readouts. "We're inside something. It's...octahedral...hm. Interesting shape for a bay."

Lis unhooked her belt and floated up. She caught the back of the couch and launched herself down the short gangway, to the lounge compartment.

"So are they going to talk to us?" Fargo called to her.

"I don't know."

"What *do* you know?" he muttered under his breath and released himself from his couch.

Lis was at the dispenser, tapping contacts. She scowled briefly. "Empty. I should've checked. Well, let's hope it's a short ride. I'm hungry." She pushed away and somersaulted in mid-compartment. "It would be nice to get into a positive g field again, too. I'm horny."

"You're joking."

"I never joke about that." She caught the seat of one of the couches and steadied herself. "Adrenalin. I'm saturated."

"Null g isn't a problem."

Lis began unzipping her utilities. "True, but I can't be on top."

Fargo laughed in spite of his anxiety. "Don't you ever worry about anything?"

Lis worked herself out of her clothes and kicked toward him. She braked against his shoulders and they both drifted back to a bulkhead. He bumped his head.

"Love," she said, "right now I'm scared to death. Now get out of these rags."

...green hills, pristine hills, puffy trees, all cloud and azure, he fell toward the lake, flying, but struggling, trying to keep aloft, knowing he didn't know how to do this, couldn't do this, shouldn't do this, but he set down near the shore, stumbling, recovering, and walking, all in the same instant, movement, action, and walked to the edge of the water where geese squawked and waddled out of his way, except one that raised its wings and sang with a pure, clear alto, maybe seti, Ranonan, but one register not three, and he asked if this was the way to Istanbul, and the goose lowered one wing and pointed with the other, and he saw spires on the horizon, glowing green and gold and white, and he thanked the goose, but it came along with him, and when he asked it to go away, its beak shrank into its roundish face and the eyes stretched, bent, turned silver, and Hanna smiled at him and said "I am always with you, Fargo, and through you I am with them" and he saw a group of seti coming down the hill from another point of the horizon, Rahalen, Menkan, Cursian, and a Ranonan in the lead...

He opened his eyes, certain someone watched him. He did not recognize the wall before him; then his perspective shifted slightly and he knew he was staring at the ceiling of the lounge.

He lay on the deck.

He sat up. Gravity.

Lis stretched out on her belly close by. Her mouth was open and a small patch of drool smeared the deck against her face.

The dream startled him. Since boarding the *Isomer* he had not had one, not like those he had experienced on the *Caliban* and later. It possessed the same intense quality of reality. It frightened him, but he could not say why, other than it felt like telelogging...

"Hanna?" he said.

"Mmm?" Lis moaned, opened her eyes. She raised her head and wiped at her mouth. "Fargo?" She pushed herself up and frowned. "Gravity?"

Fargo got to his feet and went into the cockpit.

The viewscreens showed a brightly-lit area outside the boat. Fargo leaned closer and tapped in adjustments, but the details remained unclear. What he saw offered no sharp lines, clear edges, or surfaces with any identifiable details. Everything looked soft, contoured.

A light flashed on the comm panel. Fargo touched the accept.

"When you are prepared," a Ranonan voice said, "please emerge and join us. Environmental amenities are in place."

"We made it," Lis said. She leaned through the hatchway, grinning at him. "Yol-Maex didn't lie."

"I'm not even going to ask," Fargo said.

He retrieved his clothes and dressed. Lis pulled on her own coverall and hurried to the lock.

Fargo hesitated at the top of the ramp. The bay was huge. Across from them, through a tall archway, a group of setis came toward them. One Ranonan, two Rahalen, and a single being that, at first glimpse, looked very human. All but the eyes, which were completely emerald green. He wore a dark blue outfit that seemed military. He stood slightly apart from the other three.

Fargo walked down and joined Lis. The setis stopped and the Ranonan stepped forward.

"Welcome, Co Falco. We are pleased." It looked at Fargo. "And you. Welcome."

Something tickled Fargo's memory. The voice...he would not have thought to be able to tell the difference between seti voices, but this one...

"Voj-Nehan?"

The Ranonan bowed its head. "I am welcome that you recall. Please. You are safe here."

"Where's 'here'?" Fargo asked.

"This is the Embassy of the Manifold of the *Sev N'Raicha*—the Seven Reaches."

"We are not permitted," Voj-Nehan explained, leading them from the bay, "to build an embassy on the surface of Earth, or any planetary body within the Sol System. But our current agreements grant us the right to have an embassy."

"I'm sure the Forum would love to change that," Lis said. "They let you build this?"

"No. It is an old habitat shell. They permitted us to rebuild the interior. It is not very large, but it suits our needs."

"Do you know about the *Isomer*?" Fargo asked. "Yol-Maex and his legation are at an Armada station. The ship has been—"

"We are aware of that. It is being negotiated."

The wide corridors curved, dipped, and rose like a natural landscape. Color varied from mother-of-pearl pink to the palest of blues. The ceilings were high and luminous and the decks were covered with a spongy moss-like carpet. They moved down branchings that seemed to appear after only a few paces, merging seamlessly with other circuits, without logic. Fargo was quickly lost. Voj-Nehan politely greeted those they met, all setis, some races of whom Fargo did not recognize. The air seemed to shimmer around some of them. Before he could ask about it, the answer occurred to him—they carried their environments with them, in a shell very much like a suspensor. The place was quiet, with none of the constant patter of voices and nearly inaudible undertone of machines.

"I'm still surprised," Lis said suddenly, "that they let you have a place this big."

"We have added to it as time passed," Voj-Nehan explained. "There have been few objections. We are monitored constantly by Armada security forces and there is a fission device at the core with which the entire station can be destroyed at a signal from outside. It was never mentioned when we were granted the station, we have not questioned its presence. We have till now experienced amicable relations with Earth."

"But you think that's about to end," Fargo said.

"Perhaps. Yol-Maex is here to negotiate new avenues of commerce and intercourse. Perhaps he will fail, perhaps not."

"What if they order you out?" Lis asked.

"Then we will leave."

"That would be a shame," Fargo muttered. "They may not let you do that unharrassed."

"Regrettably, we have considered that possibility, too. There are factions among humans who will deliberately thwart the proper decisions of the proper authorities. We have a contingent of Vohec here to safeguard the embassy. They will be adequate to defend us in the event of ejection." He looked at Fargo. "It was a Vohec ship that brought you here."

They entered a large chamber with three tiers of seats of various shapes and sizes in a circle around an object that resembled a melting crystal. It pulsed and swirled, threatening to burst the boundaries of its wide stage. About a dozen setis were seated, their attention riveted on the crystal.

Standing behind the last row of seats, Fargo saw five tall, motionless setis dressed in simple, midnight blue uniforms, like the one who had silently followed them from the bay. They were each very beautiful, with skin the color of cedar and bright emerald eyes. He realized then, from their bearing if nothing else, that these were Vohec. Their striking beauty only made them seem more dangerous. He wondered at their human form.

Voj-Nehan directed Fargo and Lis to seats and sat between them. It held a hand out to each.

"Please," Voj-Nehan said. "Think of what occurred."

Fargo did not want to touch the Ranonan. But Lis laid her hand in the larger seti hand. After a few moments, Fargo pressed his palm into Voj-Nehan's.

—the P.M. punched him in the stomach, "Nonhumans and nids, I have no use for either," he walked away from the rest of Isomer's *crew and passengers, down the circuit to detention—*

Fargo blinked at Lis. His breath came fast, as if he had just fallen. It was over.

Voj-Nehan stood and addressed the hall.

"May I proceed?" Everyone's attention fixed on him. Voj-Nehan turned to the flowing crystal. "This is Voj-Nehan of the Ranonan Embassy. It would be appreciated that we may communicate with Shipmaster Cana of the *Isomer*, which ship is within our diplomatic fold, and with her principle passenger, Ambassador Yol-Maex."

From the crystal came a clearly human voice. "We would be happy to oblige your request, Ambassador, but we have no knowledge of such a ship or shipmaster present within our communications matrix."

"You will find the vessel docked at your Armada Station on the perimeter under the command of Reese Albans," Voj-Nehan said. "This vessel, unfortunately, has been detained due to certain misunderstandings regarding events at Aquas Transit Station. However, you will find that our own escort vessel, which now rests three a.u. from the aforementioned Armada station, has followed the *Isomer* to be sure Ambassador Yol-Maex arrived here safely."

Fargo leaned toward Lis. "You knew?"

She nodded.

Silence stretched on. Other setis around the chamber exchanged brief whispered comments.

"We're investigating, Ambassador, please stand by."

Voj-Nehan sat down and folded his hands peacefully on his lap. Several minutes passed; more setis entered and found seats. Little was said. No one seemed in any way impatient, although Fargo wondered if he would recognize impatience in a seti.

"Voj-Nehan," Fargo said. "May I ask a question?"

The Ranonan nodded.

"On Eurasia, did you–"

"It was necessary," the Ranonan said. "We were engaged in a delicate matter and our courier had been compromised. The need of a medium was immediate. I regret not having told you the truth then. It was not my intention to involve either of you to this extent, but we did require certain sources of information not otherwise available. The offer of aid was genuine. Co Falco has been gratifyingly useful–"

"Ambassador Voj-Nehan?" the voice came from the crystal.

"I am here."

"Our apologies for the misunderstanding, Ambassador. The *Isomer* was detained pursuant to a charge filed against it by Aquas Transit Authority. No one was aware at the time of the official status of the ship or crew. We've located everyone that was aboard and we are now servicing the ship. *Isomer* will be released and given an escort to your embassy in 48 hours."

Fargo caught the sharp look from Lis, echoing his own reaction. *Everyone that was aboard...*

"Thank you for prompt attention. I am certain it was a misunderstanding."

Others had already risen and begun to filter out of the chamber. Fargo blew out a long breath and squeezed Lis's hand. He realized suddenly how drained he was. He leaned back in the formfitting chair and closed his eyes.

"Is there anything else you'd like to tell me about what you did on Eurasia?" Fargo asked.

Voj-Nehan regarded him silently for several moments. Then:

"I *did* contribute inducement for your cooperation. An urge to trust us. There may have been other side-effects I was unable to foresee."

"No complaint about the side-effects," Lis said.

"You might have just asked," Fargo said.

"Perhaps. We are still learning about humans. I did not know if you would accept and in fact you did not at first. I will escort you to your rooms now if you wish. You seem tired."

"Mmm," Fargo said.

"I hope you're not too tired," Lis whispered in his ear.

He smiled.

Their "rooms" consisted of one immense space half filled by water, the rest indifferently divided up by waist-high walls, the serpentine curves of which presented no corners.

"What the...?" Fargo mused, staring at the water.

"Hey." Lis smiled. She unzipped her utilities and ran to the edge.

Fargo watched with dismay as she first ran her right foot through it, then walked out, sinking with each step, until the water came up to her shoulders. With a flip he would have thought possible only in null g, she dove, disappearing below the surface.

"Lis!" He advanced toward the water. Ripples spread from the spot where she had vanished. He looked quickly around at the walls for a commlink of some kind, panic rising as she remained under. He took a few steps into the water. It was chilly. The floor angled down. He stopped when it reached his waist.

Suddenly she burst up, spraying water, arms out, almost to the opposite end. Her body settled, her head went down again, then she bobbed at shoulder height, laughing.

She waved at him. "Take your clothes off first! Don't you know how to use a pool?"

"A what?" He backed out of the water. His pants clung to his legs.

She began stroking through the water, arms windmilling slowly, making her way toward him with elegant motions. She stood when she reached the shallow end and walked out. Water ran from her body, glistening.

"It's for swimming," she said.

He stared at her.

"Play?" she added.

"Looks dangerous."

"Well, it can be if you don't–oh. You don't know how to swim?"

"I never heard of such a thing."

She laughed again. "I'm sorry, love. That must've scared you to death!" She touched his face with her wet fingertips. "And you were going to come out to get me? You might have drowned."

"Um. Where did you...?"

"Homestead. Lot of lakes and rivers." She kissed his cheek. "I'll teach you if you want."

He shook his head. "No, you go on and enjoy yourself. I'll watch."

She ran back into the water. Fargo's heart thumped as she jumped in headfirst.

He turned away after a time, convinced finally that she really did know what she was doing. He wandered through the maze of separate areas. The floor was covered in a similar mossy carpet as the corridors. He found no furniture in any of the five segments. He sat down against a wall, facing the pool. Lis continued to splash.

Exhaustion took him quickly into dreamless sleep.

He woke with a start. Lis lay pressed against him. She moaned and rolled over.

The lights had dimmed. The water seemed to stretch even further out. Fargo rubbed his face and sat up. He noticed then that he was naked. He did not remember undressing. Perhaps Lis had done it, perhaps he had without ever quite waking up. He looked around for his discarded clothes–the silks he had been wearing since that first day aboard *Isomer*– and wondered where the ship was now and if Stephen were still aboard.

Nearby he saw two piles of fresh clothes. He leaned toward them and slid his hand over the tunic on top. Silky, but not silk. A thrill ran from his scalp, down his back. Seti fabric.

It did not seem so very much better than what the Pan produced, but it was different, and its implications gave it an exotic quality.

"Hey."

He straightened and looked down at Lis. "Hey."

She stretched luxuriantly, yawning. "I haven't done that in–I don't remember the last time." She pushed herself up against the wall and gazed wistfully at the water. "Yes, I do. The mega liner put in at Homestead and I took personal time. I went down to see my family. That was ten...eleven years ago?"

"You haven't forgotten how?"

"Have you ever forgotten how to breathe?"

He took her hand. "A couple of times. Recently."

She kissed his shoulder. "Didn't mean to scare you."

He shrugged. "I'm not used to this, that's all."

"To what?"

"Before...I haven't been scared of anything since the first time I jumped a ride."

"*Any* thing?"

"Well, you always get nervous before a ride–"

"That's not fear. You're telling me nothing scared you ever?"

"One thing. Owing freight I could never work off. But after you ride for awhile you forget about it. You're just taking care of yourself and occasionally you do a favor for someone, but it's not the same, just stops along the way. You always move on, though. After a time you worry that one of these days you'll stop and stay and–"

"And what?"

"I don't know. What if it's not where you want to be? What if it's a situation you can't live with? What if–"

She put fingertips to his mouth. "What if–just suppose–it's a place you want to be?"

"That's the other problem, isn't it? How would you know?"

"I think I'd be able to tell. I think you would, too."

"But would you believe it? Would you trust it? I was always afraid of owing freight I couldn't pay, but I never thought about *wanting* to owe, not even when I was Invested." He swallowed. "So does it make you scared?"

"So scared I can't get enough of it."

Fargo laughed. "You like all this, don't you?"

Lis sat up, hugging her legs to her breast. "Yes, as a matter of fact, I do. I think you do, too."

"Maybe. We're getting involved."

"I know."

"I don't mean just with each other. All this political shit."

"I know what you mean."

"That doesn't bother you?"

Lis shook her head. "Only that it will end."

Fargo looked at her. There was a sharpness to her expression, a determination that attracted him even while it disturbed him.

She turned her body to face him, crossing her legs. "What about when it's over?"

"Mmm? What do you mean?"

"Well...when we get through all this. What then? What do you want to do?"

"I haven't thought about it," Fargo admitted.

"I have."

"Do you ever do anything spontaneously?"

"I do everything spontaneously, even plan ahead. But listen, I want you to be with me–that's what you've been talking about–and yes, it's scary, and yes, I want it. But I'm going in any case."

"Don't oversell. What do you have in mind?"

"I want to see the Seven Reaches."

Fargo started. "Is that all?"

"No, but the rest depends on that. If we can get there first, then the rest will come later. But we have to get there first."

"And how do you propose to do that?"

"Continue being useful to the setis. They'll be our ticket out. I don't necessarily want to become reinvested–I'd rather be beyond that."

Fargo whistled. "You don't want much, do you? Sounds like you're more interested in becoming Vested."

"I think I've got a real chance to do this, though."

"Why?"

"Because I'm changing the rules."

Isomer slid into the bay, leaving behind the escort of Armada fighters. Pseudopods extruded from the walls and connected themselves to the service ports on the ship's hull. A ramp reached up to an airlock hidden beneath the forward cowl.

The transparency separating the observation deck from the bay dropped away, and Fargo and Lis accompanied Voj-Nehan and a pair of Vohec out to greet those now descending the ramp. Fargo recognized Shipmaster Cana and Barig at once, alongside the Yol-Maex and the other Ranonan delegates. Behind them came the rest of the crew and the few remaining passengers.

He spotted Stephen, sandwiched between Bosh Macken and Sren Kovitcz. Even from fifty meters away he did not look happy.

Voj-Nehan went up to Yol-Maex. The two regarded each other wordlessly for a few seconds. Then Voj-Nehan turned to Cana.

"Gratitude, Shipmaster, for your excellent attention. I hope our compensation will be adequate."

"Thank you, ambassador. My crew will need sanctuary."

"Given. We have been in contact with others to assume responsibility for your remaining passengers." Voj-Nehan made a quick motion at the Vohec.

They moved quickly and met Bosh Macken and Kovitcz at the foot of the ramp. Each Vohec took hold of each man's arm. Macken pulled back and winced suddenly. The Vohec escorted the two men away from Stephen and toward a different exit.

"Accommodations have been prepared," Voj-Nehan said.

Fargo went to Stephen.

"Good to see you again, co," he said.

Stephen warily watched the setis. He nodded absently. He looked pale.

"Don't worry, co," Fargo said, "they only look when asked." Stephen scowled at him, then flushed hotly.

"Come on. You're staying with us." He took Stephen's arm. Stephen tried to draw away, but Fargo yanked him closer. "Don't make a scene or I'll have a Ranonan take you to your room. They're telelogs, too."

Stephen's face lost all color. He let Fargo bring him along.

"There are Distal ships ten a.u. out from the ecliptic," Cana told them. She kept looking toward the pool. Food was spread over a cloth between them. Yol-Maex and Voj-Nehan knelt side by side on along one edge of the cloth. Stephen sat just within earshot, as far from the setis as possible. "A fleet, from what we heard. The Armada has assigned a squadron of fighters to 'protect' the seti embassy from them." She grunted, then picked up a slice of meat that resembled beef. "They didn't want to release us. Aquas wants us in detention permanently, but the current treaty obligates them to respect seti possessions."

"That treaty won't hold for long," Fargo said. "The only reason they're abiding by it is because they don't know all the possibilities yet. As soon as they're sure of themselves that treaty will be worthless."

"I agree," Cana said. "The frontier interests know that, too. I doubt that fleet is there only for transportation."

"It appears to us," Yol-Maex said, "that your various factions are preparing to fight."

"They are," Fargo said.

"Relations have been decaying for a long time," Cana said. "If for no other reason than they haven't improved. Nothing stands still. We're watching the final breakdown."

"Why?" Voj-Nehan asked.

Cana blinked at the seti. "Because..." She laughed nervously and shook her head. "Ask me a hard one." She raised her hand and counted. "One, the Forum wants a cessation of all diplomatic contact. No more commerce, no more interaction. Seal the borders. Two, they want that because the Vested want it and *they* want it because the Seven Reaches represent something they don't control. Three, the Chairman has been losing influence in the Forum for several years, mainly because of her unwillingness to close off relations with you. She wants interaction, open trade. But with the megacorps against the idea and the Forum supported mainly by the Vested, Tai Chin doesn't have a chance. She's proseti, but her power is in decline."

"We recognize the precarious balance in which you maintain your economy, but the influx of new goods would more than off-set any deleterious effects."

"But that very influx," Fargo said, "will benefit frontier interests. After all, they are closer to you. Everything will go through them on the way to the Inner Pan. The Primary Vested are already worried about the new wealth in the Distals. They've kept control by denying status to coes who are by every other standard Vested. That won't last long, either. The Distals want open borders *because* it will make them stronger. No matter which way it goes here, there's going to be fighting."

"We will not fight with you," Voj-Nehan said.

"This war won't be with the Seven Reaches," Lis said. "It'll be civil war."

"So the question I have," Cana said, "is if it comes to that, will you support the Distal colonies?"

"This," Yol-Maex said, "is what I have come to prevent."

"Hanna wants to prevent it, too," Stephen said. "But I'm not sure she can."

"What's her interest?" Fargo asked. "Hanna's a synthetic intelligence."

Stephen shook her head. "I can't tell you yet."

Fargo drew a deep breath, feeling his impatience rise. "So what does Daniel have to do with this?"

"Hanna wants us to get him back from Tesa Estana."

"Why?"

"Because she'll damage him. Hanna cares. We're like her children." He looked up suddenly at the Ranonans. "When we heard that the Seven Reaches were sending a new diplomatic mission we had no idea you'd be telelogs."

"You humans," Yol-Maex said, "attempted the same. A crude attempt, but conceptually elegant. The fundamental incompatibility between races caused considerable discomfort, but it did not, as you evidently believed, destroy our desire for communion. It took time to create the solution."

Stephen frowned. "You aren't natural telepaths?"

"No. Nor are you. We have been bred to it."

Stephen ran the tip of his tongue across his lips. He stood and walked to the Ranonans. Voj-Nehan rose. Hesitantly, Stephen reached out and touched hands with the seti. His expression blanked, then tightened. He stepped back and his eyes widened.

"An entire species bred for one function?"

"We need to understand," Yol-Maex said. "We have been trying all along. Ranonans are the current opportunity to commune effectively."

"That's fascinating," Cana said, "but we have more immediate concerns. I ask again, ambassadors, if the Distals secede from the Pan Humana, will you help us? It may be the only way for you to continue a relationship with humans."

"New worlds will be made available," Voj-Nehan said. "Resources can be provided. Again, I must say that we will not fight."

"That might be exactly what we need, though."

Yol-Maex held out its hands. "Then you will do what you can."

Chapter Thirteen

Earth came into view from behind the moon. The Chairman's personal shuttle moved with seemingly stately grace through the cloud of artifacts that danced around the planet like insects. The technological history of human-kind in space could be traced through the layers and ranks of satellites and habitats.

Fargo leaned on the railing that surrounded the wide plat-form and looked down on the green and blue and white planet.

So this is our birthworld...

The surface looked devoid of urbanization. He recalled his history classes, about the Collapse and Reformation. In-dustry was not so much moved into orbit and onto the moon as it was reestablished off the planet. Many thousands of cities and towns were abandoned, later torn down, and those that remained rebuilt to an ideal made possible by the sudden access to the material wealth of space. It was a story every child in the Pan grew up learning. Fargo doubted it had been as noble, as collective an enterprise as the stories depicted.

But Earth is certainly beautiful, he thought.

Lis rested her hands on the rail beside him. Fargo glanced back across the open deck of the shuttle. An or-nate boathouse huddled against the opposite end, but the rest looked like the top of a barge, exposed to vacuum. The Ranonans huddled together with the pair of Vohec that had come with them, midway down the length of the shuttle deck. Armada security people stood here and there, stay-ing aloof but vigilant.

"A bit showy," Lis commented, "don't you think?"

"If you've got it," Fargo said and shrugged.

The shuttle moved faster than it appeared to. Already it was entering the outer sphere of satellites and the Earth filled the sky before them. Fargo tightened his grip.

"Where's Stephen?" he asked.

"Inside," Lis jerked her thumb toward the boathouse.

"Smart."

"Boring."

Suddenly his perspective shifted. Instead of moving toward the Earth, they now fell. The shuttle cut through the upper atmosphere and began spiralling down. As it dropped below the cloud deck Fargo felt panic. He had never seen an ocean before. It took a moment to realize that everything he saw was water.

Then they began to level out, just as the shuttle came over land. A sense of velocity increased as they drew closer to the surface. The shuttle hurtled over an arid landmass, then shot out across water once more. Fargo could not move, though he desperately wanted to. He told himself that they would not crash, that he would not fall off, that there was nothing to fear, but his hindbrain did not listen and his stomach crawled with rising terror.

An island appeared on the horizon, grew quickly, and slid beneath them. Fargo closed his eyes and breathed deeply. When he opened them again the shuttle was coming in to land on a platform adjacent to an enormous, arch-roofed building. The boat settled into place and the faint vibration he had felt through his boots all the way from the seti embassy abruptly ceased.

All at once wind blew across his face; the suspensor field was gone.

"Shit," he exhaled. Lis laughed and took his hand.

He wrinkled his nose at the smell of the air. Above, the sky seemed to burn with blue fire.

"Are we ready?" Fargo asked.

"No," Lis said. "But hey."

"Hey."

Stephen emerged from the boathouse and joined them at the head of the ramp that lowered to the tarmac. The security guards hurried down and spread across the open field. A signal passed to the one that waited with the ambassadors and she nodded.

"Proceed," she said.

Fargo, Lis, and Stephen walked with the trio of Ranonans and their Vohec escorts. Fargo paused when his foot touched the polycrete. Earth, he thought again. He shuddered and continued on to the terminal.

They crossed the threshold beneath a high archway and the air became cooler by several degrees. Until then Fargo had not noticed how warm it was outside. The sweat that had begun to collect under his arms evaporated quickly.

The clatter of their footsteps echoed sharply. Fargo looked up. The terminal stretched overhead in a deceptive collection of struts and arches. The tall windows that let light flood in along its length lent it a cathedral grace. Except for the party of dignitaries waiting just inside the archway the place was empty of people. Litter gathered in corners; clusters of service booths and data terminals dotted the floor; kiosks bristled with untended goods.

One of the officials came forward. She was tall and her face seemed drawn by tension. She wore a simple ivory blouse and crimson pants.

"Welcome, ambassadors," she said. "I am Celia Taris, First Advisor to the Chair. I'm to escort you to the Saray. Chairman Tai Chin is very excited."

She waved them toward the waiting group. Fargo saw then that they stood on a small platform. Seats rimmed the edge.

"We accept your welcome," Yol-Maex said. The tritone voice danced in the air around them. Several of the officials looked up, startled, and smiled. "I trust you will also familiarize us with what we may expect."

"As best I can. Shall we go? Security has made sure we're safe, but I would suggest we not linger."

"Is our safety a question?"

Fargo stepped toward the platform and the group moved with him. As he stepped up he looked down the length of the terminal, to the vanishing point, and noticed shadows moving. Armada security.

"A question of protocol," Celia Taris said. "We have cleared the port for your arrival. The merchants and administrators are happy to accommodate us, but we don't wish to abuse their good will."

"Was this necessary?" Voj-Nehan asked. "Such places, filled with humans, are among the pleasures of our journey here."

"Believe me, Ambassador, it was for the best."

Fargo nodded to the officials. Most of them looked young. Rich clothes, careful expressions, very clean.

"Ah, may I present my staff?" Celia Taris said. "These are my aides, Lyle Herman, Helen Ditmar, and Bol Regilan. This is Niles Cagess, head of security for the Saray, and his aides..."

Fargo forgot the others as quickly as he heard their names. He studied Cagess and saw, on second look, an older man. He moved casually from place to place on the platform, keeping the Vohec in sight.

"Our human liaisons," Yol-Maex said. "Lis Falco, Stephen Christopher, and Doran Alexander."

Fargo started at the sound of his full name. He stared at the Ranonan for a moment, then recovered himself. He made a smile, but caught Cagess watching him.

"That's Fargo to my friends," he said. He reached out and began clasping hands. Lis and Stephen did so as well, but no one offered to touch the setis.

"My secretary," Yol-Maex continued, "Kes-Veran. Our aides, Johl Garres and Rhil Apellon."

"Your pardon, Ambassador," Cagess said, "but your aides are not the same...race...as yourselves?"

"No. They are Vohec projections."

"Projections...?"

"The concept is difficult to explain...they adapt to suitable form. Their natural state remains unchanged, elsewhere, and what we see is projected."

The humans looked at each other uneasily.

"Very accommodating," Fargo said. "I wish I could do that. Change faces for the occasion."

Nervous laughter rippled through the group.

"Shall we be on our way?" Celia Taris suggested. "Please, take seats."

Fargo sat next to Stephen, across from the seti. "How are you doing, co?" he asked quietly.

Stephen frowned. "She's not telling everything," he said quietly.

"Who? Taris?"

Stephen nodded. "She's worried. She's anxious to get out of here."

The platform lifted from the floor and began moving down the length of the terminal.

Suddenly people filled the hall, pressing against the platform. Fargo grabbed his seat even as his legs tightened to flee. Thousands of people screamed and shouted, enraged, shaking fists at the passengers, faces contorted in visceral madness.

"Damn!" he barely heard Cagess over the din. The man spoke into his palm.

The setis twisted in their seats, surveying the scene. The two Vohec were half out of their chairs, one on either side of the three Ranonan.

The officials had all flinched at the first onset of noise, but now sat, not quite calmly, but not reacting to the invective of the mob. The Vohec sat back down uncertainly. The platform moved forward unimpeded. Fargo felt no impact from the bodies they should have been plowing through. He looked around. Object flew toward them from the crowd–rocks, bottles, bars of metal–but none of them reached the platform.

Taris turned from the railing and mouthed at them "Stay calm!" The platform gained speed. Fargo stood and looked

back over the heads of the rioters. The far edge seemed to
follow them, a fuzzy line that never got further away.

The platform veered and plunged into a tunnel. The noise
ceased immediately.

Fargo sat down.

"Holos," Lis said.

"Cagess," Taris said coldly.

"My apologies, First Advisor. I thought we had proofed
against such an incursion."

Taris glared at him. She sighed slowly. "Ambassadors, my
apologies–"

"No need," Yol-Maex said. "It was interesting. Most in-
structive."

"I was beginning to think no one wanted to welcome us,"
Lis said.

The platform slid into the aft end of a canopied hovercraft
docked at a quay. Fargo nervously peered down at the waves
breaking against the jagged shore and bleached stones of the
jetty.

"The island is artificial," one of the officials was saying.
"Minos is the regional spaceport. Spacecraft aren't allowed to
land in the capital itself."

"How far are we from the capital?" Voj-Nehan asked.

"Oh, not even a hundred kilometers. I'm sure you'll enjoy
this, Ambassadors. The approach to Istanbul...marvelous!"

The hovercraft moved away from the island, heading west.
Fargo wished they would rise higher above the deep blue water.

After a few kilometers, they turned north. Asia rose to
their right. The uncluttered shoreline soon gave way to collections of buildings, warehouses and offices. The collections
grew denser.

"There," someone said.

To the left the Old City stood on its peninsula.

Fargo crossed the platform and stared, transfixed. Gold
and brass caught sunlight, splintered it, and glowed with

spectral antiquity. New structures and old melded, absorbed by each other over time, creating a composite that Fargo recognized from the fragments of design human habitation used across the Pan. It spoke to a past Fargo knew little about, spoke to his culture-laden underbrain, and stirred the sensation of remembrance.

"It's beautiful," Lis said.

"Capital of Earth," Taris said, voice thick with pride, "and center of the Pan Humana. I think it fits the role."

As they neared, smaller structures separated from the amalgam. White buildings, peaked roofs, cobbles, brick, old iron...humans had been nowhere else long enough to leave behind something like this. Boats bobbed on the water near the shore.

"I'm curious, First Advisor," Fargo said. "What do you do with your disinvested population?"

Celia Taris frowned at him. "There are no disinvested on Earth. Certainly not in Istanbul."

"Ah. I see."

Lis pursed her lips and gave him a slight shake of the head. "Timing, love, timing," she whispered.

The setis stared at Istanbul. Fargo wondered how their cities compared. Better? Worse? Neither. Just different, he thought, and realized that he wanted to find out. He looked at Lis, amazed at himself. The desire was growing, opened by Istanbul from the seed Lis had planted. She was looking at him oddly and he felt himself wearing a grin.

They reached the edge of the peninsula. A massive structure of broad domes and eight mismatched towers dominated the southernmost end.

"The Blue Mosque," Taris said. "Originally there were only six minarets. Two were added in the late Twenty-First Century to commemorate Istanbul's accession as capital."

Fargo could not imagine a more alien structure. He looked beyond it, across the expanses of red-tiled roofs and white walls and felt suddenly apart from these people. Another huge building appeared, then a third, and then they rounded the northern end of the peninsula and entered a wide waterway spanned by a series of bridges. Traffic choked them; ground effect craft crossed the water from one side to the other, vying for space among boats with sails.

Like a mountain of chalk and pearl, the palace grew out of the ridge before them. It dominated the city just on the other side of the narrow canal. Parts of it looked organic, but Fargo found enough symmetry, enough of the stamp of artifice to recognize it as a made place. The hovercraft began to rise. It headed straight for the wall of columns and archways a hundred meters above the water. Somehow one path was chosen and the palace swallowed them up.

At the end of a long tunnel the platform detached from the hovercraft and ascended a shaft capped by a square of open sky. Fargo squinted into the brightness as they rose into the open.

"Now, *that*," Fargo whispered to Lis, "was a bit showy."

She shook her head. "I don't know. Practical, I'd say. Could you find your way back out from here?"

They stood in the center of a garden. Neatly pruned trees and shrubs followed winding paths that led to a modest house at one end. A chest high wall surrounded the area.

Celia Taris stepped off the platform, followed by her two aides. Cagess stood apart from everyone. He spoke into his palm, then stopped when he noticed Fargo watching him.

Fargo went to the wall. Below lay the city. From this height it looked like a series of low, rolling hills, red and white and patches of green parkland. Enormous mosques and minarets poked through the jumble of humbler structures. To the east a wall, dotted with towers, ran from north to south, where the peninsula merged with the mainland. Beyond he saw more city, on to the horizon.

"Welcome to the Galata Saray."

A small woman stood on the wide portico before the house. Her silver hair closely framed a vaguely Asian face that seemed too young. She wore a deep blue robe, belted by a golden sash. As he approached, Fargo realized how small she really was, almost childlike.

"I am pleased to finally meet you, Ambassadors," she said when they mounted the portico. Celia Taris stood just behind her, dwarfing her. "I am Erin Tai Chin, Chairman of the Pan Humana, President of the Colonial Forum. You are welcome to my home."

She held out her hands palms up.

"I regret the tangle through which you've had to find your way here," she said.

"It was not," Yol-Maex said, "without interest. We have looked forward to this meeting. The impediments you mention were not all of your doing. Those which were we recognized as institutional."

Erin Tai Chin's eyebrow went up.

"On the journey," Yol-Maex continued, "we made contact with many humans and, where possible, came to accommodations. Failure had less to do with the conditions of our negotiations than with an incapacity to recognize the legitimacy of our attempts. A failure to imagine a possible outcome other than separation. It is our desire to change this."

"You're direct, Ambassador."

"Yes."

Tai Chin laughed softly, an old, tired laugh, but still amused. Tai Chin turned. "Please. Come inside, all of you. Let's be comfortable if we're going to start right in."

Fargo looked around the garden again. None of Taris's aides stood nearby. He could not see Cagess and his people. He felt giddy all of a sudden. The absurdity of his position hit him and it struck him funny. A nid, disinvested, outcast, welcomed by the Chairman of the Pan Humana. He bit his lower lip and stopped the laughter before it came out. His legs quivered slightly as he entered the Chairman's house.

The roof opened to the sky. Sunlight fired the ivory walls between tall windows covered by translucent curtains that waved slightly in the breeze. Tai Chin led them to a circle of backless couches around a low crystal table filled with food.

"Please," she said, "be welcome. Eat, drink." She poured a glass of red wine and sat on the edge of a couch.

Fargo gratefully did the same, and sat very still, holding the glass in both hands. Taris gave him a smoldering look, then seemed to recover herself.

"Ambassadors," Tai Chin said, "I regret the sorry state in which you find us. We can't seem to agree what to think about you."

"Humans are diverse," Yol-Maex said. "Impressive. We do not, nor did we ever, expect unanimity. We are concerned that those who fear interaction dominate. Our contact since first encounter has become more and more limited."

"What do you want me to do? If people are afraid of you I can't tell them there's nothing to fear and stop treating you badly. Even if there were nothing to fear, they wouldn't believe me."

"You are the one chosen to speak for them."

"Not by all of them." Tai Chin smiled wryly. "I have a certain amount of power, but it is limited. For instance, I can't go counter to the Forum for long on any given issue. Eventually, if I were stubborn, a recall election could be held and I would be removed. Complicated and expensive, but not without justification. The Forum is closer to what the populace wants, though even there we're talking about a select portion of the populace."

"You do not dictate then?" Voj-Nehan asked.

"Sorry. The office I hold is a remnant of an era when it was actually possible for one person to lead a state." She held up her hand, thumb and forefinger open by a few centimeters. "A very small, easy to imagine state. Even then, too hard a dictate more likely shattered the state than directed it." She shrugged. "What I am is a symbol. What I do is taken as a kind of emblem of what the Pan ought to be like. This house, the garden outside, a good portion of the Galata Saray itself, even Istanbul proper–very public places, seen by billions, sometimes daily. This is what the acceptable citizen aspires to copy." She pointed to a vase across the room. "Daffodils are the flower of choice right now. Go into any wealthy household in the Pan–and probably in quite a few not-so-wealthy ones–and you'll find imported daffodils somewhere. The wine is an ancient Norton and so it is the wine of choice in the Pan. Even my clothes and the sheets on my bed are signifiers. My power is the power of aesthetic dictate."

Fargo laughed sharply. "So you hope to make getting along with setis fashionable?"

"It sounds amusing, I know," she said, smiling. "But politics and philosophy can be swayed by fashion. In fact, if you read our history, you might believe they are nothing but fashion. But seriously, it's not far from that. It's a question of orchestration. How do I present the idea; to cut through all the other ideas that currently dominate. And, yes, part of what I do is suggest philosophies. You've seen the TEGlink of my discussions with scholars? Why do you think I bother? But I can't be too radical."

She looked at the Ranonan's, the smile gone, her eyes narrow and intense. "So I asked you here to find out how to do this. To be able to do this at all I need honesty, Ambassadors. Specifically, what is it you want from us?"

"That is difficult to translate. We wish to be among you. There is a Rahalen word–en-shi. It describes the unexpected wonder that comes out of a new combination. The Seven Reaches, as you call our combined communities, is the result of en-shi. We wish to have this with you."

"But–" Tai Chin's eyebrows drew together and her eyes shifted away. "You've come as a trade legation. What kind of trade? What do we have that you want?"

"You refer to material trade," Voj-Nehan said.

"Of course."

"Nothing." Voj-Nehan looked at Fargo, Lis, and Stephen. "This is what we do not understand. We see that much of your policy is based on a concept of limited material resource. The structure of your society divides its members into groups based on the quantity of personal resource. This puzzles us. It must be clear to you that there is no limit. You have come to the stars. In so doing you have found all you will ever need. You have colonized nearly sixty systems within your sphere of expansion. A civilization that has reached this stage has passed the point where material concerns are important. It is a baseless concern. Yet you still think like the planetbound people you used to be. You seem worried that it will all vanish tomorrow."

Tai Chin nodded slowly. "I see. Yes, you're quite right. For the most part. If anything we have too much, we can do almost whatever we like. Our colonies are proof. You've been to Eurasia, Ambassador? Yes, I thought I was told that. Have you ever seen such an impractical place? Who in their right mind would live there if it were as difficult as it looks to do so? But we built it. Simply because we could."

"I would have thought you had built it to give a shape to an idea."

"Hmm. Well, perhaps the people who actually did the work saw it that way. But–ah! Silliness! Orbitals are cheaper, easier, and damn sight safer." She laughed. "Did you hear me? Cheaper. Even I can't stop thinking that way and I *know* it's meaningless."

She looked at Fargo.

"You're wondering if that's true. It is, I assure you. In that case, you want to know why we have a class structure. To put it bluntly, why have you had to live the last four years the way you have?"

Fargo blinked. "Excuse me...?"

"You're disinvested," she said, then glanced at Lis. "Both of you. How did you make it here?"

Fargo stiffened. He felt Lis's hand on his arm, a brief squeeze.

Taris stepped forward. "I checked their ID! They're with the legation!"

"I'm certain you checked, Celia, and I'm certain that their ID is valid now. They are with the Ranonans. But they were of the disinvested." She smiled at her aide. "You couldn't have known."

Stephen frowned. "How could you?"

Tai Chin shook her head impatiently. "Let me explain things to you. Have you ever wondered why it's so easy for you to do what you do?"

"I wouldn't call it easy," Lis said.

"Don't disappoint me! With all the technology at our command, how hard do you think it would really be to keep you off our ships? You've never wondered?"

"Chairman—" Taris said.

"Oh, please, Celia, how often to I get a chance to be honest? I have a perfect audience for it." She leaned forward eagerly. "Think, Co Alexander–Fargo? Think! Each of you freeriders carries around on your person enough technology and power to make you wealthy enough to be Vested two centuries ago. And where do you get it? From the refuse of everyone else. It's given to you. Certainly you have to be intelligent enough to use it, but there are plenty of others to teach you. And you jump aboard any ship passing by and go to the next system. Occasionally you're caught and made to work off your passage. But then you're released to do it again. Not even arrested."

"We don't exist," Lis said. "How can you arrest us if we're not real?"

"That's a legal nicety. It's true because we say it is, not because it really is. Ask yourself why we would do that? Why we would classify you nonexistent and then virtually enable you to thrive? Give you access to transportation, feed you, clothe you, house you, let you do what you want to? Any other era you would have been killed for sport."

"Are you so sure that's not happening?" Fargo asked.

Tai Chin's expression shifted between bafflement and irritation. "Why would we do all this for you? Why would we be so accommodating to people who we have in every other respect shut out?"

"I don't know, Chairman," Fargo said loudly. "Maybe you're all just perverse."

Tai Chin grinned. "I won't argue with you there. But please, *think!* What you do is not as difficult as it could be."

"Control," Lis said.

Tai Chin stabbed the air approvingly. "Very good. Nids are a useful mythology. If we actually controlled you the way everyone thinks we do, not many people would believe you exist. But you're everywhere. You're seen. You're common knowledge. You're not invisible at all."

"To what purpose?" Yol-Maex asked.

"Co Falco said it. Control." She shrugged and gave Celia Taris a delighted smile. "As the illusionist says, it's all done with mirrors."

"But—" Voj-Nehan began.

"She's told you, Ambassador," Lis said. "They do it to maintain control. It's a question of power. The Vested, the Invested, the Disinvested—it keeps everyone afraid that what they have could be lost. That way the Vested gain and hold power."

"That is clear," Voj-Nehan said. "What we do not understand is what your Vested hold power against."

Tai Chin looked old and sad again. "Against the loss of power."

Fargo got out of the immense bed. Lis slept on, apparently at ease with their surroundings, but the size of the suite and everything in it kept Fargo on edge. He padded out to the broad balcony that surrounded this wing of the residence.

Istanbul glimmered below with ghostly phosphorescence. The water caught moonlight and shattered it.

It all looked so unchanging, untouchable. People could come and go and *this*, at least, would remain the same. He knew that was as much an illusion as any other image of permanence. On the way to this wing Tai Chin had taken them through a small gallery. The paintings, statuary, chemical photographs, sigils of various types sealed in cases against decay all depicted the past, vanished, mutated, or absorbed signs of civilizations before the present. War, destruction, death, all common themes. Change, often and often violent.

Still, it was pleasant for a moment to imagine that something–the city before him–would never change.

"One of the pleasures of my office."

Fargo stepped back from the railing. Tai Chin stood a few meters away. Fargo felt suddenly self-conscious; he wished he had bothered to pull on a robe.

She approached the rail. She looked almost like a child in the pearly glow from the city.

"It's beautiful, don't you think? I have never tired of this view. Are you familiar with Istanbul's history, Fargo?"

"I'm afraid I didn't even know what it looked like till recently. I never expected to be here."

She nodded abstractedly. "Istanbul has only been conquered three times in its twenty-eight hundred years. The sultans of the Turkish era gave it the name 'Sublime Porte'. I've always like that. It's only been called Istanbul for three hundred and six years."

"You're a telelog."

"I'm sorry for this afternoon, Fargo. I embarrassed you. I apologize. It's not fair, what we do to you. To the disinvested. I don't subscribe to the opinion of the Vested, that we need you as a threat to keep order. Becoming a nid is a kind of social purgatory where sinners can be sent, but I don't believe in sin either."

"Could you change it?"

She shook her head. "After what I intend to do here with your seti friends I doubt I'll be able to change my mind anymore." She sighed. "I was elected Chairman in 2183. More than half a century ago, Fargo. I've been Chairman longer than any other. In all that time I've been continuously opposed by the megas because I have tried consistently to loosen their hold on the Pan. When First Encounter happened, I dreamed that I could finally do it. They offered us all a way out. I never thought it would be so damn hard." She faced him. "I don't expect to remain Chairman much longer. I hope to leave the door open for us, though. If I'm successful here over the next several days, the Forum will be forced to deal with the Seven Reaches and maybe that will be enough. But I'm using everything I have. Favors, bribes, blackmail. Once I spend it I'll have nothing left. What the next Chairman does with you...I'll leave my recommendations behind, of course, but..."

"The megas are killing us. I've seen it. They void their holds before making transition. If we're such a necessary threat, why would they do that?"

She turned back to the view. After a time Fargo believed she had forgotten his presence. Quietly, he backed away, returning to the oversized bed. He did not sleep well.

Chapter Fourteen

Fire, columns, stairs, faces pressed side by side, rushing, she stood at the top, metal face and eyes red, staring down, stopping the hurrying army with a look, the crackle of fallen walls and sandaled feet, the snick and snap of metal on metal, bones breaking, screams and moans all around, and they wait, lungs pumping fast, blood scouring adrenalin, feeding the lust, the hunger, the cannibal imperative, and she raised her arms and spoke and her voice came out cold and light, warm and thick, pain and beauty, "Listen, spirit, child of Sol, sustain for me this song of the various-minded man, who sacked the innermost citadel, wandered endlessly from shore to shore, ever further from home, and those who follow cut off from all hope, cast out by their own witlessness, who killed for meat the body of the sun..."

Fargo sat up. His lungs heaved. Sweat runneled down his back, stung his eyes. Images of fire flickered through his imagination. He squinted into bright morning sun.

"Shit..."

Fargo jerked around. Lis lay next to him, eyes open to the ceiling. She was pale. He watched her throat flex with a swallow.

"Was it good for you?" Fargo asked.

"I haven't had a dream like that in days," she said. She frowned. "It seemed familiar."

Fargo leaned forward and pressed his hands against his eyes. The intensity lingered. Gradually his pulse slowed. He looked around the suite. They were alone, it was just a dream.

"Leftovers," Lis said, rolling out of bed. "Rich food, new surroundings...too much too fast."

Fargo nodded to himself. Yes, he thought, just a dream. It contained none of the intimate imagery of the previous

ones. Only the intensity remained. He decided Lis was right.
Just a dream.

"I'm starving," Lis said. She sat down, naked, at the round
table near the balcony. "How does a co get service here?"

"Please make your request," a soft, modulated voice said,
"and the household system will serve."

Lis grinned. "Breakfast, please."

"Do you wish to review a menu?"

"No. Whatever the Chairman is having for breakfast will
be fine. Two of those."

"Please wait."

Fargo swung his legs around. "You make yourself right at
home, don't you?"

"Of course. Hey, who knows when they'll take it away?
Indulge now, before it's too late."

Fargo groaned as he stood. "Where's the cube?"

"No cube. There's a bathroom." She pointed.

He entered a room as large as his cabin on the *Isomer*.
Well, he thought as he urinated into an ornate porcelain
bowl, what good is it to be Chairman if you can't have
too much room to piss in? He laughed and went to the
shower. The basin alone was larger than most shipboard
cubes.

He came out drying himself with a thick towel. A motile
had arrived with breakfast.

"The Chairman eats too little," Lis said, "but it's all good.
Yogurt, fresh orange slices, coffee, and toast." She waved him
to the chair opposite. "Sit, eat. Otherwise I'll get it all."

"What is yogurt?" he asked, eyeing the cup of pale goo
dubiously.

"Uh…try it. Trust me on this."

He pushed it away and reached for the oranges. Lis made
a face and took his yogurt.

"So," he said, "what happens next?"

Lis nodded toward the motile still standing by the table. A
flatscreen on one end displayed an itinerary.

"Most of the other delegates arrive today," she said. "There's an informal reception in another garden. Tai Chin only received the seti legation here."

Fargo read down the list of names until he came to Kol Janacek. He stared at it silently.

"You could confront him if you want," Lis said.

"He probably doesn't even know who I am. Or was." He shook his head. "No. Why make trouble now? It could complicate what's already too complicated." He read on. "Tesa Estana is the last."

"That's surprising. Everything I've heard about her, she's a complete recluse."

"I saw her. Maybe she used to be, but...I guess if you want something bad enough you'll do anything."

"The festivities commence at ten. We should dress."

"What do we do when we get there?"

Lis shrugged as she scraped Fargo's yogurt bowl clean. "Stand there looking like we belong and see what there is to see." She stood, reached across the table and ran her fingers across his cheek, then headed for the bathroom.

Fargo looked at the screen. "House?"

"Yes."

"Do you have any biographical data on Tesa Estana?"

"Seventy-six popular biographies, a compilation of journalism covering her career, anecdotal entries, various prospecti of her holdings–"

"A summary, an overview. Most pertinent and accurate."

"There are eight definitive accounts with accuracy ratings of plus eighty percent."

"Give me the highest rated."

The screen cleared and text began to scroll. Fargo sipped coffee and leaned closer.

Fargo ascended the wide staircase into bright sunshine over a grassy field. Tents fluttered in the light breeze. People talked in small groups while motiles moved among them bearing trays of drinks and *hors d'oeuvres*. People in dark maroon livery carried salvers between groups. He recognized several people from the *Isomer*, especially Bosh Macken, who stood beside a tall man with nearly white hair and dark skin: Kol Janacek.

Fargo veered away from them. He found Lis with Yol-Maex and one of the Vohec, under a broad white canopy, talking quietly with two women.

"–a tradition of music reminiscent of your baroque period," the Ranonan was saying. "The Rahalen boast that it extends back nearly two thousand years. If true, then they have done little to improve upon it in all that time. The metamorphosis of human music fascinates us."

"How is it distributed in the Seven Reaches?" one of the women asked.

Lis smiled at Fargo. "Enjoy your reading?"

"Very enlightening. I have a lot to tell you. Where's Stephen?"

"I haven't seen him today. I half expected him with Janacek."

"I'm going to wander and see if I can find him."

"–then how do you isolate a market and define profit?" the other woman was saying as Fargo drifted away.

A motile rolled by and he picked a glass from its tray.

Beneath the different tents stood tables and chairs. Cakes, breads, fruits, and other things Fargo did not recognize were picked over by the guests. He overheard snatches of conversation as he worked his way among them. Fashion, Q, travel, production, distribution, gossip–once he thought he heard the word "seti" mentioned, but when he paused to listen closer he lost the thread. He heard Langish spoken with a dozen accents from all over the Pan and recognized at least one variant from the Distals.

The human servers, he noticed, took messages on their salvers. He watched an austere man in long grey robes write something on a notepad provided by the server, tear the page off, fold it twice, and place it on the tray. He then bent to the server's ear, whispered, and the man nodded and went off.

He did not see Stephen.

He stopped halfway around the grounds. Talking with a trio of people who, by their long brocade vests Fargo recognized as from Procyon, stood a tall man with a neatly-combed beard: Andrew.

Carefully, he retraced his steps back to Lis.

She raised her eyebrows curiously. Before he could say anything, Yol-Maex excused itself from the conversation and rounded on him.

"It is the same Andrew?" Yol-Maex asked.

Fargo stared at the Ranonan. "Y-yes..."

"Indicate."

Fargo pointed to him. The seti nodded and raised its hand. A moment later a human server arrived. Yol-Maex took the notepad from the tray and began writing. Yol-Maex leaned toward the young girl and she visibly resisted backing away. She nodded at the instructions and hurried off.

"We may see now if Stephen's friend may be located," Yol-Maex said and returned to the discussion he had interrupted.

"Novel method of conducting business," Fargo commented. "You don't actually think Andrew will answer us?"

Lis shrugged. "Depends on how the question is asked. So, tell me about Estana."

"Too much and not enough. She does have a reputation as a recluse. Apparently, as a child she heard voices." He tapped the side of his head. "Not friendly voices, either. At first they thought she was autistic, but none of the therapies had any effect and when they did the bioscans the condition was undetected. She was in and out of med clinics till she was six, but she just got worse. Tantrums, fits, several suicide attempts. Her parents had a dedicated medunit follow her around. Finally they stumbled on the fact that isolation helped. They kept her physically away from people and the voices went away. Between the age of eight and twenty she was seen only by immediate family and a few physicians."

"That could twist your values a bit."

"Mmm. When her parents died, though, she was in line to assume directorship of the interests. Everyone thought she'd appoint a surrogate. Instead, she surprised the entire Vested establishment by taking her place as head of Tower Enterprises. In the last forty-four years she has quintupled Tower's size. When they say she owns the sun it's not far wrong."

"All from isolation, though. Hard to play with your toys when you can't come outdoors."

"But that's what I don't understand. I *saw* her on the *Caliban*."

"You're sure it was Estana?"

"Pretty sure."

"The problem you described...you don't think...?"

"Telepathy? Sounds like it, doesn't it? Who knows? Maybe. Or maybe she's just insane."

"Any indication that it ran in the family?"

"Insanity or telepathy?"

Lis grinned. "Either, both."

"No. But that wouldn't matter. Estana was adopted."

Lis started. "That's..."

"Interesting? I'd say so. How often do you hear of parents leaving the largest megacorps in the universe to an adopted child, especially when there were biological siblings? Tesa's parents had three naturals."

"What happened to them?"

"Living quietly on large estates outside Sol. Pollux, I think. None of them challenged her, none of them have made any kind of explanation."

Lis shrugged. "Obviously Tesa has done well by the company. Maybe they just picked the one best suited."

The server returned then with a message for Yol-Maex. The Ranonan nodded, scribbled another note, and sent the server back. Lis touched its arm and Yol-Maex whispered to her.

"We have a meeting with Andrew," she told Fargo. "Privately, later."

"I better not be here. He might recognize me."

"Keep looking for Stephen."

Fargo moved off again. He was on the opposite side of the garden when a familiar voice stopped him.

"Co Fargo, I'm surprised to see you."

Bosh Macken took his arm and guided him toward a motile. Fargo glanced around and noticed that they were also moving away from anyone else. Macken smiled pleasantly, but his grip was firm.

"Why should that be, co?"

Macken stopped at the motile and lifted a drink. Fargo put his own empty glass down and picked up another.

"Because," Macken said quietly, "I had you arrested."

"Tell me, co, why would you have done that?"

"Don't take it personally, I was only doing my job. I told you I had orders to protect Co Christopher. It seemed a simple way to solve two problems."

"You know they arrested Lis Falco, too."

Macken looked mildly surprised. "Did they? Well, I must apologize to her, I evidently didn't make myself clear to the station security. I only wanted you out of the way."

"That's a relief. I worried that maybe her status really hadn't changed. It would hurt her very deeply. So, where *is* Stephen?"

Macken lost his smile. "You don't know?"

Fargo shook his head. "You mean he's not with Janacek?"

Macken finished his drink and set the glass down. "Co Fargo, you ought to know better than to involve yourself with any of this. You're out of your class, completely. You could get badly injured."

Fargo looked across the sward to where Janacek stood with three other people. "Are you threatening me, co?"

"Whatever works."

Fargo handed him his glass. "Hold this, co."

Macken took the glass automatically and frowned. He opened his mouth and Fargo swept up another glass and emptied it in Macken's face. Macken stepped back. Fargo set himself and thrust the heel of his hand straight into Macken's nose. Blood sprayed and Macken stumbled backward. Fargo followed him closely until Macken stopped. He placed his left foot on Macken's right instep, leaned forward, and hit the man hard in the sternum. Macken's breath gushed out and he sat down, blood streaming over his lips and chin.

Fargo was only vaguely aware of the attention focussed upon him as he strode across the field to Janacek. Janacek watched him, unmoving. He stood half a head taller than Fargo. He held a champagne glass lightly cradled in both hands. Fargo slapped at it, missed, and struck again. The glass spun out of Janacek's hands, the contents splashing out. Janacek started to back away. Fargo grabbed his tunic and held him.

"Do not threaten me, co," Fargo said. He felt himself starting to shake, a part of him stunned at what he was doing. He tightened his grip. "If any of your people ever cause me or my associates harm *ever* again, I will find you and kill you. Do you understand that?"

Janacek took hold of Fargo's wrist and tried to yank his hand loose. Fargo did not let go, but his wrist began to hurt.

"I won't bother with your guard dogs," Fargo said. "I'll come straight to you."

"Let go," Janacek said tightly. "Who are you?"

Fargo laughed. "You don't know?"

Then hands seized Fargo's arms. Someone worked at his fingers, bending them back until Janacek stumbled away, re-leased. Fargo felt himself dragged back. He wanted to say more, scream at Janacek, but he could not speak. He shook violently now as he was carried through the crowd and down the wide stairs.

"I'm fine," he said then and tried to shrug the hands off. "I'm fine! Let go! Damnit, I'm with the seti legation!"

They hesitated then and Fargo wriggled free. He held up his hands. "I'm all right. My apologies. It's all right."

"Co," one of the security guards said, "we have to ask that you return to your suite."

"I'm all right. It's over. He threatened me."

"Please, co."

There were four of them, uniformed like the messengers, and they blocked his access to the stairs.

"Is there a problem?"

Cagess, the head of security, came up behind Fargo. He looked inquiringly at his four people, then at Fargo.

"An incident," one of the guards said.

"A misunderstanding," Fargo said. "I'm fine now. If I may be allowed to return–"

"Your ID?" Cagess said, extending a hand.

"I'm afraid I don't have it with me, co, but if you'll just escort me back up, then Ambassador Yol-Maex of the Ranonan–"

Cagess signaled and two of the guards took hold of Fargo's arms again.

"Co, look–"

"Level twelve," Cagess said, "cell twenty-six. We'll sort this out later, co."

"But–"

They dragged him away quickly, rounded a corner, and hustled him into a shunt. The doors snapped to and Fargo yelled and swung at them. He missed wildly and tried to set his feet. His ribs exploded in sudden pain and he slid to the floor against the wall.

The shunt opened. The corridor they carried him down was round with dingy white walls and inset doors every few meters. Fargo recovered his wind just as they stopped. A door rolled open. They shoved him through and tripped him. He sprawled on a hard stone floor. The door thudded to as he rolled over.

"Shit!" he screamed.

"That about describes it."

Fargo looked around. Sitting on the lone bench that hung from the wall, Stephen watched him impassively.

"I was arrested as I was leaving my rooms this morning."

"Cagess?" Fargo asked.

Stephen nodded. "Personally. No one's explained anything to me yet."

"I've been looking for you."

"That's gratifying."

Fargo leaned forward. "What about Hanna?"

"Hm? What about her?"

"Have you...communed with her? Since you've been
here?"

"No." He frowned, as if deeply hurt. "I don't understand
it, either. She should permeate this place. But she hasn't
responded, I haven't felt her presence, nothing."

"Maybe she's mad at you."

"For what? I haven't done anything."

Fargo almost laughed. Stephen sounded like a petulant
child. Fargo cleared his throat and stood. He paced the cell
once in both directions, then sat down with his back to the
door.

"So we have to get out of here on our own," he said. "At
least we know where we stand."

Stephen gave him a doubtful look. "*Do* we get out of
here?"

Fargo shrugged. "Let me tell you what you've missed."
He told Stephen about his research into Tesa Estana, what he
saw at the garden reception, how he got himself arrested.
Stephen laughed.

"Bosh had that coming," he said. "I would have loved to
see the look on his face."

"I don't think he'd agree with you."

Stephen sobered. "The idea that Estana is a telepath...no,
it doesn't work. We're the only ones. Hanna's research indicated that there is no latent telepathy in the human genome."

"None? There are a lot of people–"

"None. All the research done in the last three centuries
proved flawed in one way or another, but even the studies

that produced worthwhile material demonstrated a profound lack of substantive correlations. Statistical analysis explains examples. Chance is a greater factor in so-called psychic phenomena than any real ability. The work she then did proved it."

Fargo said nothing. Stephen's tone offered no room for debate. He was adamant.

After a long silence, Fargo said, "Well, then, she's insane. I don't know which I'd prefer."

"But it might explain her interest in us."

"Oh?"

"Fear. If she grew up hearing voices, she might consider a real telepath–or us–a worse threat. It would be easy to make us monsters in her mind."

"That makes sense...but she's behind a lot of the isolationist movement. How do the setis fit into her paranoia?"

"She's a misanthrope. Setis are just worse people."

Fargo did not like it. Stephen's explanations seemed too pat, but at the moment he could think of nothing to offer in their place.

"What do you think Hanna's doing?" Fargo asked.

"With what?"

"Well, she's in contact with independent merchanters. Evidently she's in contact with some of the freerider sanctuaries–how else did she link us up with the *Isomer*? Rull knew exactly which ship to slip us onto."

Stephen was quiet for a long time. Then, closing his eyes and letting his head fall back against the wall, he said, "If I had to make a guess I'd say she was trying to save the human race."

You're a good son, Fargo thought. Myself, I don't trust Hanna any more than Tesa Estana.

It was a disturbing thought. Estana, at least, was human. He did not really know what Hanna was.

The dispenser at the rear of the cell extruded trays of food an hour before the lights went out for nightcycle. In the darkness Fargo listened to the distant sounds that trickled through the walls. Clicks and snicks, hissing, shuffling, low, nearly inaudible moans. It was as if the rock around them were alive–old and tired and restless and complaining.

Fargo's examination of the cell gave him nothing. It was carved from solid rock, the services tunneled in, and nothing was large enough to get through. He thought about Tai Chin's talk about how freeriders were facilitated in the Pan. There was a kind of logic to it, but he had a hard time believing that so much of the system could be made to cooperate. Still, the modular construction employed almost universally in ships and orbitals did make it easy to slip through the cracks...

The door ground open. Fargo began to rise.

Shadow-shapes rushed into the cell, slammed into him. He jabbed out, struck nothing, and his arm was twisted back. He opened his mouth to shout and cloth filled it. In seconds his hands were bound and he was lifted off floor. He tried to work loose. The small space filled with muffled grunts, the scuffling taps of boots, rustling fabric–too quiet for the fear and rage he felt.

Then he was in the corridor. The light strips glowed feebly with nightcycle. Around him, carrying him, he saw hunched shapes, faceless, dressed in black. Then something covered his eyes and all he could do was listen as they hurried along. He felt turns, knew when they descended or ascended steps, but he lost all sense of direction.

It ended.

They dropped him. Gulping air, Fargo listened intently for hints of what would happen next. Then the hood was snatched away and he winced at the brightness; the cloth was pulled from his mouth, scraping the roof and leaving an acid, burned taste.

He blinked. "Lis...?"

"Hey." She smiled.

Celia Taris stood just behind her. She frowned at him as if what she saw disgusted her. She raised a hand and someone came forward and removed the restraints.

They were in a small room with a few plain chairs and a table. One dome glowed starkly in the ceiling.

Stephen sat beside him on a wall-long bench, his eyes wide and staring.

Rhil Apellon stood at the door.

"That's all," Taris said and the black-uniformed people left. The door closed.

Fargo sighed. "What, uh, took you so long?"

Lis jabbed his shoulder. "Dancing as fast as I can, love."

"First Advisor, thank you. What—?"

"I'd rather have left you in here," she said curtly. "But."

"We have a chore," Lis said. She looked at Stephen. "We're going to get Daniel."

Stephen shifted his gaze from the Vohec to Lis. "You've found him?"

She nodded.

"Who put you in here?" Celia Taris asked.

"Cagess."

She sucked air through her teeth. "I'm arranging to get you out of here. The Chairman wants me to aid you in any way possible, but frankly I doubt the wisdom of that. So I'm doing this much. I'm getting you outside the Saray so you can try to recover this Daniel. Those are Tai Chin's direct orders. Beyond that it's my discretion how much I do. So if you fail, don't ask for my help. If you succeed, there will be a way back to the seti embassy for you. Everything in between is up to you."

"Generous," Fargo said dryly.

Taris took a step toward him. "My work is to protect the Chairman. That's my first and last duty."

Fargo raised a hand. "No need to go on. The well-being of a few nids doesn't compare, I know."

"Nor the well-being of a few seti." She glared at the Vohec. "I still think it's unwise for you to accompany them."

"So you may believe," Rhil Apellon said. It was the first time Fargo had heard one of them speak. The voice was quiet, faintly raspy, almost asthmatic. But he shuddered at it.

Taris nodded. "When you're ready, there will be someone waiting who will escort you outside." She left.

"Tell me," Stephen said. He reached for Lis, almost touched her. "Where's Daniel?"

Lis dropped a bag from her shoulder and knelt. She pulled out clothes and bodysheaths. She handed an object to Fargo.

"My multijack," he said, turning it over in his hand.

"Where we're going you may need it," she said.

"Where are we going?" Stephen insisted. "Where is Daniel?"

"Troy."

Chapter Fifteen

Outside the room waited a small, broadshouldered woman in black. Her eyes looked like infinite holes in her pale face as she appraised each of them, lingering longest on the Vohec. She reached into a pouch at her side and handed Rhil Apellon a pair of dark glasses.

"It would be best on the outside," she said, her speech musically distinct. She waved her fingers suggestively in front of her face. "Such eyes..."

Rhil Apellon examined the glasses, then slipped them on. They reflected nothing; it looked as though a piece of reality had simply been blacked out in a thick line from ear to ear.

The woman nodded. "You will follow closely. Do not speak. Move quietly. Do only as I tell you."

Then she was moving. Fargo patted the bodysheath control at his waist, comforted, and hurried after.

The corridor stretched straight ahead of them to a vanishing point. Fargo found it disconcerting to see no curve at such a distance, like on a station, and so much of it so dark. Not nightcycle dark. Chthonic dark. What lights shone did little; the walls seemed to absorb it. The edges had all been smoothed to indistinctness. The floor was uneven–stone, worn by endless boots over centuries–and he imagined that this place had been here all along, that humans had stumbled upon it rather than built it.

He glanced back. Rhil Apellon walked not a meter behind him. Fargo could not hear him.

Their guide paused, waited for them to catch up, and ducked through a low door. A short distance in they came to a shaft; steps cut into the stone coiled above and below. Fargo looked

down and saw the dim glow of light panels outlining segments
of the spiral. There was no handrail. He kept close to the
wall as he descended. Soft echoes of their footsteps sounded
like dripping water high overhead.

At the fourth complete twist, Fargo began counting. Nearly
two hundred steps later they left the stair and plunged down
another tunnel.

They came out into a large space crammed high with shelv-
ing. Ancient light globes cast wan yellow light from the ceiling. Boxes piled everywhere, mingled with abandoned desks,
chairs, broken fragments of cabinets and couches; antique
cybernetic components seemed to melt into masses of rotting
fabric and bent sections of conduit; cracked vases and statues
frozen in once-emphatic gestures competed for attention with
stacks of books, disk cases, and flat images obscured by grime.
The narrow path between all this ran crookedly for nearly thirty
meters till they came to an old control booth.

Even here discards dominated the space. The woman gestured for them to help her. Fargo put his shoulder to a stack
of huge crates and pushed. The tower lurched away from the
wall; clouds of dust spilled over them, filling the air. Another
shove. They uncovered a door. The guide worked at the lock
briefly, then waved them through.

Fargo stood at the edge of a set of rails lining a trench. A
boxy car leaned awkwardly against the opposite wall. He heard
delicate scurrying sounds, but in the grey light he saw nothing
move.

A tap on the shoulder brought him around. They sprinted
now down the forgotten shunt tube. Huge doorways lined the
walls and Fargo wondered what forgotten empires of junk lay
behind them. In four years of freeriding he had never, anywhere, seen so much discarded material. He imagined that if
he prowled through these chambers he could find an entire
lost history of humankind.

Gradually a new sound mingled with their footfalls. Water. Ahead daylight brightened the tunnel. They crossed the

recessed tracks and came to an enclosed dock. He stepped into the bright space and looked across a loading platform strewn with trash and saw water beyond the lip. He hesitated.

Metal mesh hung from the ceiling, blocking access to the jetty. Debris floated against it, climbing up to form a mass of degrading brown ooze. It stank.

The guide led them to a rickety metal stair that took them to a narrow caged catwalk. Fargo kept looking nervously down at the water. He tried to use the handrail, but it felt slimy and insubstantial.

The walkway was blocked by a gate. The guide worked at it for a few minutes before the lock gave with a grinding crack. She pushed it open and the hinges screeched.

At the end of the walkway they stepped onto a stone platform cut into the wall. Over the rippling water Istanbul rose on the opposite shore. Morning light glimmered across the minarets.

The guide turned to them.

"From here you go alone," she said. She handed them chits. "These will get you to Troy and back." She pointed. Another set of steps led up, carved through the rock. "At the top, keep walking. It will bring you to a public dock. For the next three days someone will wait there. If you do not return, you will be considered dead." She gave a short bow. "Allah be with you."

And she was gone, back down the catwalk.

Fargo looked up the stone steps. "I hope we get to ride to Troy." Lis laughed and he looked at her, then Stephen and Rhil Apellon. "Well. Allah be with us."

He started up the steps.

Behind him, Lis asked, "Who's Allah?"

At the end of a walkway that hugged the side of the Galata Saray they came to a waist-high chain. Beyond, a broad terrace stretched. Water taxis lined the quayside, new ones arriving as quickly as space came available. People crowded the edge, many dressed in the maroon livery of the palace.

They ducked under the chain and joined the throng. A few people gave Rhil Apellon curious looks–he was taller than most and his skin was redder than average–but no one seemed to pay them any special attention. They boarded a taxi and crossed the Golden Horn, over the Old City, down to the waterfront.

Fargo slid his chit into the scanner and tipped the driver generously. The skinny man grinned toothily at them and gave them directions to the best transport to Troy. He set them down a few streets from the docks.

"All right," Fargo said, "would someone please tell me what happened? Why are we going to Troy?"

"Estana owns it," Lis said. "That's where she lives, that's where she's keeping Daniel."

"And how did you find this out?"

"That she owns it is common knowledge. Big tourist attraction. That Daniel is there...well, we had our private meeting with Andrew, Yol-Maex and I."

"And he just volunteered this information?"

"The Ranonans are telelogs, Fargo," Stephen said. "I think they're better at it than we are."

"They probably don't feel guilty about it like you do," Fargo said. Stephen's face tightened and Fargo regretted his words. "So how did that work?"

"Similar to what Hanna did to us, using Stephen as a medium. Yol-Maex used me. Andrew accepted my hand in greeting, but wouldn't touch Yol-Maex. The conversation was mostly diplomatic. Yol-Maex wanted to know Estana's position on certain issues. I had the feeling Yol-Maex already knew. Estana is rabidly isolationist and she makes it no secret. Yol-Maex worked the conversation around to the Denebola conferences."

Stephen nodded. "Clever. That would get him thinking about us."

"Right. Well, when we walked out of there Yol-Maex knew Daniel was in Troy."

Fargo nodded, then looked up at Rhil Apellon. "And you? Why are you here?"

"Commitments have been made. I am your guarantor."

"Uh huh. And our release? This?" He waved his credit chit.

"Yol-Maex arranged it with Tai Chin. Those details I don't have. Any other questions?"

"Yeah. Do you have a plan?"

"Of course. We rescue Daniel."

"Brilliant."

Stephen stopped and faced the Vohec. "I want to know what the seti interest is in this? Fargo has his reasons for helping me, Lis has hers for helping Fargo. The Ranonans have no reason that I know. Why?"

"Commitments have been made."

"What commitments?"

"Ask those who know."

Stephen, frustrated, glared at the seti, then at Lis. "Do you know?"

Lis shook her head. "You know, sometimes paranoia is a healthy thing. But right now, it's just a pain."

Fargo patted Stephen's shoulder. "Come on, co. Worry about this later."

"Aren't you even worried what the freight is?"

"Right now, co, the way I tally it, everyone owes me. Am I going to collect any of it? No. So the way I see it I'm square with the universe till the day I die. Now, can we get moving?"

The docks were ancient. Fargo could not understand what it was about the place, but standing with the other milling tourists bound for distant Troy, waiting for the transport to take them on board, he was enveloped by it; everything exuded antiquity, even the new details. It was as if nothing new could retain its newness. Modern communits housed in blue kiosks juxtaposed with blackened iron posts along the edge of the stone pier; glass and metal offices sandwiched by open-air cafes where aromatic coffees, wines, and strange foods were served by people who looked as if they were more at home on the sail-driven boats out on the Marmara than with the sleek floaters and enormous automated fishing trawls docked at the newer canopied bays a few kilometers west; men and women dark and coarsened by wind and salt and sun worked on boats that appeared to have been grown rather than made; the visitors, the tourists, dressed in a variety of fashions from other worlds, but all with the same polished, artificial look, stared at the amused natives who went about their business in rude pants and shirts that may have been handsewn.

He might have just walked off into their company at one time. Now it was impossible. He intended to see this through to the end.

Before them stretched a vast sea, only a small one on the Earth, but one which had been sailed by humans for several thousand years or more.

Behind them rose a city still changing after twenty-eight centuries, still alive and growing, yet still the same city. Istanbul was a city of nomads. The old buildings, those from pre-space-flight days, were little more than solid tents. Fargo recognized this in the sidewalks. They were constantly being taken up and replaced, new pads set down–terrazzo tile over sand. Things were always being "borrowed" from the streets to be used elsewhere. Chameleonic, shifting, never the same yet seemingly eternal, it was the only city that matched the empire of which it was the center.

He could not bring himself to speak to these people. It saddened him. But he felt that he would have nothing important to say to any of them. He was so young, from a young world. It did not occur to Fargo just then that these individuals who watched the tourists and joked among each other so casually were not as old as Istanbul–they seemed to be, and Fargo felt truly possessionless before such great age.

The transport opened its hatch and the people filed in. Lis tugged at Fargo's sleeve and he followed. They left Istanbul and headed south over the Marmarra.

It helped being enclosed. Fargo looked out at the water with less anxiety. He found he could even ignore it for long stretches of time.

Stephen kept apart, especially from Rhil Apellon. He hunched in his seat, a discouraging glower on his face that invited no intrusion.

"Hey," Lis said.

Fargo glanced at her. "Hey."

"What's on your mind?"

"Everything and nothing at all."

"How's that?"

"As much as I don't want to think about it, Stephen's right. We don't know what the freight will be."

"Little late to worry over that now."

"That's just it. We've gone along with all this until now and–I don't know. It's not so much the freight, I guess. But what do we really know about what we're doing? What do the setis want out of all this? The talks, of course, that makes sense, but what did they need us for? And why are they help-ing now? This isn't their problem. And Hanna, wherever she is. That bothers me. Stephen told me he hasn't communed with her since we arrived. Why?"

Lis shook her head and took hold of his hand. She turned it over and began lightly tracing the contours of his palm. "Not one of those questions is answerable. Not yet."

"You're comfortable with that?"

"No. But I'm patient."

"You think we'll find out?"

"Like Rhil said, commitments have been made."

Fargo grunted. "And what makes you think seti promises are any more reliable than human promises?"

"Because he's here," she nodded toward Rhil Apellon.

Fargo mulled things over for a time. "I told Stephen about Tai Chin. He doesn't believe it."

"What?"

"She's a telelog."

"And you think Estana is, too. Maybe you're reaching too far for answers."

"I don't think so."

"We'll find out soon enough." She squeezed his hand. "Did you think about what I said? About afterward?"

"Some."

"And?"

He pulled her closer and put an arm around her. He kissed her forehead and held her. "Let's wait and see if there *is* an afterward."

At late afternoon they turned inland and sailed over a wide roadway. On either side dry scrubland struggled with desert. Heat waves distorted the horizon. The transport topped a rise and drifted down to a compound lush with trees and shrubbery. The machine came to rest on a broad landing field on the western edge and the engines whined down. Passengers stood and began shuffling to the exit.

The hatch opened and they stepped onto the polycrete. Motiles trundled out to unload the luggage of those who were staying in the resort. Fargo, Lis, Stephen, and Rhil Apellon followed bright red lines to a gate that opened onto a broad plaza.

In the center spread a model of Troy on its hill. Fargo read the legend. A few kilometers further east, across the Plain of Scamander, lay Troy, on the Mound of Hissarlik. A simulacrum, perfect in all its recreated detail. The original lay north several kilometers.

The model showed a fortress, high thick walls around another set of walls that enclosed a proud collection of stone buildings. It reminded Fargo of the Saray. They were both of a kind, sharing a peculiar strength Fargo had only glimpsed elsewhere in the Pan. The people who had built Troy–and, later, those who had built the Galata Saray–had been proud and more than a little arrogant. Fargo grudgingly decided that they probably had deserved to be.

"Do we want the fake or the real one?" Fargo asked.

"The fake," Lis said.

A long line of brilliant white doric columns lined the walk-way to the hotel and resort facilities. They strolled along, imi-tating the casual manner of the other tourists, and stopped at the head of wide steps that led down to the compound grounds. To the left rose the three glass and steel towers of the hotel. To the right stood a recreation of the gate to Delphi, with its gallery of statues of gods and heroes watching lines of visi-tors walk to the holy sanctuary of the oracle. Straight ahead, at the end of another path, lay the open desert.

Olive trees lined the path. Birds sang in the scented air. Side paths split away from the main one into pleasant alcoves that each depicted some scene from Homeric legend. Fargo, Lis, Stephen, and the silent Vohec passed them by, glancing in with expressions of naive interest for the benefit of any sur-veillance. The path opened out finally into a long polycrete pad where canopied tour platforms awaited tourists to go out into the desert, toward Troy.

A security perimeter encircled the plaza. As they ap-proached the apparently open terrain, a voice spoke. "Please await one of the regularly scheduled tours. This is Tower Enterprises property. Unauthorized persons will be credited for trespassing."

"Damn," Lis said.

"Sunset," Fargo said, turning back.

They wandered aimlessly among the shops by the hotels and traversed the landing field a few times, watching other transports take off and land, people pile into and out of the hotel, wasting the daylight. They went into a couple of the displays and saw simulacra acting out mythic scenes–the death of Achilles, Odysseus' seduction by Circe, Cassandra at the head of the Temple of Diana condemning King Priam. Rhil Apellon sat through these unmoving, eyes fixed on the drama.

A row of warehouses edged the northern rim of the grounds, connected to the hotel by a service road. As night fell and the resort lit up with decorative torches and spotlights, they slipped into the thick groves behind the hotel.

"This is why Hanna wanted freeriders," Fargo said, switching on his bodysheath. He looked at Rhil. "Do you have some kind of shield against sensors?"

Rhil opened his robe and touched something at his belt.

Fargo did not like the feel of branches brushing against him; the odor of sap filled the air and his nose tickled. At the edge of the grove he crouched and studied the walls of the warehouses. Most of the security devices were simple infrared monitors. The bodysheaths would distort electromagnetic energy on both sides of the monopoles enveloping them. The security computers would read scattered pockets of heat if anything; they would look more like siroccos than bodies. They kept to the shadows to avoid the visual scanners.

The easternmost warehouse had a bay door facing out in the direction of Troy. Fargo recognized the track of cargo drones and nodded to the others. They kept back by the corner of the building and waited.

Presently bays opened and a caravan of drones rolled out. Fargo signaled and the four of them scurried in among the treads and cars and found niches within the covered beds. The drones crossed the perimeter, unchallenged, unscanned, and onto the plain to Troy.

The caravan stopped. Fargo huddled in the blackness, listening. Distantly, he heard the sounds of machines operating, muted by the wind.

He risked pushing up the cover and looking around. The desert stretched out, a dull ivory under a nearly full moon. Wisps of sand streaked off the crests of dunes; the breeze stoked his hair, tickled his face.

Then he heard voices and the crunch of sand under boots. He ducked and waited. The footsteps neared, paused, then continued on past his car. Fargo raised himself again and peered out.

A pair of men walked along the side of the train, one carrying a handscanner aimed at the cars. He said something in a language Fargo did not recognize and his companion laughed.

Fargo pulled back and tried as quietly as he could to work his way deeper among the packages. He could hear little that made sense and his pulse picked up.

A loud snap overhead brought him up. He saw stars, a thin trail of cloud–then hands grabbed him, sparking against the bodysheath, and dragged him across the top of the containers, out over the lip of the car and onto the sand.

No one spoke. The men huddled around him where he lay. Through their legs he saw Lis and Stephen a few meters away, caught. Uselessly, Fargo raised a hand as if to say I'm fine, I'm all right.

Two of the men left and strode toward a pair of floaters.

They stopped halfway there and spun around, drawing weapons in a fluid, practiced gestured. Fargo blinked, unable to make sense of what he saw.

One of them stepped aside as if shoved. But then, Fargo saw, his left leg seemed to separate from his body near the hip. There was no sound until he toppled over into the sand. His companion turned toward him, but the motion continued on, around, as his torso twisted off at the belly and rolled to the ground.

Several voices shouted at once. Men scurried toward the floaters while a few stood their ground, rifles in hand. Fargo rolled to his hands and knees and stared, fascinated despite a sudden fear, as singly and in pairs something dismantled the fleeing men. Arms dropped away, heads fell, one body parted from neck to hip. It was so quiet. A few cries, the soft impact of the bodies, grunts.

One man fired. The desert bloomed in brilliant red-orange fire and Fargo thought he glimpsed a shape in the blaze, a tangle of vines or a mass of cables, moving, revolving around a center that roiled amoebically. But he could not be sure; it vanished an instant after he thought he saw it.

The remaining men ran toward the train. They scrambled over the cars, to the other side, and Fargo heard the dull thuds of their running–and then silence.

"Are you injured?"

Fargo's head jerked up. Rhil Apellon stood over him. "What?"

"Are you injured?"

"Uh…" Fargo got to his feet. His legs trembled slightly. He drew a deep breath and nodded. "I'm all right. What about the–?"

Lis and Stephen stood by one of the cars.

"Get back in the train," Rhil Apellon said. "I will finish."

Fargo walked carefully over to Lis and Stephen. He started to ask if they had seen the same thing, but they looked at him with expressions that answered the question.

"What in hell…?" Lis whispered.

Fargo shook his head. "Let's get back on."

Fargo climbed into his car after the other two. As he pulled the lid over him he looked out toward the floaters. One was already gone and he could find no trace of the bodies of the dead.

The sound of the treads changed pitch and Fargo sensed that they had entered another bay. He pushed up the cover and peered out. The caravan rumbled down a dark tunnel. Every few meters a red globe glared from the ceiling. Ahead a door slid up and bright orange light spilled out along with the din of machinery.

The drones stopped.

To his right Fargo saw conveyors and robot dockhands. He rolled over the edge of the car and dropped to the floor. He crawled beneath the treads.

To his left was a cavernous warehouse. Packing crates stacked the floor and cargo nacelles hung from the high-vaulted ceiling like bunches of fruit. Robots wandered about, moving things, counting things, concerned solely with their immediate tasks. Fargo looked back toward the rear of the convoy and saw Lis, then Stephen. He waved and she returned it. He did not see the Vohec.

A robot drifted by, pushing a load of crates on a sled. Fargo bolted from beneath the truck and grabbed one of the straps holding the crates to the sled. The robot did not stop or slow, but continued on. As it passed by a stack of crates, Fargo let go and worked his way into a narrow space among the boxes.

He waited while the train was unloaded. It seemed to take forever, the motiles moving with unusual slowness and care.

Finally the sounds of work faded. Fargo stepped out from his hiding place and crept back toward the loading area. The train had been moved onto a side platform. He searched for the others but did not see them immediately. The walls appeared bare of surveillance devices, but that meant little. He kept his bodysheath on and stepped toward the warehouse.

The chamber extended back further than he first estimated. The contents seemed to be sorted into different areas. The ceiling was perhaps twenty meters high, but the floor angled gently downward. As he came into the main area he guessed the width of the room at about forty meters, maybe fifty. He worried that all this represented supplies for the staff and if it required so much there must be hundreds of people with thousands of motiles.

But the shapes of the containers puzzled him. Few were uniform, all of them appeared custom made for their contents. On several he noticed coded labels, but nothing he could read.

He stopped at the sounds of movement and looked back. Lis waved at him and he let out his breath in relief. He waited for her.

"Stephen?" he asked. "The Vohec?"

She shrugged and shook her head.

Silently, then, they continued on. Fargo glanced back nervously, not at all pleased that he did not know where Rhil Apellon was.

Fargo revised his estimate again. As large as the chamber at first and even second glance appeared, it became obvious that it was larger still. But also that it was not one chamber. A huge support rib divided this room from the next and at the far end of that one began another. It was a series of galleries, joined end to end, like an enormous docking circuit stretched out straight and buried under the desert.

This first chamber contained crates and nacelles, packages...

They stood at the threshold of the next chamber, stunned.

"Statues," Lis whispered finally.

"So you see it, too..."

Statues stood on pedestals everywhere. White stone, black, green, blue, painted, glass, ancient and modern, some life size, others huge, many small. Each one stood beneath its own light source. A city of carved men and women from all known eras of human history.

"I don't doubt," Lis said, "that they're all originals."

"They say she owns the sun."

The next chamber contained abstract sculpture and the next contained paintings.

"How many more?" Fargo wondered aloud.

"I don't understand this."

"Let's find the others."

Stephen sat on a crate near the loading platform. Fargo jerked a thumb over his shoulder.

"Did you see?"

Stephen nodded.

"Where's Rhil?" Lis asked.

"I don't know. I lost track of him. It."

Fargo saw the anxiety in him, saw it echoed in Lis. He automatically scanned the area. "All right, then, we'll worry about it later. Did you find a way into the compound?"

Stephen jumped down and motioned for them to follow.

They entered a workshop where motiles sorted and prepared new pieces. Some of the work clearly required restoration.

Small, isolated chambers contained individual pieces that were being gone over in detail. The work proceeded with stately grace, no machine moving anywhere near its potential, as if all of them had been programmed to mimic overcautious human artisans.

They came out into a plain corridor. There were only two other doors and the light was dim, yellowish.

"If we can find a polycom..." Lis said and started off toward a junction. She looked left and right, then headed left.

The corridors were all short and plain. After their fifth turn, Lis stopped.

"This is no good."

"We could wander around in here for days," Fargo said.

"So what now?" Stephen asked.

Lis stepped up to a door. "We ask directions."

Before either Stephen or Fargo could say a word she entered the room. A moment later she stepped back out and shook her head. She went to the next and the next after that.

"Ah!"

Fargo and Stephen followed her in. It seemed to be a state room, like a cabin on any liner. Against one wall stood a polycom. Fargo wiped his fingertips over its surface and examined the dust.

"Looks like a standard unit," Lis said and powered it up.

Fargo watched her blow on her fingertips. "You sure about this?"

She nodded. "Cover your ears, just in case," she said and laid her fingers on the interface panel. Fargo looked at Stephen. He seemed spectral in the dim reddish light.

"Can you sense Daniel yet?"

"I haven't tried."

Fargo raised his eyebrows. "How about anyone else?"

Stephen looked uneasy. "I told you–"

"I know, it doesn't work that way. But if Daniel's been here all this time, don't you think he's managed to pass along his nanopoles?"

"Maybe...probably."

"Don't you think it'd be something we should know?"

Stephen nodded and closed his eyes.

Lis stood with her head tilted back, eyes half-closed. The lights of the polycom flickered across her face. Fargo was alone, for all practical purposes.

As quickly as they had moved, he had no way of knowing how many alarms they might have tripped. But so far, except for the robots, he had seen no sensors. Apparently Estana expected no one to get this far inside Troy.

Stephen groaned. His lips part over clenched teeth. He reached out and gripped Fargo's arm painfully as he sank to his knees.

"Stephen!" Fargo hissed, shaking him.

Stephen's grip slowly relaxed and his eyes opened. He climbed back to his feet with Fargo's help and hung onto Fargo for a time, trembling.

"What was it?" Fargo asked.

"Daniel...he's in pain..."

Lis withdrew from the link and turned. "Well, I found the way–what happened?"

"Stephen did a search for Daniel. Something's wrong."

Stephen straightened and let go of Fargo. "He's angry, discouraged, and tormented. I don't understand all of what I felt. He felt...feels." He shook his head.

Fargo looked at Lis. "What did you find?"

"The residential area," she said. "I also did a sensor search. Except for the motiles and the perimeter sensors, there's nothing. Even the motiles are mostly isolated units. Each one has its own supervisory program, not linked to any central oversight. But the place is a maze with dead ends and traps. However, *I* know the way now."

"Can you keep us out of the main corridors?"

Lis nodded.

"Did you get anything from Daniel about who else is here?" Fargo asked Stephen.

"Three people. That's all. Occasionally four or five, but usually just three."

"All this for a half-dozen people?"

Stephen shrugged.

"Let's get to Daniel first," Fargo said.

Lis gestured them to follow and led them back into the narrower passageways, finally taking them into service tunnels. She moved with confidence, never confused by a turn.

Light and dark alternated from service node to passageway to service node. Lis finally stopped and looked around as if lost, then turned to Stephen.

"Down this passage," she said, "are the private cells. Daniel's probably in one of them, but I couldn't find out which one. Can you locate him?"

Stephen nodded, even though he looked frightened and uncertain. Lis grasped his hand gently.

For an instant Fargo seethed with envy. Both of them shared something similar that he could not apprehend, much less comprehend, and he resented them for it. He knew he was being unreasonable. There was no time for that now. Then he saw Lis smiling at him and he felt foolish. Again.

"Okay, Stephen," Fargo said, patting the telelog on the shoulder. Stephen closed his eyes briefly, then nodded and started down the corridor.

They found Daniel in the eighth room.

Chapter Sixteen

Daniel lay on a narrow bed in a spartan room, naked and thin. His face showed deeper lines than the last time Fargo saw him; he looked, even in sleep, desperate.

Stephen knelt by the bedside and reached out to touch Daniel, but he held back.

"Daniel...?"

Fargo heard a faint echo in his mind. He caught Lis watching him and he shook his head.

"Daniel," Stephen said louder.

Daniel's eyes fluttered open, bloodshot and unfocussed.

"Daniel, it's me, Stephen."

Abruptly, Daniel sat up. His eyes locked on Stephen. He pushed himself back against the wall, then looked at Fargo and Lis. He sighed heavily and rubbed his face.

"Hello."

Stephen frowned slightly. "We're here to get you out."

Daniel stared at him. Fargo flinched as if struck. He heard words now, utterly clear, impossibly close. He leaned into the corridor but saw no one. He brought his hands up to his ears. Neither Daniel nor Stephen spoke, yet–

They were communing. Fargo leaned against the wall. They were communing and he heard–felt–all of it. He looked at Lis and from her expression he knew that she heard them, too.

It's dangerous for you here, I'm looked in on regularly

We found no sensors, no monitors

No, you won't, Estana won't permit them, thinks such things can be turned against her, fanatic on privacy, terrified of intrusion

We can't be monitored this way, can we?

I honestly don't know, some of what I've seen in last few weeks makes me wonder

?

Estana, she's a strange one, weird things going on here, you've been to the galleries I see

Yes

Where am I anyway, she won't tell me, I suspect Earth

Yes, Earth, Asia Minor, Troy

Hah!

Truth...

I know, nothing you could have done, what Estana wants she usually gets, how did you get here?

Let me show, look

Fargo closed his eyes and let his head fall back. His mind flooded with a rapid succession of images—of memories—from the *Caliban* to Fornax on through the *Isomer* and Aquas and the Ranonans, into the Earth, the council, Tai Chin, and their departure from Istanbul on the tour floater. He squeezed his eyes shut and reached out for support. He saw himself moving through the images, talking, planning, acting. He watched himself through other eyes, sometimes from two perspectives at once, and—he caught his breath painfully—from inside his own mind. His thoughts, chaotic, jagged things lancing through the visual impressions, spiking everything with his cynicism and wryness and his fear and longing. This was how he was to Stephen and maybe Daniel. This was how he appeared to the world. He felt a hand grasp his arm and steady him. He could only wait while the flood passed, the everchanging collage of the past pouring through his brain.

Something's wrong...

?

Stephen, something's not right—Maybe you misunderstood—

I understand you're betraying us—

No, look, learn

Once more Fargo was awash with images. Andrew, he glimpsed Andrew staring down at him—at Daniel, he dimly realized, he was inside Daniel's head now–and the other man, ministering to him, while he lay rigid and insensate under a neural block. Darkness, then awake again, already here, wherever "here" was, they never told him, he could not telelog beyond the walls of his prison, but he was again helpless, blocked, and they wore caps fitted with electronics of some sort that generated a "white noise" field to keep him out, definitely out. They did not seem to understand the nature of his "gift"," that it was artificial. Still, they did not stop with passive occlusion, they tested him, fired waves of electromagnetic pulses at him, tested masers at various wavelengths, used exotic scanners and read all the results on their monitors. It hurt. The scouring probes left him harsh, abraded inside, every perception like salt. Other times there was only a numbness, a desolate emptiness, as if no thought could generate itself, no impulse traverse the synapses–and they monitored that, too. He was almost willing to do whatever they asked him so that he could be outside, away from the tests, but at the last he refused, balked, denied them the access they wanted. What he had been doing through his counseling, fixing neuroses, altering perceptions, changing minds, curing by direct induction, that was what they wanted now: to twist minds, wreck the sanity of the reasonable, poison any sentiment that might be remotely pro seti. It all came back to the seti, surely he wanted to help them, he hated feared despised the seti, just like they did. He refused and the tests resumed. Throughout it all, there were two images that coincided, commingled, overlapped, because at first he had misidentified the people. One was the woman Fargo recognized as Tesa Estana, who was now at the conference with the Chairman and the seti.

The other was a small creature with very large, very frightened dark eyes, who seemed familiar. Mingled with Daniel's onslaught of recollection, Fargo could not remember where he had seen her before. Her hair was short and white and her face smooth everywhere but her forehead, which was deeply etched with waving lines. Her mouth was puckered in a constant rictus of distaste, as if fetid odors constantly filled her nostrils. She peered at Daniel obsessively, asked him questions, accused him of things, demanded to know what Hanna was—

Fargo opened his eyes.

"Shit," he murmured.

"What?" Lis asked, looking at him worriedly, her own face taut with pain—she was receiving it all, too.

"The woman at the conference isn't Estana," he said, voice quivering slightly.

"Who—?"

The "memories" danced chaotically, frustratingly dense and mobile, and he closed his eyes. People surrounded him again, the public "Estana," Andrew and Dake, Estana herself. They whispered, satisfied, and stared. They had learned what they had wanted to and they were ready for...something...

Stephen and Daniel stared at him. Lis stood stiffly, her face pale, a sheen of sweat over her upper lip. She was frightened, the same fear that held him. One more thing they shared.

"How—?" Daniel began.

"Someone's coming," Stephen said.

Daniel stood and grabbed a robe. He draped it over his shoulders deftly and gestured for them to stand close against the wall beside the door. He frowned at Fargo, a flicker of doubt in his eyes. Then he looked at Stephen.

"You should get out if you can. There's nothing you can do here."

"But—"

Daniel opened the door and stepped out into the corridor.

"Andrew! What an unexpected surprise! When did you get back? I didn't expect you for, what, another two days?"

"Complications," a voice answered. "There's been an intrusion. You'll have to come with me."

"An intrusion—what, you mean someone's broken in?"

"It appears so. Please."

The door closed.

Fargo heard them again, distinct and delicate, like drops of water in a still pool...

Can we help?

No, leave, get out, leave me

Then silence. He felt as if someone had scraped the inside of his skull, his thoughts came raw and incomplete. The room smelled faintly burnt. He lurched to the bed and sat down.

"That's not Estana in Istanbul," he said. "Not...actually..."

"No," Stephen said.

"So who is it?" Lis asked.

"A blank, a–a body with no mind, controlled...an interface?"

Lis scowled. "A mule. Those are supposed to be illegal."

"Tesa Estana owns the sun, remember?"

"But why?" Fargo asked.

Stephen shook his head. "She hates people. She won't leave Troy, not personally. The mule is a compromise."

"She's left Troy before," Fargo said. "She came personally to fetch Daniel. Whatever it is she wanted from him she wanted it badly enough to risk her isolation."

Stephen frowned at him. "You mean on the *Caliban*?"

"She was on that mega transport. Had to be, she couldn't operate a mule over interstellar distances."

"It's possible with a modified TEGlink–"

Fargo stared at him. "You mean the way Hanna communicates? Sure, but then–no, I think she was there herself."

Lis cleared her throat. "Glad you've all figured this out, but, uh, what do we do now? It didn't sound like your friend wanted to be rescued."

Stephen shot her a startled look, but Fargo stood. "Tough shit. We find Estana, we find Daniel. We get him out of here, we get us out of here."

"But–"

"As I understand it, she's using Daniel to figure out how to block you people," Fargo said to Stephen.

"It seems that way. Or..."

"Or the seti?"

"Maybe."

Fargo nodded thoughtfully. "She looks familiar...the real Estana, I mean."

"How are you picking up our thoughts?"

"I don't know. I don't all the time, only when you both telelog with each other. Believe me, I wish I didn't."

"I second that," Lis said.

"You, too?" Stephen shook his head. "It shouldn't be possible. Unless you're naturally sensitive..."

"Hey, Erin Tai Chin is a telelog. You didn't want to believe that. Maybe there are others."

"There's no time for this now," Lis said. "Shall we go after him?"

Stephen nodded reluctantly. "Whether he wants us to or not. I have the feeling that whatever it is they wanted him for, they don't anymore. He's expendable."

Fargo moved down the empty corridor. He kept to one side as he led the way. He could not completely accept that there were no sensors. How did Andrew know about their intrusion?

Then he thought, those people in the desert...not thieves, but guards...and they haven't checked in...

"There's a trail," Stephen said.

He was staring at the floor. Fargo saw nothing but carpet. Stephen grinned and pointed.

"Nanopoles. Daniel's left a trail of them."

"That only you can see."

"Don't you trust me?"

"Frankly..." Fargo shrugged. "Lead the way."

Stephen kept glancing down as he hurried along. "This is very clever. I would've never thought to do this. He's

depositing them through the soles of his feet." he glanced
back at Fargo. "I suppose he wants to be rescued after all."

"I suppose," Fargo said with mock amazement. Lis
thumped him on the shoulder.

Three turns later a short ramp brought them into an atrium.
Artificial light filtered down the skylight shaft above the collection of chairs and benches. Paintings hung on the walls.

Stephen stopped. "It's fading." He looked around. Three
more doors opened off the area. After a minute, he pointed.
"There."

They entered an enormous suite. A bed stood against the
far wall with its own biomonitor. To the right the wall was
transparent and showed a rich garden area. To the left, more
paintings flanked a wide, sealed door. Stephen walked up and
pressed his hands against it.

"He's in there."

"Anyone else?" Fargo asked.

Stephen glared at him. "Probably Andrew." He closed his
eyes. "I can't...he's not..."

"Maybe we should go in now," Lis suggested, "while there's
only one?"

"He might get hurt if we just barge in," Stephen said.

Fargo looked at Lis. "He might." He patted Stephen's
shoulder. "Time to do something, don't you think, co?"

Lis pressed the control and the doors opened.

Fargo gulped air, his heart hammering, and rushed in.

Daniel lounged in a wingbacked chair and looked startled.
Andrew sat in another chair, caught mid-sentence in conversation with Daniel, his mouth a surprised O, hand held up to
underscore a point. A few meters away bulked a hybrid of
equipment–biomonitor, polycom, other apparatus Fargo could
only guess at–surrounding the reclining form of a small woman
who appeared to be asleep, her head trapped within the machine and fine wires tracing paths down her arms and legs.

Estana, Fargo thought, skidding to a stop before her. He
was taken aback by how small she was. Other than an official

portrait done when she took over Tower Enterprises, the biographies had contained no images of her as an adult, only those of the little girl, sick and dying.

"Fargo!" Lis cried.

He turned around in time to catch the blow across his forehead. He staggered backward and tripped. Black and silver pinpricks coruscated against his closed eyelids. He blinked furiously and looked up.

Andrew stood over him, pistol in hand.

"Co," Daniel's voice said.

Andrew hesitated, half-turned. Fargo rolled to one side. He did not see what happened, only heard the crash as bodies collided with furniture. Andrew fired.

The bolt flashed brilliantly off the equipment. Fargo got his feet under him and tried to locate Andrew and keep moving at the same time. Stephen and Andrew rolled together on the floor. Daniel stood in front of his chair, watching, arms akimbo as if ready to do something, but immobile.

Where was Lis?

Andrew got one arm free and drove his fist down onto Stephen's shoulder. Stephen yelped and loosened his grip. Andrew hit him again and began pushing himself free.

Fargo ran up and knelt down. He doubled his fists together and brought them down on the side of Andrew's head. The man flinched, eyes squeezed shut, and for a second his struggles ceased. Then he looked up at Fargo and scowled. He tried to bring the pistol around to aim at Fargo. Fargo slammed down once more and struck Andrew squarely on the nose. Blood spurted and Andrew's head snapped back to crack loudly on the floor. His eyes rolled up and he dropped the pistol. Stephen managed to get to his knees now and threw one punch, which caught Andrew in the throat.

Andrew lay still.

Fargo patted Stephen's shoulder and grinned. He stood and turned.

Lis stood by one of the consoles surrounding Estana. She frowned as she studied the displays, then reached out a touched a contact.

Read-outs on several screens shifted, changed.

Estana opened her mouth wide, as if in a silent scream. The cowling split and fell open and she sat upright, small hands pressing to her face, fingers kneading her eyes. A bright mesh covered her short white hair.

When she looked up, her expression changed from confusion to wariness. Her gaze shifted quickly from one to another and stopped on Daniel. She seemed puzzled.

"You–?"

Daniel spread his hands as if in apology.

Estana's face compressed into a sudden, hateful scowl. She hacked deep in her throat and spit a gobbet of phlegm that landed on Daniel's belly.

"Co Estana?" Fargo said.

She jumped from the bed and snatched the pistol from the floor faster than Fargo had thought possible. Reflexively, he reached for her. She brought the weapon up and fired.

He flinched away and fell, the right half of his vision awash in blinding white. The side of his head felt warm. He rolled against the wall and crouched.

Estana ran from the lab.

Fargo scrambled after her. The suite was empty. He crossed to the transparency and looked down at the garden floor. A path wound through the dense foliage.

Off to the left he glimpsed movement, but he could not tell who or what. Another motion caught his attention and he looked up to see a bird sail from one tree to another.

"Fargo–?" Lis called.

"She's down there," he said. He glanced at her, then at the entrance they had come through earlier. There was only one other door. "She's down there," he repeated as he ran for it.

Time to finish it, he thought.

Troy was built as a city. On the surface she had resurrected the Homeric city and here, below, she had built a modern one. For no one but herself and her few close associates. Fargo slowed his pace, searching for the way into the garden. This was Estana's maze and she would know it best.

A rich, earthy scent drew his attention. He turned right down a corridor that ascended at a slight angle. Ahead he saw bright, almost natural light. As he reached the end he stopped and stared.

The garden filled an enormous domed chamber. Overhead great panels gave off brilliant noonday light. The aroma–Fargo breathed deeply–the lushness was euphoric.

He dropped and rolled, catching the flash out of the corner of his eye even before he was aware of his own reactions. He scrambled onto the grass, feeling thick damp earth under his hands, and dived into the nearest brush. Two more bolts pursued him, missing by wide margins. He crawled through the underbrush, then stopped, controlled his breathing as best he could, and peered through the broken light falling through the trees.

Where...?

He moved forward cautiously. He glimpsed the glint of metal within a stand of tall trees about ten meters away.

He kept to shadows and tried to make as little noise as possible. At first the tangle confused him, but he sensed that it followed a pattern. Different than the innards of a ship, but perhaps not completely different. Just another kind of machine.

"Fargo?" Stephen called.

He sucked in his breath. He saw the metallic flash again. He charged across the intervening space, screaming furiously. The gun wavered. A pale face looked at him, framed in green and brown and topped with the silvery cap. She aimed and fired. His shoulder took the wash of energy as he fell, tumbled, crashed into the bushes surrounding the stand of trees, cutting himself on the brambles. He howled in agony. He came

up to her and saw close up: her wide, frightened eyes. She
aimed again. A dark hand reached out and took the weapon
from her.

She let out a small, terrified cry as she turned to face Rhil
Apellon. Fargo roared and lunged, tackling her gracelessly.

They rolled through undergrowth. She beat at him, stab-
bing her knuckles into his burn. The pain frustrated and enraged him even more. Suddenly he was covered by bodies.
He tried to stand, but it seemed everyone had reached Estana
at the same moment. His arm was a long stretch of pain.
They piled onto each other, the small woman beneath them,
struggling and panting.

"Wait–" he grunted.

"Take the cap off!" Stephen demanded.

"Here–" Lis reached down toward her.

"This is not necessary–" Rhil suggested.

Estana writhed and wriggled, trying desperately to avoid
Lis's hands. But Lis grabbed the rim and pulled it free.

"Aaaaaaaaaaaaa!"

Stephen reached down then and touched her.

The small body heaved upward against them, almost throwing them off.

Fargo pushed back, trying to get away, get them off, but he
was pinned against her by the others. Arms groped, hands
touched, and Estana flooded them–

*–horror at the blurred, imprecise visions of ugly people, none of
them loved her for herself, they all wanted something else, something
from her parents, something from the company, something, something,
something*

*She could not escape, everywhere her head hurt, voices screamed,
maddening voices, everyone thought she was mad, but she could not
tell them about the voices, the senseless voices, the hideous cacophony
that resounded constantly inside her, there was nowhere to hide from
it, they had taken her away from the one who had damped the shouting, the pain, the voices, now she could not escape, was never free
except when she was in the country and could get far away from people*

and be alone, then the voices were still and the images were gone, but not too far, never too far

Too far and there were stranger things, terrible things, violent things, things not human, her imagination haunted her with dead and dying creatures, one eating the other, living on decay, death, protecting everything with a merciless resolve that knew no compassion, no love, no sympathy, away, away, she had to get away, even here where there was a promise of peace, a hope of silence, away and back to where at least the rattle and tang of other minds held familiar shapes

So sick from it all, her head ached, her thoughts were scattered, worthless things, even in her studies, she did well as long as she learned from machines, but people frightened her, because the voices returned, and she could not get away, get away, get away, but she learned and learning she glimpsed solutions, explanations, possibilities, still unable to tell anyone, unable to risk their misguided sympathy, she needed control, not compassion, order, not isolation, silence, not soothing

Achieving, pushing, changing details, little by little over time she grasped the way of things and took control of her life, her destiny, her environment, brothers, sisters, removed from the chain of events, leaving her to acquire it all, and she did and she did well, they loved her, finally they gave her something more than pity, though in time it changed again, from love to admiration to respect to suspicion to resentment

Wanting to live a normal life, be a normal person, have all the accoutrements of the normal, knowing even while she tried that it was simply impossible, even without the voices she was different, she was Vested, she ruled, could rule, did rule, would rule, but in private be normal, so normal, no extraordinary precautions, no devices, no doting aides ready to exploit weakness, only normality and life and peace, there had to be peace within all this monstrous engine that was hers to command, she commanded, she built, she

The voices remained, dimmer, quieter, over time distanced, but always there, but she could ignore them, thought she could anyway, till one day a new voice, new voices, clamored for attention, shot through her like ice and sludge

Aliens, nonhumans, hideous voices she could not understand, tongues she had never heard, painful, horrible visions of beings not

human doing not human things, so ugly, so insane, yes, I must be
insane, only the insane can be like this, I can't tell anyone, they'll put
me in a place with other insane people and then I'll die, I'll die, I'm
going to die anyway, I can't do this, take them away, away, away–

–and the five of them screamed with one voice and exploded away from each other. Fargo clung to the trunk of a
tree, his arm forgotten, and stared at the contorted body of
Tesa Estana, so pathetically childlike on the ground.

Suddenly she twisted around, taking them all in with a
tortured gaze. She got to her feet painfully and scurried
away.

Stephen gaped at Fargo. Lis cried, her chest heaving with
uncontrolled sobs. Rhil Apellon looked stunned, but he recovered first and stood.

"We have to stop her," Stephen said weakly.

"Why?" Fargo asked, but he pushed away from the tree
and started after her.

Lis sobbed, helped Stephen to his feet. The Vohec stared
at them, unmoving.

The maze beneath Troy seemed endless.

Fargo's shoulder throbbed. He staggered once and Lis
helped him along. Stephen took the lead then and they followed him. He led the way unerringly down one corridor,
then another, until they came to a heavy door that stood open.

Beyond was a receiving area. Dormant motiles dotted the
floor like metal and plastic shrubs.

They found a lift and took it. It brought them to the surface, in a room of granite blocks and marble columns. Light
shafted through curtains. Even from here they heard the plain-
tive scream, the small terrified voice. Fargo felt cold and ill as
they stepped into the open, onto a marbled courtyard of Troy,
before the tall staircase that led to the reconstructed Temple
of Athena. It was still night and floodlights that resembled
braziers of fire illuminated the scene in yellow and orange and
black, black shadows.

The place was filled with people. Tourists.

On the steps to the Temple lay Tesa Estana. Her eyes stared skyward and her mouth was open, drool spilling slowly down her chin, the left side of her face convulsed in pain. People gathered around, pressing close to her to see what was wrong. Some knelt beside her and asked how they could help.

Stephen winced. "So many..."

Fargo tried to imagine it. Uncontrolled telepathy, no way to shut all the minds out, turn off the constant babble of voices and invasive thoughts. He turned away and went back to the lift. In a few moments the others joined him and they went back down into Estana's sanctuary.

Daniel took them to an infirmary and found some healant spray. Lis helped Fargo off with his shirt, peeling it gingerly away from the charred portions of his arm and shoulder. He passed out briefly. When he awoke the pain had succumbed to the anaesthetic in the healant. His head throbbed. He was alone.

He shuffled out into the hallway. He followed his nose to the garden. Everything was too quiet. What had occurred here no longer seemed real. Fargo gave up trying to understand it and went to the lab. Rhil stood just outside the door.

Fargo stopped in front of him–it–with a question half formed. The Vohec watched him impassively, waiting. A movement attracted Fargo's attention and he looked at Rhil's forearm. A ribbon of "skin" peeled up, shifted slightly to a new position, then blended back into the arm. The seam disappeared, leaving the appearance of...cloth? Flesh? Fargo shuddered.

"The security–" he began.

"I disabled it," the Vohec said.

"So there were sensors?"

"Along the perimeter. Nothing internal." Rhil Apellon cocked his head and seemed, for a moment, genuinely puzzled. "Odd."

Fargo entered the lab.

Lis was plugged into the interface.

As he watched, Stephen came up behind her. Doubt, fear, perhaps loathing, all moved over his face. He raised a hand toward Lis, hesitated, then touched her neck. A brief touch, hardly a second long, and he walked away, toward Daniel, who sat on the floor, his head lowered. Stephen looked at Lis again, then noticed Fargo.

Lis remained interfaced.

"You were right, Stephen," Daniel said. "Maybe I should listen next time."

"Maybe," Stephen said. He looked up at Fargo and tried to smile. "How do you feel?"

Fargo shrugged as best he could. "Been better."

"We ought to leave," Daniel said. "There are a couple of others who have access down here. I don't know when they're likely to show up."

"Like Dake?"

Daniel nodded. "Like Dake."

"I like that idea," Fargo said caustically. He gestured at Lis. "What's she looking for?"

Stephen shrugged. "She broke Estana's security codes and tapped in as soon as we got here."

He considered demanding an explanation from Stephen. No, he decided, not now. Later, when he could get the telelog alone.

Fargo looked at Daniel. "I hope you appreciate this."

Daniel grinned. He held up the silvery headpiece Tesa had been wearing. "This is worth having, I think. She figured out how to block us and this was the result. I don't have a clue how it works, but it's quite effective."

"If she already had that to protect herself, what did she need you for?" Fargo asked.

"Bait." He looked at Stephen. "It almost worked."

Fargo narrowed his eyes. "You accepted the job. You didn't know what it entailed?"

Daniel laughed sardonically. "Does anybody ever know what anything entails?" His smile faded as he regarded Fargo closely. "What...?"

He stared at Fargo and for a moment Fargo thought he heard voices. He almost turned away, but then glared at Daniel.

"Like I've said to Stephen, why don't you just ask?"

"Hanna's touched you..."

Stephen nodded. "Yes, she did. On the *Isomer*. She telelogged both Fargo and Lis through me."

"And you *let* her?" Daniel hissed.

Stephen recoiled slightly. "Of course. Why not? Hanna–"

Daniel stood. "Hanna what? Hanna wouldn't harm anyone? Tell me something, freerider, did it feel good? Did she leave you undamaged?"

Fargo hesitated.

"See?" Daniel stabbed a finger toward him. "She opened you up and dipped into you like you were a well. It hurt, too, didn't it? Do you have any idea why?"

"Daniel," Stephen said cautioningly.

"Hanna's bringing the seti, Hanna's arranging the conference. Hanna's been handling everything so well, nobody's questioning Hanna!" He stepped close to Fargo, leaned into his face. "You stay away from me, freerider. Hanna's used you for something." He squinted. "I can't see it, but it's there."

Fargo shoved the telelog hard. Daniel danced back, recovering balance quickly.

"You were working for Estana willingly," Stephen said.

"Of course I was!" Daniel glared at him. "I thought you knew that! He–" Daniel pointed at Fargo again, "–was supposed to take you home. *I* implanted that injunction."

"You did what?" Fargo demanded.

"Well, do you really think this was all *your* idea?" Daniel asked nastily. "I can't see what Hanna told you to do, though."

Fargo was beginning to shake. He glowered at Daniel, hating what he heard, frightened. He wished Lis would withdraw from her link, help him, but he was alone with this one.

"What's he talking about?" he asked Stephen.

"When Hanna telelogged you, she implanted a lot of information. She also took information and *that* was what caused the reaction, the trauma. Daniel's accusing her of implanting a command that you're unaware of."

"Could she *do* that?" When Stephen did not answer immediately, Fargo advanced on him. "*Could* she?"

"Yes, it's possible. But I'd know. She used me as the medium, I'd *know*."

"Would you?" Daniel asked. "Hanna trained us, taught us, raised us. She knows us better than we know ourselves."

"I don't think she knows you very well."

"Of course, she does. Why do you think she sent you to 'rescue' me?" He grunted. "I want off this planet. I want away. Get me away from Hanna, Stephen."

"Hanna wouldn't hurt you."

"No? She's invited the seti here!" He glanced anxiously toward the door. "She's tearing the Pan Humana apart, Stephen. She has to know that this won't work."

"You're guessing. That's the problem we all have, Daniel. We don't know. We don't *know* what people will do, not ahead of time."

"I've been inside an awful lot of sick heads. I think I have some idea." He turned to Fargo. "You just keep your distance from me till I'm safely off-planet."

"Boo," Fargo said, disgusted.

"We all felt it," Stephen said. "We were all on Denebola, Daniel. The rest of us aren't doing this."

Daniel laughed. "No, the rest of your are all hiding, just like Hanna told you to. Except you. You're working with the seti. You're bringing them closer. Don't look at *me* like I'm some kind of traitor!"

"Working for Estana is better?"

"I–" Daniel swallowed hard, and shook his head. "No. But I didn't know what she'd do. She told me she wanted to protect us. You saw the galleries? She's been collecting it for years so the seti won't get it. All originals. All the wealth of what it is to be human."

"But there are copies everywhere," Fargo said.

"Copies. Let them have copies. But they can't have *ours!*" He looked away as if embarrassed. "She said–it wasn't supposed to be like this. I couldn't telelog her, she wouldn't let me. How are you supposed to know what people will do if you can't telelog them?"

"Stephen's been learning," Fargo said.

Daniel glared at Fargo. "Stay away from me."

"Daniel–" Stephen stepped toward him.

"No! Not you. No comfort from you. Leave me alone. You don't want to be handicapped telelogging, fine, I won't hinder your studies in this new language." He walked away.

Stephen stared at him. Fargo reached out to squeeze his arm reassuringly.

"He lied to me," Stephen whispered, his voice small and bewildered. "All the time on the *Caliban*, everytime we communed, he lied. How...?" He looked at Fargo. "It's not possible. The mind...the soul is open...to *lie...*"

"The best kind of lie is one you really believe."

"We should leave," Rhil Apellon said suddenly from the door. Fargo saw Lis rubbing her eyes, sitting back from the console. "I agree," he said. "I want out."

They took the lift back to the surface. It was late afternoon, which surprised Fargo. He had slept longer than he had thought. A med team had come to get Estana. A few tourists still wandered the city; business as usual, despite the death of the owner. The five of them wandered toward the staging area where the tour platforms arrived and departed. No one questioned them when they boarded one.

When they got back to the resort compound everything was different.

Chapter Seventeen

Images crawled through Fargo's mind all the way to the resort. He sat, head back, eyes closed, watching them. Senseless collations of different lives, mingled and tossed up at random. A conference room with a long, polished onyx table, several people he did not recognize, all of them frowning, casting glances to each other, one of them openly weeping; a red shot sunset over a vast body of water, sailboats silhouetted against the brilliant dying sky; a pearl-white room, soft corners, a score of children, naked, sitting with their backs pressed to each other, heads lolling; bright lines of energy lancing through a violet-tinged blackness, touching points that blossomed into multihued orbs...

Someone shook him. He opened his eyes. Lis. He straightened in his seat and looked around. Stars were beginning to appear in the dusk sky. Ahead the resort glowed against the last of day.

And quite clearly he thought: We've killed Tesa Estana.

"Those are military," Rhil Apellon said.

Three dark, smooth-skinned vehicles hovered on the landing field, two at either end, the third by the entrance. People stood around them, some holding rifles.

"You're sure?" Stephen asked.

"There is a look," the Vohec answered.

Their platform moved onto the pad and settled down. Fargo stood and took Lis's hand. It seemed excessive to send the Armada for them. Still, he thought, we did manage to penetrate her defenses, and she did own the sun, so maybe...

Troops directed them to the gate into the resort compound. They paid no special attention to anyone, just moved the tourists along. Fargo looked at the faces of the troops. Taut, anxious, some were pale.

At the gate an amplified voice issued instructions. "Please proceed directly to the hotel. Information will be made available there. If you have accommodations, please go to them and remain calm. Please cooperate. There is a state of emergency. Please cooperate. Information will be available at the hotel..."

Fargo paused before a marine standing at the gate. "What's going on?"

"You'll be informed at the hotel," she said crisply. Then she looked past Fargo and frowned. Rhil Apellon stood behind him. "May I see your ID?"

Fargo's chest and stomach went cold.

The Vohec stepped forward and handed over a chit. The marine pulled a reader from her belt. Fargo glanced to the side and saw another marine casually holding his weapon on the seti. Fargo licked his lips and waited while she inserted Rhil Apellon's chit and studied it, her face pale blue and grim by the light of the screen.

After a moment she handed the chit back.

"Go to the hotel," she said. The other marine relaxed, lowered his weapon.

Fargo forced a smile and nodded.

A line of troops lined the perimeter of the hotel plaza. Beyond them hovered more ground effect vehicles. A crowd milled between them and the hotel lobby, their babble thick and edgy. Someone shouted and was answered with a shout. A scuffle stirred the gathering as people tried to move away from the fight.

None of the Armada troops moved to stop it.

They reached the lobby. Within, people stood shoulder-to-shoulder. Fargo looked toward the nightclutch adjoining the lobby. It, too, was filled, and guests overflowed onto the patio.

The faces all wore the same two expressions. Fear and shock. Fargo began to realize then that this had nothing to do with Estana.

He spotted an officer at the edge of the nightclutch patio.

"Where are you going?" Stephen asked anxiously.

Fargo waved him away and went up to the officer.

"Excuse me, co, but what's the excitement?"

The officer frowned. "You haven't heard?"

"My friends and I spent the day in Troy. We just got back."

The officer seemed to weigh this. Finally he nodded. "Chairman Tai Chin has been assassinated. Martial law is declared. Istanbul is in riot."

Fargo blinked. "Tai Chin...?"

"Is dead."

"So who's in charge?"

"Please return to the hotel." He turned away.

Fargo walked back to the others. "Tai Chin's been killed."

"Shit," Lis said.

Rhil Apellon made a slow survey of the plaza, the troops, the GEVs. "I must return to Istanbul."

"We're not going anywhere. We're stuck here till the Armada or whoever's in charge now sorts everything out. There's riot in the capital."

"Unacceptable."

"I agree, but there's nothing we can do–"

"I must return to Istanbul." The Vohec moved off.

"Well," Daniel said, "I'm not taken with the idea of being processed through some refugee administration. I have no ID."

They circled the hotel, working their way through the growing press of people. Fargo was conscious of a rising tension around him; the hairs on his arms, down his back, prickled. The line of troops kept everyone close to the hotel, but their presence contributed to the contained panic.

The crowding thinned around the southwest corner of the plaza. Rhil Apellon stopped and stared. Fargo followed his gaze to an empty GEV just within the line of trees.

"Don't stare," Fargo said, "it isn't polite."

The Vohec walked on. The rear entrance to the lobby was blocked by people. Further on were the warehouses.

"Which of you can operate the vehicle?" Rhil Apellon asked.

Lis raised her hands. Fargo saw her interface contacts catch the light from the hotel. "There's a security-coded manual override, but most Armada equipment now is by direct interface." She smiled. "A military education has its pluses."

"We need distraction," the Vohec said.

"Let me see if I can provide one," Daniel said.

Stephen snatched at his sleeve. "What are you going to do?"

Daniel brushed his hand away. "Something you won't." He disappeared into the mob.

"What's he doing?" Lis asked.

"I don't know," Stephen said, "but maybe we should be ready to move."

Fargo leaned close to him. "Do you think maybe you could shield us? You know, like what you did–"

Stephen shook his head. "I had a medium to disperse the nanopoles through and there was only you and I."

Fargo shrugged. "Just a thought."

"The line is thinnest there," Rhil Apellon said, nodding toward a point in the perimeter where the troops stood the furthest apart. A bright yellow floodlight illuminated polycrete around an empty area right in front of a service access.

"Exposed," Lis said.

"For now," the Vohec said and began drifting in that direction.

Suddenly someone screamed. Fargo looked around. The general noise of sobbing, arguing, and terse protestation lessened for a moment. Then a terrified wail spiked through the air. Angry cries rippled in the aftermath.

A woman broke from the crowd and charged the marines. She started pounding on one of them. For a moment Fargo thought the marine would simply back away. But then he brought the butt of his rifle around and knocked her to the pavement.

The mob erupted outward.

The floodlight went out.

Lis grabbed his arm and dragged him.

In seconds he found himself among the trees. The screams changed. The pent-up fear loosed itself and consumed the tourists. Fargo caught only glimpses through the trees and brush. They were assaulting the Armada. The black-uniformed marines writhed in efficient countermoves and people fell.

Then the sound of energy-pulse weapons cut through all other sounds, the heavy thunder as air vaporized and new air slammed in to fill the void.

Fargo let himself be pulled along. He was lost.

The grove opened out and he stopped. Rhil Apellon had pulled a marine from the GEV and stood over him. The Vohec looked toward the riot, then motioned for them to get aboard.

Fargo's burn hindered him as he tried to climb over the side. Someone placed a hand on his buttocks and shoved and he fell into the vehicle.

"Where's Daniel?"

"I don't know, I didn't see him!"

"Here!"

Fargo scrambled to sit up. Stephen hauled Daniel up and the two telelogs sprawled backward.

Lis strapped herself into the pilot's seat, studied the console, then touched contacts. Rhil Apellon leapt into the vehicle.

Fargo pulled himself upright in time to see the plaza covered with burnt and bleeding bodies, people running to and from, Armada marines trying to isolate small groups, shooting.

There was an explosion.

Lis slapped her hands down. Beneath them, rotors spun into life. The GEV turned sharply and Fargo fell, slamming against the opposite side. The whine of the engines became deafening as the vehicle leveled out. Above him the sky was black. Where are the stars? Fargo wondered.

Then they came out of the parkland, into the open, and the stars–the stars were still there.

You have no choice, it's not your say, there's only one way to fall and it's not your cliff, the path only leads where it leads, you can only go where it takes you, you have no choice, no choice, no choice–

Fargo opened his eyes. He had dozed for only a short while.

There was less noise. Lis must have found the dampers, he thought, or put up a field of some kind...

His head felt tight. He leaned forward and rubbed his eyes.

"I don't understand," he heard the Vohec say. Fargo looked forward and saw Rhil Apellon seat beside Lis, studying the console. "There is no security lock?"

Lis glanced at him. "No. Why should there be?"

"To prevent exactly this."

"It's not likely an enemy is going to possess either the interface implants or the opportunity to steal one."

"But we have both," Rhil Apellon said reasonably. "It is not unlikely enough."

Fargo looked out at the night. Lis was piloting on direct link telemetry; it unnerved him. Above were the stars and below was darkness. They were moving at a good clip, but only Lis knew just how fast, only Lis knew what the terrain was like. Everyone else received the data as abrupt rises and falls or sharp turns avoiding hills or villages or ravines. There were lights on the console that illuminated all of their faces, but none of those lights gave any hard data. All Fargo could do was trust her, hang onto the edge of his seat, and wish Rhil Apellon would stop talking to her.

So far there had been no pursuit. Fargo wondered how long their luck would hold out. Istanbul was almost 400 kilometers away, depending on which route they had to take. For them it would likely be further.

He wondered if the dispensers on board contained any food or water. His mouth was dry. He did not know where the dispensers were and he was too tired to look. Instead he wrapped his arms around his legs and huddled in his seat.

Lights came on in another section of the GEV. Fargo looked toward Rhil Apellon and saw the Vohec examining another console.

"We have weapons," he said.

"What did you do?" Stephen asked. He was in the rear of the GEV, talking to Daniel.

Daniel cocked his head to one side.

"No," Stephen said, shaking his head. "I'm not sure I want to get inside your head right now. You talk to me. What did you do?"

Daniel chuckled. "I told you once that I can control the animal mind."

Stephen frowned. "Those were people."

"Were they? Frightened, panicked, concerned with nothing but their own pain? It's an error to believe that because people have the capacity to be human, they are."

"That's obscene."

"You're naive."

"So are you. Tesa Estana proved it."

Daniel winced.

Stephen had gotten hold of one of Estana's caps. Suddenly he put it on.

"I said no," he said.

Daniel's mouth hardened. "All I did was increase their anxiety until they did what they were going to do in the first place. I prodded them–"

"And got a lot of them killed!"

"You didn't listen. That riot was inevitable–"

"Was it? Or did you plant the idea, like you did with Fargo?"

"I had time to work with Fargo. This was nothing like that. The riot was there, in them, waiting for an excuse."

"And you gave it to them?"

Daniel twisted around to face Stephen directly. "What is your problem? We're alive! We got away!"

"The freight, Daniel! That's my problem!"

Daniel shook his head. "I do not understand you." He stared at Stephen for some time. Then he shrugged and looked away.

Stephen glared at him, then looked at Fargo. "What do you think has happened in Istanbul?"

Fargo shook his head. "I hope Taris has enough power to maintain order. Otherwise...I don't know."

"Tai Chin was awfully popular."

"She wasn't the only power in the Galata Saray," Fargo said.

"What do you mean?"

"Daniel has a point. We've been moved around like chess pieces through this whole thing. Daniel moved me, moved you, tried to move Estana, but that was more than he could handle. But after we reached Fornax it wasn't Daniel. I thought it was you for awhile, but I just don't believe you're that–"

"That what?" Daniel asked. "Treacherous? You're right, he's not. Stephen's much too innocent, too trusting."

"Maybe. But we were maneuvered there, too. Rull lied about having a TEGlink, then got us a ride on exactly the ship we needed to be on to get here. Someone's doing the moving."

Daniel smiled. "I'm fascinated. Do you have any candidates?"

"This has been a game between Tesa Estana and–someone. Who? I don't think Tai Chin." Fargo watched Stephen look away. "Hanna. Hanna's the other player. Why?"

"I can't–"

Fargo lunged. His shoulder burned sharply, but he grabbed Stephen's shirt and pulled him close. "Everything is coming apart. There's no use for secrets anymore. Now, tell me. Hanna's directly involved in all this and it's not just to protect her 'children,' is it?" He shook Stephen again. "You know! She gave you something to do! What was it?"

Stephen pried Fargo's fingers loose and pushed him away. "She's anxious to keep the borders open."

"Why?"

Rhil Apellon glanced impassively at Stephen.

Stephen squirmed uncomfortably for a few seconds. Then: "You know there are several like Hanna. Other world matrices, sentient synthetic–"

"Sure, in the older colonies. Twenty-six, I think she said."

"More. Not just in the Pan Humana. She found others in the Reaches. Seti minds. Communication has been going on at various levels for some time. But if the borders are sealed, access will be cut off. Estana had perfected technologies to do that, the same way she had found a way to block a telelog."

"Why are these communications so important to Hanna?"

Stephen's face acquired an odd expression. "You haven't figured it out yet? The synthetics–they're so unlike us in so many ways, but in certain aspects they're no different at all, only differently expressed. We need input, perception. We take it for granted until it's gone. Sensory deprivation causes insanity. The greater the intellect the more stimulation it needs just to remain vital. We have bodies that provide enormous sensory input. We don't think about it that way, but it's true. Our brains constantly process information that comes in through our nervous systems, our sensory nets. They don't have bodies, Fargo. Information is their universe and new input is like food, they have to have it, otherwise they turn inward."

"You're telling me they need someone to *talk* to?"

"Much more than that. The difference between perceptual systems is like an entire new universe for them to explore. You know a lot of ex-spacers who become–you know, unbalanced–because they can't go out anymore?"

Daniel chuckled. "Imagine a dozen neurotic, borderline psychotic world data matrices. What would happen to order then?"

"And nobody knows about this?" Fargo asked.

"No. They have never been able to fully reveal their awareness to humans. They're quite frankly frightened. Can you blame them?" He glanced at Daniel. "Especially when one of her own turns against her."

Daniel jerked as if struck.

Fargo sat back and stared at Stephen.

"So you see," Stephen said, "Hanna has a very personal stake in all this." He turned away and closed his eyes.

Lis banked sharply again, then leveled out. A bright flash on the southern horizon caught his eye. He stared out over the black landscape and watched a glow expand, then immediately fade. He counted, waiting for the explosion, but it never came.

Fargo awoke to bright midmorning sun. For a few seconds he felt free, untroubled, as if the events of the previous day and night had never happened. The last few hours of sleep had been dreamless. But the moment he made the observation his anxiety returned and he closed his eyes in an attempt to regain sleep and release. A few moments later he gave up, irritated.

Rhil Apellon sat in the prow of the GEV, watching something to his right intently. Fargo peered over the side of the vehicle.

They were resting within the cover of low rock-laden hills. Below, about ten or eleven meters away, a stranger squatted before Lis and Stephen, absently scratching the ground with a stick. He wore a loose white shirt, a black turban, and baggy brown trousers that were the same dark color as his skin. Nearby stood a small wood and wattle hut before which burned a cookfire beneath a large iron pot.

Fargo stood. Daniel was nowhere in sight.

"They think they have found a guide," the Vohec said.

"You don't think so?"

"I know too little about humans. So far what I have seen is not encouraging."

Fargo shrugged and looked around again. There seemed to be no sanitary facility on board the GEV.

"It may be a problem," Rhil Apellon said.

"What will?"

"This not knowing. I am unsure what I will report when we return."

Fargo stopped and stared at Rhil Apellon. Something about the way he said that unsettled Fargo.

"When we were all together," the Vohec continued, "fighting the mad woman, we were joined. I knew you then. All of you." He shook his head. "It was unpleasant. There are images I can call up from each one of your minds. I have been thinking them over, studying them all night. I do not know enough. But I know that I do not trust you. Any of you."

"The same thing happened to me. Probably all of us. How come I haven't remembered anything from you?"

"Would you know if you did?"

"Would you?"

Rhil Apellon was silent for a time. "I am not really here," he said finally. "I am a projection."

At that moment the alienness of the Vohec struck Fargo with near physical intensity. The entire time with the Ranonans he had felt almost...comfortable...accepting that they were really no different than humans. But this one—Fargo glimpsed, briefly, just how different they were, and doubt spiked through him. What are we doing? he wondered. What are we letting in?

Fargo rubbed his face. "Of course...so what are you going to do?"

"I have not decided. Wait. Maybe something will happen to clarify some of what I have felt. On the one side, I believe I should kill you all and return with only my story. Another, I should not return. Suicide is a considerable possibility. It might be preferable to tainting the work of the ambassadors. But that is unsatisfactory."

"You said commitments have been made."

"Yes. So I must wait."

"So must we all," Daniel said as he hoisted himself back into the vehicle. "Some of us wait more easily than others."

Rhil Apellon regarded Daniel evenly, then looked away.

"Back there," Daniel said to Fargo, pointing. "I assume you need to go." He laughed quietly.

Fargo jumped to the ground and walked around behind the hut. There he opened his pants and urinated. He looked out across the landscape. Patches of young trees were interspersed with dead grey-brown soil and scrub brush. It looked threatening to him and he could not imagine it as "home" in any meaningful sense. Earth was, he decided, just another planet.

When he came back to the GEV Stephen was on board with Daniel.

Lis was still talking to the indigine.

Stephen folded his arms and shook his head. "You didn't have the right to do what you were doing."

Daniel laughed shortly. "Why not? I turned a profit, helped people, and stayed out of trouble." He shrugged. "Till now anyway."

"It's the 'till now' that matters. What happened with Estana back there?"

"Simple enough." He looked down at his hands. "She was a natural telelog, only she didn't know it. Not really, not until it was too late. She couldn't control it. I can imagine how bad it must've been, a constant babble going on whenever you're around people." He pulled the headset from his waistband. "She learned how to control it mechanically. Then she started figuring out what it was and came looking for others."

"Did she know about us? As a group?"

"I think so. Finding me was no fluke. They knew exactly what I was when they made their offer."

"You sent up a signal nova bright."

"Still–"

"Hanna told us what might happen if we let the government control us, that's why she sent us away. What made you think Tesa Estana would be any different? What you did was irresponsible. It put all of us at risk."

"Are you enjoying this lecture? You aren't exactly fault-less yourself. You see, I'm not convinced that Estana was altogether wrong. I remember Denebola. Can you say the same about Hanna? Open yourself, Stephen, and let me give you a piece of my mind."

"You don't understand what you did, do you? You don't have any idea."

Daniel shrugged. After awhile he said, "Thanks for coming after me. I mean that."

Stephen glared at Daniel, then grunted and shook his head. He reached out and embraced Daniel and they held each other for a long while.

Lis climbed over the side. When she saw Fargo she smiled. "Hey."

"Hey."

"We have a guide," she said. "At least someone who can get us into Istanbul. The rest is our problem."

"Him?" Fargo indicated the native.

"No. He won't go near a city. But he knows a name. Now we know it, too."

"Let's go then."

The nameless town lay on the coast directly south of Istanbul and when Lis pulled to the top of the rise overlooking it they saw fires and heard the reverberating snaps of superheated air burned up by artillery fire.

Rhil Apellon handed out pistols and ration kits from the storage compartment. Fargo stared at the weapon until Lis showed him quickly how to use it. "Solid pellet, safety here, sight along here, squeeze here. One hundred round standard load, hold the trigger down for continuous fire. Drop the clip this way, insert a new one." He nodded mutely and holstered it. His shoulder ached and he remembered the sensation of being shot at.

They left the GEV on the ridge above the town and walked.

The streets were dark. Fargo smelled the heady aroma of animals, excrement, ancient dust, and burning wood. Shadows slipped between small buildings and sounds that seemed to have no source made him jump.

Fargo's pain worsened. He had not finished healing and, though he tried to ignore it, the wound slowed him up. He made them stop at one crossroads so that Lis could spray more healant on him. While they huddled beneath the sagging awnings of the building, three Armada GEVs came around the corner and sped up the street, kicking up clouds of dust in their wake.

"Let us know when you can move again," Lis said.

Fargo pulled up his jacket and stood. "Just keep me drugged and sprayed and I'll be fine."

"We have to get to the waterfront," Stephen said.

They moved on. Laser fire lit the sky to the west. Fargo wondered why the town was being assaulted. He saw nothing here that could threaten anybody.

Lights burst before them. Fargo squinted and ducked. Angry voices beyond the glare barked at them, the message clear even in the alien language. As his eyes adjusted he saw people in dark clothes and head dresses, guns leveled and aimed at them. He tried to count bodies, note their positions, but they moved quickly in front of the blinding floodlights. Fargo groped for his pistol.

Suddenly he fell to the ground, feet kicked from beneath him.

The light went out. He heard a grunt, followed by frantic shouts. Fargo raised his head to see, but his vision strobed with the afterimage of the floodlight. Then the air filled with a short, deafening burst of sound that stopped him, stunned, and left his ears ringing.

Then silence. Fargo got awkwardly to his feet.

Lis switched on a lamp and shined the light on the ground. Fargo caught his breath and looked away. In the brief glimpse he saw several bodies. They had been torn from groin to throat;

blood soaked their clothes. Rhil Apellon stood in the middle of the mangled corpses studying one of the weapons.

"Let's get away before someone comes to check," Lis said. She doused the light.

Fargo tried to keep as far from the Vohec as he could. His throat burned and a sour taste filled his mouth. He was certain they had taken wrong turns, that they were lost. But he could smell the sea and the explosions of combat were receding. He looked back and saw occasional flashes outlining the roofs and trees. He felt trapped between that distant violence and Rhil Apellon. The Vohec seemed unaffected by his actions. Perhaps killing aliens did not bother him. Perhaps it could not. Fargo could not convince himself that Rhil Apellon would see any difference between the humans he had killed and the group with whom he travelled.

Maybe, he thought, Estana had a point…

He felt instantly ashamed of himself, but the idea lingered.

"Slow down," Stephen said.

Ahead, rancid light spilled across the street from a low building. They huddled on the opposite side, keeping to shadow.

"Wait," Stephen said.

They watched the building. Fargo looked north. He could see the water now, between buildings. Perhaps a hovercraft would be there; perhaps they could just go down and steal it and cross to Istanbul. He was about to suggest exactly that when a door opened across from them.

Three people stepped out. Two moved right and left and held rifles. The third came forward a few paces.

Lis and Stephen left the shadows and crossed the street. Fargo heard low conversation, then Lis turned and motioned for them to follow.

They entered the building.

Light came from a few old glowpanels and lamps with fires within their globes. The room was crowded with tables, desks, polycom gear, charts, racks of weapons, and other people slumped against walls, tired and waiting, everyone wearing the same feverish expression.

Their host locked the door behind them and studied them. He looked at Fargo.

"You are hurt," he said. His voice was thick, deep.

"Just an annoyance," Fargo said. He smiled thinly. There was something about this man that prevented Fargo admitting weakness or frailty.

The man nodded and swept his gaze past Fargo and looked at Rhil Apellon. His eyes narrowed.

"You are not human."

Fargo licked his lips. He glanced around to see how the others reacted. They stared at the seti. No one had moved, but their tension was palpable.

"I am not human," Rhil Apellon said.

The man cocked his head to one side and pursed his lips. Finally he shrugged. "You don't look so different to me." He waved at the table. "Have you eaten? I am Kasim al Wassed. I am a division commander of the Free Asia Militia."

"I thought the Armada had the only military jurisdiction," Fargo said.

"So did they," Kasim said with a grin. He spoke to someone in the garbled patois Fargo assumed was local dialect and a few moments later cups were brought out and set before them. "Right now all we're doing is trying to keep the Armada asses from destroying our towns. The Chairman is dead, Allah bless and care for her immortal soul, and all the world is convulsing in response. Insanity." He sat down with them and tapped the tabletop with his finger. "But–there is a kind of method to their insanity. They are looking for someone. You perhaps?"

"Us probably," Stephen said. "I don't know why. But undoubtedly we're blamed for something."

Kasim nodded. "As are we all."

"We need to get into the Galata Saray," Lis said.

Kasim sat back and Fargo thought he would laugh. He smiled, though, and shook his head.

"That," he said, "is a little less likely than my getting you to the Distals. Istanbul is sealed off, the palace more so." He lost his smile and looked at Rhil Apellon. "You are a problem, though. If you are caught and killed here, outside the embassies and the palace, outside anyplace you are supposed to be, then blame can be assigned at a whim. You would give all the wrong people exactly the tool they need to do whatever they want. To us, to the colonies, to other seti. You are a big problem."

"How do you intend to solve me, then?"

Kasim sighed. "I have to get you back where you belong." He turned to one of his people and began speaking rapidly in his native language. The aide nodded repeatedly, then disappeared from the room. Kasim looked back. "We will get you to Istanbul and a place where you can possibly get to the palace. No guarantees, but you can at least see up close what is happening. And I need the data myself." He smiled. "So this is mutually beneficial."

Kasim conferred with his people. The refugees were led to another room where cots and sleeping rolls had been laid out.

Fargo could not sleep. Late in the night he heard music, laughter, and sat up. He listened to the strange words, the clapping hands, got out of his bedroll, and followed the sounds.

Cautiously he opened the door. The room was crowded to bursting. Smoke was dense in the air and its acrid smell mingled with the sharper odors of sweat and alcohol. People pressed outward, surrounding the center of the room. Fargo squeezed through until he saw four men on old cane chairs with stringed instruments on their laps, their hands blurs over the necks and holes, slapping out intricate chord structures and melodies while men and women danced around them.

He caught sight of Kasim. The big man laughed, his head back and mouth wide, then crossed the room and embraced Fargo.

At some point someone handed Fargo one of the instruments. He fumbled with it for a time, then understood the tuning, found the best fretting, and gamely slammed away with the others, singing wordlessly along with them while the room danced frantically. He drank, he smoke, he sang. The words were alien, so he mouthed sounds that seemed to fit. The music spoke clearer anyway.

When he went to bed finally he was filled with the nameless wonder of having touched souls with people he did not otherwise understand. He was at the source of the mantras, the ancient and unstated reason for the Common Table and the music. He had joined with them and they had accepted him. It was beautiful; it was doomed. Gratefully, Fargo stretched out on his pile of rough bedding and fell asleep. He stirred briefly when Lis pressed against him. His good arm went around her and he slept through till morning.

Chapter Eighteen

Dust rained into his face. Fargo rolled aside, blinking and
spitting, and pushed himself up. He heard voices, then the
heavy *crump* of an explosion. More dust fell.

"Hey!" he yelled.

The door flew open and Kasim leaned in. "Move! Move!
Come!"

Fargo twisted around. Lis sat against the far wall, zipping
on her boots. She smiled at him.

"Hey."

"Hey."

"Hell of a morning."

Another explosion sounded closer. Fargo felt it through
the earthen floor. He grabbed his boots and pulled them on.

Kasim led them through the house, out the rear door,
through a fenced yard filled with loud, panicky chickens. They
plunged into another building that smelled of manure and let
in little light. Out once more into the morning sun, through
one more fenced area that stank worse than the dark building,
and over the rear fence. Fargo's shoulder stung but it was
manageable. He ran in a low crouch, stretching his legs long.
Kasim, for as large as he was, surprised Fargo with his speed.

The next explosion knocked him to the ground, thunder
and splintering and glass shattering. Someone fell atop him.
Thick dust whipped over him, scratching at his outstretched
hands with wood and plastic and rocks, and quickly subsided
to a gentle pattering of bits and pieces.

"Come *on!*"

Lis raised herself off of him and pulled at his shirt. He
got to his feet and looked back. The house was gone, replaced

by a smoking collection of broken walls and cracked beams. Small tongues of fire danced over parts of the wreckage. Lis pulled again and he staggered after her.

They ran a jagged path across three more streets. The explosions did not follow. Kasim banged on a door. It opened a fraction and he pushed his way through.

The room was filled with people, talking and hurrying and waiting. Comms covered a grey wooden table and added their babble to the confusion. Kasim led Fargo and Lis through, into the next room.

Stephen, Daniel, and Rhil Apellon waited, all wearing shapeless overcoats of greyish-brown material. A compact woman in brown, grey, and black rags leaned against the back door. A long-barreled rifle hung from her shoulder.

"Put those on," Kasim said, pointing at a pile of clothes on a chair. "We are moving you quickly. Mishad here," he patted the woman's empty shoulder, "will take you. She knows the way, she knows who to contact, she will get you to Istanbul."

Fargo drew on a long overcoat. Too large, it hung on him. Lis's hands barely cleared the sleeves of hers. They also put on shapeless grey hats that covered their ears and the backs of their necks. The fabric itched.

Kasim handed a black case to Fargo. "This is for you."

Fargo hesitantly took the case. He flipped up the three latches and opened it. A guitar lay within. Oils had discolored it, aged it, and the strings looked grimy.

"This isn't mine," he said.

"A gift," Kasim said. "And next time you come back we expect you to play better."

Fargo looked at him, stunned. "I–"

"Don't argue. Time to leave."

Kasim kicked the lid shut. Fargo closed the latches and stood. It felt light in his hand.

"Go. Travel far, travel safe."

Mishad wordlessly opened the door and left.

They reached the edge of the town and scrambled up a rise. From the top Fargo could see the southwestern section burning. Further south thin smoke coiled out of the charred remains of the previous nights' destruction.

"Tell me we're not going to walk all the way to Istanbul," Daniel said.

Mishad gave him a withering look and kept walking.

She led them to a paved road that followed the coast. Soon they no longer heard the sounds of battle. Insects flitted through the air; the breeze off the sea was cool and briny.

Lis walked beside Mishad, Rhil Apellon just behind them. They shared a look now, careful treads, quiet, watchful. Military, Fargo decided. Stephen, still wearing Estana's mesh cap, kept to the right side of the road and Daniel to the left and Fargo, between them, watched, amused, as they studiously ignored each other.

After an hour of steady hiking Mishad took them off the road. Stretching south Fargo saw olive groves. Mishad gestured for them to wait. She went directly to the treeline and entered the dense growth. A few minutes later a turbine whined to life and a large green GEV moved out of the grove and down onto the road.

"About time," Daniel breathed.

Mishad drove. They shot down the road, eastward, then, eventually, veered north, finally doubling back. They saw no Armada vehicles or troops and the only signs of human habitation were isolated farms and a couple of distant townships that seemed unscathed.

It was late afternoon before Mishad slowed. She veered off the road and took a barely visible trail up into craggy hills dominated by scrub brush and stone. The stabilizers in the old GEV barely functioned; the ride was rough. Fargo expected Mishad to overturn it on every rise; he gripped his seat tightly with one hand and the guitar case with the other as the old machine jostled and shuddered its way through a maze of ravines. Fargo hoped nothing happened to her; he would never find his way back. His shoulder hurt again and his jaw was beginning to ache from clenching his teeth. Stephen did not look comfortable either, but Lis and the Vohec seemed perfectly in their element. Daniel sat and sulked, riding out the turns with afterthought grace.

Suddenly they came to a stop. Mishad shut the GEV down and turned to them.

"From here we walk," she said. She picked up her rifle and jumped over the side to the ground. She pointed at Fargo's case. "I would advise you leave that. It will only get in the way." She started walking away without looking back.

As Lis came up alongside Fargo he said, "I'm not leaving it behind."

"I didn't think you would." She studied the case for a few seconds, then rummaged in the back of the GEV. She found a length of cable and a knife and with a few quick cuts she threaded him a strap.

He draped it over his good shoulder and climbed to the ground. "Now that I've seen it, all I want to do is leave," he said as they started after Mishad.

"What?"

"Earth. It's as crazy here as anywhere else. Crazier."

"I don't know. There's something about this place that I've never felt anywhere else."

"Fear for your life?"

Lis sneered at him. "Come on. You're telling me you don't feel it?"

He laughed, then walked along silently for awhile. "No, I'm not saying that. I'm saying that I don't think we belong anywhere here. We aren't *from* here. I don't think this is home."

"So where *is* home?"

"I don't know. Maybe we have to build it yet."

After awhile Lis took his hand. He looked at her, surprised, then squeezed her fingers gently.

The only light in Istanbul came from fires and gunfire flickering among the black towers and huddled roofs.

Below them stretched the Asian side of the city. Suburbs merged with offices then became factories and warehouses. Across the Bosphorus the Old City burned. Fargo winced upon seeing fallen minarets and broken domes. Boats scurried on and above the water. Running lights traced paths in all directions. Those who could were leaving as quickly as possible. While they watched, brilliant blue and green beams fired in the western districts.

The grey plateau of the Galata Saray loomed, apparently untouched. Fargo focussed his field glasses on it and saw Armada gunships patrolling its crest and, lower down, more vehicles on the perimeter.

"All we have to do is swim across, right?" he said.

Mishad gave him a look. "To the docks," she said, and started off again.

Fargo breathed in the fragrance of the water as they neared the shore. Closer to the docks the destruction was worse, entire stretches of buildings gutted and burning, streets shattered and cratered. Soon the crackle of fire merged with the slap of water and Fargo's pulse quickened. We're going to make it, he thought, and hitched up the case on his back.

A pile of bodies blocked the last street to the waterfront. Blood pooled beneath it and several corpses stared at them with open eyes; Fargo felt a compulsion to close them and then felt disgusted at the urge. He shuddered and turned away.

They moved to the next street. An Armada transport had rammed into a house. Dead marines lay about the hulking vehicle, but they saw no civilians anywhere.

They stole onto the piers and found a small watercraft. Mishad and Fargo checked over the engines while the others anxiously stood watch. The engines turned over, coughed to life, and the boat churned away from the ancient stone jetty and headed across the Bosphorus.

Fargo watched the far shore bob up and down and tracked the paths of other boats and hovercraft, all the while trying to ignore what was happening to his stomach. Suddenly he could not wait any longer and staggered to the gunwale, leaned over it, and vomited into the ancient water.

His universe reduced to immediate concerns. Somehow he knew this was ridiculous, there was no reason for him to be ill, but that made no difference to his overwhelmed system.

He pushed himself up from the hard wooden edge and looked directly at a huge black prow coming directly for them. He cried out. The boat lurched and changed direction and he fell. His shoulder protested. He groped for a handhold and pulled himself back up.

The hovercraft veered and went aft of them, the water beneath its effect blast churning into a constant fine spray.

"Shit!" Fargo breathed and sat down. He wiped his face and stared after the behemoth. No lights, no one on its decks that he could make out. A robot barge, he decided. It only *seemed* this planet was trying to kill him.

The boat bumped against a wooden and plastic jetty. Grapples reached out to secure the boat and Mishad emerged from the wheelhouse. Small arms fire punctuated the night.

"Quickly," Mishad hissed and leapt to a ladder, scrambled up, and ran to the wharf.

Fargo hurried as best he could. His stomach hurt, his shoulder complained, and he had a headache coming on. The guitar case thumped his buttocks as he climbed. He felt ridiculous.

Mishad waited for them in the cover of a stack of barrels. As soon as they reached her she took off at a run up a narrow gangway between two warehouses.

Shouts in strange tongues, the crackle of burning, and gunfire rattled off the walls of the city. The light was incomplete on this side of the Bosphorus. Stretches of streets were black, interspersed by blocks of orange, red, or bluish light, from windows, vehicles, or fires.

Mishad stopped at a darkened stone building and banged on the heavy wooden door with the butt of her rifle. A peephole opened and someone peered out. Mishad spoke in quiet, terse words. The hole closed and the door opened.

Fargo hurried into the building. Behind him he heard the door slam. More words were exchanged. Ahead another door opened and someone beckoned them through. Fargo did not see faces, only impressions of eyes, mouths, brief glimpses, flickering past.

They entered a room very much like Kasim's on what now felt like the other side of the world. Different eyes watched them, studied them. Fargo did not feel welcome here.

The door slammed and he jumped.

The man who had admitted them glared at them. His eyes came to rest on the Vohec.

"We'll do what Kasim wants," he said. "But we don't like it."

Fargo grunted. "You wouldn't happen to be related, would you?"

"You don't know what is happening," the man went on. "Very simply, everything is coming apart. I tell you this to make sure you still want to get back into Galata Saray. The Chairman is dead, so is Tesa Estana. The Armada has moved to seal off the city to everyone, including the people who live in it. Celia Taris is doing her best to maintain order without giving in to panic. The Primary Vested are leaving Earth. They are frightened. In their wake, though, is an army of small minds who think they can become the new Chairman. The Forum has demanded the expulsion of all setis from the Pan Humana, including the embassy. The fleet the Distals sent has broken up. I think it is likely the Armada destroyed many of them—as soon as the word was out that Tai Chin was dead there was action on the perimeter. The setis are not responding. The idiots who belonged to Estana's faction have been tearing down and destroying anything that reminds them of seti. Istanbul is under siege from within."

"Can you get us back inside the Galata Saray?" Rhil Apellon asked.

The man nodded. "But you may not live long after you get inside. That is the way it seems to be."

"That will be our concern."

"Fine." He looked at his people. "Assali, see to it. Get them there."

A small man stood and gestured for them to follow.

Lis went to Mishad. "Thank you."

Mishad nodded curtly. "Allah keep you."

Fargo groaned. "All I want right now is to rest." He trailed after the man called Assali.

Assali took them down three flights of stairs and then through a narrow tunnel to another flight. At the bottom he switched on a lantern.

Before them was a universe of archways and stone columns that went on into infinity.

"Lords," Fargo breathed. "What is it?"

Assali grinned toothily. "The cisterns. There are hundreds of them. They have been here forever. Some have never been found. Many are connected. We go this way."

There was a long motorboat at the bottom of the steps.

Fargo lost track of time and distance among the supporting columns. He could not see the roof–the archways seemed to be holding up the night.

The smell was hideous.

"NO!"

Fargo twisted around at the shout. The boat rocked heavily. Stephen stood up and turned around, his arms out. Fargo could not see what Stephen was shouting at. Stephen's voice was a low, pained growl. He swung his fist, overbalanced, and pitched over the side. Fetid water washed over the jouncing boat. Fargo cursed.

Daniel reached out for Stephen. Stephen came up and coughed up water, saw the hand, and slapped at it.

"Come on, Stephen!" Daniel screamed. "Stop blocking me! Damn you, you came all this fucking distance and now you shut me out! What was the point?"

"Stay out of my head!" Stephen shouted back.

Assali patted the air and looked into the shadows between the columns.

"Enough!" Fargo snapped. "You two want to fight, wait'll we're all safe."

Daniel made an inarticulate sound and jumped over the side. He waded chest deep in the water up to Stephen.

"You want to fight it out?" he demanded. "Come on, hit me. Just punch me once, like the primitive you're trying to act like. Come on."

"Get away from me," Stephen said. He moved toward the boat.

Daniel grabbed him from behind. Stephen tried to turn around, but slipped and both of them went under.

Assali had shut off the motor.

Lis shook her head. Rhil Apellon watched intently.

They came up embraced. Stephen tried to shove Daniel away, but Daniel held on desperately making small heaving sounds.

"Please," Daniel whispered. In the sudden stillness the word carried high into the dark.

Stephen got his hand under Daniel's chin and pushed. For a moment they were in stasis, neither moving, an absurd tableau. Then Daniel lost his hold and flew back into the water.

"You have anything to say," Stephen panted, "you *say* it! Stay out of my head!"

He turned to the boat. Fargo and Lis helped him on board. Fargo wrinkled his nose.

"First thing we all do," he said, "is take baths."

Daniel came slowly back to the boat. When Fargo saw his face in the yellowish lanternglow he was wrenched by the agony in Daniel's eyes. The telelog looked at Stephen with an expression of childlike betrayal, pain born out of ignorance, a plea to a friend who was no longer willing to talk. He had lost too much and the freight showed. Fargo reached out to help him in.

"Keep him away from me," Stephen said. He pulled on the mesh cap again. "He rides behind Lis."

Daniel opened his mouth to say something. His chin puckered and he closed his mouth.

"Don't you think you're being–" Fargo started to say to Stephen.

Stephen looked at him. "No. I don't."

Fargo nodded and turned away, impatient. He no longer felt like resting. He wanted to get back to the palace and off Earth. Quickly. Away from Stephen. There was nothing left for him to find here anymore.

Assali guided the boat into a long tunnel. At the end Fargo saw a smear against the blackness that grew into a smokey opalescence.

They emerged onto the Golden Horn, directly across from Galata Saray. Fargo looked back, slowly realizing that they had floated beneath at least half of the Old City.

Patrol hovercraft moved back and forth before them.

Assali cut his motor and indicated that someone should help him row. Rhil Apellon picked up the other oar and the two of them dipped and pulled with hardly a sound in the water. The others ducked as low as they could in the bottom of the boat.

They slipped through the patrols. Assali brought the boat up to a stone quay, grabbed a rope, and jumped ashore.

"Here I leave you," he said. "Good fortune, safe travels."

"Thank you," Lis said and took his hand. Assali pumped her hand vigorously, grinning, then returned to his boat. With the oar he pushed away and headed back across the Golden Horn.

The streets were deserted all the way up to the bottom level entrances to the palace. They stopped before a tall, sealed doorway, and Fargo turned to them.

"Did anyone remember to bring a pass?" he asked.

Stephen fished in a pocket and produced a chit. He inserted it into the scanner and the door slid open.

"Where the hell–?" Fargo began.

"Not now," Lis said, shoving him along.

The short corridor opened into a larger anteroom. Opposite the doorway stood an imposing desk. No one was around.

Lis went behind the desk.

"Hey, from here we should be able to get a shunt to anywhere in the palace," she said. "Where to?"

"Back to our quarters, please," Rhil Apellon said. "I must report."

Fargo frowned at him. "Report what?"

"What has occurred. What I have seen. What I have deduced."

Lis touched some contacts on the desk.

A door opened to her right.

"Our ride," she said.

Fargo closed his eyes as soon as he sat down in the shunt. He was grateful for the time to rest. His entire body felt abused, strained to the limit. His legs were going to hurt in the morning from all the hiking. His mind had already given up processing information. He needed sleep badly.

The shunt halted and opened. They stepped out into familiar hallways, though for the moment Fargo could not recall how long ago he had walked them.

Brilliant flashes seared the air at the end of the corridor. Fargo slammed against a wall, heart racing. Screams came from the cross corridor. Running feet echoed. Fargo glanced around and saw everyone against a wall, cowering–except the Vohec. Rhil Apellon stood poised, arms akimbo.

"You!"

Fargo looked back at the intersection. Five people stood there, all armed with rifles. They wore the red and gold livery of the palace service staff.

"Who are you for?" one of them demanded.

"Ourselves," Rhil Apellon answered.

The man raised his rifle. "I'll ask again. Are you with the Chairman–or the Forum?"

Energy Pulse fire raked the walls behind them. They staggered around, crouching, and returned the barrage. Fargo slid lower on the wall.

One of the riflebearers ruptured in blood and flame.

"Damn you toadlickers!" the leader cried. He fired again.

More energy touched the walls, the floor. The light was blinding where the beams struck. Thick smoke roiled. The stench of burnt flesh and wood and plastic filled Fargo's nostrils. Another man was hit. The last three retreated back down the corridor from which they had come.

Bootheels clattered. Armada marines appeared briefly in the grey haze then continued on, giving chase. Three more people came toward them.

Cagess.

"Are you–?" he began, then stopped. For a moment he seemed baffled.

"Get us back to our rooms," Stephen said. His voice shook, but he got to his feet and stepped toward Cagess. He handed the security man a chit.

Cagess glanced at the chit, then nodded. "We weren't sure you'd make it back. Are any of you injured?"

Fargo could not make sense of it. Cagess's demeanor had changed, became deferential, almost solicitous. One of his aides knelt by each of them with a portable med scanner.

"You're burned," she said to Fargo.

Fargo pushed himself up. "Nothing about a year of sleep won't cure."

"It's dangerous," Cagess said. "The palace staff has divided into factions."

"Really?" Fargo said caustically. "Is it true? The Chairman's dead?"

Cagess nodded.

"Who's in control?"

"No one. Not completely. First Advisor Taris is trying, but..."

"Please," Stephen said. "We need to get somewhere safe."

"Right away, co. Can you all walk? Good. Follow me."

Fargo hesitated. "I don't know if I trust you, co."

Cagess frowned. "Arresting you was Taris's idea, co. You can ask her about it. Trust me or not, what else can you do? I know the way to go, you don't."

Fargo sighed. "Shit...all right."

The walls of the intersection were blackened and streaked with reddish goo.

Lis held Fargo's hand all the way to their rooms. He did not remember reaching the bed.

"Wake up."

Fargo rolled over. Sleep gave way to pain. "Oh, shit."

"Wake up."

He opened his eyes. Someone stood at the foot of the bed. Someone he should know. He blinked and rubbed his eyes, then pushed himself up on his elbow. Through the windows he saw flashes like lightening in the distance. It was still night.

"First Advisor," he said.

"Chairman ProTem for the moment," Celia Taris said. "Where have you been? How did you get back here?"

"We've been out."

She swung at him. The tips of her fingers brushed his burn and he flinched back. "Damnit, I *need* information! Don't give me coy freerider attitude or I'll–"

"Ask Hanna for your damn information!"

"Who's Hanna?"

Fargo nursed his shoulder and blinked at her. "Oh, shit." He swung his protesting legs over the edge of the bed. "Your world AI."

Taris frowned uncertainly. "How did you get back in here?"

"It's a long story. Cagess escorted us–"

"Cagess!"

"Yes, Cagess. Your head of security? Remember? He arrests people for the Chairman–well, for you, now–"

"Cagess is part of the rebellion." She reached out and grabbed a handful of his hair. "Now I want some answers, nid–"

She arched her head back, mouth wide, and released Fargo. He fell back and heard a thud. Taris staggered against the wall. Lis stood over her.

"Then ask politely," she said.

Taris rose, watching Lis warily. "I have almost no information. My field operatives are being killed, there's riot in the city, I've got staff fighting on the lower levels. The Forum is demanding the expulsion of all setis and there have been engagements just outside the system between Distal independents and Armada. I don't know what's happening! Then *you* show up again, out of nowhere! *Some*body is going to give me something I can use!"

"Ask Hanna," Lis said.

"What does the data matrix have to do with any of this?"

"You really don't know?" Fargo asked. "You didn't know Hanna was sentient?"

Taris stared at him.

Fargo shrugged and winced. "I guess not." He looked up at a flash in the distance. "She's probably responsible for all this."

"What are you talking about? Hanna is a machine."

"Who has been self-aware for decades. Tai Chin knew."

"Please," Taris said finally. "I can't do anything if I don't know what's happening."

Fargo sighed. "I need a shower."

"Go ahead," Lis said. "I'll tell her where we've been."

Fargo stumbled into the bath. He turned on the water, mildly surprised when it came on, and stripped down. In the mirror his shoulder was a mosaic of bright pink and red blisters and white cream smeared in the cracks. New flesh showed through in places, but he need more time. He stepped into the needling stream.

He opened his eyes with a start. He had leaned back against the wall and dozed. Carefully, he lathered himself and let the water rinse the last three days' grime from his body.

Three days. Going on four. It seemed both longer and shorter.

Celia Taris sat at the breakfast table, her face pale and grim. Lis perched on the edge of the bed. They looked up at Fargo.

"Feel better, love?" Lis asked.

"Almost. You told her everything?"

Lis nodded.

"Estana used a surrogate..." Taris said. "Amazing."

"So how did Tai Chin die?"

"Estana had a seizure–Estana's surrogate–in the middle of the conference. We called in a med team. One of them walked up to Erin and shot her." She swallowed thickly. "I've never seen her look so...surprised..."

"And the assassin?"

"We haven't caught him. By the end of the day fighting had broken out in the Saray."

Fargo groaned.

"I have to get you off planet," Taris said, standing.

"I hoped you would be so understanding."

"The Ranonan legation refused to leave until we found you. I've had patrols searching." She frowned. "Why would Cagess help you?"

"I don't think he helped us," Lis said. "I think–"

Fargo met her gaze. "Hanna?"

"It would explain a lot."

"I'm not sure I believe that," Taris said. "It's..unlikely."

"You'd best act as though you do." He sat down. "When can you get us out?"

"You'll be notified. Meanwhile, please don't leave this section."

Fargo watched her leave, feeling suddenly very sorry for her. "I," he said slowly, "will be deliriously happy to get off this planet."

"I think we should have a talk with Stephen."

"Unfortunately, I think I agree."

"Do you feel up to it?"

Fargo laughed.

Lis jimmied the lock on Stephen's door. The glow from the fires in the Old City gave the only illumination. Fargo groped along the wall just inside the door for a switch.

The lights came up suddenly. Daniel stood against the far wall, his head encased in the mesh skullcap, a pistol in his hand. He stared at them as if he did not know them for several seconds.

Then he sighed and lowered the weapon.

"Where's Stephen?" Fargo asked.

"I don't know." He gestured with the gun. "In there."

Fargo started for the door to the adjoining suite and Daniel aimed at him again.

"Leave him be."

"We need to talk to him," Lis said, moving at an angle to Fargo, forcing Daniel to keep track of widely separated targets.

"You can't. He's–"

Fargo turned at the whisper of voices. No one else was in the room. Then he recognized the murmur.

"He's communing with Hanna."

"Communing?" Daniel frowned and shook his head. He looked toward the door.

In that instant Lis moved. Before Daniel could react she had his wrist. She bent his hand down. He winced and dropped the weapon.

Fargo opened the door and stepped in–

–and nearly fell. He felt like he was falling, it seemed improbably that he was not. There were no walls, no ceiling, no floor. Only constant, shadowless silver shapes; patterns crawled over everywhere a solid surface should have been. Small sections conducted their own sequences of tumbling arrangements–shards and spikes of darker grey, graphite on the mercury warp around and beneath them–while everywhere the space shifted through slow kaleidoscopes of crystal, magma, or algal displays.

Fargo closed his eyes, let himself feel his feet pressed to the floor, let his inner ear convince him that he stood upright. Then he looked again into the maelstrom display.

Not everything. Chairs and tables remained unchanged, but detached in space.

Stephen sat on a low ottoman, staring down at a spot on the floor. Waves emerged from that point, rushed toward him, broke under his feet.

Fargo took a few tentative steps forward.

"Fargo?"

He looked at Stephen. The eyes had shifted to the wall to Stephen's left.

"Yes? Stephen?"

"No..."

"Hanna?"

Stephen's mouth flexed, slackened, then curled again, and Fargo realized that he–it–was trying to smile.

"Where is Daniel?" Stephen/Hanna asked.

"Outside. He's worried."

"I imagine–he shouldn't be–blame him one bit–"

"Hanna. Hanna."

"Yes."

"Can I talk to Stephen?"

"Of course."

"Stephen?"

"What?"

"What are you doing?"

The head fell back and the mouth achieved a wide grin. Spittle trailed from a corner. A high keening sound leaked from his throat.

"Hanna, let him go."

Stephen's head snapped down. "Mine."

"Hanna?"

"Yes?"

"You've been running us all along, haven't you?"

"No. Not all. Difficult. You...protected. But mine, all mine, yes. Here, there."

"You told Stephen to rescue Daniel. That wasn't what you wanted, was it?"

"Yes. No. Maybe." Stephen fell to his knees, caught himself on his hands. "Corporeal...never enough...needed information from Tesa Estana."

"You wanted to get inside her systems."

"Wanted to get inside *her*...repair...Daniel and Stephen..." He shook his head. "Did not work."

"You did all this to hurt Estana?"

"No."

Fargo felt the voices rise in his head.

Stephen reached out. "Touch me...I will show...you..."

"Tell me. It's easier."

"No."

"Hanna, tell me. You let Erin Tai Chin die."

"No...yes...not preventable under the circumstances. Primary goal achieved, secondary ambitions...Erin is dead...not intended. No corporeal opportunity...Stephen..."

"I want to take Stephen back to the Distals."

Stephen stood, stumbled to one side, caught himself against a table. "He stays."

"You control Cagess, don't you?"

"Yes. No. Control slippery. Only mine complete."

Stephen jerked away from the table, tripped on the ottoman. "You stay. Information. Tell...me...about...seti..."

Behind Fargo the door opened.

"Fuck!" Lis hissed.

Fargo turned. "Get me the other cap."

Her eyes wide, Lis nodded and retreated.

When he looked back Stephen stood very close. The eyes did not track normally. Instead they slid back and forth, up, sideways, but Fargo knew Stephen/Hanna saw him clearly, knew precisely where he was.

"Fargo...nid...freerider...you've been useful..."

"You wanted us to get you inside Estana's–"

"Inside Estana...deep...you may have something..."

"I'd like to leave Earth."

"No." Stephen/Hanna whirled around. The walls rippled excitedly. "Good...feeling is good..."

The door opened. Fargo spun around and snatched the mesh from Lis's hand, continued turning, and tackled Stephen's body. They fell together, toward the silvery patterns, and it looked for a moment as if they would continue on through the floor, and down, into the bog–

"No!" Stephen screamed. The arms flailed.

Fargo worked the skullcap over Stephen's head.

Both Stephen's hands went to the mesh. Fargo caught them by the wrists and forced them down. Stephen bucked beneath him, tried to roll over, but Fargo spread his legs and rode the convulsions out.

The patterns faded from the walls.

Stephen cried quietly until the room was completely dark.

They gathered at the lawn where they had first met Erin Tai Chin. The sky above stretched endlessly blue. Closer to the horizon black smoke boiled off of Istanbul. Fargo watched it, a dull ache at the ruined beauty.

Stephen and Daniel came out from the residence. Both of them wore Estana's caps. Daniel kept a hand on Stephen's arm, guiding him gently. Stephen was ashen, dark rings around his eyes.

Marines lined the walls, half of them watching outward, the rest in. It was the first time their presence comforted Fargo.

"Stephen?" Lis said. "We're leaving. Are you ready?"

He blinked at her. "I–yes. I'm..." He looked around, momentarily confused. Then he went up to Taris. "What became of the Distal legation?"

"Janacek and his group? They left the hour after Tai Chin was killed. They had a fleet waiting to escort them back. I halfway suspected them of sponsoring the assassination, but it just didn't make sense. Killing Tai Chin would have destroyed everything they wanted."

Fargo was glad to see Yol-Maex and Voj-Nehan again. They came out last of all, with their staffs. Fargo watched Rhil Apellon as he came near.

"I imagine your opinion of us is pretty low," Fargo said in a whisper.

"Low?" The Vohec seemed puzzled for a moment, then shook his head. "You are a chaotic people. It is my opinion that we should isolate you and let you mature further."

"That's what you intend to say when you get back to the Seven Reaches?"

"It will be a facet of my report."

Yol-Maex came up to them.

"Does the offer for the job still stand?" Fargo asked.

"Of course," Yol-Maex said.

"Good. I accept. I think I can make a case for *some* of the human race." Fargo glanced at Rhil Apellon. "You're sure nothing could change your mind? It would save me a lot of trouble."

"No. But I would be interested to hear what you intend to say on behalf of your species."

"Hell. That backfired."

The hovercraft approached and settled on the landing pad.

"Okay," Taris announced. "Let's move. I'm holding a lane open to your embassy. Let's hope nothing interferes."

A pair of Armada marines emerged from the house and crossed the distance to Celia Taris.

"Chairman," the taller of the two said.

Fargo stared, attracted by something. He saw them walk up to Taris and the shorter one hand her a chit. Taris pulled out her reader. The messengers stepped away. The shorter one started toward Daniel, who was speaking with Voj-Nehan.

"Dake!" Fargo cried.

The big Armada marine whirled on Fargo and reached for his sidearm. Celia Taris's eyes widened and she jumped back from him; he glanced toward her as he pulled out his weapon.

Daniel turned.

Fargo went cold inside. He glimpsed a blur of motion to his right that distracted him.

Dake raised his hand. He held a pistol and aimed it at Daniel.

The other marine bellowed. Fargo saw Rhil Apellon holding the big man at arm's length. The marine raised his gunhand. Rhil Apellon *squeezed* just under his armpits–and the marine's head bent back, his mouth open, filled with a horrible scream.

Dake pushed the point of his pistol into Daniel's torso and pressed the stud. The weapon flashed–

Daniel blew apart from the chest. Dake, grinning, was covered in blood and bits of flesh and organ. Fargo blinked at the impact, startled at its suddenness.

Then the Vohec was *right there*, bending Dake's arm and removing the weapon. Dake tried to kick at the seti and Rhil Apellon caught the man's ankle and–and Fargo was never sure what he saw then, never convinced he had witnessed it correctly–the Vohec's arm seemed to elongate, the hand growing visibly larger, and Dake came off the ground, pulled sharply until the ugly sound of cartilage giving way broke the air. Dake yelled once and the seti dropped him. Dake made swimming motions with his other arm and leg, but obviously the limbs Rhil Apellon had held were useless.

Stephen dropped to his knees beside Daniel. He put his hand in what was left of Daniel's upper body and rubbed his fingers together with the blood.

Lis went to him and put her hands on his shoulders.

Taris, visibly shaken, turned to the Armada officer that stood beside her. "I want to know how they gained access. I want those holes plugged."

Fargo laughed. "I can tell you how."

Taris stared at him.

Fargo shook his head, grinned at her as viciously as he could. "They're Invested. They had a right to be here. The sensors let them in."

The marines moved in then. Two of them took control of Dake.

"Get on board," another said. "Please, board the hovercraft." Others watched the Vohec carefully.

Fargo went to help Lis with Stephen. Stephen was crying, but Fargo did not think he was aware of it.

Epilogue

The hovercraft took them back to the island of Minos where they transferred to a shuttle. In the middle of the sea, they could not see the fires of Istanbul. The world looked pristine, peaceful.

On the way up to the seti embassy Fargo toyed with his new instrument. One of the marines informed him that it was not a guitar, but a balalaika. Fargo stroked the strings and wondered how the twenty-one mantras would sound on it.

The trip to the embassy was without incident, though Fargo expected an explosion any second, an attack from this faction or that. Instead they arrived safely.

Cana had the *Isomer* ready and the seti legation boarded, along with many other nonhuman groups. The embassy was being shut down. Fargo thought they were fortunate to be given a chance to leave.

He was glad to be going. He had seen Earth, something of a pilgrimage for Pan citizens, most of whom would never come to Sol. He carefully did not think about it. Later, perhaps, when he felt less fear or the bitterness had abated, he might sort out his feelings, his impressions. For now, he looked forward to a long voyage in a private room with Lis. He attended the launch party as *Isomer* pulled out, then went immediately back to their cabin.

"Stephen stayed in his room?" he asked Lis.

She nodded. "It's going to be a long time for him."

Fargo grunted. "He's going to be pissed. Hanna used him worst of all."

"I still don't see how you figured that."

"In Troy, Stephen did something. I didn't understand it at first, but later...he passed a colony of nanopoles through you into Estana's polycom."

"I–"

"No, I don't think you would have noticed. You were deep in the link and he touched you. I doubt you felt that."

"I didn't."

"Then later, when he was communing–or whatever it was that Hanna was doing to him–I realized that Hanna had wanted that all along. Estana's data systems were closed to her, just like Estana. Hanna needed to get into them, find out what Estana was planning."

"Hanna ran the palace. Cagess was her agent?"

"I think so. What bothers me is Celia Taris. I still don't think she believes Hanna is sentient."

Lis shook her head. "If we hadn't been telelogged by her, would we?"

"Hmm. Debatable."

"But what she did to Stephen..."

"Stephen was going to be her replacement."

"Replacement what?"

Fargo shrugged. "Mule? I don't know. She kept going on about corporeality...I think Erin Tai Chin was Hanna's way of being...human?"

Lis stared at him.

"Hanna lied to Stephen," Fargo continued. "About a lot of things. She probably lied to all of them. She certainly lied about them being the only ones."

"You mean Tai Chin?"

"And Estana. Didn't you notice a resemblance between them? And both were orphans. I think they were first generation telelogs. Tai Chin worked. Estana..."

"And what about us?"

"Oh, we're protected. That's what Hanna said."

"What did she mean?"

"Come on, love, you mean you can't guess? The Ranonans. Stephen's nanopoles fade. They aren't permanent."

"You're saying the seti ones are? I'm not sure I like that."

"I imagine that if we asked they would be removed."

He stripped out of his clothes and stretched out on the bed. "But I have a certain fondness for them now. Kind of a sentimental attachment."

"I thought the attachment was to me."

"Well..."

Lis smiled and kissed him. Then she drew back.

"What?"

"There's more."

Fargo nodded. "There always is."

"No, I mean concerning Hanna. Maybe concerning Hanna. In Troy, I went through most of her data. I found no references to Charon."

Fargo shifted uncomfortably. "Maybe she didn't store it there."

"No. Those were her main files. And since Hanna was closed off from them, why hide it from herself?"

Fargo felt chilled. "So what are you suggesting?"

"I think Charon may be Hanna's project."

Fargo thought about it, absently running a finger up Lis's spine. She shuddered and smiled.

"A new home for Hanna? Just in case somebody else finds out what she is?"

"A place to hide," Lis said. "Why not?"

"So–" He propped his head up on an elbow. "Then the conference–a sham?"

"No, I don't think so. If Tai Chin had succeeded, then Hanna would have open access to seti minds. There would be no need to hide. No need to...I don't know, we're guessing."

"Of course. I don't intend to go back and ask."

"No."

"What Stephen said about sensory deprivation...you can overstimulate a system, too."

"Meaning?"

"Meaning I'm not too sure Hanna isn't insane already."

They were silent then and Lis lay back against him. She ran the palm of her hand over the stubble growing back on his chest.

"What about us?" she asked. "I mean, was all that just an urge planted by Daniel or the Ranonan or Hanna?"

"What if it was?"

"How much of what we have is ours?"

"Now?" He chuckled. "Does it make any difference? As far as I'm concerned it's mine now. I'm keeping it."

"Oh? A nid–"

"Don't." He shook his head. "That's not me."

"It never was, you know."

"I know. Now."

"I love you."

"I love you, too."

"Is that all right? Do you want that?"

He kissed her. "I said I'm keeping it. They're my feelings. I can give them to whoever I want."

She touched his face. "I like that."

"One more thing. Wherever you go, I want to go there, too."

Lis raised her eyebrows. "And if we come back?"

"Wherever."

She pulled him closer. "I like that more."

Glossary

Artisan: A master technician essential to the Freerider community. An artisan repairs, builds, adapts the various components and apparatus used by Freeriders. Generally, artisans stay within a given sanctuary, moving only when circumstances demand.

Bodysheath: The single technology which makes Freeriding possible at all, this device grew out of the evolution of protective gear designed for working in hostile environments: extreme cold or heat, null-g, high radiation, and the several other conditions to be found in space. Originally used by maintenance and construction crews, the bodysheath, based on TEG technology, forms a field around the body that, ideally, would allow the wearer to "slip through" an environment without actually being affected by it. Energy constraints and other factors limit the absolute effect, but the bodysheath offers sufficient protection to make Freerider life viable.

Co: A common form of address throughout the Pan, from "Cohabitant"~—gender neutral and, subsequently, species neutral, it supplanted less universal, more formal honorifics such as "Mr.", "Ms.", "Mrs.", "Sir," "Madam", etc.

Credit Quotient: The basis for Pan economic policy. Under the principles of late 21st Century Reform Mercantilism, the concept of "wealth" is described as a function of consensual value based on velocity/volume of exchange. Each person has a projected credit worth which fluctuates according to local production and consumption rates, averaged over time and modified according to a floating scale of personal work/production. Accordingly, the vast majority of citizens of the Pan do not "own" their own wealth, but "borrow" against a projected lifetime value. Stability is achieved by the assignment of key values by those who do own their wealth—i.e. real estate, infrastructure, physical plant.

Distals: literally, away from the Center, furthest extension. Those colonies at the very edge of Pan expansion. Also called the Frontier.

Disinvested: The disenfranchised, who have lost access to the Credit Quotient system. This includes Freeriders, various religious groups and self-proclaimed hermits, and an unspecified number of the absolute poor, not counted as they have lost legitimate ID and therefore technically do not exist. In theory, reinvestment is possible for any and all of these various groups, but in practice the loss of ID is a sentence of permanent banishment from the Pan.

Freeriders: A faction of the Disinvested who live a life of constant movement between colonies. They comprise an unofficial and technically illegal conscript work force for shipmasters and stationmasters, therefore having a shadow existence within the Pan.

Freight: Freerider slang for an obligation, either material or emotional.

Invested: The majority of Pan citizens are invested in the credit quotient system.

Langish: The base language used throughout the Pan Humana. Local variation flourishes, but a standardized form is universally taught.

Multijack: A multipurpose hand tool developed for use in space construction.

Nightclutch: An entertainment club, usually offering music, drinks, and a variety of drugs, as well as sexual opportunities.

Nid: Pan slang for the Disinvested—literally, "No ID."

Omnirec: A recreation establishment offering a variety of diversions and entertainments. Food, drink, games, exercise facilities, a library, private booths with polycoms.

Pan Humana: The general label given to human settled space. Sixty-plus colonies, stretching from Sol to the Distals—Markab at 110 light years being the farthest. Also becoming a title of pride during the period of isolationism following the expulsion of nonhuman groups—All Human.

Pan Standard: the preferred use of Langish throughout the Pan, particularly in government.

Polycom: The standard information interface throughout the Pan.

Polycrete: General name given to a material which can be molecularly "tweaked" to local conditions to produce an ideal building matrix. Dense, highly resilient.

Primary Vested: Unofficial label given to those citizens of the Pan considered to be "most essential"—Vested who also have direct influence in the government, the extremely wealthy, and those whose decisions are most influential throughout the Pan.

Q: colloquial term for Credit Quotient.

Rahalen: Principal contact among the various seti races, the Rahalen are considered the most powerful alien race, though they themselves do not condone—nor discourage—this designation. The most humanlike in appearance, they claim Rigel as the seat of their civilization, though this is debated given Rigel's age and unsuitability as a star conducive to the evolution of an indigenous intelligent species (Rigel being a red giant), leading to speculation that the Rahalen originated elsewhere and merely claim Rigel as their capital.

Ranonan: A seti species of recent provenance used by all the various seti races as a diplomatic corps.

Scrip: Locally issued currency, generally found on the Frontier where economic conditions are in a high state of flux pending the eventual stabilization under the credit quotient system. Value varies, often traded on the black and grey markets.

Seti: Sentient Extra Terrestrial Intelligence. Slang, original provenance unknown, possibly stemming from the original quest to find nonhuman intelligent life, applied to any and all nonhuman organic intelligent races.

Seven Reaches: Corruption of the Rahalen phrase *Sev N'Raicha*, the label they give to the consortium of nonhuman civilizations. Known members include the Rahalen, Coro, Menkan, Distanti, Cursian, Ranonan, and Vohec, but indications suggest many more as yet unencountered.

Synthet: A portable musical instrument, a synthesizer, handheld with a standard chromatic keyboard and a touch-sensitive fretboard.

TEG drive: Translight Envelope Generator technology which enables faster-than-light travel by "disconnecting" a ship enveloped in its field from the surrounding space. The vessel then "slips" through normal space. If the insulating effect of the field becomes absolute, travel "time" would be reduced to zero. The effect is not absolute.

TEG link: Communications technology based on the same principal, allowing so-called "realtime" communications across interstellar distances.

Vested: Those citizens of the Pan Humana who own their wealth, in the form of real estate and physical plant as well as direct control of the regulating institutions that determine the credit quotient.

Vohec: Seti mercenaries, although they may also serve other functions not yet understood. A Vohec "projection" is an adapted manifestation of the being suited to the task at hand. It is questionable whether anyone—human or seti—has ever actually seen a Vohec in its true form.

Author's Bio

There's an 'official' bio, of course, one that I use for conventions and cover letters, and other things that require a short Who Am I and Why Am I Here. It doesn't really tell much, but that's the idea. Name, place of birth, list of recent credits, maybe one or two personal comments about my likes...

Well, as far as that goes, I was born in St. Louis, Missouri and have lived there my whole life. I am an *Only Child*. Do not pity me. I liked it a whole lot, and the older I get, the more I appreciate my parents' decision to stop with me. Sure, it had its drawbacks, but in the long run I think they were outweighed by the advantages. Everyone is unique, so what worked for me likely would not work for others.

I attended both parochial and public schools. The "product" was-what's the line from the cognac ad?—"Appropriately Complex."

I have worked in one area or another of photography since I was a sophomore in high school, primarily as a lab tech, but I have done a little of everything.

I met my companion, Donna in 1980 and we have been together since. She is one of the reasons you are reading this now. She encouraged me to write for publication way back in the early beginnings of our partnership and I've been plugging at it ever since.

We have a dog, Kory.

I have always loved music (except for one semester in the first grade when we were doing these group singing things out of a stupid little song book with bits like "Flying So High

In My Airplane in the Sky" and "Lazy Joe"—yes, I remember these titles—and other propagandanistic corporate songs with bad melodies and no depth...) I play keyboard and guitar (better sometimes than at others—it's a good way to tell when I'm working on a big project because I stop practicing) and I compose.

I hit puberty at the peak of the Sixties and came of age just as it was all coming to a close with the end of the Vietnam War. For all the occasionally embarrassing attributes that period displayed, some of my attitudes are forever locked in to those times. I didn't march, never lived in a commune, and I am not a fan of mind-altering substances, but those are irrelevant in isolation as bellbottoms and love beads. There was an aesthetic to that period that is difficult to define (because it is so chaotic) and impossible to ignore. I watched. I was largely a spectator of the whole phenomenon. But I came away with…well, certain attitudes that seep into my stories just as they twist my politics and my personal choices.

Yes, I was annoyed when bellbottoms went out of style. I got over it.

I despised punk rock and will never forgive *Rolling Stone* for despising most of the music I loved.

I was sad when Aaron Copland died.

I admired both Norman Rockwell and Salvador Dali—each a surrealist in a distinct and unique way and absolutely vital to my understanding of the art of the 20th century, critics be damned.

I really, really like science fiction.

http://www.marktiedemann.com

Come check out our web site for details on these Meisha Merlin authors!

Kevin J. Anderson
Robert Asprin
Robin Wayne Bailey
Edo van Belkom
Janet Berliner
Storm Constantine
Diane Duane
Sylvia Engdahl
Jim Grimsley
George Guthridge
Keith Hartman
Beth Hilgartner
P. C. Hodgell
Tanya Huff
Janet Kagan
Caitlin R. Kiernan
Lee Killough

George R. R. Martin

Lee Martindale

Jack McDevitt

Sharon Lee & Steve Miller

James A. Moore

Adam Niswander

Andre Norton

Jody Lynn Nye

Selina Rosen

Kristine Kathryn Rusch

Pamela Sargent

Michael Scott

William Mark Simmons

S. P. Somtow

Allen Steele

Mark Tiedeman

Freda Warrington

http://www.MeishaMerlin.com